CODE: TSUNAMI

A Port Stirling Mystery

BOOK 3

KAY JENNINGS

Code: Tsunami/Kay Jennings –1ˢᵗ ed.

ISBN (Hardcover edition): 978-1-7339626-6-7
ISBN (Paperback edition): 978-1-7339626-7-4
ISBN (e-book edition): 978-1-7339626-8-1

Publisher's Note: Code: Tsunami is a work of fiction. As of this publication date, the events and circumstances that occur within are a product of the author's imagination, with assistance from the wealth of research surrounding the real-life Alaska 9.2 earthquake of 1964. While certain locales may draw on real life, they are used fictitiously to add authenticity to the story. The cast of characters, with the exception of real-life political figures, are fictitious and are not based on real people, businesses, or organizations.

Cover design, Port Stirling Map, and Family Trees Design: Claire Brown
Interior design: Steve Kuhn/KUHN Design Group

Printed and bound in the USA
First printing 2021
Published by *Paris Communications*
Portland, Oregon, USA

www.kayjenningsauthor.com

OTHER BOOKS BY KAY JENNINGS:

Shallow Waters

Midnight Beach

*For Marcia (1945-2005) and Annette (1949-2020),
my warrior sisters.*

CODE:
TSUNAMI

KOUSE FAMILY

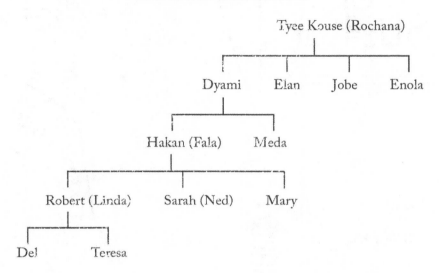

Tyee Kouse (Rochana)

Dyami — Elan — Jobe — Enola

Hakan (Fala) — Meda

Robert (Linda) — Sarah (Ned) — Mary

Del — Teresa

CARMICHAEL FAMILY

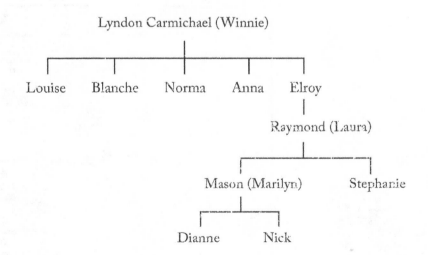

Lyndon Carmichael (Winnie)

Louise — Blanche — Norma — Anna — Elroy

Raymond (Laura)

Mason (Marilyn) — Stephanie

Dianne — Nick

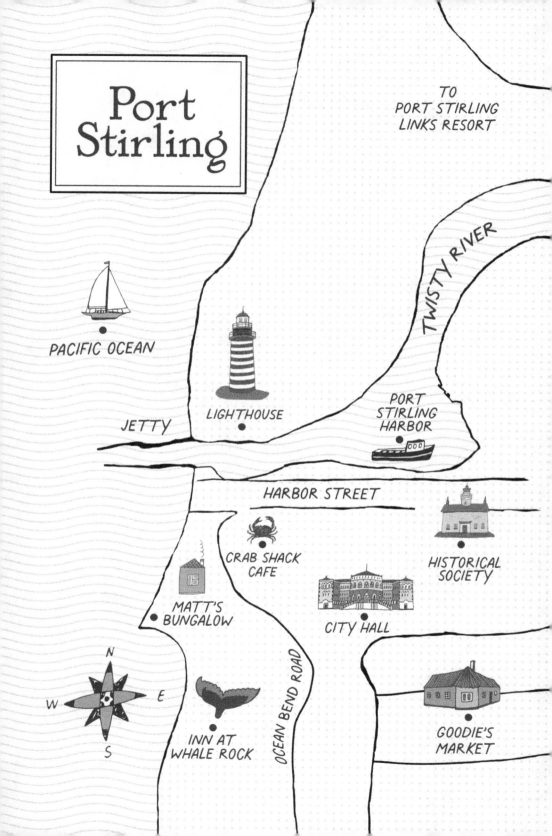

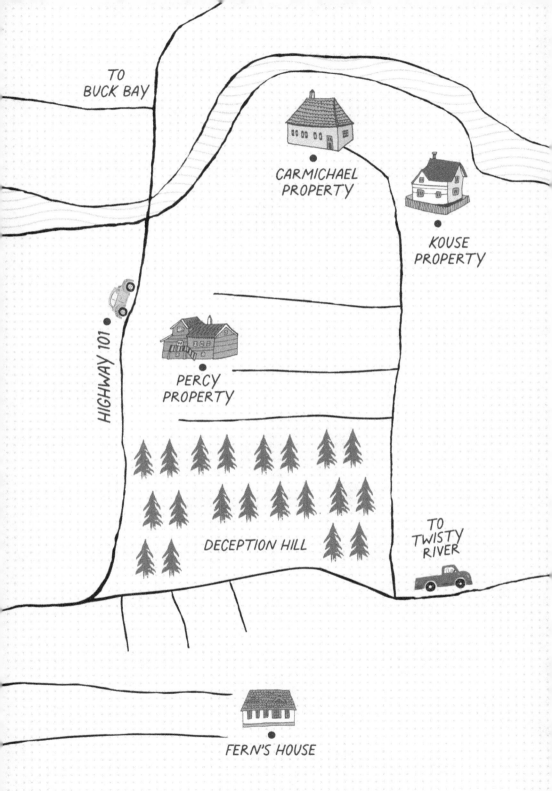

CHAPTER 1

Matt Horning heard the roar before he felt the violent shaking of his bed. It sounded like ten fighter jets flying directly over his house. His eyes flew open, but it was so dark nothing changed. He swung his feet from under his covers onto the floor. At least Matt thought it was his floor, but why was it rolling and moving up and down?

He tried to stand up, supporting himself by grabbing the bed's headboard. No use; the cottage was swaying wildly back and forth. The buckling floor threw him into the wall, and the sharp pain in his left elbow told him that arm took the brunt of his fall. He reached out for the side of his bed, and tried to pull himself up by the sheets. But again, the raging bull that his floor had become tossed him aside like an amateur rider.

Earthquake! I'm stark naked and need to find my jeans.

He climbed back onto his bed, and clawed his way across it to where he remembered leaving his clothes earlier. The bed reminded him of riding on the Tilt-O-Whirl at the Texas State Fair when he was a kid. In the pitch dark, Matt felt for his clothes on the armchair a few feet from his bed. The floor lamp beside it crashed to the floor.

Forgot that was there.

He sat on the edge of the bed, and pulled on his jeans despite one savage pitch that sent him tumbling back to the middle of his bed. The Chief of

Police of Port Stirling, Oregon, had never felt so helpless in his life. Bare-footed and widening his stance, he was finally able to stand on his hellish floor. With his hands out in front of his face, he lurched drunkenly toward his bedroom's big picture window in the blackness.

The window exploded.

• • •

Further inland from the beach, Fern Byrne was also in bed, but wide-awake reading a book by former President Trump's fixer, Michael Cohen. It was so morbidly fascinating, she'd kept reading past her usual 10:00 p.m. lights-out.

Suddenly, she heard a slow rumble and her nightstand lamp fell onto the floor, landing softly on the oatmeal-colored wool carpet. She watched horrified as her lamp rolled away from the bed and crashed violently into the wall six feet away. The slow rumble became a growling howl that Fern at first thought was near-by thunder. Then it sounded like a train com-ing through the house, and, after a few seconds, moving through. Boom!

What the heck was going on?

The room went dark. Her bed had turned into a vibrating, oscillat-ing beast, and Fern dropped her book and held on to the side of the mat-tress like she held on to armrests during a turbulent plane ride. But still, she was tossed onto the floor, her head narrowly missing the corner of the nightstand, and her pale yellow cotton nightgown thrown upwards over her head.

Oh. My. God. It's the Big One. I've got to get to higher ground…now!

Realizing that it was going to be difficult to stand up on her undulat-ing, yo-yoing floor, Fern rolled over to balance on her hands and knees, and felt the air moving as her floor-length draperies swayed wildly from side to side. From all fours, she wobbled to a swaying stance, spreading her feet wide apart. She grabbed hold of the oak railing at the foot of her bed, and held on furiously as she worked her way to the other end of it, and closer to her walk-in closet.

The rustic alder closet door was swinging on its hinges and hit her in the face. She swore, but kept moving forward, reaching for the light switch inside the small closet. Nothing.

Okay, the power is off. I need my flashlight.

Fern, like many Oregonians, thought she was prepared for The Big One. She had an earthquake preparedness kit all packed, with hand-cranked radio, flashlight, phone charger, a battery-operated radio, long-burning candle and waterproof matches. Her favorite, must-have toiletries and a small first-aid kit were packed in the outside pocket of the bag. When Fern joined the Port Stirling police department earlier this year and realized she had more community responsibility now in the face of an emergency, she'd added a 50-foot nylon rope, a whistle, work gloves and face masks, a Swiss Army knife, safety eye goggles, a Mylar sleeping bag, and a small tent. She had a separate bag stored next to the emergency kit packed with bottled water, canned foods and a manual can-opener, protein power bars, freeze dried food, and water purification tablets. A small backpack with a change of clothes completed her 'grab and go' preparation.

However, Fern stored the kits in her garage, which now seemed miles away. In spite of being tossed around her closet like a rag doll, she needed to get dressed in the dark. Instead of trying to rummage around in various drawers for clothing, Fern lunged for the hook on the back of the closet door where she'd hung her clothes earlier—they'd have to do for now. She again took a wide stance and leaned against one waggling wall as she pulled on her jeans, black tee, and black V-neck cashmere sweater.

A basket of clean laundry that she'd earlier placed on top of the small island in the middle of her closet had toppled to the floor, spilling its contents. She floundered around until she was able to scoop up some socks, putting on one pair (she hoped they were a pair), and shoving two more in the waistband of her pants.

Fern gauged that a few minutes had passed, maybe as many as five. Surely the severe shaking would stop soon. Somehow, she had to get to her garage, get her shorty weatherproof boots on, and get her car out of the building. She knew the automatic garage door opener wouldn't work with the power off, but there was an emergency release cord, and she had used it before during Port Stirling's famous storms.

Suddenly, the undulations and the roar stopped. Although her legs still felt rickety, the floor was stationary. The howling had turned into a dead, calm silence. This was even more frightening.

• • •

Port Stirling police detective Jay Finley was shooting pool in the back room of the Port Stirling Tavern in the old part of town with a couple of buddies. Near the port, the tavern's elevation was only eleven feet above sea level, like all of this original area of town.

Jay, a native Oregonian like his co-worker Fern Byrne, knew immediately what the relentless tremors meant. *The Big One. Holy shit.*

Before the tsunami warning would even sound its ominous blasts, the tall, skinny 28-year-old cop and his pals were in his police car headed for higher ground as fast as he could drive. Which wasn't too fast because the road kept buckling in front of him.

• • •

Oregon State Police trooper "Big Ed" Sonders and his considerably smaller wife, Milly, were conked out asleep at their Twisty River-front home in a valley about 35 miles southeast of Port Stirling. Highly respected and beloved by all the local cops he worked with in Chinook County, Sonders covered the south coastal region.

The Sonders' yellow lab, Max, also in dreamland in his doggie bed at the foot of his people's bed, was the first to wake. He staggered to his old feet, and barked his way to the sliding glass door that opened to the riverside patio.

"What the hell?" asked Ed, coming awake with a start at his dog's growling.

"What's wrong?" said Milly, sitting up in bed.

"Uh-oh," replied her husband of twenty-two years. "Are we having an earthquake?"

Just then, a strong jolt threw Max against the door, and he whimpered loudly. Ed was out of bed in an instant, and stumbled, unsteady on his size fifteen feet, to comfort his dog. In the pitch darkness, he heard rather than saw water sloshing up against the glass door. Water that should be one hundred feet away from his patio.

"Get up, honey," he said as calmly as he could manage, "we need to get out of the house."

• • •

By the time the shaking ended—which seemed to last forever—everyone west of the Cascade Mountains, bisecting the large state, was fully awake. The violence of the tremors could not be ignored, and even mild shaking was felt on the Oregon/Idaho border, 450 miles east.

When the initial ground shaking finally stopped at 11:38 p.m., parts of the western half of the state were no longer recognizable. Several buildings which formed Portland's skyline had collapsed, igniting gas explosions and fires. The dome on the state capitol building in Salem smashed into millions of pieces. The old interstate bridge on I-5 connecting Oregon and Washington ended up in the agitated Columbia River in several large chunks.

The destruction in the Willamette Valley was not fair or even logical in some places. Sometimes older buildings that had been retrofitted survived and newer ones, supposedly earthquake proof, crumbled alongside them. The oldest stone building on the University of Oregon campus stood tall and proud, while the new science complex was moved two feet off its foundations.

Further east and south of the valley, results were mixed. A busy street in downtown Bend saw every third or fourth building disintegrate, leaving grotesque gaps between standing, untouched structures. In nearby Redmond, it was business as usual with no serious damage. Southern cities like Grants Pass and Medford survived mostly unscathed, although it was later revealed that the course of the Rogue River at Grants Pass had been slightly altered.

The only thing that was starkly clear and unarguable in the aftermath of the 2021 Big One was that the Oregon Pacific coast had taken the brunt of it. The Cascadia subduction zone—a roughly 700-mile fault line—moves up and down, not sideways, and the vertical jolt from a major quake can create walls of water that gather in height and speed as they race toward shorelines. Residents living directly along the almost-400-mile Oregon coastline had less than thirty minutes to reach higher ground before the 40-foot surge of water traveling at jet plane speeds slammed into the full length of the coast. Not all of those poor souls made it.

• • •

Matt Horning, originally from Dallas, Texas, until starting his new job on the Oregon coast nine months earlier, had never actually experienced an earthquake. Oh, Dallas would have an occasional mild quiver, rarely over 2.0 in magnitude, and most people never even felt it.

As Port Stirling's chief of police he'd undergone earthquake and tsunami training early on in his tenure. The city manager, Horning's boss Bill Abbott, lived directly on the Pacific, his house 200 feet back from the beach, and his deck only about ten feet above the sand. Abbott knew the potential danger, and was adamant that all city employees be well-trained on what to do if the worst case happened.

But even with all the studying, workshops, and community forums Matt had attended since his arrival in Port Stirling, he had no clue what the real thing would feel like and actually entail. The force of his huge picture window exploding, and the shocking velocity of it knocked him back on his ass.

He sat stunned on the floor of his bedroom, which had finally stopped gyrating. Picking some shards of glass out of his left arm and hand, Matt appeared to be otherwise all right. His instincts were to run, to get out of the cottage as fast as he could, but he chose his way carefully across the glass-covered floor. He rounded the corner of his massive stone fireplace, still solid and standing firm, to discover that the rest of his cottage was missing.

Gone. Walls and windows collapsed. Furniture turned into sticks and scattered around. Refrigerator toppled onto its side out near where the bluff-top fence had been. Partial roof over the kitchen, but the living area was exposed to the night sky and an eerie, but beautiful full harvest moon. His back yard with its two Adirondack chairs, once a wonderful 300-foot perch from which to view six miles down the beach, was also gone. In its place was a new jagged earth outline that might not be finished rearranging itself. What remained of his house, namely the bedroom, was now hanging precariously over the liquefying and land-sliding bluff.

Glass on his bare feet or no, Matt Horning took off running, sprinting as fast as he could, toward the Twisty River valley and away from the demonic Pacific Ocean.

· · ·

Fern Byrne was able to back her baby blue VW Bug out of the garage after some jiggling of the stuck door. So far, her one-story, small ranch house remained intact. She threw her preparedness kits in the trunk, pulled on her boots, grabbed a parka off its hook near her car keys, and took off, not bothering to even attempt to close the garage door.

Her driveway and cul-de-sac had buckled fiercely in places, but she could see well enough with her car's lights and the bright moonlight to avoid the worst areas. She was dismayed to see that her newly-seeded front lawn now had a small mountain of earth smack dab in the middle of it. Like a gigantic mole had come up under the grass.

She and the Port Stirling police department had trained to head to a high place at the first tremor of a quake. The likelihood of a coastal tsunami was probable, perhaps a few feet of water, but also perhaps much more than that. They had agreed to take the old highway inland toward Twisty River, the county seat, to where a 500-foot elevation hill marked the dividing line between the beach and the river valley. The hill was called Deception Hill, and that's where Fern headed now.

She hesitated for a moment when she reached Highway 101, thinking that she should cross it and head west to Ocean Bluff Road to make sure Matt got out safely. But she knew her boss and lover had unmatched survival instincts and smarts, and he was likely already ahead of her. She turned north instead, and headed for Deception Hill.

• • •

Detective Jay Finley had been promoted to his current rank six months ago after he had played a key role in solving the tragic murder of Port Stirling's former mayor's young daughter. The young detective didn't have all the answers yet about his job, or life, for that matter, but he knew one thing: if there was one chance in a million of a tsunami striking his town, he didn't want to be anywhere near sea level. Jay had seen the projections of the potential damage of what even a small tsunami would do to Port Stirling.

On the way to their town's pre-ordained meeting point on Deception Hill, Jay called his parents' home. They lived inland about thirty miles from Port Stirling, still in Jay's childhood home. He knew they would be asleep at this hour, and he was hoping like hell his phone call would wake them. His mom answered, raspy-voiced but alert.

"Is that you, mom?" Jay asked.

"Jay! Are you all right, honey?"

"I'm fine. Headed to Deception Hill now with Harlan and Justin. That's where we're all supposed to meet in case of emergency. Are you and dad OK?"

"We're fine. Shook up, but not hurt. Dad was thrown out of bed onto the floor, but he's OK. He'll have a big bruise tomorrow. He likes to keep one leg out from under the covers, so he was close to the edge. Guess that bit him in the butt tonight, huh?"

"So it shook good where you are, too?"

"Oh my, yes! This was a big one—biggest in my lifetime, for sure. Scared the bejesus out of me. I'm still shaking. What are the roads like? Are you being a careful driver?"

If Jay had a dollar for every time in his life his mother had asked that question, he could retire. "Of course I am. The roads pretty much suck," he told her. "There's debris and crap everywhere, trees down, and lots of the pavement is cracked and buckled. It's your worst nightmare out here.

You and dad should go outside the house with flashlights and take a good look around. Make sure everything is secure and the house is solid. OK?"

"We were on our way to do that when you called. We can see that we've got some fallen trees in the backyard, but they missed the house. Tell Justin we'll go next door and make sure his folks are good. We've got lamps and dishes and so forth strewn all over, and your dad wants to check the foundation, all the windows, and the roof. This is gonna be quite the clean-up."

"Mom, this is important—are you listening to me?" Jay said urgently.

"Yes, Jay. What is it?"

"Please, please tell dad to *not* go up on the roof. With the magnitude of this quake, there will likely be several aftershocks. They could be substantial. He needs to stay on the ground, got it? In fact, if you can stand it, you should probably stay out in the backyard the rest of tonight, in case there is any more action."

"I already told him that about going up on the roof, but I'll reinforce what you said. S'pose it wouldn't hurt to camp outside until dawn. I'm more worried about downed power lines than our house collapsing, though. There's not a light on anywhere."

"Yeah, same here. Dark as hell."

"Maybe this is hell," she said, her voice quiet.

"Yeah, maybe it is. Maybe it is." And their connection suddenly went dead.

CHAPTER 2

Jay was the first to arrive at the town's designated meeting point. City Manager Bill Abbott pulled up five minutes later with a woman that Jay presumed was his wife. She looked familiar, and Jay thought he might have met her at last year's city holiday party.

"Mr. Abbott, thank God you're OK!" Jay exclaimed, wrapping his boss's boss in a bear hug. At six-foot-three, the gangly detective towered over the shorter and much stouter city manager. "Mrs. Abbott," Jay risked, nodding in her direction.

"Detective Finley, isn't it?" she responded, trying a smile that didn't quite take. She looked ghostly pale in the darkness, and seemed agitated. "Please call me Ruth, and then I can call you Jay."

"Deal," agreed Jay.

"We're good," Bill jumped in, giving his wife an affectionate squeeze, "but our home wasn't so lucky. It collapsed."

"What do you mean, sir?"

"The ground underneath our house liquefied. Just turned to mush and took the house and everything in it with it." Tears began to roll down his face. "We were lucky we made it out, and that one of our cars was parked out in front instead of in the garage," he choked out.

Jay stood stunned, and stared at them, speechless for a long moment. Finally, he said, "I'm so, so sorry. I can't believe this." He jammed his useless hands into his jeans pockets, and looked down at the now enemy ground beneath his feet.

"Believe it, Jay," Bill said, wiping his eyes with his shirt sleeve. "And there's more bad news to come. Everything we could see on the drive away from the beach was destroyed. Leveled. People were running away, many in their nightclothes. Didn't even stop long enough to change. Too scared. We stopped and picked up as many as we could fit in our minivan." Bill Abbott pointed to the six people still huddled in his vehicle, their faces etched in horror—Jay hadn't noticed them, and they hadn't said a word.

"You lived right on that point north of the inlet, right?" Jay asked, remembering how Matt had been concerned about Abbott's location during the hunt for the smugglers in the big raid five months ago.

"Yes, we were well north of the Anselmo operation, but you can bet your bottom dollar I was out on my deck every night checking the horizon," Bill said, referring to the ship involved. "I would've guessed then that those crooks were more dangerous to us than Mother Nature," shaking his head.

"This is awful. Do you think anyone was killed?"

Collected now and squaring his shoulders, Abbott looked intensely at the young detective. "Yes, we're going to have multiple casualties. Likely hundreds if not more. Granted, except for the moonlight, we couldn't see much, but I'm afraid that everything near the beach is gone. And we heard the tsunami siren as we turned east and inland. Thank God our system worked. But if there is any water at all, say two-to-four feet as most projections say…"

Mrs. Abbott interrupted her husband and finished his sentence, "Then the lower part of town and the port and waterfront area will be completely flooded. And that's if the old town didn't get obliterated during the earthquake."

"And if people don't take the earthquake or the warning seriously, it'll be even worse," Bill said.

"People know what to do," Jay said. "We headed for higher ground the minute the shaking stopped," indicating his two buddies standing behind him.

"God knows, I love our Port Stirling citizens," Bill said, "but some of them aren't as smart as you folks. And even some of the smart ones are stubborn as hell. Remember that old coot up on Mount St. Helens? He refused to leave even as the volcano was rumbling. I'm afraid we have more than our share of Harry Trumans in Port Stirling. Colorful, lovely people, but stubborn as mules."

"But they wouldn't stay put, surely, when they heard the tsunami blast," Jay said and it came out as a question more than a statement. "I know these people, and they won't be stupid," he argued.

"Scared people do dumb things," Fern Byrne said, coming up behind the Abbotts. She went straight to Jay and gave him a voracious, heartfelt hug.

"I'm glad to see you, Jay-ster," Fern said.

"I'm happy to see you, too, Red," Jay grinned, breaking free of her tight grip.

"I told you not to call me that," said his red-haired, freckled co-worker, who had been called by that nickname as long as she could remember. Didn't mean she liked it. Any more than she liked 'string bean' because of her tall, slim body that hadn't changed much since high school, even though she was now closer to 40 than 30.

Fern motioned to three people standing beside her. "This is Lisa, Sharon, and Ron. I don't know their last names," she smiled. "I picked them up walking on the highway."

"We couldn't get our car out of the garage," Ron grunted. He had grime on his face, and cuts on one arm. "Damn door was warped and it wouldn't budge. Fern's an angel."

"We're all in this together. Mr. and Mrs. Abbott, I'm so relieved to see you," Fern said, shaking hands with him, and giving Mrs. Abbott a quick hug. "You live right on the beach, don't you?"

"Lived," Bill corrected. "I was telling Jay here that our home was destroyed. If we hadn't been up watching the late show, we'd be under our collapsed second story now. We made a run for it, and barely made it out before the ground gave way."

Fern's hand flew to her mouth and an involuntary gasp escaped. "Oh, no!" She unwrapped the scarf around her neck, pulled off the wool hat she was wearing, and put them both on Ruth Abbott. "I'm so sorry. This might help you stay warmer." And then, looking around frantically, Fern said, "Has anyone seen Matt yet? Is he here?"

"We all just arrived," Jay said. "Five minutes ago. He'll be here any minute, I'm sure." He sounded more confident than he looked.

. . .

Oregon State Police trooper Ed Sonders and his wife, Milly, dressed quickly in the dark, scooped up Max, their elderly dog, and left their house through the front door. They settled Max safely in the back seat of Ed's state car in the driveway, and then set out, flashlights in hand, to survey their house and riverfront property.

After about twenty minutes, Milly said, "I don't see any cracks in the foundation anywhere, do you, hon?"

"Everything looks good to me," Ed replied. "Siding is fine, windows OK. I can't see the top of the chimney, too dark, but from here it looks like it always does. Remind me to call our builder tomorrow, and tell him he did a great job," he smiled at his wife. "Let's take a look around back. Watch your step—I heard water closer to the house than it should be," he said, taking her by the hand.

They inched their way together around the side of the house, carefully picking the way. About ten feet from the back corner of their house, a loud crack off to their right sounded like a gun shot, and the ground beneath them shook mightily for a couple of seconds.

"What the hell?!?" Ed exclaimed.

Both flashlights swung to their right, illuminating a sad sight. One of the two 100-year-old oak trees on their three-acre property had crashed to the ground, giving up to the forces of nature after a century.

"Oh, no," cried Milly, who dearly loved both oaks. She'd planted red tulips around the base of each tree when they had built their home here six years ago.

"I'm sorry, Mil," Ed said, wrapping her up in his big body. The top of her head came to his massive barrel chest. They stayed like that for a while, as Milly broke down against her husband.

"We could rebuild our house, I guess," Milly said sniffling, "but we can't rebuild that tree."

"True," agreed Ed. "But we can sure as hell plant another one as soon as we figure out how bad this quake is and what we're dealing with as a state. Are you up to keep going?"

Milly smiled at her gentle giant of a husband, his kindness always a touch point in their long relationship.

She grabbed his hand and said, "Let's go," and they continued around to the back yard. Which was now a swimming pool.

"The river is not supposed to come up this high," Ed deadpanned, as they stared gaping at the normally placid fifty-foot-wide river that was now over 200-feet wide and swiftly advancing. Noisy, muddy, and turbulent, it covered their stone patio, and lapped at the glass doors outside both their bedroom and the great room area.

"Quick!" Milly said first, springing into action, "let's grab the pellet bags from the barn and stack them against the doors. It might help keep the water out."

. . .

Downstream sixteen miles northwest in Twisty River, it was already too late for Patty Perkins and Ted Frolick, still newlyweds seven months after their wedding, to keep the river out of their house.

After meeting during the Emily Bushnell murder case, seventy-something Ted had fallen hard for Twisty River Police Department Detective Patty Perkins, a few years his junior. Both had been lucky in their first marriages, and had assumed they'd met the loves of their lives, and would remain alone.

But Cupid wasn't having it. They were wed shortly after Emily's murder investigation concluded, figuring there was no point in waiting at their ages. Ted kept his bungalow and beloved garden on Ocean Bend Road overlooking the Pacific in Port Stirling, but they mostly lived in Patty's home just outside Twisty River, the county seat, and where her office was located. The two towns were only 18 miles apart, and keeping two separate residences worked for them.

Patty was recognized as one of the leading detectives in southern Oregon, and she wasn't yet ready to retire. Her boss and every one of her colleagues on the county crime team hoped that day wouldn't come for years. Ted, now retired from teaching, tended both homes and properties in between the travelling that both world travelers loved to do when Patty wasn't working on a case.

On the night of September 23, Ted and Patty were tossed from their bed like almost everyone else near the Oregon coast on that fateful night. Patty came to rest on her butt, her padding there softening her landing. Ted wasn't so lucky. He was thrown against the knotty pine wall, broke his arm in two places, and suffered a concussion when his head hit the wood. When the shaking stopped, Patty jumped to her feet and helped her husband, crumpled against the wall, stand. He was woozy, and winced in pain, cradling his broken arm, but she got him over to an armchair by the window, and the two settled there for a while, deciding what to do next.

"Look at me," Patty directed, leaning in close to his face. "Follow my finger with your eyes, darling," and she moved her finger side-to-side and up-and-down. Ted's eyes followed her finger. He was concussed, but would be OK in a few days, she surmised.

But his arm was another matter. "Stay here, and try to relax. I'm going to have a look around and see if we have any issues, and then we'll get you to the hospital."

"OK. Are you all right?"

"I'm fine. Scared shitless, but no harm."

"It takes more than a stupid major earthquake to rattle my wife," Ted smiled at her.

"How big do you think this one was?" she asked her scholarly husband. "Big."

Patty poked around the house as best she could in the dark. Used to high winds and the power going out frequently at the beach, Ted had an array of battery-operated flashlights, and Patty grabbed the biggest one from the drawer in her nightstand. She left another one on Ted's lap, with instructions to stay put until she returned to the bedroom.

Her old farmhouse built in the 1950s was solid and low to the ground.

The one-level home sprawled 2,800 square feet on six acres with about 500 feet of Twisty River frontage. Patty and her first husband, Pat, always had a large vegetable garden between the house and the river where the loamy soil was a gardener's dream. She and Ted had continued that tradition this summer. Ted was overjoyed at what he could grow in this prime spot, and, still eating fresh vegetables and fruit out of it in late September, expected their harvest to keep going most of the mild winter that Chinook County usually experienced. They'd had eggplant fresh from the garden for dinner earlier tonight. Unlike at Ted's place at the beach, eggplant thrived here in this protected, sunnier little valley.

From what Patty could inspect, the house looked like it had survived the violent shaking intact. She ran her hand over the two-sided brick fireplace that dissected the living room from the kitchen, and everything was still where it should be. Some furniture and certainly all the lamps had been tossed about, and there wasn't a single painting or mirror remaining on any of her walls. A corner curio cabinet holding her collection of carnival glass had toppled over, and her collection was a bye-bye, every piece shattered on the hardwood floor.

"Shoot," she grumbled. It would not be the worst thing that Patty discovered that night.

It was now about twenty-five minutes since they'd hit the floor and the shaking had stopped. Patty went back to the bedroom, reporting the damage to Ted. She slipped into clothes by flashlight, and then helped him into some pants and shoes. They decided it was too risky to attempt to free his arm from his PJ top. Patty threw a jacket over his shoulders, and they made their way to the garage through the kitchen.

The garage was connected to the house via a short breezeway. Patty went out the kitchen door first, shining her flashlight on the ground so Ted could be careful where he stepped. It took a few moments for her to realize that she was wading in water up to her ankles.

"What on earth?" she started to say, before a strong waist-high wave knocked her down.

"Look out!" Ted yelled, too late.

Because Patty and Ted were eighteen miles inland from Port Stirling, they hadn't heard the tsunami warning system blasts. The sirens alerted residents of the coastal town that the quake might be followed by the two-to-four foot wave that all the experts predicted would hit the low-lying sections of Port Stirling.

Virtually no one was expecting the gigantic surge of water that slammed into Port Stirling and the Twisty River basin, burying the older part of the village, and causing the river to run backwards as it propelled the wall of water inland more than 50 miles upstream.

CHAPTER 3

The cities and towns in Oregon alongside the Pacific Ocean's Ring of Fire regularly conduct earthquake and tsunami training drills, and community informational workshops. The Cascadia Subduction Zone "megathrust" fault runs between Northern Vancouver Island and Cape Mendocino, California, about 700 miles in total. It separates the Juan de Fuca plate from the North America one. The Zone is between 70–100 miles off the coast of Oregon.

Most people understood the risk that earthquakes and volcanic eruptions posed for this breathtaking part of the world. While they technically knew what to do if the earth started moving, it was also true that most people fell into the "it will never happen here" category. And, a subsection of that group who lived in Port Stirling were, as City Manager Bill Abbott predicted, woefully unprepared for the events of September 23, 2021.

The shaking lasted for five minutes and twelve seconds…an eternity for an earth movement. The cause? A magnitude 9.1 Cascadia Subduction Zone earthquake at a depth of twenty-five miles, its epicenter about seventy-five miles southwest of Newport, Oregon.

At daybreak most of the horrific damage to Port Stirling, and the loss of life was becoming visible. The older part of town along the waterfront was flattened—not a single building survived the shaking of the earthquake.

As the sun rose, just the occasional lone chimney stood above the muck and slime of what had been just hours before a thriving business district.

Luckily, because the quake struck at 11:32 p.m., most of the businesses that made up this part of the village were empty. Cafes, restaurants, souvenir shops and the like that catered mostly to the tourists were closed up for the night, and employees had gone home.

The waterfront promenade disappeared completely, and every boat in the harbor, including the Coast Guard cutters, sank or cut loose from moorings and vanished. Infrastructure surrounding the port was also gone, and pieces of the wharf would materialize days later several miles inland.

Pavement buckled and disintegrated completely in many places. One SUV was found in a 30-foot drop of what had once been Main Street. The Port Stirling Tavern, one of two establishments still going strong at 11:32 p.m. collapsed about fifteen minutes after the shaking stopped. In ten terrifying, ghoulish seconds, remaining customers and employees, who mistakenly thought they were safe, were entombed under the walls, falling roof, and debris. Fourteen people died at this location.

At the Harborside Café and Art Gallery, six people were killed instantly when the second floor gallery where they were just wrapping up an evening show and wine-tasting collapsed onto the ground floor in a thunderous, shuddering heap.

But those may have been the lucky ones, because what happened next was almost unbelievable. Twenty-eight minutes after the city's tsunami warning system blasted out its ominous missive, the first surge produced a forty-foot wave that ravaged what was left of Port Stirling's oldest section, and crashed ashore on most of Oregon's 400-mile coastline, triggering landslides, and liquefying most of the beach-front property. In the first hour after the earthquake, Oregon's shoreline dropped four feet, and it wasn't done yet.

The second surge wave was the assassin. Some who miraculously survived reported the monster was over 150 feet high and moving at jet plane speed.

When early residents of Port Stirling decided to expand the village beyond the sea-level port, they took advantage of a small hill adjacent to the city's core. At an elevation of roughly 300 feet, it ran along a ridge to the south of the older town, and adjacent to the ocean bluffs. City hall, all three of the town's schools, the library, and most of the retail services were located in this area. Many of the buildings here were also completely destroyed during the earthquake, or suffered extensive damage from the tsunami, and would likely take months, if not years, to repair. City hall, where the police department and emergency services were located, had been retrofitted ten years ago to withstand earthquakes, but still, one wall of the building crumbled. Guess the retrofit didn't go as high as magnitude 9.1.

Of the approximately 1,200 Port Stirling households, over 500 were displaced within two hours, with another sixty or so families forced to leave their homes in the next twenty-four hours. The death toll was unknown within the first few hours, but it would be heartbreakingly significant for the small coastal village.

And the debris! What on earth would the clean-up involve? Thousands of dump-truck loads, for sure.

• • •

City Manager Bill Abbott was busy connecting with every city employee or citizen who made it to the meet point on Deception Hill, which, so far, was about thirty people. For a man who had nothing left but his life partner, the clothes on his back, and his vehicle, Abbott was remarkably calm.

But as they all edged closer to the brink of their hilltop perch and looked toward Port Stirling, it became increasingly difficult to remain calm. Everyone gasped, the few children still awake began to cry, and a piercing scream came from a young woman near the front. Ruth Abbott grabbed her husband's hand, and let out a low moan.

From their 500-foot elevation viewpoint and with the nearly-full moon reflecting brightly over the churning, diabolical Pacific Ocean, their small group watched in horror as the tsunami's wall of water raged through town and toward them. It hit the jetty first with such power and force that the rock barrier and the 1901 lighthouse never had a chance. They were demolished in an instant. A collective wail washed over the crowd as they watched their beloved beacon disappear into the roiling sea.

But Mr. Tsunami was just getting started. Next to go was the small port that gave the village its name. Ships were tossed around like apples as the wave crashed fifty feet above them. The angry water, black in the night, had an eerie white crest on top that made it look like a building—a massive, endless skyscraper hurtling inland at tremendous speed.

Suddenly, the mouth of the Twisty River rose up about three stories high, and, for a moment, seemed to completely stop in air. Mr. Tsunami pushed against the river's natural flow, a bully beating up on a smaller child. The wall of cruel water hovered over the gentle river and violently thrust it inland, gathering force as it progressed. As the small group watched helplessly, their amiable, mellow river became an unrecognizable brute.

The old, historic part of Port Stirling was now covered by the Pacific Ocean. Jay shivered when he realized where he'd been only an hour ago. *Please God, let everyone have taken my advice to head to higher ground when the quake hit!*

All the lights in town had been extinguished, and the only sound was the roar of the mighty water. The harvest moon glowed over the water, as if to say "Hey, I'm still here", and all were grateful for it.

"Stay calm, everyone," Abbott implored the small group, huddling even closer together. His eyes darted toward town, and the road up the hill, now beginning to fill with more and more cars and trucks. "We're safe. The quake has stopped, and the water can't reach us."

The monster waves had, in fact, stopped down the hill from them. But what Abbott didn't tell them was that the nasty water had covered much higher ground than all of the city and state projections had shown, or prepared for. He swallowed hard.

• • •

"Does anyone have a notebook or paper and something to write with?" Abbott asked. "Let's all sign in and get a list going for those who will join us soon."

"I've got a notebook and pens in my car," Fern said loudly from the back of the pack, waving her arm at Abbott, and hurrying toward her VW. She kept busy going from person to person, signing them in, smiling at each individual and trying to offer up some soothing words.

"Ah, Dr. Richards, so nice to see you here," Fern said, approaching Paul Richards, Port Stirling's pediatrician. They had met at little Emily's funeral.

"It's nice to see you made it, too, Fern," Dr. Richards replied. "This is my wife, Sydney, and my son, Dustin."

Instinctively, Fern hugged all three of the Richards. Somewhat surprisingly, the teenage son returned Fern's hug, and even seemed to cling to her briefly. This was going to be especially terrifying for the children, Fern thought, and she furiously blinked back tears. It wouldn't do anyone any good if the police broke down.

"If anyone needs medical attention, I've got my bag and first aid in our car," Dr. Richards told Fern.

"Wonderful news. I'll ask as I sign in folks, or if I see anyone who looks like they could use some help. I'm really, really happy you're here!" she said.

"It looks like we might all be here for a while," Jay said loudly to the gathered group, moving to stand next to Bill Abbott. "I'm Detective Jay Finley with the police department, and I want to suggest that we take an inventory among us for survival items."

Abbott nodded his support, and Jay kept talking, making sure his clear voice carried to the back of the group. "While Officer Byrne makes a list of all of us who are currently safe, I'll start another list of who has what supplies, quantities, etc, and I'll go first. I had my squad car with me, and we keep emergency items in the trunk at all times. I've got first aid, flashlights, flares, and a couple of earthquake preparedness kits." He paused and looked sheepish. "To be perfectly honest, I've never opened them, and I have no idea what's inside."

That drew a laugh, releasing some of the tension in the air.

"Do you have any guns, Jay?" asked a tall young man standing off to one side of the group.

"Yes, but we won't be needing guns," Jay answered firmly. "Why do you ask?"

"I have my hunting rifle in my truck," the young man replied. "Seeing as it's getting close to hunting season."

"Well, right now, I'd rather you had a pizza in your truck," Jay grinned at the crowd. Jay was known for the copious amounts of food he could eat. "But we'll note your rifle, just in case. Got anything else in your truck?"

"Tent. Sleeping bags. Cook stove. Lanterns. Stuff for camping."

"Awesome," chimed in Bill. "We're all on a camping trip for a few days. That's how I'm thinking about this mess. Anyone else got camping gear?"

At least twenty hands went up. Turns out most of Port Stirling had been readying their rigs for hunting season. The first thing tonight that went right! At least, they would have some shelter from the mild, but still fall weather.

"Let's get some tents set up and make some beds for the kids," Abbott said. "Those of you with lanterns, please place them in a circle, and let's put the tents around them."

Abbott watched while several people in the group did as he suggested, and the lights helped banish some of the gloom.

"My cell phone is not working," Abbott lamented. "By any chance, does anyone have a working phone?" He grimaced as he said it, pretty sure he knew the answer.

He waited for a hand to go up. Not a single one did.

"'Fraid of that. The quake likely knocked out the system."

A voice from the group said, "My brother-in-law works for Seal Solutions. They've been training on this earthquake crap, and they'll get us back operational as quick as they can."

"I will hold that thought!" Abbott said. "I see Dr. Richards is here," he continued. "Does anyone need medical attention? Any cuts or scrapes? Bumps on your heads?"

Shaking of heads.

"Great," he said. "While the tents get going, let's see what kind of skills we have so far in our group. Any cooks, or construction workers, or…"

A voice from the crowd interrupted Abbott, an older woman, "Excuse me, Bill, but is Matt Horning here yet? You're doing a wonderful job, but I was hoping our police chief would be here, too."

Jay and Fern traded anxious glances, and Bill looked pleadingly at Jay.

"We haven't seen him yet, Lydia," Jay answered, "but I'm sure he's on his way to meet us here." Jay and Lydia had met back in January when Lydia's Border collie had discovered Emily Bushnell's body in the tunnel on the beach. That experience had bonded the older woman and the young officer for life.

"So, he knows this meeting location?" Lydia persisted.

"Yes, ma'am—Matt was advised of this site as Port Stirling's meeting place at the last earthquake readiness meeting. Don't worry, he knows where to go, and he should be here any minute." He swallowed hard and felt his Adam's apple noticeably shift.

"Doesn't Chief Horning live right on the bluff in that rental cottage?" asked another voice from the crowd. A murmur went up.

"He does," confirmed Abbott. "But so do a lot of us who made it and are here now. My house is now in the Pacific, probably on its way to Japan, and here I stand without a scratch. Let's don't worry about the chief. As he's shown us every day since he arrived in Port Stirling, he's very resourceful. He'll be fine."

"There are some cars coming up the hill now," Fern interrupted. "I'll go check in these people. Maybe Matt is with them." She bounded down the road, casting a quick glance back at Jay, and took her nervous energy with her.

. . .

Patty Perkins struggled to her feet, sputtering and spitting out water she'd swallowed after being knocked down by the wave. Ted grabbed her arm with his one good arm, and held on tight to keep his beloved wife from being swept away.

"What the fuck was that!?!" Patty exclaimed once she stopped coughing and regained her balance.

"Come on! Back inside the house! Move it, lady!"

Patty didn't hesitate and followed her husband who was moving faster than she'd ever seen him scurry back through the kitchen door. Once he helped Patty inside, he slammed the door behind them, and the newlyweds grabbed every towel they could find and stacked them up against the door to keep out the surging water.

"You stay here and rest for a minute while I go secure the patio doors," she instructed her concussed husband. She pulled out a kitchen chair away from the table and said, "Sit down here, please. I'll be back in a minute."

Dripping water, Patty hustled from memory to the hall bathroom in the darkness and plucked several bath towels out of the linen closet. She was calm enough to nab the older towels on a lower shelf rather than the new ones she'd bought after their wedding and placed up higher.

I never liked these towels anyway. She shoved them up against the patio sliding doors overlooking the river, as water was now seeping into the house. She then dashed to the opposite side of the house facing the meadow and the Twisty River valley beyond. All seemed secure on that side…at least, for now. Patty made her way back to the kitchen and to Ted's side.

"Tsunami," Ted said plainly. "Backed up the Twisty River all this way inland. Port Stirling and the beach must be destroyed." His lower lip quivered, and Patty knew he was thinking about his cottage on the bluff.

"We don't know for sure how bad it is, so let's don't go there quite yet, OK?"

"If the water made it this far, it must have been at least 50 feet high when it came ashore. Picture that, Patty." Wide-eyed, he turned to look at her, and they both burst into tears and clasped their hands together, their foreheads gently touching.

"Tell me how you're feeling, honey," Patty recovered. "We won't know until daybreak whether we can get you out of here and to the hospital, so, for now, call me Nurse Patty. How are you? And tell me the truth."

"My head hurts, but I don't feel as light-headed as I did earlier. An Advil would be nice," Ted said.

"What about your arm?" she asked, carefully rolling up his sleeve to get a better look. She took the flashlight off his lap and held it up to his arm. She couldn't see any bone poking through anywhere, and figured that was a good sign.

"Well, I won't be pitching in the World Series anytime soon. Or lifting my coffee cup, for that matter. It's aching and torn up pretty good, I fear. I'm a little miffed at that wall right now. Better make it two Advil."

She smiled and kissed him on the cheek. "I'll get you some, darling, and this time I'm taking the flashlight so I don't have an encounter with that mean wall. Be right back."

After she tended to Ted as best she could, Patty scrounged around for some matches, and lit her gas cooktop. No water came out of her faucet, but they kept gallons of bottled water in a kitchen cabinet for such an emergency. She boiled water and made instant coffee. The two of them sat side-by-side at their round kitchen table, and talked softly about next steps.

Flashing the light at the wall clock in the kitchen, Patty said, "Since it's still about five hours until dawn, let's go back to bed and try to rest. I doubt if either of us will sleep, but resting seems like the smart move under the circumstances. What do you think?"

"Agreed. If you've secured the river-side doors as best you can, I don't see that there is anything further we can do until it's light. We have some sandbags in the garage left over from last winter, but there's no way in hell I'm letting you go out there again in the dark. And I'm useless right now," he sighed.

They had promised to never lie to each other, so she left his remark unanswered—he was useless right now against whatever force they were dealing with. And Patty suddenly felt tired to the bone. She stood and quietly and kindly helped Ted stand. Together, they made their way slowly down the long hallway and back into their bedroom.

. . .

Ed and Milly Sonders, whose home was surrounded by huge old trees, their status unknown until it got light out, had decided to spend the remainder of the night in their minivan. Ed secured the doors on the river side of the house, and then drove the van out to a clearing about 200 yards from their home. Milly grabbed some warm blankets and their pillows, and they, joined by Max, of course, bunked down huddling together against the chilly night air and their fears.

When daylight entered through the van's windows, Ed tried to stretch his long, big body without waking Milly or Max. But there was really nowhere for his six-foot-four length to go. Max, understanding his master's conundrum, whimpered and crept closer to Milly, trying to get out of Ed's way.

"Guess we're all awake now," Milly said, her eyes blinking into the sunlight.

"Sorry, hon, but I need to move. Cramping up."

Ed reached for his shoes, and opened the van's side door and climbed out. Max jumped down right behind him, and bolted to one of his favorite small trees near the house.

"I'm going to the house and put on the coffee," he said, sticking his head back in the van. "You OK?"

"I'm fine, just laying here thinking about things. I'll be there in a minute."

"Take your time. I'll look around and see what we're dealing with. Are you warm enough?"

"I'm quite cozy, if it weren't for the horror that's undoubtedly happening around us," she looked up at her husband. "Maybe we should sleep in the van more often."

"Yeah, next time there's a killer earthquake. Right behind you," he grinned. "I'll be back soon with a steaming cup of coffee for you. C'mon, Max, let's go boy."

Man and dog circled the house, dog sniffing frantically at everything, and man's eyes getting wider and wider.

"Good Lord," Ed said to himself. The front and sides of his house looked normal, no tree damage, no cracks or missing shingles, and the chimney looked like it always did. A twenty-foot pine tree had fallen, its roots freshly sticking up in the air, but it was far enough from the house that it did no damage.

But the back of the house, the side fronting the usually placid Twisty River, was another story. The stone patio that Ed had laid by hand six years ago was gone. As was all of their outdoor furniture, BBQ, flower planters, and Max's doghouse. The gentle grassy slope down to the river had disappeared. In its place was mud. Brown, icky mud mixed with water still lapping near the house. The small trees growing along the riverbank were also gone, the much wider river now in their place. Mud, and a river still five times its normal size—that's all there was to see.

Ed knew that it must have been a raging river flowing backwards during the night to do this kind of damage. And he immediately understood that it meant a giant tsunami had followed the big earthquake and had come ashore at the Twisty River's mouth in Port Stirling. If the wall of water was powerful enough to do this much damage this far inland, Ed also knew that it was possible there wasn't much left of that beautiful little village.

He needed to get to work.

CHAPTER 4

Fern separated from the rest of the growing group, grateful that daylight had broken at last. She squinted into the sunlight glinting off the reds, yellows, oranges of the surrounding trees, preparing to drop their leaves and get ready for yet another Oregon fall. It was a lovely morning, cloudless blue sky, and still.

Fern loved this time of year; most true Oregonians did. In a coastal village like Port Stirling, September and October often brought the best weather- warm days, mild nights, and not much wind. That would change by Thanksgiving, when the rains would begin in earnest, followed by a string of winter storms, one after the other blowing in from the southwest. There was a reason why the Hawaiian Islands saw a lot of Oregonians in the winter months, but during lovely September, this was a good place to be.

But today, Fern despised the chaos Mother Nature had deposited on her community. She stood on the edge of the hill, surveying what was left of Port Stirling and beyond to the Pacific Ocean. She could see nothing but destruction. Impassable roads, cracked and buckled pavement, flattened buildings—all covered with thick, wet sand. Debris everywhere, and not just the usual high-tide seaweed and driftwood; huge logs and trees cast aside like toothpicks. Cars on their sides pushed up against collapsed buildings. Large blobs of mucus-like foam covering almost every surface. And something else she couldn't make out from this distance, but Fern had a horrible feeling that her town was also covered with thousands and thousands of dead fish. The air smelled briny, as one expected with the sea covering the land, but it had even more of a fermented whiff than usual.

Oh, sure, the Pacific was its normally blue and beautiful self again this morning, but last night it was a cobra-headed behemoth, smashing everything—and everyone—in its evil path.

Where is he? Where is he?

She felt a hand on her shoulder. Jay.

Without turning, Fern said, "We have to find him, Jay. We have to go and find him."

"My thoughts exactly. You OK?"

"I'm fine. Extremely pissed off, but physically fine."

"What's our plan?" Jay asked. Even though he'd been a cop longer than Fern, he knew that her smarts and instincts were the best in the department, right up there with Matt's.

"I think we need to first help everyone here with some breakfast," Fern said, pulling a strand of thick auburn hair behind her ear, her hand shaking a little. "It sounds like we've got good supplies from almost everyone, which is a huge relief. Let's check with Bill and see what the three of us can organize."

"I don't want to be in charge of this effort," Jay said quietly, bending close to Fern's ear, "but it looks like everyone is counting on us."

"No question. We're it, and we don't have a choice. And we will step up," she said. Her jaw was clenched, and she had a steely look on her face that Jay had only seen once before.

"I wish Matt was here," Jay replied. He looked so morose that Fern hugged him.

"Me too. But he's not, and he might need our help." She squared her shoulders and looked him in the eye. "So let's do this, partner. Give these nice folks some freeze-dried coffee and pour two big ones for us. I'm not going to let Matt Horning die out there because of a stupid wave."

"I have some beef jerky in my preparedness kit," he answered, "and if you're nice to me, I'll share some with you." He grinned at her.

Fern breathed in the fresh, morning, tree-scented air with its hint of dead fish. "How the hell did we get here?" she smiled a shaky smile back at him. Arm-in-arm, the two cops marched back toward the group.

. . .

The resilience of the human spirit never failed to amaze Abbott. He looked around the survivors, now grown to about 160 people as the night wore on, and his heart warmed at what he saw. People had their camp stoves out and lit. Fires had been built with wood foraged from the surrounding area, and it made a difference against the morning chill. The smell of hot, strong coffee wafted through the air. Kids were running around, in and out of the trees, playing hide & seek. Today would bring a harsh reality, but for now, it was indeed a camping trip.

. . .

With only the light from the moon, and breathing hard, Matt Horning kept running until he reached Highway 101. Only once did he look back toward his cottage and the Pacific Ocean. His home was no longer there.

He didn't take time to mourn the loss. Once the shock of what was actually happening wore off, and the ground beneath him stopped shaking, Matt concluded that he needed to get his shit together, and fast. It was obvious to him that Port Stirling had sustained a major natural disaster with this earthquake, and people would need him. Houses didn't slide down the bluff into the Pacific every day, and there would need to be a strong recovery response from city leaders, like the police chief. Just because he had no shoes, and except for the rising moon he was engulfed in darkness, didn't mean he was powerless. *I'm young, I'm strong, I'm smart, and I will help fix this awful thing.*

Pausing to get his bearings with the position of the moon, Matt put the time at about midnight. His wristwatch, a beloved gift from his paternal grandfather, was likely on its way to a watery grave about now.

Think. Which direction is the pre-arranged meeting point in case of a disaster? Obviously away from the ocean. Think! You went over this stuff with your department last month. Deception Hill—that's it. East of town toward Twisty River.

Matt slowed his run to an easy jog, feeling a sharper-than-usual pain in his football-injured knee. He headed north on the highway to where he remembered the turn-off to the Twisty River road was. He turned occasionally to look over his shoulder with the thought of potentially hitching a ride, but no cars had come by in five minutes. *Am I all alone in the universe?*

He kept jogging, and it felt good to be moving toward his destination now that the ground tremors had stopped. He was increasingly anxious about his co-workers and neighbors. Fern and Jay would be fine because they both lived inland, but he feared for some of his Ocean Bend Road neighbors…had they all escaped their homes in time? Lydia Campbell and her dog, Mr. Darcy? Bill Abbott, his boss and friend? Had Vicky finished up her shift at the Inn at Whale Rock? Where did his favorite waitress live? He didn't know. Sylvia, his department admin, and her beautiful family. *Please God, let these people I love all be safe.* Matt figured he'd write a check for $50,000 on the spot if Ed Sonders would drive up right now.

Even in the darkness, Matt could see that the destruction was severe. The highway pavement had gaping cracks every few yards, and nearby buildings were leveled. It was clear the power was off all over town. All was quiet. *One foot in front of the other.*

Now on the eastern edge of town, he turned inland off the highway onto the smaller road to Deception Hill, and the dark night got even darker. As he started the climb out of town, the forest blocked out the moonlight, and it was pitch-black. He stepped off the pavement onto a carpet of fallen leaves and sat down to rest for a minute, letting his eyes adjust to the murkiness of the witching hour. The air was fresh and brisk, and he breathed in deeply, recovering from his running. Matt rested, comfortable in the knowledge that he was nearing the meeting point.

Just then, Port Stirling's tsunami warning system blasted, startlingly loud in Matt's ears. He jumped to his feet at the first sound of the sirens, understanding immediately that he needed to race to the higher ground ahead of him. For the second time in thirty minutes, he took off running, heading uphill. But this time, his luck ran out.

● ● ●

Fern was now officially worried about Matt. It had been about eight hours after the initial quake, and a little over four hours since the tsunami waters had receded. And still no sign of him at their designated meet.

Their group ate breakfast, and had a meeting led by Bill Abbott where they discussed a plan on how to proceed. The survivors agreed on a course of action: they naturally wanted to inspect their properties, and help their fellow citizens who might not be safe.

Abbott had assigned three people in addition to himself—Fern, Jay, and Abbott's long-time assistant Mary Lou, who had arrived just after the tsunami sirens with her husband—to lead four groups, and they had divided up the crowd equally. Each of the groups were assigned a section of the town on a map that Jay hastily drew.

"Our first priority is search and rescue," Fern told the assembly. "Now that the water has receded and we've got daylight, we'll hunt for other survivors. If it's as bad as it looks, we might not get any help from the outside world for a few days, so it's up to us to find and take care of our own."

"Fern's correct," Abbott said. "I was awake all night, and I didn't hear or see any planes or helicopters overhead. That tells me that all of Oregon is in trouble, maybe even all of the west coast. So we are responsible for Port Stirling, and here's how we're going to proceed. Search and rescue, number one. Number two, we'll keep this camp together. If you discover today that your home is intact, please bring food and supplies back here before you start your personal home cleanup."

"What kinds of things should we bring here?" asked a voice in the crowd.

"Anything that will help out the camp in terms of food, shelter, fire, light, hygiene," said Abbott. "Those of you whose houses are OK can stay if you choose to, but you also have an obligation to the greater good."

Jay added, "Kind of consider this a modified martial law. We're going to operate this search and rescue with public safety in mind. We can't stop you from going back to your homes, but if the structure is dicey at all, you should return here before nightfall. Understood?"

Nods from the crowd.

"Please keep in mind that we might discover some people who need medical attention, or who are traumatized in some way," Fern said. "Normally the police would tell you to not touch or move anyone, but we won't have that luxury today. Be as careful as you can, but bring them here. Bill, I would suggest that we leave Dr. Richards here in case we need to attend to any injured. Paul, is that OK with you?"

"Yes," Dr. Richards agreed. "My wife can assist me if we need to treat anyone, but my son can go with a group—he's strong and could be of help." Dustin smiled shyly.

"I'd like to go search with a group," said a voice from the crowd. "I'm Rick, and I'm a nurse at Buck Bay Hospital. I can perform triage if needed in town, and decide who needs to be moved to camp."

"I thought I recognized you, Rick," said Fern. "That sounds like a good plan. Thank you for volunteering." To the crowd, she said, "We'll also need a few of you to stay behind and take care of the young children."

"I want to emphasize that all we care about today is search and rescue," Abbott said. "Do what you feel you need to do, but remember that there are probably fellow residents out there who need our help. We're the lucky ones—we got out safely. Some may be trapped under rubble, some may be too injured to move. We have to find those people, and we have to find them as quickly as we can now that it's light. I don't want to scare you older kids any more than you already are, but you can be a big help, too. Look and listen, and if you see anything, tell your parents. OK?"

A few kids started clapping their hands together, and it spread through the crowd until every person was clapping. Bill wiped a tear off his cheek, gave a forceful wave, and said, "Let's go, then."

· · ·

Fern and Jay had slept a few hours in sleeping bags that they'd placed near the entrance to the parking lot, in the hopes that Matt would see them when he arrived. But it was now clear that he hadn't made the meeting point during the night. For whatever reason.

"Bill, I want to take my group along Ocean Bend Road, and make sure everyone is out of those homes and the hotels and motels," announced Fern. "OK with you?"

"Sure, and I appreciate that, Fern. That area is a little raw for Ruth and me. It's the most likely place for people to be trapped or injured, so take Rick with you. Sounds like you know him."

"I do. He lives down the street from me. Works in the ER."

"And, make sure your group has some tools and whatever equipment people might have with them. Take Gil Moretti with you. He's a construction guy, and I'm sure he'll have tools in his rig. Check with him."

"I know Gil," she answered. "He's got a big truck here, so my group can go in that vehicle."

"Any sign of Matt yet?" Abbott asked.

Fern looked down at the ground and mumbled, "No, I'm afraid not. Very worried."

"He's OK," said Jay firmly, coming up behind Bill with the town map. "I don't know where in the hell he is, but he's OK."

"He should have come straight here," said Abbott. "That was always the plan." He rubbed his stubbly cheek.

"Maybe he's helping people in town that didn't leave in time," Jay said, and there was a defensive tone in his voice. "You both know how tough he is. This won't get him. I'm positive."

Fern snapped her head up. "You can't say that, Jay! This was a killer earthquake, followed by a killer tsunami. He could be dead twice, for all we know. All I know for sure is that I'm going to look for him *now*."

She started to move toward her group, and Bill put his hand on her arm. "Start looking on the beach under the bluff, Fern," he said quietly, leaning in close to her ear. "All our projections showed that landslides were likely to occur. Matt's cottage may be in the Pacific like my house. I just hope he's not still in it."

CHAPTER 5

Matt Horning heard the roar behind him, and turned to look at the single most frightening thing he'd ever seen in his forty-four years on this earth. At the instant he realized he was to be swallowed up by a three-story wall of water, his thoughts were of making love to Fern earlier tonight.

Thank God she left my cottage to return to her home before the quake hit. Then the beast walloped him and hurled him forward with all its might. He flailed as he tumbled like clothes in a dryer, an unsuccessful effort to regain his balance. Water clogged his mouth, his nose, his every pore, and all was blackness. The violence seemed to go on and on, and Matt wasn't sure which way was up or down.

Then, he was floating—upwards to the surface. Or was he? He was dizzy. So very, very dizzy. And so tired. *Was it time to let go?* Just let go of this world, and float into the beyond.

If I could only rest for a minute. Close my eyes and sleep. He shut his eyes and floated peacefully.

Something is poking me; stop it, and let me sleep. Leave me be.

Matt flung out his arm to push the poking thing away, and his hand hit something hard. He opened his eyes, and in the murky water could see an outline of something next to him. A tree. A tree floating by. Instinctively, he reached out and put his arms around it. A sharp branch jabbed him in the stomach, but he clung to the tree with every ounce of energy remaining in his body.

Together, the tree and Matt drifted to the surface, buoyant in the calming water. Gasping for air, he climbed fully onto the tree now, his head and shoulders lifted above the water. Sputtering and spitting, he discharged a mixture of sea water and brown foam. The tree was precisely the right size, big enough to support him, but small enough that he could hold on with ease, and hold on he did.

Matt and his new best friend glided across the top of the water for what felt like forever, eventually coming to rest on the forest floor. He waited, still, not daring to move off the tree. The only sounds were his breathing, difficult and wheezy, and the rippling water as the tree gently rocked in the outgoing tide that sucked the ground under him. He put one foot down and touched the solid but squishy earth.

When he knew he could, Matt swung one leg off the tree and stood, with one hand resting on the log for support. His bare feet touched less than an inch of water, and the muck of mud and forest combined. He was shaky—to be expected. Certain he had on a sweater when he left his house, his upper torso was now bare. He reached down; *pants still on, that's a relief.* He shivered.

The tree had come to rest on an incline, and Matt scrambled up it in the blackness, grabbing shrubs and weeds to pull himself up on the steep sections. He thought his lungs might burst. When he believed he had climbed fifty feet or so up the bank, he stopped, looked up at the full moon peeking out between the treetops. It illuminated the hateful water below him, and where once had been only forest, there was now a lake. But he was in the midst of a Douglas fir grove, and there was no point in trying to find his way out to any kind of civilization until daybreak.

Matt made a bed of fir boughs, leaves, and pine needles on a soft spot of the forest floor, laid down and covered his cold, bruised, and battered body with more tree boughs as best he could.

And then he fell into a deep, deep sleep.

• • •

A squirrel played with Matt's curly black hair, thinking that perhaps he could use it somehow. Awakened by the movement on his head, Matt swatted and sent the squirrel flying.

Daylight. I appear to be alive.

He sat up, and everything hurt. He felt woozy and light-headed. But he was in one piece, and although weak and thirsty, he knew what he had to do. Remembering where the moon was last night when he laid down to sleep, Matt started walking in what he was fairly certain was the direction of the road up to Deception Hill. His knee was now screaming at him, and one arm hung limp with pain.

He came out of the forest and hit the road after about thirty minutes of agonizing walking. The tsunami had carried him south of the road but further east, so he knew he didn't have long until he'd arrive at the meet point.

A red Ford Expedition was coming down the hill toward Matt. He realized what a scary sight he must be, and he was sure he didn't smell real good either. But he'd never been happier to see a vehicle. People! Matt began waving his arms as best he could, wincing at the sharp pain in his left shoulder.

The Ford screeched to a halt alongside Matt, and the driver's window opened.

"It's about time you showed up," said his boss, Bill Abbott, with a wide grin. Abbott simultaneously jumped out of his car, and rushed up to Matt, embracing him in what could only be called a bear hug.

"I'm glad to see you, too," Matt said, returning the grin. "I thought I was a goner last night." Flinching in pain, he extricated himself from Abbott's embrace.

"I thought you might be. I had visions of your house sliding down the bluff into the ocean," he said, shaking his head as if to clear the picture out of his mind.

"What about your place? You obviously got out safely."

"It was close. Real close. Ruth and I were watching TV in the family room at the front of the house instead of in our upstairs bedroom like we usually do. When things started shaking, I grabbed her hand, and we ran out the front door. Car was parked in the driveway, and we took off as fast as we could. One time I was happy I'd left the keys in the ignition. We'd gone about 100 yards when our home slid into the Pacific. If we had been upstairs in bed, we'd be at the bottom of the ocean right now."

"I barely made it out. I was sound asleep, and the first thing I knew, I was thrown out of my bed. Came around the corner from my bedroom, and guess what? Rest of my house was gone, and I just started running away from the bluff. My garage, my car, and my police car all went over the side with the house. All I've got is what you see," Matt said, spreading his arms out wide.

"Yeah, we need to do something about that before your ass freezes off. Get in, we'll go back to the camp and get you some help."

Both men climbed in. The only other time that Matt had been in Abbott's car was the morning he picked him up at the Buck Bay Airport in January...the morning that Emily's body had been found on the beach. That had been a little over eight months ago, but, today, it felt like a lifetime.

Abbott turned around to the back seat where some people Matt didn't recognize were sitting. "This here's our Chief of Police, Matt Horning," Abbott said as an introduction. "We'll go back to the camp and see if we can find him some clothes, and then we'll resume our search and rescue operation."

"I know you," said the small boy sitting between his two parents. "You're the cop that shot that bad guy. I saw you on TV." He beamed at Matt, and jumped a little in his seat with excitement.

Matt leaned around his seat, although the move sent tormenting jabs throughout his body, and gave the kid a high five, also excruciating. "What's your name, son?"

"Troy," the boy answered.

"Let that be a lesson to you, Troy. Don't be a bad guy or I'll have to shoot you, too." He winked and pointed his finger at Troy, who immediately burst into giggles. His fit continued while his parents introduced themselves and shook the chief's hand.

"Several people are worried about you up at the camp," Troy's father told Matt. "What happened to you?"

"I was making good progress, but the tsunami had other plans for me,"

Matt said, wondering how many times he would have to tell that story today. Not a pleasant thought.

"Oh, my," gasped Troy's mother, reaching forward to touch Matt's arm. "Was it awful?"

"About as bad as it gets, I reckon," Matt admitted. He only slipped into Texas talk when he was tired. "If it hadn't been for the right tree coming along at the right minute…well, I'd rather not think about what might have happened. But I'm OK now, or will be if some nice person will lend me a shirt."

"I don't mind if you don't put on a shirt," Troy's mother said and smiled at Matt.

Troy's father looked at his wife over the head of Troy, his eyes narrowing in puzzlement as if to say "Where the hell did that come from?"

Abbott roared with laughter and said, "Well, I mind, and we'll find him something to cover up with."

. . .

"Thanks for the ride," Matt said placing his hands on Abbott's open window. "And, Bill, I've told you to quit leaving your car keys in the ignition, dammit," Matt smiled at his boss.

He looked around the encampment, amazed at how organized everything looked considering his own past eight hours. He saw Jay first, who ran toward Matt like he'd been shot out of a cannon, grinning and laughing in relief. Chief Horning and Detective Finley embraced, and it was a toss-up as to who was the happiest.

"I thought you were halfway to Hawaii by now," Jay said, still laughing. Kinda crazy laughing.

"Now you know, it takes more than a killer earthquake and the Empire State Building of tsunamis to take me out."

"Where have you been all night? My God, I'm glad to see you!"

"No clue. Somewhere in the forest down there," Matt pointed at his hotel for the night. "I thought I was almost here, and then the water hit me from behind."

"We watched it from up here. Terrifying," Jay said. "I can't believe you made..."

"Matt!" A scream from the other side of the campsite. Fern came running, making Jay look slow in his streak to their boss.

Matt, relieved, teared up. Her aura of youthful good health made him forget his own battered body. Fern laughed, and, simultaneously, started crying big-time. Jay, unusually sensitive for the gangly cop, stealthily stepped away to give them some privacy.

Locked in an embrace that had no room for even air between them, Matt whispered in her ear, "I told you things were going too good."

Fern smiled through her tears, her face blotchy. "You did. You said it last night. And I told you to not jinx us." She felt the knot of tension slowly leaving her body. Gently, she touched the bruising around his black eye.

"Not sure you can blame me for a once-in-a-millennium earthquake, although I was right," Matt said, playing with a strand of her shining auburn hair.

Fern broke apart, and assessed him with a cool eye. "Are you all right? Tell me the truth. You don't look so good."

"I'm cold as hell, hungry as hell, and beat up, but I'll be fine. You? You look darn good. And I love you, by the way."

Fern squeezed his arm, and said, "Same here, cowboy. I got out of my house fast, and made it up here before the tsunami siren went off. My house suffered a little damage from the quake, but if the wave didn't make it too far inland, I think it'll be OK. We couldn't see from here how far the wave went on the upper part of town. But," she hesitated, "do you want to hear about your place?" She asked the question quietly, lowered her chin a little, and looked up at him with wide eyes.

"I know," Matt said. "I saw the bluff disintegrate as I was running toward the highway."

"I'm so sorry, honey. I don't know what else to say."

"It's OK," he said shrugging, but there was sorrow in his eyes. "There isn't anything to say. Stuff can be replaced, though. Between us, I'm lucky to be alive. I was dead-to-the-world asleep—due to your earlier visit—and I barely made it out in time. It took me a few minutes to realize what was happening, even with all the training we've had. Not proud that I was so slow to react."

"In one way, it was lucky it hit late at night, especially when you see what happened to the port and lower part of town. People were home, not downtown. But I worry about people like you who were asleep and naturally would have reacted slower than those of us who were still awake."

"When the tsunami hit me from behind," Matt said slowly, "I thought about how grateful I was that you'd insisted on going home last night. I knew you would be safe. Not sure we both would have made it out if you had stayed." He drew her to him again, and hugged her tightly.

"Finally, that damn district attorney did something good for us," Fern teased. "If he hadn't called a 7:30 a.m. meeting in Twisty River this morning, I would have stayed with you. Oops, guess I missed his meeting."

Matt laughed. "The visual of him getting knocked out of bed like I did is a hoot. Do you suppose he was wearing a suit at the time?"

"No doubt," she laughed, too. The uptight, ambitious D.A., David Dalrymple, had been a thorn in Matt's side since he'd arrived in Port Stirling. Fern knew her former boss had resented the spotlight that Matt's brilliant detective work on two cases had stolen from him. And when she left the county to take the job with the Port Stirling police department, his resentment toward Matt—and now her—had grown even stronger.

"What could you two possibly be smiling about?" Jay asked with raised eyebrows, coming toward Matt with some clothes.

"You mean, other than the small fact that the three of us are alive this morning?" Matt asked. "If you must know, we had a visual of David Dalrymple being thrown out of bed wearing one of his suits," Matt confided. "Fern was supposed to have a meeting with him this morning."

"OK, that is funny," Jay snickered. But then, the smiles left all three of their faces as they contemplated the road ahead. "Wonder how bad it is inland. Guess we'll find out today. Here," Jay said, thrusting his found treasure at Matt. "I brought you some extra clothes Mitch Dugger had in his camper. He was going to head out deer hunting this weekend, and has a bunch of stuff. Happy to loan to you."

"The kindness of strangers," Matt quoted. "Guess I'd better get used to it for now until I can get my act together." He pulled on a clean tee shirt, heavy wool sweater, and white sweat socks.

"He doesn't know if the boots will fit," Jay added, "but if they don't, there's a couple of other guys that have extra shoes and boots. We'll find something that works for you."

Matt stuck a foot into the rugged grey boots. "About a half inch too big, but these will work. Thanks, man. Point out this guy so I can thank him."

Jay gestured toward Mitch, standing by the campfire.

"OK, now that I'm not half-naked, we need to get to work. All hands on deck. Tell me the plan while I borrow a cup of that coffee over there."

CHAPTER 6

att Horning, Bill Abbott, Fern Byrne, Jay Finley, and Olive Joiner, in her role as the only Port Stirling city commissioner at the meet site, sat in Bill's car.

"I am officially calling to order the first meeting of the Port Stirling Earthquake Response Team," said Olive. "Jay, do you have anything to write on? Could you jot down a few notes in case we ever have to remember this meeting?" She brushed back her short, wavy gray hair, tucking one side behind her ear. Her small, tasteful gold and diamond earrings were in place as always.

Olive was in her seventies, but looked fifty. Fit and wiry, she was also always unwaveringly calm and composed. Abbott was happy that she had been the commissioner who joined them, mainly because the current Oregon governor was her younger sister. And that could come in handy in the days and weeks ahead. He knew his constituents, especially the men in town, didn't always think highly of the governor, and blamed her for almost everything that went wrong in Chinook County. However, Abbott knew, in more circumstances than not, it was a simple case of men not liking taking orders from a woman in power. He didn't care if their governor was male, female, or Martian—he'd take help right now from anyone who could deliver it, and he knew that Olive would be foremost in the governor's mind this morning.

"Does anyone's cell phone work?" started Matt. "Moron that I am, I didn't think to grab mine when I left my house."

"Perhaps because your house was in the process of falling 300 feet into the ocean below?" Olive smiled graciously at him. She lived on the east side of Ocean Bend Road and had watched in horror as the bluff began to slide. She'd jumped in her Mercedes sedan, throwing preparedness kits that she truly never expected to use in the backseat, and drove inland faster than she'd driven since she was a teenager. Portions of the road had buckled, and she was eager to return in the daylight and assess how bad the damage was.

"Yeah, when my bedroom window exploded, getting out of the house seemed the most important thing," Matt said. Fern winced.

"No, no one's cell phone is working," answered Abbott. "We all tried last night, and then again at dawn, and we've got nothing. Zilch."

"Which totally sucks," added Jay. "It would be nice to call for help. Get some kind of backup in here to help us."

"My guess is that everyone knows by now that we're in trouble," Matt said. "Our big problem is that we don't know how widespread the earthquake damage is. Is all of Oregon in trouble? Most of the Pacific Northwest? I suspect, based on our training, that most of the coastline got hit hard by that damnable tsunami. I saw it up close and personal, and I swear it was three stories high. It had to damage most of the coast. It had to." He shook his head.

"Agree," said Abbott. "Even the projections we had that showed us a shorter duration earthquake, and a thirty-foot wave wiped out the entire Oregon coastline, complete damage. And our earthquake was long and violent, and our tsunami was much bigger than thirty feet. Projections also showed further inland to the Willamette Valley and beyond to the Cascades with strong shaking, landslides, and widespread, but more moderate damage. I think we have to assume that roads and infrastructure all over the state took a hit, at least to some degree."

"So, we're on our own," Fern said.

. . .

An uneasy silence came over the group as the ramifications of Fern's remark kicked each of them in the gut.

Finally, Matt said, "I think so." He massaged his sore shoulder, and made an attempt at sitting up straight. To Abbott he said, "My priorities are to first canvass the town, and make sure that if anyone is trapped or in trouble we help them. That's probably what you were on your way to do when you found me, right? Search and rescue?"

"Yes. We've divided up into four teams," Abbott said, "and divided the town into four areas. Everyone is anxious to go."

"OK, people should also get supplies that we need here, but no looting," Matt said firmly. "Please make sure that your team members understand that this is about *all* of our survival, and that we'll be stronger together."

"Our town wouldn't do that," Jay said. "Looting."

"When people are scared, frightened for their very lives, they'll do anything," Matt said. "It's up to us to keep the peace. Law and order, that's our job. And we do that by helping them, making sure that people are safe and have the necessities. We can do that and we will."

"We should also stress to people that until we can get the standing homes and buildings inspected for earthquake damage, they shouldn't enter them, or at the very least, get in and out quickly if they must," Abbott said. "We can't really enforce state or federal guidelines on every structure in Port Stirling with just the five of us, but we can ask for their cooperation."

"That's right," said Olive. "With this big of a shaker, the projections said we should expect aftershocks." She shuddered. "Just because our home is still standing this morning, doesn't mean it will stay standing. What a fucking nightmare."

The four city employees all turned to look at their city commissioner. None of them had ever heard her swear before.

"What?" Olive said. She had paled and slumped in her seat, looking her age. "I just call it like I see it. And it *is* a fucking nightmare."

. . .

Turns out, Olive was right. As the groups fanned out across Port Stirling, they soon learned the extent of the devastation. Some people went home to a pile of sticks and bricks where their house had been. Some people's homes in the older part of town had been completely washed away by the tsunami's force—all that was left was mud and debris and dead fish. The fish covered much of the lower part of town, and the stench was just beginning. The port that gave the town its name was also gone, infrastructure disappeared and nothing but water in its place.

But the water this morning softly lapped at the shore and pooled in various-sized puddles here and there, eerily quiet now. The Pacific was calm under a sparkling blue sky, and seagulls returned overhead, their squawking the only sound as they dive-bombed the dead fish, swallowing them whole as fast as they could.

What was most stunning was how the actual geography of their village had changed. Much of the bluff adjacent to Ocean Bend Road had liquefied and slid into the ocean, taking the majority of the ocean-front homes with it. In Port Stirling alone, more than forty houses—almost all occupied by full-time residents—had joined Matt's bungalow three hundred feet on the beach below. The tsunami had broken up most of the structures and sent the pieces scattering. The coastline was now further inland than it had been yesterday at this time. The "town" had shrunk.

Buildings, roads, water and sewer services—either destroyed or facing serious damage. Utility networks not working. City hall, although at a higher elevation than the older part of town, had its north side damaged, the side that took the watery remnants of the giant tsunami that barely reached it. The building was repairable, but in the meantime police and fire departments would be operating in the parking lot.

But, inevitably, the worst of the devastation was the number of bodies the survivors pulled out of the rubble. Family members, lifetime friends, tourists enjoying the best of the Oregon coast in the beautiful fall season, the earthquake didn't discriminate in this village of approximately 3,000 people. As they began their search and rescue operation, first counts of the dead, with Police Chief Matt Horning in charge of that grim detail, numbered twenty-four. Those bodies were found under the collapsed buildings, mostly in the older part of town next to the port.

While the three other search and rescue groups were going door-to-door, Matt's group was unable to take that approach…because there were few doors left standing in the older, lower elevation section of town they were searching. Jay, working with Matt, insisted they go first to the area of the Port Stirling Tavern, explaining how many people had still been in the building when he left. He feared, rightly so, that several of them ignored his pleas to run to higher ground. Jay was able to identify most of the dead in that location.

"I recognize all but two," Jay told Matt, as they carried the dead out of the rubble and placed them in a makeshift morgue in the tavern's parking lot, now with its asphalt divided into pieces damp with slime. Jay slipped on a slick spot, and injured his groin trying to not drop the body of the bartender Kristin Breen, a friend of his. "Dammit!" he yelled. "Gimme a freakin' break here."

Matt rushed to his side, and helped support the body while Jay regained his balance. Kristin had a bloody gash on her forehead that had splattered most of her face, and her spiky blond hair was matted with a creepy mixture of mud, foam, and blood. And in a heartbreaking twist, Matt noted a doorknob in Kristin's right hand. Swiftly, he covered her hand with his sweater so Jay wouldn't realize that his friend might have been close to surviving the building's collapse.

"How many more?" Jay cried through his grief, leaning on Matt. He was exhausted, but he took a last distraught look at Kristin's blood-soaked face, and then turned back toward the rubble.

"What was that noise?" Matt said, putting his hand on Jay's arm to halt his progress. Both men stood stock still and listened to the silence. A low whimper.

Eyes wide, Matt and Jay stared at each other, frozen, both willing the other not to flinch until they heard it again. A soft moan, more distinct this time. In concert, they moved toward the sound, about ten feet away. A louder moan as the two cops scrambled to a heap of broken lumber and began frantically tossing pieces of wood off the pile.

• • •

Fern, along with Rick, the nurse, and Gil, the construction guy, concentrated on the Ocean Bend Road area, as she had promised Abbott she would do.

Was it only last night I was in bed with Matt on this spot? Fern thought, as she stood on the edge of the road, hands on her narrow hips, looking toward the place his snug cottage had stood. In this morning's bright sunshine, there was now only the stone fireplace remaining, and it was perilously close to the new cliff.

The road was nearly impassable in some places, but Gil's truck managed to carry their group most of the length of it. It was weird how structures on the east side of the road, away from the bluff, had escaped the worst of the quake's tremors. Some homes and motels had collapsed, while others appeared untouched. A few had missing roofs, some buildings had been moved off their foundations, and almost all had blown-out windows.

Fern kept a running account of 'destroyed' and 'repairable' on a legal pad she always kept in her car. A life-long resident of Port Stirling, she knew almost every house and business along the popular road, and was able to put a name to most. As they went door-to-door to hunt for survivors, she started a third list of 'inhabitable' properties, with a thought to where they could re-locate the people who would inevitably be homeless this morning.

The only people Fern's group encountered were residents who had escaped last night and were now returning to check out the damage to their homes. Most were sobbing openly, and shoulders drooped from the long, sleepless night. Many had lost everything, especially those families on the west side of the road with the ocean-view properties. There were competing emotions that bounced between 'We're lucky to be alive' to 'What are we going to do now?'

Fern instructed the people they talked with to return to the encampment before sunset, and tried to assure them that they would get the help they needed going forward. Her grit and determination were infectious, and the survivors nodded in agreement.

Returning to Gil's truck after talking with a displaced family, Fern's group continued south on the road, where the destruction, if possible, was getting even worse. "Looks like I'm going to be real busy," smiled Gil, who owned the town's largest construction company.

Fern glared at him, her cheeks reddening. "This is hardly the time to gloat. These people have lost their homes. Have you no empathy at all?"

"Just stating a fact."

"Well, how dare you. You will do what the city manager tells you to do. You may or may not get rich in the next few months, but you will help out the public good first."

"You can't tell me how to run my business, little lady," Gil said. "I have rights. It's a free country."

"Oh, no?" Fern answered, ignoring his stupid insult. "I can make sure the city and county reject your building permit applications. I can spread the word that you aren't worth hiring. And, if you don't dot all your I's and cross every single T, I can arrest you on the spot. For a little lady, I can actually do quite a lot to make sure your business suffers. I'd stay on my good side if I were you." She slammed her legal pad down on the seat.

"Sure, I'm going to help out folks," Gil backpedaled. "I didn't mean it the way you took it." Her fault, of course.

"Good. Then we understand each other. Pull over at this next house on the left. It belongs to a friend of mine and I want to check on him."

. . .

"There's someone under here!" Matt screamed at Jay, as the two worked side-by-side. They continued digging desperately under the timber and rubble, hands becoming raw even under the gloves they'd found in the trunk of Jay's squad car.

An arm with a tiny tattoo of a rose at its wrist appeared first, with a manicured hand at the end of it. Purplish-gray nail polish. Jay howled, "Justine! Justine, can you hear me?"

A moan came from close to where Jay's knee was resting. He scooted back a few feet, and he and Matt kept clawing at the rubble where they figured the woman's head should be. Crisscrossed two-by-fours covered her face, and Jay gently pulled them off of her.

A poof of air came out of Justine's mouth. Her eyes were closed, and her nose was smashed against her wounded face. Her dark hair, that Jay remembered had been casually piled on top of her head last night while they played pool, was now down around her shoulders in a tangled mess.

"Justine! It's me, Jay. Stay with us! Keep breathing! We'll get you out of here. You're safe now. Stay with me, Justine."

Matt pulled at the debris covering the rest of her body as fast as he could do safely, while Jay put his arm under Justine's head and cradled it. Matt unearthed her and scooped her up in his arms, all in one motion.

"Careful!" Jay shrieked.

"I am!" Matt wailed at him.

Justine barely opened her eyes, and blinked at the sunlight, but Matt could tell she wasn't all there.

· · ·

Fern wound her way through the driftwood-littered front yard, and knocked on Ted Frolick's door. She gaped at the small stone bungalow as if she was seeing a mirage. In a way, she was. It was about the only structure on Ocean Bend Road that appeared untouched by the quake.

When Ted didn't answer the door, she tried it, but found it locked. Fern knew that Ted and Patty mostly lived on Patty's farm in Twisty River, and she hoped that's where they were now. Just to be sure, she walked around the side of the house to Ted's garden in the back. Kitchen door was locked, too. Other than the gate hanging off its hinges, and one cracked window in the kitchen door, there was remarkably no other damage. The multi-colored roses in bloom along his back fence were the prettiest thing Fern had seen in the last twelve hours.

Her group continued on their assignment, and helped ferry tourists whose hotel and motel rooms had been destroyed to the encampment for safety. Most had slept part of the night out in the open in a large RV park behind one of the bigger hotels. Many were from California and knew that you didn't go back inside any buildings following a quake. One young couple from Oakland told Fern they came on vacation to

Oregon to decide if they wanted to move here. They wanted to get away from earthquakes.

"Yeah," was all Fern could think to say.

. . .

Matt and Jay carried Justine to a clearing where they'd placed a tarp. Matt performed CPR on her while Jay sprinted to his car to get his first-aid kit. She was breathing, but Matt took her pulse and her heart rate was slow. She lay still with her eyes closed while Jay carefully cleaned off her face with alcohol. He could tell her nose was badly broken, and he avoided that area.

One ankle was mangled and positioned at a funky angle, also surely broken.

"I take it you know her," Matt said.

"Yeah, went to high school with her. We ran into her last night at the tavern, and the four of us had a beer together and shot some pool."

Matt was worried that Jay was approaching shock. Understandable. "I'm sure she beat you, right?"

Jay took his eyes off Justine's face and stared at Matt like he'd forgotten he was there. "I know what you're doing, man. I'm fine. And, yes, she beat me."

"Well, you don't have to be a badass to beat you at pool."

"True. What are we gonna do?" Jay returned his gaze to his friend.

"You stay here with Justine. Keep her still and talk to her. I'll go look for the nurse who's with Fern. They're covering Ocean Bend, and I'll find him and bring him here. He'll know what to do."

"Sounds good."

"But then, we'll need to set up a temporary infirmary of some sort. My guess is Justine won't be the only survivor in bad shape we find today."

"How are we going to do that?"

"Don't know. But I'll think of something. Give me your car keys."

"Hurry, boss. Please hurry."

CHAPTER 7

Matt knew that Fern's group planned to start at the north end of Ocean Bend Road, so he picked his way down the road by the library that dead-ended at Ocean Bend. It joined the bluff road about halfway down its length. It also brought him close to his cottage, but he drove past with just a quick glance at it. His stomach fluttered when he saw the stone fireplace, now near the edge.

He found Fern in front of the Inn at Whale Rock, and was pleased to see it still standing, although with some serious damage. Matt's heart skipped a beat when he thought of his favorite waitress, Vicky. He hoped like hell she had been safely home last night at 11:32 p.m. and not in the Inn, but he'd have to check on her later—first things first.

"Hi. What are you doing here?" Fern asked, removing her sunglasses. The wind was picking up, blowing strands of red hair across her face.

With urgency, he said, "I need Rick. He's with you, right?"

Fern didn't answer Matt but turned, cupped her hands around her mouth, and yelled "Rick! Over here."

He ran from where he'd been about to climb through a broken window in the restaurant.

"What is it?" he asked, joining the cops.

"We need you down by the port. Jay and I pulled a survivor out of the rubble, but she's in bad shape. We did CPR, and are keeping her still and warm, but we need your pro help."

Rick didn't hesitate. He ran to Gil's truck and pulled his medical bag out of the back.

"Let's go."

"Do you know who it is, Matt?" Fern asked.

"Justine somebody. Jay knows her. Went to school together, and saw her last night. They're friends and he's upset."

Fern covered her mouth with her hand, and teared up. "Awful," she croaked. "Anything I can do?"

"Keep doing what you're doing, and listen and look carefully. We heard a faint moan, and that's how we found her." He took Fern by the shoulders. "There will be more. Go as fast as you can, but be conscientious."

. . .

As he drove Rick, Matt said, "We're gonna need some sort of temporary hospital. What do you suggest?"

"When you get to the highway, turn right instead of left, and pull into the drug store," Rick said. "The owner of Summers Pharmacy gave me the back door code in case I ever need to get in due to an emergency. Guess this qualifies."

"Hope it's still standing."

"Yeah, there is that," Rick said. "But even if the building is damaged, we might still be able to get some things I will need."

"Like medicines? Do you know what to look for?"

"I'm not a pharmacist, but, yeah, there're some basics like pain killers, antiseptics, bandages. I've got some of those in my bag," he said, patting the black bag on his lap, "but my supply won't last long if we have major casualties. I'm thinking we might also score some portable cots, I know Sam had some at some point. I didn't see him at the meet site this morning, did you?"

"Sam?"

"Summers. He owns the pharmacy and lives in town."

"I don't know him. Sorry." Matt pulled into the store's parking lot, and both men were relieved to see the pharmacy intact except for one thing:

a section of its roof was laying on the parking lot pavement about thirty yards away.

The front door was wide open. Matt and Rick leapt from the car and sprinted to it.

"Sam!" Rick said as they entered the pharmacy and saw the owner. "You're a sight for sore eyes."

"I was hoping you and Paul Richards survived," Sam smiled and hugged the tall, muscular, nearly bald nurse. "Are you OK?"

"I'm good," Rick said. "Shook up like everybody, but I live inland on the north side of town, and made it to the meeting site easily last night. My place is pretty much OK. This is our police chief, Matt Horning. He had a more eventful night."

"It's great to meet you, Sam," said Matt, quickly shaking hands with the stooped-over older man wearing black glasses. "I'll buy you dinner next month and we can chat then," he smiled. "But right now, we're in an awful hurry. We've pulled a survivor out of the rubble, and she needs Rick's attention. Will you be here for a while?"

Sam spread his arms to encompass the mess in his store. "All week, I'd say."

"OK then, we're going to grab whatever Rick needs now, and then we'll come back after we treat Justine. We need whatever you've got that will help us make a temporary infirmary. Keep track and the city will reimburse you."

"No problem, chief. Let's use my parking lot for the hospital. I'll start setting up with whatever I've got that might be useful. It won't be perfect, but it will do until you can get people to Twisty River or Buck Bay."

Matt clapped his new best friend on the back. "You're a savior, Sam. See you soon."

• • •

Rick took charge of Justine, with Jay serving as his assistant. She was alive, but her pulse was weak, and she was unconscious.

While the nurse and Jay worked on her, Matt continued searching through the rubble of the tavern. If Justine made it out alive, maybe there were others. He worked until he was covered in grime, and all of his muscles strained, but sadly, it was a recovery operation, not further rescue. In all, he pulled out over a dozen bodies, listening and looking carefully for signs of life that weren't there.

The rest of his group, spread out throughout the lower part of town and the port area, fared no better. When they met back at their vehicles, it was clear to Matt they'd found no survivors, only bodies. Among the rescuers, there were bouts of weeping and obvious signs of human distress.

Some eyes flashed in anger, and there was a lot of "How could this happen? Why were we so unprepared?"

There was no point trying to explain that the city *was* prepared, Matt thought, based on what information the scientists gave them. Because of the geography, Port Stirling was always going to be vulnerable to an upper-range earthquake. The loss of life was devastating, but he knew it could have been so much worse if the quake had struck earlier in the day.

But saying that now to his group who were witnessing horror and tragedy all around them, wouldn't help. All he could do for them now was sympathize, get through Day 1, and try to help people rebuild their lives.

They transported Justine up the hill to Summers Pharmacy, and Sam was ready for her. He had arranged three portable cots in a line, two of which had medicine drip bags attached to lightweight movable racks. A card table holding packaged medications was next to one of the cots. He had arranged some clothing items—mainly robes, PJs, and a few sweaters—on a display rack nearby. Once Rick returned, Sam was planning to dash home and pick up his large family camping tent. It would provide some protection during the night.

"Oh, my," Sam said, looking at Justine's pale face and mangled leg. She had awakened just before Rick and Jay loaded her into one of the larger SUVs in their group. Her eyes barely open, she whispered, "Thanks, Jay." Rick told her to not talk, save her strength, and that she was going to be fine. Jay sobbed, and squeezed her hand.

• • •

Once Rick had Justine stabilized, with a big assist from Sam Summers, Matt turned his attention to Jay. "You OK?"

Both cops had aged in the past sixteen hours, but Jay looked especially drawn now, and appeared to have already lost weight under the ordeal. "I'm not coping very well, am I?" asked the distraught detective.

"Neither am I, to tell the truth," admitted Matt. "Not sure anything could prepare us for this. But we need to keep going, if you're up to it."

"There might be more like Justine," Jay said, and gazed off into the distance. Matt wasn't sure if Jay meant that in a good way or bad.

"Yes, there might be. We've only got a few hours of daylight left." He let that hang in the air because he wasn't about to order Jay back to work, not when he might be seriously traumatized.

Jay put both hands on his knees, breathed in to the count of five, exhaled noisily, and pushed himself up off the chair the pharmacist had kindly provided for him. "It smells like fish around here," and then, "Let's go."

. . .

Feeling confident there were no more survivors to be found in the port area, Matt's group had moved around Port Stirling Point to continue their search while the two cops took Justine to safety. When they rounded the rock outcropping that separated the older part of town from the beach and bluffs beyond, the villagers could not believe the carnage on their beloved beach.

After the pause to take in what their eyes were seeing, they began crawling over the wreckage on the beach, frantically working to beat the incoming tide. Some of the cliff-top homes had slid down the liquefied bluff, almost intact and looking like they'd just been relocated from ocean-front to ocean. But many others were nothing but heaps of lumber, stone, and broken glass.

There were vehicles of all sorts, some half-in and half-out of the surf. Furniture littered the beach, and hundreds of lamps looked like a new breed of seashell scattered about.

Matt's group of twenty or so were beasts and kept going, aggressively sorting through the remnants of their friends' lives. Fern's group had come up from the south end of the long beach, and worked side-by-side with

Matt's group. They had set up the second makeshift morgue of the day, this time finding a flat, rock-free area at the top of the surf line in some sand and grasses.

Miraculously, most of the beach-front residents got out in time, bolting from their homes at the first earthquake shudder. Several of those lucky people were now helping to carry their dead neighbors to the morgue, their backs aching after the long, terrifying day.

Working alongside his master, Lydia Campbell's Border collie, Mr. Darcy, had sniffed out one positive story after alerting his owner to tragic results earlier. The pooch had discovered nine bodies during the afternoon, but his last find helped raise the spirits of the dispirited group—a teenage boy alive.

Mr. Darcy was sniffing around a house near the surf that had been torn apart by the waves. About five yards up from the water in a jumbled stack of wood, he started barking and leaping around. Lydia ran to her dog and immediately yelled, "Jay, over here!"

Lydia pushed some debris to the side, and uncovered Spencer Thomas, age fifteen, knocked out but breathing and with his legs twitching. She knew the boy—he lived two doors down with his parents and eighteen-year-old brother, Zach.

"Spencer! Can you hear me, honey?" Lydia asked the boy, holding his face in her hands, while Jay freed his lower body and shifted him carefully to get him out of the encroaching surf.

Lydia patted Spencer's cheeks, gentle slaps on each side, and continued saying his name. After a few seconds, he opened his eyes. "Mrs. Campbell," he spoke softly. "What happened?"

"I'll tell you later, Spencer. Do you know Detective Finley? He's going to help me and Mr. Darcy move you further up the beach. Does anything hurt?"

"Don't know," he whispered. "Maybe everything."

It took four men, legs buckling after the interminable day, to carry the hefty teenager around the point to one of their vehicles. Spencer Thomas was patient number three at the Summers Pharmacy outdoor infirmary. All three would survive, but someone would have to eventually tell Spencer that the rest of his family didn't make it.

Jay scratched Mr. Darcy behind his ears, and then put his arm around Lydia Campbell's shoulder. "Well, that's karma if I've ever seen it," he said to the elderly woman. "You and Mr. Darcy couldn't save Emily, but you've saved another child's life."

CHAPTER 8

Although the destruction and, especially, the death toll was horrifying, there were signs that the human spirit to survive was alive and well in Port Stirling. Exhausted and aching all over, Matt was growing increasingly irritable that he had no way to communicate, electronically or otherwise, with his town's residents. While the search and rescue groups continued working both on the beach and inland, Matt gathered Jay and Fern, saying "C'mon. We're going to make an amazin' new police department."

"How exactly are we going to do that, boss?" Jay asked. Drained beyond belief, his shoulders slumped and he adjusted the passenger seat in his squad car to the reclining position. Only his cowlick stood at attention. "You drive," he said, tossing the keys to Matt.

"Fern has a tent in her preparedness kit, don't you Detective Byrne?" he winked at her.

"I do. I am always prepared."

The three drove to the parking lot of Goodie's Market, next to Highway 101 in the high part of town. The largest market in the village was still standing and appeared to suffer little damage except for a few blown-out windows, and one rather huge tree that had crashed through the back part of the roof.

While Matt and Fern erected her tent where it would be visible from the highway, Jay managed to craft a sign from a cardboard box he found behind the market. It instructed everyone to stop and sign in, below big letters that read 'Port Stirling Police Department'.

And they did in droves.

Reunion hugs were plentiful amid smiles and tears. Matt was especially happy to see Vicky, his favorite waitress and buddy from the Inn at Whale Rock's restaurant, down the road from his bungalow. He'd never seen her outside of the restaurant, and was surprised to see her wearing jeans and a big parka. The jeans were tighter, and her boot heels were higher than they should be considering the circumstances, but Matt knew that was Vicky's style all the way, and he had to smile.

"Oh, my God, Tex," Vicky exclaimed. "I was so afraid you'd ended up in the Pacific!" She clung to him.

"Almost did. I thought the same might have happened to you. Were you working last night?"

"I had closed up for the night, and was headed home when the quake struck," she said. "I live inland, between Ocean Bend Road and the highway in a small development. I just pulled into my driveway when it started rockin' and rolling. Never been so scared in my life. Were you home?"

Matt repeated his story to his good friend, and her eyes widened. "Is it bad on Ocean Bend?" she asked.

"Bad," Matt told her. "Whale Rock is standing, but barely. All the windows are gone, and the tsunami left a real mess. I would say it's salvageable, but it's gonna take a while and some real elbow grease. The ocean-front cottages on the bluff are gone."

Vicky gasped. "I was afraid to go down there and check this morning. The highway is in bad enough shape, and I didn't dare drive on any side roads."

"Yeah, we're going to ask people to avoid going anywhere west of the highway until we've had a chance to check all the structures. Today we're just looking for survivors."

Vicky looked down at her boots. Quietly, she said, "Did we lose many?"

Matt decided this morning when he made it to the meet site that he would level with people and not pull any punches. If they were to survive as a community, and he knew they would, everyone would need the truth.

"Twenty-four dead so far, and thirty-one reported missing," he told Vicky. "But we still have a lot of inspecting to do."

Uncharacteristically for the tenacious, seen-it-all-woman, Vicky began to sob.

"You're safe, everything is going to be OK," consoled Matt, holding her to his chest.

"Is… your group… intact?" she asked between gulps.

"Yes, thank the gods. All present and accounted for at our meet site with the exception of Walt, my sergeant," Matt said. "But he lives on the road to Twisty River, on a little hill further inland, and he decided to stay put with his family for now. He's got three little ones. I stopped at what remains of city hall, and was able to retrieve our government walkie-talkies, and I just talked to him. He's fine."

Vicky stepped back and made an effort to pull herself together, wiping her tears away. "What about Big Ed? Heard from him yet?"

"No, but it's not like he can pick up the phone and call me, is it?" Matt said. "This is gonna drive me nuts… not being able to call anyone. But we know at least two of our network of cellphone towers are down, so might as well get used to it. I've communicated with all of the local police and firefighters on our frequency, but Ed is too far away. I haven't been able to reach him yet, but I'll keep trying."

"I'm sure he's OK," Vicky said, pulling on one earring. "Guessing we probably got hit about the hardest of anywhere in the state, don't you think?"

In spite of her attempts to appear brave, Matt saw the fear in Vicky's face, and took her hands in his. "Yeah, we took a real blow, but you know what? We'll bounce back. We may have lost some good souls, but the heart of this community is beating strong. I know I can count on every single person in Port Stirling, just like I know I can count on you."

She looked up at him with moist eyes. "Always, Tex. Always. Now let go of me. I'm going in Goodie's and make sure they know how to manage the food they've got."

"That's my girl," Matt smiled. "You make a good point. There's bound to be some panic shopping. If anybody's in there, tell them I've deputized you, and you'll be in charge of rationing out their stocks. That all right with you?"

"Might as well be. I don't have another job at the moment," she said wistfully.

"Good. That will free up my team to keep searching for survivors. When you've got things organized here, go to the other markets and do the same thing. Is your car running OK? Here, take a walkie-talkie and let us know what you find."

"My Honda won't ever die," she said with a smile. "I slept in it last night because I was afraid to go in my house. I take care of it and it takes care of me. Speaking of sleeping, do you have a place to go tonight?"

"Haven't thought that far ahead," Matt admitted. "Guess I'll bunk with Jay if he'll let me—his house is still in one piece."

"Oh, for God's sake, Tex," she whispered, "the whole town knows you and Fern are a hot item. Just stay with her."

. . .

Halfway through his harrowing drive toward Port Stirling and just entering Twisty River, Ed picked up his walkie-talkie, pressed the PTT button and said, "This is Oregon State Police trooper Ed Sonders. Is anybody there?" He took his finger off the button and waited.

"Ed! It's Patty Perkins. I'm so happy to hear your voice! Where are you?"

"I'm driving into your pretty little county-seat town. Where are you?"

"Trapped in my house," she said. "The river rose up something fierce a little after midnight, and flooded us. I'm OK, but Ted's in trouble. Broken arm and concussion, I think. My guess is that the earthquake was centered off the coast, and generated a substantial tsunami that raced up the river."

"Yep. That's my calculation, too. It pushed water up to my place as well, although it sounds like we didn't get it as bad as you folks here. The shaking was epic, though. How can I help?"

"Ted needs medical attention. Can you check and see if our hospital is in business? We don't have any power; can you tell if there is any in town?"

"I don't see any lights, and the stoplight isn't working. It doesn't look good. I'm only about five blocks from the hospital so I'll go there now and check on their status. Give me your address. I'll come by once I know what the situation is. Is Ted in much pain?"

"I've got him stabilized as best as I know how, and he's a trooper. But he's not comfortable, that's for sure. We couldn't do a thing while it was still dark because of the water. But looking out my window now, it looks like the river has subsided. Not sure my car will make it out of the garage, though. Lots of mud and muck."

"Stay put. Let me see what I can do. Give me fifteen minutes."

"Thanks, Ed. Really appreciate you."

The good news was that the small Twisty River hospital was indeed open and accepting guests, operating with a skeleton crew, and a diesel generator. The bad news was that the road to Patty and Ted's home was dicey at best.

Ed approached the bridge over the Twisty River cautiously, parked his vehicle on the town side, and inspected it as carefully as he could from his vantage point. Studying both sides of the river, Ed was surprised that the bridge had survived. The usual lush green vegetation on the river banks was now a sea of mud. Shrubs and small trees had been mowed down as if someone had come through with a machete. A good-sized fir tree, its roots sticking up in the air, was lodged up against one of the bridge supports. The current was swirling and strong, and seemed determined to keep piling up branches and sticks around the big, stuck tree. Instead of its usual beautiful blue-green color and babbling sounds, the water was muddy brown with whitecaps, and the continuous thump of debris hitting the supports caused a continuous rumble. The air smelled damp.

But he couldn't see any cracks in the supports or on the surface of the bridge itself, so he decided to go for it. Climbing up into the cab of his RAM pickup truck, a better choice today than his OSP sedan, Ed patted the dashboard and said out loud, "Don't tell Milly we're doing this, OK?" He'd promised her to "be careful" when he left their house, and driving across this bridge with a still-raging river below was not a careful act.

Ed drove his truck up the entrance ramp, and eased the front tires onto the bridge, peering through his windshield at the road ahead. So far, so good. In the middle, he risked a glance out his side window and over the rail to the water directly below him. Water that was usually about twenty-five feet below the bridge was now only ten feet or so below him, churning and seething. *Best to not look down.* He kept driving, slowly but dogged. *No other traffic; am I a fool?*

He cleared the river on Patty's side, and realized he'd been holding his breath. The turnoff to her house was about 500 yards ahead on the left. According to her directions, their place was only about one-half mile off the main road. Her road had clearly been covered in water during the night, but it was receding now, leaving behind a brown slime that Ed's truck had no problem navigating. He pulled up at the front of their house, but didn't attempt the driveway. Patty was right; there was still too much mud and junk in the area surrounding her house. He would go the rest of the way on foot.

"I'm always happy to see you, but this may be the happiest!" Patty exclaimed from her covered front porch, waving with both arms. There were three hanging baskets with begonias and azaleas still blooming in this mild fall season, and two chintz-covered rocking chairs facing out to the meadow and valley beyond. Ted stood beside her and he, too, waved vigorously at the trooper with what Ed supposed was his good arm.

"Hope you've both got some good boots," Ed said as he approached them, looking down at the mud dangerously near the top of his boots. He leaned forward to hug Patty, and gently tousled Ted's mane of white hair. "How are two of my favorite people doing?" he asked.

"Patty's perfect, as always," replied Ted with a smirk. "Me, not so much. Think I've cracked my arm and probably my hard head, too. How are you, Ed?"

"I'm sorry to hear that. Me, I'm doing well. My lawn and all my outdoor furniture are gone for good, a few trees down, but otherwise we're fine up the river. Thought I'd better get to work, and see what we're dealing with."

"Port Stirling must be a disaster," Patty said, shaking her head. "I slept a little last night after the quake, but I kept imagining a wall of water coming off the Pacific and slamming into that perfect little town. It must have been absolutely terrifying."

"Yeah," Ed said. "Hope like hell their warning system worked." Silence while all three contemplated what would have happened if the sirens hadn't gone off.

"Let's get you to the hospital, Ted," Ed said, regaining his composure. "I checked there on my way into town, and they are up and running. Only one doc and a skeletal crew so far today, but they told me they'll take care of you. You're going to have to walk out to my truck—I don't want to get stuck in your driveway."

"That's no problem," Patty said. "Let us grab our boots and coats. I packed overnight bags for both of us after you called. You wait here, Ted, and I'll lock up."

"Bossy, isn't she?" Ted grinned.

"Part of her charm."

Patty and Ted tried to scrape the calf-high mud off their boots before climbing into Ed's truck, but he said, "It's hopeless, don't worry about the mess. We're all going to be dirty for weeks."

All three settled into Ed's truck, and he backed onto the road. "I might suggest that you close your eyes when we get to the bridge," Ed said, and added, "Don't worry, I'll keep mine open."

"Why?" Patty demanded, her head whipping around to look at him. "Is there something wrong with the bridge? Is it safe to drive over?"

"I'm here, aren't I?"

"That's not much of a confirmation," she chided. "Maybe you got lucky."

He laughed. "Maybe I did. Guess we're about to find out."

Ed navigated the short distance to the river, and then nudged his truck forward and nosed the front end up onto the bridge.

"Holy Moly!" bellowed Ted. "Would you get a look at that river!"

Patty exhaled as Ed came off the ramp on the other side. "I always knew that someday I might regret living on a river," she said. "That day is today."

They got Ted situated in the hospital, and waited while they took him to X-ray. They had one battery-powered portable X-ray machine, and it would do the job for now. The test confirmed that he had indeed broken his arm in two places. The ER doctor who examined him also diagnosed a concussion, and it was agreed that Ted would spend at least one night there while they set his arm and observed him for any further symptoms.

"I've got to go to Port Stirling with Ed, honey," Patty told her husband. "Will you be all right?"

"There are undoubtedly people there who need your help right now more than I do," he said, taking her hand. "Will you check on my place?" He looked at her with somber eyes. Patty knew how much he loved his little house on Ocean Bend Road, even though it looked like a junk pile from the road because of Ted's vast collection of driftwood and beach finds out front. But inside was a cozy, tidy, well-furnished home, and a backyard garden that surprised everyone who got invited in to see it. The house was across the road from the ocean-front properties, but he could still hear the sea with his windows open.

"Of course I will. But I fear the worst," she said softly.

"The odds aren't good," Ted agreed. "But that little house is solidly built. I give it a chance. You be careful. If it's risky at all close to Ocean Bend, let it go, and we'll check it another day, once I can get out of here. Promise?"

"I promise. I know you think I'm Superwoman, but earthquakes and huge tidal waves scare me. I'm not about to take any unnecessary chances. Ed and I mainly want to connect with the police there, make sure they're OK, and see if there is anything we can do to help."

"How will you find them?"

"Once we get closer to town—*if* we can get closer to town—we'll try them on the walkie-talkies. We have our own frequency. If they don't answer, then I don't have a clue."

"Doesn't Matt Horning live on the bluff?" Ted asked. "Across the road and down a little from my house?" Ed and Patty exchanged a quick look.

"Yep," Ed answered for them. "Right out on the edge of the bluff with a view that will knock your socks off. I've spent some good times there in a chair with a brewski in my hand. Hope like hell it's still where I left it."

. . .

Ed and Patty had to move some small trees off the road between Twisty River and Port Stirling, and in one area, drove off the road for about twenty yards to get around a big fir the two of them couldn't budge. But they were able to get through. Relief washed over both of the cops when they had connected with Matt on the walkie-talkie, and they agreed to meet at the police department's tent on the highway. But when they crested the hill east of Port Stirling that relief dissipated.

The ravaged town that laid before them was barely recognizable, and they both swore under their breaths simultaneously.

"Where to begin?" Patty asked hypothetically.

"The same place we began in January with Emily Bushnell's death, and again in April when Clay Sherwin was murdered," Ed said. "With Matt Horning."

And Patty could not argue with that.

CHAPTER 9

Things were humming in the corridors of the Federal Emergency Management Agency (FEMA), both in Washington, D.C. at headquarters and at the Region 10 field office in Bothell, Washington. HQ didn't know at the first news of the earthquake whether or not the Bothell office was operational, because the office's power and mobile networks had been knocked out. While the Puget Sound area also sustained big damage from the quake, their geography offered more protection from the tsunami that ran rampant from the Cape Mendocino Peninsula to the northern tip of Vancouver Island.

Johnny Johnson, Regional Administrator for Region 10, which encompassed Oregon, Washington, Idaho, and Alaska, slept through the earthquake at his Bothell home. A former military commander with over twenty years of active duty service in places you don't want to go, he had taught himself to sleep through almost anything. Fortunately, Johnny's wife was a lighter sleeper.

"What the hell was that?" she said, waking up and shaking her husband. She reached for her bedside lamp, but it wouldn't turn on. Johnny sputtered and woke up, just in time for a second jolt. The couple had been in bed early tonight, lights out at 9:45 p.m. "Sweet Jesus!" he bellowed. "Earthquake!"

• • •

Seventeen hours after the earthquake and tsunami, 2,650 of Port Stirling's approximate 3,000 residents had been accounted for and were in good shape. The latest count had thirty-eight known dead, and over 400 still missing, many of them unaccounted-for tourists.

"What we don't know," Matt said to Ed and Patty, who showed up at the police department's temporary tent on the highway, "is whether the missing are safely at home and don't need attention, or whether they are unable or unwilling—for whatever reason—to make their presence known. We've organized patrols to start doing house-to-house checks. I've deputized some citizens to act on our behalf."

"That's smart," said Patty. "You never know what the patrols may uncover. What do you want us to do?" She nodded at Ed.

"There are apparently some boats smashed to smithereens on what's left of the jetty over by the lighthouse. We've been up to our eyeballs here in town with search and rescue, and I haven't been able to free up anyone to check it out. Could you two make your way out there and see if there are any people who need help? Ed, is your vehicle able to get through the gunk?"

"Up to a point. If it's no worse than the road between Twisty River and here, we'll be fine. Do you know if the bridge on the highway is OK? The tsunami must have walloped it pretty good."

"We've got several people at the meet site who live north of town, and they all crossed it. Said it was beat up some, but withstood it. The worst section is between here and the bridge. Apparently some of the road is missing, but folks say it's passable, you just have to be careful. I think you can make it out there."

"So, we're not completely cut off from the rest of the world," said Patty. "Good to know. What about south of Port Stirling? Do we have any info?"

"Haven't heard yet," Matt said. "I don't think our walkie-talkies have enough range to talk to Sheriff Les down in Silver River, but I'll keep trying when I have time. I'm more concerned about the road between here and Buck Bay. I've been trying to reach Bernice at the hospital, but no luck yet. If you two can drive further north of town from the lighthouse, please try Bernice. We're going to need our county coroner, and I hope like hell she's OK."

"Bernice will be fine. Next to this one," Ed said, yanking his thumb in Patty's direction, "she's the toughest person I know. And one of the smartest. But she'll be busy. Considering what that wave did here, I can only imagine the force of it slamming into the narrow bay up there, and there's a lot more people in that town than down here."

"But, as I recall, most of Buck Bay is at higher ground than Port Stirling," Matt said. "We were a sitting duck. Totally vulnerable."

Patty hugged Matt for the second time today. "We'll be all right," she said. "It's just a little water and some mess to clean up."

Matt and Ed laughed, but Matt could feel that "little water" from last night towering over him and swallowing him alive. It was a feeling he would never entirely shake.

. . .

"I've started a list of missing persons," Jay told Matt. "People are telling us about folks they haven't been able…"

Jay was interrupted by a low rumbling noise, and a sharp rolling of the ground beneath his feet.

"Aw, shit!" Matt swore. "Aftershock." He reached out to steady Jay, who swayed and looked dangerously close to falling. Screams and moans came from the battered, ragged residents nearby.

But no one panicked. The assembled group of about twenty-five people moved out of Goodie's Market and the PD tent into the open, and waited out the shaking. The first aftershock, lasting about one minute, would turn out to be a 6.9 earthquake, substantial compared to anything but the one last night.

"OK, folks, here's the drill," Matt said, rubbing his shaking hand through his curly, dirty hair. *Don't panic, dude. Stay calm*, he told himself, but he was afraid. "Everyone calmly return to your vehicles, and immediately drive to Deception Hill. We don't know if there will be another wave or not. Move to high ground now, and help anyone along the way. Got it?"

No one spoke, and all moved quickly to their cars in the creepy quiet.

Highway 101 was suddenly a thing again, as all residents who had returned home during the day headed back to the meet site.

As the sun started to drop into the Pacific, signaling the end of Day 1, the huge group on Deception Hill settled in to wait and watch. Roughly thirty minutes after the big aftershock, a small wave about two feet high came ashore and promptly petered out. In relief, everyone smiled and began chatting.

"This is starting to be annoying," Ed Sonders said to Matt.

"Annoying. Yeah, that's the word," said Fern, standing close to Matt. Jay and Patty nodded in agreement.

"Let's go home, Patty, before it gets too dark," Ed said. "We'll be back in the morning. You three stay safe tonight."

"Will do, and thanks," said Matt. "Tomorrow is a new day. I hope."

• • •

Day 2 was, indeed, a new day…but not exactly the day Matt had hoped for. After a rough night with little sleep at Fern's house, they'd organized their groups again, and returned to the temporary PD in Goodie's parking lot.

Ed and Patty showed up about 9:00 a.m., bringing reinforcements from the Twisty River police department, Patty's co-workers, with them. Bill Abbott had spent his second night at the encampment, and came with his group. They reviewed yesterday's action, and developed the plan for today. As they were about to disperse and begin door-to-door searches, a helicopter appeared overhead.

All present waved wildly at it, jumping up and down with their arms in the air. It circled briefly, and then landed smoothly in the parking lot. A stocky, grumpy-looking man, about fifty years old with a crewcut climbed out first, and approached the tent.

"Who's in charge?" said Johnny Johnson to the assembled.

Abbott stepped forward and reached to shake hands with Johnny. "City Manager Bill Abbott," he said. "And you would be…?"

"I would be the guy who's going to save your asses," barked Johnny. "Johnny Johnson, administrator of Region 10, FEMA at your service."

"Hallelujah!" said Abbott. "We need help. Our poor town was ravaged, first by the quake, and then that huge tsunami."

"Do you know yet if you've lost any people?" said Johnny.

Abbott turned to Matt, and said to Johnny, "This is our police chief, Matt Horning. He's in charge of search and rescue, and has the count."

"Thanks for coming, Mr. Johnson," said Matt.

"My job," snapped Johnny. "I oversee operations and administer policy implementation. I'm also in charge of the Region's tribal nations."

"We've got thirty-eight dead, several injured, and over 400 still missing after our first day of searching. What, specifically, can FEMA do to help us?" asked Matt. "We haven't worked with you before."

"We focus a lot on preparedness, but too late for that now."

"We were prepared," said Abbott, a defensive note in his voice. "But a village at sea level can't *prepare* for a 150-foot tsunami."

"Right. So now we're into response and recovery, and hazard mitigation. We'll bring in manpower for search and rescue, set up an emergency shelter, and make sure the survivors are taken care of."

"That's great," said Matt.

"You need to know that much of my region is in the same boat as Port Stirling, and my resources are thin. HQ is marshalling additional help from the other regions, but that will take another day. The coasts of Oregon, Washington, and northern California are the worst hit…it's dire in every populated area. The quake did a job on Portland and Seattle, too."

"We were afraid of that," said Matt. "Appreciate you coming here so fast."

"Your governor called my boss yesterday, and specifically requested a team in Port Stirling. Her sister lives here, or some damn thing," Johnny said. "Only reason I'm here instead of a more populated town."

Matt and Bill exchanged glances.

"We do appreciate your help," said Bill. "We've made a good start on finding survivors, and taking care of our own, but there's only so much we can do alone."

"We'll keep working, too," added Matt. "And maybe we can let you move on soon to help other communities." He tried his best to sound gracious.

"My boss wants me here, and I'll be here until the job is done," Johnny

growled. He pointed to an emblem sewed onto his khaki-colored jacket—
it read 'FEMA'. "See this? This means your government is here to help."

. . .

Once FEMA and the Port Stirling leadership developed the plan for
Day 2, Ed Sonders and Patty Perkins were dispatched to the north of town
to see if there were any survivors among the wrecked boats. Matt's instructions to the pair were the same as last night: see if there were any dead and/
or injured, and then continue north on Highway 101, and determine if it
was passable to Buck Bay.

Although the going was dicey in a few places, Ed's truck made it to the
lighthouse access road, and they headed toward the water, which sparkled
in today's warm sunshine. But as Patty got out of the truck, and started
hiking toward what had once been a scenic jetty and lighthouse, she felt a
chill. Too practical to be superstitious, she nevertheless was uneasy.

"Something's wrong here," she said to Ed, trying to keep up with his
lengthy strides.

"Yes. There's been a major earthquake and tsunami," he deadpanned.

She punched his arm. "Something sinister. Can't explain it."

"You have a feeling?" Ed didn't discount women's intuition, but it was
unexpected coming from 'show-me-the-facts' Patty.

"I do. Something weird. I feel cold and disturbed."

"Do you want to wait in the truck while I search the boats?"

"Of course not, you goofball. I'm just warning you. Something's off."

"And that makes *me* a goofball?"

. . .

As they approached the lighthouse, they encountered a woman. She
was wearing suspendered fishing waders and boots, which seemed like sensible attire for today, and was spryly climbing over the rubble of the historic lighthouse. Its giant stone foundation blocks had been picked up by
the monster wave, turned forty-five degrees in the air, and rammed down

200 yards away…and most definitely not in the order they were originally assembled. The tower had crumbled, and there was no sign of its historic lighthouse lens or trumpet fog horn. They were never seen again.

"Hello!" Patty called out as they approached the middle-aged woman. She turned, shading her eyes from the brilliant sun, and returned Patty's greeting.

"Patty Perkins, and this is OSP trooper Ed Sonders," said Patty, reaching out to shake the woman's hand. "Are you OK?"

"Just dandy, considering. I'm Mae Walters." She squinted at Patty. "I think we met last summer. Aren't you the detective that's overseeing the relocation of the young women who were trafficked last April? I came to a meeting you ran to update the community."

"Yes, that's me. Still working on finding homes for a few of them. Ed here has helped, too. His organization suffered casualties in the raid. Do you live in Port Stirling?"

"Uh-huh. Been here for ten years, and I run the historical society, which, until last night included this pile of rocks you see here today. She never had a chance out here alone on the jetty against that wave. I live up on the west side of Deception Hill, and I watched her get hit. Worst thing ever, heartbreaking." Her nose reddened, and tears pooled in her eyes.

"We could tell when we turned off the highway onto the access road that this grand old lady didn't make it," Patty said, her voice quiet out of respect for the loss. "I'm so sorry, and I have a feeling we're all going to be saying that a lot the next few days." Patty placed her arm around Mae's shoulders and gave her a squeeze.

"The first time I saw this old lady was when I was about five years old," said Ed. "My dad and I climbed to the top, and I thought it was the coolest thing I'd ever seen." He looked around now. "Shame. Just a shame."

"We're part of the official search and rescue teams for Port Stirling, and we're here to see if there are any people trapped around these ruined boats, or any survivors on the jetty remains who need help," said Patty. "Have you looked around out here at all?"

"Yeah, I did when I first got here. Looked everywhere I could without risking my own skin—the rocks are slimy and tricky. I didn't see anyone, but I can't guarantee I might not have missed something. I'll help you look some more, but watch your step."

The three of them poked around near the water as best they could for the next hour. There was no sign of human activity. The boats were all completely destroyed. They salvaged some pieces of wood and fiberglass floating with the names of two boats, and Ed put those in the back of his truck. Mae spotted a distinctive steering wheel, very nautical looking and made of wood and brass. "Someone might recognize this," she said and added it to Ed's pile. They had no way of knowing whether the boat's owners were safe or at the bottom of the sea—a devastating realization.

"I hope this won't sound frivolous to you, and I know that we all have more serious considerations right now, but I want to see if I can retrieve the lighthouse stone marker with the date they laid the foundation," Mae said. "That's why I came out here. Wanna help sift through this debris?"

"Sure," said Ed. "I'd like to save something of her for future generations."

"I'm in," said Patty, "but only for a little while. We need to keep moving."

"It should be relatively easy to find," Mae told them. "The foundation was cut from local stone, and I know the date, 1901, was carved into one of them. So we're looking for the lighter colored stone, not the bricks. Got it?"

Ed walked about fifteen feet away, where there was a small pile of the local stone, and began to pull off pieces to study. Patty and Mae went the other direction to another area with the light stones.

Patty spotted it first.

"Ed, I think you'd better come over here," Patty said, her voice shaky. "What?"

"This," she said, pointing down into the ground where a human skeleton lay prone at the bottom of the rubble, the back of its skull clearly visible. The skull had a hole in it, precisely the size a bullet would make.

Peering over Patty's shoulder, Mae screamed and jumped back.

"What the hell is that?" Ed said under his breath.

"I believe it's a human skeleton who met an untimely and most likely unpleasant death," said Patty matter-of-factly. She was known for her calm demeanor in a crisis, and for her often wry understatement. "And we needed this today like we need a hole in our *own* heads. Got any rope or crime scene tape in your vehicle?" she asked Ed.

"Yeah, I'll get it," and he scrambled back to his truck.

"Has this...has he or she...has it been here since the lighthouse was built, do you think?" Mae asked Patty.

"I was about to ask you the same question. What do you think?"

Mae thought while staring at the remains. Finally, "I don't see how it could be any other way. This foundation has been in place since the day it was laid down in 1901. It was solid stone throughout."

Patty ran her hand through her short sandy hair. "So, it's been here for 120 years?"

"Looks that way to me," said Mae. "No one could have dug up this place and buried a body here. It did stand neglected for a few years, but the Coast Guard always kept their eye on it. Someone would have noticed."

Ed came back with crime scene tape, stakes, and a hammer, and the three of them set about roping off the site.

"From now on, I promise to take your feelings seriously," Ed said to Patty.

When they'd finished, Patty looked up at Ed with her hands on her hips. "What in the name of Beelzebub are we going to do with a 120-year-old skeleton?"

CHAPTER 10

Wat do you mean you found a skeleton?" Matt said into the walkie-talkie, and the eyes of Fern and Jay, standing nearby, widened.

"Who are you talking to?" Fern whispered in Matt's ear.

"Patty. Shhh." He put his finger up to his mouth, and turned his attention back to the phone.

"I see. Did you get ahold of Bernice?" Pause. "OK, here's what you do. You and Ed drive as far north as you can get, and keep trying Dr. Ryder's phone. Ask the woman—what's her name?—ask Mae to stay there while you try to get in range of Bernice. Do you know if we have any, like, archaeologists around here? Someone who digs up old stuff?"

"Mae said she might know someone who could help us," Patty reported. "Honestly, I'm at a loss on this one. Ed and I do agree, however, that the skull is our best clue. There's a hole in the back of it, and we both think it could be a bullet hole."

"I assume the skeleton is accessible," Matt said. "But I think you should rope off the area and wait for either Bernice and her crew—if they're still alive—or Mae's expert. I have no idea how to investigate a crime scene that old, do you?"

"Nope. Ed and I are standing here looking at each other like a couple of dummies. We even briefly considered covering the body—skeleton—back up and forgetting we ever saw it."

"You couldn't do that anymore than I could," Matt said. "Every victim deserves justice, no matter how long they've been dead."

"Well, we don't actually know it's a victim. Maybe it just laid down and died, all on its own."

"What's your gut telling you?"

"I have a vivid imagination, you know."

He laughed. "Yes, I know, and it comes in handy from time to time."

"My gut feeling is that this poor soul was forced into a grave face down and shot in the back of the head. Left to rot."

"If there is a remote possibility that's true, then all the more reason why we need to find out what happened. At least try, right?"

"Of course. And Ed feels exactly the same way. We both want to poke around and see if we can find a bullet or a weapon of some sort, but it feels like we might be destroying evidence from one hundred years ago. And, it's not likely we'll be in a hurry to arrest the perpetrator. We've roped it off with crime scene tape. No one is out here anyway—the place is a friggin disaster, everything smashed to bits and covered with icky ocean foam. It's creepy."

"And you with your hubby in the hospital," Matt said. "Sorry about this, Patty. I sure as hell didn't see this coming."

"Well, at least this death can't be blamed on your arrival in Port Stirling," she sent a smile through the walkie-talkie. "These bones have been laying here since way before you got to town."

"I want you to tell that to Bernice if and when you see her," Matt laughed. "She blames me for our wave of violence since I took the job in January. Something about karma. Changing topics for a minute, are you springing Ted today?"

"Yeah. We're picking him up about 4:00 p.m. He looked good this morning."

"That's great. Give him my best. If you reach Bernice, I need to know if the road between here and Buck Bay is passable, and if she can get here to take a look at your find. Tell her to call me when she gets in range. I'm sure she has the police frequency."

"Where are you staying?" She was concerned about Matt. He'd suffered a bigger trauma than he was letting on, and it might jump up and bite him at night.

Matt hesitated. He and Fern had been so careful to keep their relationship discreet while he figured out a way around the city's human resources policies. He had to be with her during the nights, but he didn't want the whole county to know.

He said, "We've coordinated an effort for everyone who's checked in with us here today to put a white paper or cloth on their front door if they have a bed and bathroom that someone displaced could use until we get everything organized. There's a bunch of houses inland that are good."

"You didn't answer my question."

"I've got it covered. I have lots of places I could go."

"I'm not your mother, but it's important you not be alone these first few nights. When you stop helping everyone else, you might need some help yourself."

"I'm OK, Patty, and…"

"Why don't you come home with me?" she interrupted. "Ted and I have plenty of room, and we could put together some of his clothes and toiletries for you."

"That's sweet of you, but I need to stay in Port Stirling. My town needs to know I'm going to be here for them every step of the way."

"They already know that."

"I've got a couple of people here whose houses are intact, and who have room for me. I won't be alone, I promise. I do have friends, you know."

"How is that possible?" she laughed. "All you do is work."

. . .

The rest of what they were now referring to as Day 2 went as well as Matt and his co-workers could have hoped. Residents remained resolute in their hunt for fellow survivors, and the arrival of FEMA on the scene gave everyone renewed energy and an emotional lift knowing they weren't alone.

Turns out Bill Abbott had been waiting for this disaster all of his professional career. If ever a city manager had risen to the occasion, it was

Abbott. His lengthy tenure in the village meant he knew almost every resident, or at least one person in nearly every household. He had the respect of his town, and each and every one responded to his call for help.

Once the official search and rescue teams were in place, Abbott asked for volunteers for clean-up crews, and over 400 people showed up for this thankless task. Food was inventoried—Vicky, who also knew almost everyone, took control of this task. She gathered the cooks and chefs in town as they came to the check-in site, and assigned them jobs to gather ingredients and prepare food for the newly-homeless. Campfires were built, propane stoves were lit. Because of the year-round tourism to charming Port Stirling, they had the cooks and the food stores ready to go in a crisis of this magnitude. Some of the markets and resort pantries were destroyed, but supplies were healthy. Without electricity and once the generators ran out of propane, the situation would become more difficult, but, for now, people might not have a shower or a bed for a few days, but no one would go hungry.

Construction crews got organized, and the hardware stores opened their doors once they were able to repair their own damage. Lumber men—and they were all men—prepared to cut the trees and logs that the tsunami had dropped everywhere, and produce lumber that could be used to rebuild once it dried out. The town could absorb the displaced households for now, but new shelter would be paramount by the time winter set in.

As luck would have it, there was an out-of-town construction crew working on the new addition to Port Stirling Links. The golf course resort had sustained serious damage with its ocean-front location, but the worst was to the course itself. Because the golf course was the star attraction, the lodge and separate accommodations were far back from the sea, and while there was water damage and some structural issues from the earthquake, it could all be repaired. Once that had been accomplished, the resort owner offered his stranded construction crew as volunteers to work with the locals in town.

In addition to Summers Pharmacy, the one other drug store in town had been mostly flattened in the quake, but its two pharmacists were called on to help those who needed medical attention. There were only two general practitioners in town, and one of them was missing. The missing GP was Bill's neighbor, and Bill was afraid he and his family hadn't made it out of their ocean-front home. Matt was trying desperately to contact anyone in Buck Bay to learn if the big area hospital was in business or not. He and Abbott were counting on Patty and Ed to connect with the northern town.

Essentially, the entire town mobilized, and the mindset was to take responsibility for each other. Considering their individual circumstances, Matt thought it was a beautiful thing.

· · ·

Dr. Bernice Ryder finally answered Ed and Patty's continued effort to reach her on the police frequency.

"I'm here!" Bernice exclaimed into the squawking walkie-talkie. "Is that you, Ed?"

"It's about damn time," Ed said gruffly. "Starting to worry about you. Patty's here with me."

"Where are you?"

"Between Port Stirling and Buck Bay in my truck. Matt wanted us to keep driving north until we came into radio range."

"Is it bad down there?" Bernice, early fifties with a sensible manner, and no-nonsense to a fault, wouldn't want them to sugarcoat reality. In addition to being Chinook County's medical examiner, she was also a scientist, and when she was woken by the powerful earthquake at her home in Buck Bay, she knew immediately what the next few weeks would look like. And when, standing outside on her deck on the hill above the bay, she saw the approaching tsunami take out the control tower and runway of the small Buck Bay airport nestled close to the bay, and slam hard into the bridge spanning the narrow part of the bay, she realized that the region was really in for it.

"As bad as it gets, Bernice," said Ed. "Port Stirling never had a chance. Too low-lying and defenseless. Dozens dead, and hundreds missing so far."

"Oh, no!"

"Yeah, most of the recovered dead died in the earthquake in collapsed buildings, and we think the tsunami is responsible for the bulk of the missing."

"Are you doing search and rescue?"

"Yeah. And FEMA showed up this morning, which will really help. The tsunami made it upriver all the way to my place, and Patty and Ted almost floated away in Twisty River. You can imagine what Port Stirling looks like. It's a mess of the first degree."

"You live where?" asked Bernice.

"About thirty-five miles inland from Port Stirling. Southeast. On the river. The quake jolted us out of bed, and our laid-back river became a brute. Did some real damage to our property."

Patty motioned to Ed to give her the walkie-talkie.

"Bernice, it's Patty. Are you OK?"

"Yes," Bernice told her long-time friend, setting her tortoise-framed glasses down on her desk, and rubbing the bridge of her nose. "We had some major damage to homes and buildings on the bay, and the wharf area is wiped out. We don't have any power, but the hospital is on generator, and that's where I am. The drive here this morning was a bitch, but I made it in to work. We received patients throughout the night, but no one is critical—mostly a few broken bones from being tossed around during the quake."

"So if the road is passable, you'd be able to come down to Port Stirling and look at a find I made earlier today."

Dubious, Bernice said, "What kind of *find?* Don't tell me our new police chief has ended up with yet another dead body?"

Patty laughed. "He said you'd say that. I'm vouching for Matt—you can't blame this one on his arrival in town. Our corpse has been dead for one hundred years or more. We found a skeleton in the remains of the old lighthouse, which—as we're calling it—'Mr. Tsunami' took out last night. Mae Walters of the historical society said it must have been there since the foundation was laid in 1901."

"Wow," said Bernice. "I'm simultaneously intrigued and horrified. I'd like to see it, but I'm needed here. How about I try to make it down there as soon as it's light tomorrow morning? Not like it's going anywhere if it's been there that long."

"Don't be vulgar, dear," Patty said to her smart-mouthed buddy.

Takes one to know one. "That didn't come out as compassionate as I meant it," Bernice put a sheepish smile into the walkie-talkie. "Please let Mr. Dead-Bodies-Follow-Me know I'll call him on my way once I get within signal range."

"Be nice to him, Bernice. The man was nearly killed last night, not once, but twice. His house went over the bluff, almost with him in it, and then he was tracked down by the tsunami on his way to the Port Stirling meet site. He had to cling to a tree and ride it to the end, or he would have drowned for sure. I'm worried about our favorite police chief."

"Oh my God," gasped Bernice. "Does he live in the ocean-front section?"

"He did. Most of that bluff is gone, toast. He's lucky to be alive, and I suspect that factoid will hit him soon. So play nice, OK?"

"I love the guy, Patty, and my snark is my perverted way of showing affection. I'd walk over hot coals for Matt Horning. I'll be so nice to him he'll probably think I've gone bonkers. Any truth to the rumors about him and Fern? Hubby thought he saw them at a restaurant up here last week, and said they 'looked cozy'. And are she and Jay safe, too?"

"I think they're lovers, if that's what you're asking me," Patty answered. "But the two of them are cagey and not telling anyone anything. And, yeah, I talked to both Fern and Jay this morning, and they're good. The two of them have taken control since this friggin disaster started, and PSPD is lucky to have them both. You'll find the police department set up in a tent adjacent to the highway by Goodie's Market. City hall has some damage, and it's being inspected for structural issues, so until that's complete, they're hanging out up on the hill by the highway."

"Good, I'll find them. And tonight I'll read up on Carbon 14 testing and stable isotopes."

"Huh?" said Patty.

"If you've got bones, I'd better understand what they can tell us."

CHAPTER 11

Day 3 began with a joint FEMA and PSPD meeting. Matt and Bill weren't in love with Johnny Johnson, but were still grateful for the help. His emergency responders would be in Port Stirling by noon. It had been agreed, after some discussion, that their first job would be to build a proper temporary structure to house the wounded. Matt thought Sam Summers and Rick were handling their patients just fine, and let Johnny know that.

"A pharmacist and a nurse outside in a parking lot?" Johnny said with raised eyebrows.

"They're pros," said Matt. "And so far we only have three survivors pulled out of the rubble. I think it makes more sense for your crew to keep searching with us."

"We build things, chief. That's what we do. You'll see. And, at this point, it's unlikely you'll find any more survivors. It's policy to deal with the injured."

"But you hear stories all the time about people surviving for days and being saved," Bill argued.

"Yes, but the odds don't favor it. I think it's more important to take care of the living," Johnny said, and walked away, dismissing Matt and Bill.

"OK, then, I guess it's his way," Matt said to Bill, shrugging his shoulders.

• • •

Bernice's arrival at the cop tent was met with multiple hugs. After receiving an update on their progress, she asked, "Do you want me to determine the cause of death on all your fatalities?"

"We know the causes of death," Fern whispered.

"Crushed in collapsed buildings or drowned in the tsunami," Matt added. "Would be a waste of your time."

Bernice nodded, and there was a moment of silence.

"Then let's go look at your murder mystery," she patted Matt on the back, and the two set off for the crime scene.

"Why are you being so nice to me?" Matt smiled at Bernice as he pulled himself up into her older-model Toyota Tundra pickup, wincing at the pain in his arm. "And, I never figured you for a pickup driver." He looked at the small-framed, athletic woman dressed casually but chic, in a crisp white blouse, black slim-fit pants, and a deep purple cardigan. The cardigan had large, square, high-tech looking silver snaps.

"It's my husband's truck. I drive a beautiful BMW convertible, but we decided that today was not the proper day to take it out for a spin down an earthquake-ravaged coastline. I hate driving this thing, but the beloved spouse was right. And, I'm only being nice because Patty made me. Said you'd had a close call Friday night. Two, in fact, and that I should handle you with kid gloves. That suit you?"

"No, it does not," Matt replied, staring straight ahead.

"Thought not. So, if you're OK and I'm OK, let's get to work. What do you say?"

"I say 'thank you'. We've got so much to do to make this town right again. How the hell are we going to handle a dead body, too?"

"From what Patty and Ed told me, at least this one isn't as gory as the last two. And we won't have such a rush this time to stop a killer."

"Yeah, there's that," Matt agreed. "But we need to give it our best."

"Of course! You know me better than that," she chided.

"Will you be able to get a read on how old the bones are? I've got Mae Walters at the historical society and Sylvia in my department standing by to research any old mysterious deaths. But they both said they need a starting point."

"How much do you know about radiocarbon dating?"

"I know that it's possible to test the amount of carbon-14 in bones, and that the results can tell you when the person died."

"Can tell us *approximately* when the person died," she emphasized. "It's more reliable when we're talking thousands of years ago, but if your skeleton was more recently deceased, it's get trickier because of our burning of fossil fuels and above-ground nuclear tests in more recent decades. Portland's got an AMS—Accelerator Mass Spectrometry—and it can measure the amount of carbon-14 left in a bone fairly accurately. We'll be able to get close to a date when your skeleton stopped taking in carbon-14. All I need is a bone fragment."

"Patty says it's almost completely intact, skull and all. Weird, huh?"

"We'll also be able to do stable isotope testing, and that will give us a picture of the provenance of your skeleton."

"You mean where it lived?"

"Yes. We can compare it to an isotopic composition of a known sample—someone who died in Chinook County, for example. And, will the dietary history compare to that of a missing person on file around here? Bones renew themselves, and they can tell us a lot about who the person was and where they're from. It's exciting, actually. I've never had a chance in real-life to analyze an unknown skeleton. It should be fascinating to see what we learn, don't you think?"

"Fascinating," Matt said dryly. "I have to help physically and emotionally rebuild our entire town, but, yeah, an interesting dead body…bring it on."

Bernice drove carefully through the standing water and debris on the buckled and cracked access road to the lighthouse, and her truck handled it easily. They could see the yellow crime scene tape as soon as they pulled into the small parking apron. The rubble of the former lighthouse contrasted with the brilliant blue sky and the threat of the crime tape to create an unsettling dystopian view of the future.

"This is awful," said Bernice quietly. "Climbing this lighthouse is the first thing kids around here do when they're old enough to make it to the top. I did it when I first arrived in this county."

"I did it, too, just a month or so ago," said Matt. "My sergeant, Walt, organized a department BBQ out here in August, and it was a lot of fun. I was the only one who hadn't climbed to the top—even Sylvia did it a few years ago."

"Ha!"

"Yeah, it was a rite of passage for me, I guess." They got out of the truck, and Matt looked around the entire site. "I remember sitting on a giant flat boulder right over there," he pointed. "It's not there anymore, and I don't see it. That rock weighed at least 800 pounds. Sure glad I wasn't at the top of the lighthouse last night when that wave struck. It was bad enough where I was."

"What was it like?" Bernice asked gently. "Can you describe it?"

"Have you ever been to New York City?"

"Yes. Why?"

"You know those canyons that the tall buildings create down the streets? Imagine that you're standing in the middle of one of those streets and coming straight at you is a wall of water that fills the entire canyon, and is as high as the skyscrapers. That's what it felt like. When it crashed over me, I knew I didn't have a chance."

Bernice's hand flew to her mouth and she let out a little gasp. He reached over and patted her on the shoulder.

"It's OK, I'm here, aren't I? Somebody somewhere decided it wasn't my time. A small tree, about the size of that log"—he pointed to a washed-up log about a foot in circumference at their feet—ran into me, and I grabbed hold and held on. It floated to the surface, and I went along for the ride. It felt like hours, but it was probably about thirty seconds until we bobbed up."

"Jesus, Matt."

"Yeah. But that's not the worst part."

"What's worse?"

"What's worse is that by now the word of this—and I'm guessing here—this record-breaking earthquake and tsunami has hit the outside world, and my family in Texas probably thinks I'm dead. And I have no way to contact them and reassure them. It sucks."

"Knowing the little I know, I'd say all of Oregon and Washington, and probably most of northern California are all without power," Bernice said. "And who knows what happened to the cell phone towers. Communication-wise, we're cut off. There's bound to be some bridges and roads destroyed between us and the valley, too. I think we have to presume we're on our own, at least until FEMA kicks it in gear."

"Yep. That's our assessment here. And I'm not sure our regional FEMA guy is the best this country's got. So, you or the hospital don't have any satellite phones either?" he asked.

"Nope. Rumor is that Sheriff Johnson at the county might."

"Haven't heard from Earl yet, but you should see Bill Abbott in action—it's a thing to behold!" Matt smiled.

"Doesn't surprise me at all. He can act like a buffoon at times, but, believe me, it's only an act. He's one sharp cookie. Wish we had both him and you in Buck Bay instead of the dingbats I have to deal with." She shook her head.

Matt laughed. "Let's look at our skeleton now. You ready? You should have some fun today."

He climbed out of the truck, and his head started spinning. "Whoa," he muttered, grabbing on to the truck door as his legs buckled.

"What's the matter?" asked Bernice.

"Dizzy. Big-time dizzy. Give me a minute."

Bernice raced around the truck, and propped up Matt as best she could. "Try to focus on something off in the distance. Do you feel nauseous?"

"Yeah, a little bit." His face was white.

She leaned him up against his truck seat. "Breathe in. That's good. Now out."

They repeated this drill for a minute, until Matt said, "Better." He stood up gingerly, but looked stronger. "I'm OK."

"You sure?"

"Yeah, let's go."

"OK, but you need to check in with any medical personnel in Port Stirling, and promise me you'll rest once we're back in town."

"Yes, ma'am."

They stepped gingerly around the bones. "You didn't tell me it was prone—face down," she said.

"I didn't know. Odd, don't you think?"

"It's certainly unusual. It tells me it's probably male, and it might be a cultural clue. In certain cultures it's a show of disrespect."

Bernice pulled on her latex gloves, took a brush out of her black ME bag, and knelt down close to the bones. She dusted around the skull, working painstakingly. Leaning in close to the hole in the back of the head, she then shifted to look at it from a different angle.

"Bingo!" she exclaimed.

"What?"

She carefully poked her index finger into the hole and wiggled it around gently before slowly pulling it out, moving an object along with it. A bullet.

"What do you know," Matt said. "Looks like we have a murder victim."

"Shot in the back of the head and left to die where he fell. Nice."

CHAPTER 12

It was starting to get dark, and Fern was concerned because Bernice and Matt weren't back from the lighthouse yet. When her group disbanded after going door-to-door all day to head to their own homes—some with fellow citizens in tow who needed a bed—Fern had run into Goodie's Market to see what food supplies she could buy.

In a sense, Port Stirling had been lucky; the markets, restaurants, and resorts were well-stocked because fall was always a popular time for tourists. Vicky figured they had enough food for several weeks, not counting people's own preparedness kits. Even where the buildings had fallen, some of the canned and frozen foods were salvageable. No one knew yet if the Buck Bay Airport or the roads used to truck in supplies were operational or not, so the fact that their town was self-sufficient for now was a huge relief.

But the big saving grace was the primary water main that brought the town's water down from the reservoir in the hills east of town had been spared. Bill Abbott had sent a crew up there on Day 1 to inspect it, and they reported only a few minor repairs were needed. The reservoir's dam had held. They would re-inspect it after yesterday's aftershock, but so far, so good. Individual neighborhoods had broken pipe issues, both water and sewer, but overall, it could have been much worse.

Fern bought two rib-eye steaks—Matt's favorite—some fresh produce, and a healthy supply of wine and beer. The starting-to-thaw frozen meat would need to be cooked soon, and fresh produce would be limited in the near future to what locals still had in their early fall gardens.

Deep down, she wanted to load up her car with all the fresh food she could, but it went against her values to hoard. *Save some for the next guy.* She paused at the seafood counter, wondering how long it might be before the town's fishermen could resume their work. Did any boats survive? She threw some cod from the previous day into her shopping cart, but she also knew that her parents, whom she checked on briefly this morning—they were tough as nails and both fine—had a freezer full of fish and seafood. When Fern had asked her dad how long their generator would last, he had replied "Don't know. We've never needed it longer than twenty-four hours previously." She figured that people all over town were asking themselves that same question about now.

The first two nights with Matt had been equally wonderful and awful. He was the tough, smart, caring, and funny man she'd fallen in love with, and they'd gone to bed early, elated to be together, and each thrilling to the touch of the other. But Matt had rough nights. Falling asleep quickly, only to be awakened by nightmares.

Fern soothed him, and they both fell asleep again. Only to be awakened by another nightmare. He kept apologizing, and she pulled him closer to her, putting her arm around his shoulder and nestling his head under her chin. He threw one of his legs over hers, and snuggled up until he literally couldn't get any closer to her. This morning shortly before dawn, they had both fallen into a deep, deep sleep, and it was nearly 9:00 a.m. before they woke. They had quickly dressed, grabbed some cereal from Fern's pantry, and headed to the police department tent.

Her plan tonight was to feed him well, including a couple of his favorite beers. They'd been so exhausted after the first two days of search and rescue by the time they'd retrieved her stuff from the camp site that neither of them (both good cooks under normal circumstances) felt like cooking or eating much. Fern had left behind her preparedness kits (minus the battery-operated lights, candles, and matches she knew she'd need at home) for those who didn't have a habitable home to return to yet. Perhaps if they had a more 'normal' night, relaxing with a drink and a well-balanced meal, Matt would sleep better. She could tell he didn't feel great, but he wouldn't stop.

Fern had always had ambitions, even as a young student who understood that the way out into the big, wide world was through education. She had excelled at Stanford, and thought she'd carved out the life she wanted in San Francisco, away from Port Stirling.

But life had a way of making a point, and had done so for Fern via a bad love affair that segued into a crushing job loss. She felt that she was settling when she came home to Port Stirling with her tail between her legs. But then her life plot twisted in yet another direction when Matt Horning showed up last January.

Actually, in three different directions. First, she found a new profession in crime investigation that came out of the blue with her involvement in the Emily Bushnell case. Fern's background in psychology had made her a valuable asset on that case, and the new police chief saw something in her.

Emily's murder had also exposed a raw nerve in Fern, and she realized how much her small town and the people she'd grown up with meant to her. She would always love to travel the world and see new, exciting places and cultures, but Port Stirling was her home. She loved the look of it perched on the edge of the Pacific Ocean, the smell of the sea air, the bounty of the land and water, and the slow vibe of the village.

More than anything, she loved the way its residents took responsibility for each other in this remote part of Oregon. That quality seemed to be lacking in much of the rest of the U.S. these days, and Fern valued it more than ever. Today, she had seen it in action over and over again—her townspeople putting the public good ahead of their own interests.

Her only beef with her town, as a woman who valued privacy, was how everyone knew everything about your life. Or, at least, thought they did. Which brought her full circle back to Matt. After the Anselmo case was resolved, local tongues put Matt Horning and Fern Byrne together in the same sentence—even before it was real between the two of them.

She was determined to keep their relationship personal, and she knew that Matt was hinky about the fact that, technically, she reported to him in the department. They both understood that if whatever was going on between them now turned out to be the real thing, they would have to deal with work. The city policy was clear. If they both worked in, say, sanitation, they might get away with it, but not in law enforcement.

Fern hadn't worried too much about it over the past months because they were careful about their time together. And she wasn't completely clear about her feelings for him yet. Did she only think she was in love with Matt because he'd saved her life? Yes, she was certainly physically attracted to him—black curly hair, cheekbones to die for, fit, muscular body, and those gorgeous deep blue eyes—but was it real love? She loved his mild Texas twang, and how he genuinely cared about people. She loved his work ethic, how he handled his authority, and how smart he was about most things. She loved how he smelled, sort of showery, soapy clean. She felt safe in his presence, and wanted to tell the world about them. But how do you know if it's real love?

Fern had decided that you know for sure when you wake up like she did the morning after the quake, thinking and worrying that he might be dead. It was a pulverizing, soul-squeezing pain that inhabited her body. Her sudden vision of her life without him going forward was an empty, hollow life. No joy. No sharing.

No love.

She knew now. And she wasn't going to let go. Ever.

• • •

Dr. Bernice Ryder bagged the bullet she found lodged in the skeleton's skull, along with a bone fragment, and she and Matt headed back into town, making sure first that their crime scene was secure.

"There's not a big hurry on this one, Bernice," Matt said, as she carefully drove the pickup around rocks, debris, and standing water. "Obviously, Port Stirling is going to have a rough time before we can start putting it back together. I'll be anxious to hear what you discover about our new friend, but I've got a lot on my plate."

"Agreed. I probably shouldn't have even come here this afternoon, but this one was too enticing to stay away. I'm intrigued, and will get some analysis underway as quickly as possible, but the doctor title in front of my name is more in demand currently than the ME."

"Do you know if your airport is operational?" he asked.

"It's not, I'm afraid. The tsunami took out the control tower and the runway. I watched it happening."

"Why on earth was your airport built alongside the bay so close to the ocean?"

"Seems stupid now, doesn't it?" Bernice agreed. "But at the time it was built, it was cheap land in a good location. We didn't have as much information about earthquakes as we do now."

"Live and learn," he said. "Can it be repaired quickly? Or will they have to start over?"

"The water level in the bay was still high this morning when I left home, so I'm not sure what things will look like once the water recedes. It could be that the runway will be repairable, but the control tower is a complete loss."

"Good God," he said, and was quiet for a moment with the visual in his head. "Please tell me that your warning sirens went off, and whoever was working in the tower made it out."

"Yes, but he had a close call I've heard. He ran down all the stairs during the earthquake, jumped in his car, and took off immediately for higher ground. Just made it in time."

"Whew," Matt said. "I bet we hear that story a lot the next few days."

"Do you have a safe place to stay for the next few nights? Wouldn't be surprising if we have another aftershock."

Matt looked sideways at her. "Why are all the women concerned about where I'm staying?" he said.

His defensiveness brought a smile to Bernice's face, and she tried to not laugh. "We need you, honey, now more than ever, and we want to make sure you're out of harm's way. That's all. And, you're clearly not 100 percent."

"I borrowed clothes and boots from a guy at the meet site, I picked up a toiletries kit that the pharmacists organized, and I have a bed, shower, and kitchen at my disposal. I'm fine."

"Where?" She looked over at him and smiled sweetly.

"At Fern's house," he said, defeated. "She's got an extra room."

"Of course she does."

CHAPTER 13

Bill Abbott expected the best from his town, and they had delivered. Everyone who wanted one had a roof over their head, and food and clothing had been pooled and parceled out to those in need. All available building materials had been assembled, crews assigned, and work was underway on the most important structures and infrastructure needs.

FEMA had helicoptered in medical personnel, and began assembling trailers. They had ended the search and rescue component of their operation.

By the end of the first week, city hall was functional, if not yet comfortable, and most of the water and sewer pipes were under repair, if not already fixed. The local utilities were working 24/7, but restoring electricity and communication networks would take several weeks...lines and towers were down all over the state. FEMA and neighboring states were expected to bring in utilities help, but they hadn't arrived yet. The aftershocks continued for three weeks, but they were minor. Frightful, but mostly harmless.

. . .

The Chinook County Sheriff's Office, under the direction of Sheriff Earl Johnson, had recently purchased satellite phones. They had only used them once, on a recent search-and-rescue operation when their landline and cell phone services were acting up.

Sheriff Johnson, who all the oldsters around thought bore a striking resemblance to football legend Mike Ditka, tried to phone all of the county's four police chiefs immediately after the earthquake. When none of them answered, the sinking feeling in the pit of his stomach told the sheriff that things were bad. After Ed and Patty, he had been one of the first local law enforcement officials to arrive in Port Stirling, and had a similar reaction to theirs when he crested the hill east of the village. Port Stirling looked like a bomb had gone off in the heart of town.

The sheriff and Matt Horning had worked closely together on the Anselmo case and the two men from different eras, and with two distinct styles and personalities, had become close friends in the intervening months. And while the earthquake had ravaged Twisty River where he lived, the sheriff knew that Port Stirling would be in even bigger trouble.

Sure enough.

Earl was relieved to see Matt. "You're a hard man to track down," the sheriff said. "You A-OK?"

"Dead tired and a little beat up. Like everybody here," Matt said. "I have a budget request in for a satellite phone. City council said it wasn't a high priority. Think they're changing their minds now?"

"This is the second time I've been grateful that I was smart enough to buy these," the sheriff replied. "I got through to the governor's office, and told her folks in Salem that Chinook County needed some help pronto."

"How did they respond?"

"She knows the coast is in big poop. But it's no picnic in the rest of the state either. Her staff told me the entire Pacific Northwest is pretty much in shambles. It's gonna take a while. But the coastal towns will be prioritized because of the fatality numbers and the displacement. That big-ass wave hit everywhere. She's responsible for deploying the National Guard, and she also called the head guy at FEMA."

"It feels good that she has our back," said Matt. "The strong young bodies are a godsend. And the feds are helping with temporary structures, emergency shelters, stuff like that."

"You've had to deal with the feds too much lately. First, the State Department and now FEMA. What's the regional honcho like?"

"Johnny Johnson," Matt said. "We have a saying in Texas that comes to mind: All hat, no cattle."

Earl chuckled. "Is he in your way?"

"Not today. He set up a trailer for himself. 'Command headquarters'. Haven't seen much of him. There's another matter I need to talk to you about, Earl," Matt changed direction.

"You mean other than your little town has just about been wiped off the face of the planet?"

"You'd think that would be enough, wouldn't you? But no, we found a human skeleton in the ruins of the old lighthouse. Face down, bullet hole in the back of the head with the bullet still lodged in the skull."

"What the actual fuck?!?"

"Patty and Ed found it. I'd sent them out there to see if there was anyone in trouble where a bunch of boats crashed onto the jetty. Instead, Patty stumbled across a bunch of old bones. Weird, huh?"

"How old is old?" the sheriff asked.

"Don't know yet. Bernice and I went out to investigate and secure the scene. It looks like the bones had to have been there since the lighthouse was built over the skeleton. She took the bullet and a bone fragment and is running some tests. You don't know of any one-hundred-year-old-plus unsolved crimes, do you?"

"Not off the top of my head, no. Wonder if our county records will show any old missing persons cases? What year was the lighthouse built? I can never remember dates."

"1901, they tell me. Patty and Ed talked to the director of the historical society, and she's going to look into it, too. Can you check county files and let me know if you come across anything that might be relevant?"

"Be happy to," the sheriff said. "Because we don't have enough to do right now."

"Yeah, we needed a century-old murder mystery to make this month more interesting, right?"

The sheriff and the police chief compared notes on the loss of life and ruin, prioritized the tasks that needed attention first, and Johnson left Port Stirling promising Matt to get the word out that they needed help. The sheriff also left one of his precious satellite phones with Matt, with the admonition to not tell the other police chiefs in the county. "I like you the best," Earl grumped.

. . .

As with most natural disasters in the U.S., people across the country responded immediately, and help poured into the states of Oregon and Washington. The financial donations helped, but what really made the difference were the people who showed up; flying as close to the west coast as they could, and then driving the rest of the way.

Organizations like Habitat for Humanity, Doctors Without Borders, and several National Guard units from other states arrived in Oregon within a few days, all ready to pitch in and go to work to help the survivors. Although many dispatched to the larger population centers, a few national volunteers trickled into Buck Bay and Port Stirling.

Once they were back in their headquarters at a patched up city hall, Matt had asked Walt and Fern, along with a FEMA employee to set up and organize their small conference room to handle the outside volunteer help. It was up to the officers to prioritize the need, and then schedule the volunteers according to their skills.

Huddled in the conference room now, Fern said, "We need to get some of the motels and rental properties operational. If nothing else, we need more accommodations for the out-of-town volunteers. How about we assign the National Guard and Habitat for Humanity a few properties that can be salvaged and see if they can make them habitable in the short term? Or slap together some new temporary structures?"

"I talked to the National Guard commander, and their first concern is making sure there's no looting," said Walt.

"Have we seen any evidence of that?" said Fern.

"Nope, and I told them that," Walt said, sounding indignant. "The head guy said when people get desperate they do desperate things." He shrugged. "I guess."

Two bright rose spots appeared on Fern's cheeks, a sure sign she was about to lose it. "Well, we're not letting our folks get desperate, are we? We're taking care of everyone. And he knows that, for God's sake. What's he think? That someone's going to rob the bank or some of the stores? News flash! Most of them are flattened and don't exist anymore."

"Yeah, unless someone really wants a pair of shoes covered with mud, I don't see looting as our biggest problem," agreed Walt.

Steadying her voice, Fern said, "Will you talk to him about my idea to start rebuilding some of the motels? There is one on the east side of the highway that's mostly standing and didn't experience much damage. The wave barely made it to there, and they only had some minor flooding on the ground floor. I think the second story is intact and habitable. If they could rip out the ground floor carpet and put down some new wood that would be a good start. The Costco in Buck Bay has donated some mattresses, and we need to find some buildings that could take them with a little work."

"That sounds good. There's another motel as you start up the hill out of town, and I went by there this morning. It's in pretty good shape, too, except for a couple of small cracks in the foundation."

"Terrific," said Fern. "That sounds like the perfect job for your commander and his dudes."

"I'll go find him and…" Walt started to say, but was interrupted by a knock at the door. One of the most beautiful women he'd ever seen poked her head inside the conference room, and politely said, "May I come in?"

Walt rushed to open the door for her, saying "Of course." The petite, slender blond was wearing nurse scrubs, but Walt could tell she had a killer body under her clothes. Her wavy blond hair was past her shoulders, and its soft shine illuminated her heart-shaped pretty face, the kind of face that would even look good with no makeup. Perfect features fell into place, and her skin reminded Walt of a summer peach.

She extended her hand to Walt and said, "Hi, I'm Susie Longworth." Her voice was as soft as her hair, and Walt clasped her hand in both of his big, clumsy ones. "Walt Perret. Sergeant Walt Perret, Port Stirling Police Department. What can I do for you, Miss Longworth?" He knew he was staring, but he couldn't seem to stop.

She came fully into the room and noticed Fern who'd risen from the makeshift desk she and Walt were using.

"Officer Fern Byrne," Fern said, reaching over the desk to shake hands with the woman.

"It's nice to meet you both. I was told at the front door you might be able to help me."

"That's why we're here," smiled Fern. "Are you a disaster volunteer?"

"Yes, ma'am. I organized a small contingent of my fellow nurses—we're from Dallas—to come here and help y'all. What a horrible thing to have happened to your perfect little town. I'm sorry. The whole world is so sorry, and we want to help you." Her eyes reddened, and Fern hoped their visitor wouldn't cry—she was tired of people crying.

"We appreciate your help, more than you can know," Fern said graciously. "We've set up a temporary hospital—and I use the word loosely—in a tent up on the hill, and they could really use some help. I can give you directions. Do you have a vehicle?"

"Yes, we flew to a small town called Medford—do you know it?—and rented an SUV for the drive here."

Fern and Walt laughed. "Medford is one of the larger cities in Oregon," Walt told their visitor. "Port Stirling is a small town. But I'm sure compared to Dallas Medford is tiny. How was the drive here? We've heard it's hairy all over the state."

Susie nodded, and her eyes widened. "Oh my goodness, yes, hairy is the word I would use. Trees down, cracked roads, debris everywhere. You've got yourself a real tootin' mess, I'm afraid."

Fern gave her a map of Port Stirling, and circled city hall and then the location of Summers Pharmacy and the temporary hospital. "Here's where you are now, and here's where you should go. They'll be happy to see you and your colleagues."

Susie smiled and said, "Thank you."

Fern studied her for a moment, and imagined that Susie looked like a Texas cheerleader at a pep rally.

Susie took the map and said, "There's one more thing I need from you. They told me at the front that you would know where I could find Matt Horning."

Fern pursed her lips. "He's not here right now. Can I give him a message?"

"Darn it. That's too bad," Susie said, and she looked disappointed. "I tried to phone him, but I guess his cell phone isn't working."

"No, all the towers collapsed in the earthquake," Fern said, drumming her fingers on the desk.

"Well, just tell him that Susie is here to help him, and he should come and find me when he has a minute."

"Does he know you?" Fern inquired.

"He'd better. We were married."

CHAPTER 14

Dr. Bernice Ryder had already put in a ten-hour day before she came to her lab in the basement of the Buck Bay Hospital. She'd sent the bone fragment from the skeleton to the nearest lab that did radiocarbon testing, on the campus at Oregon State University in Corvallis.

She'd forgotten that the lab had acquired a new mass spectrometer through a generous grant from the National Science Foundation a few years ago. It was much closer than Portland, and an easier trip for Bernice's assistant, Curt, who had to make the drive in what would surely be adverse conditions. It turned out that the Buck Bay hospital did have one precious satellite phone, but Bernice didn't dare send it with him, so she had no way of knowing yet if he'd even made it as far as Corvallis, or if the lab was still standing.

But their skeleton, who Bernice was calling Arthur for now, justified her effort, and earthquake or no, she would get some answers for Matt's questions. Analyzing the minerals in the bone fragment would not reveal everything she wanted to know about Arthur, but it would be an excellent start on learning about him and his life.

She'd taken photos of the bone fragment before Curt left for Corvallis with it, and stared at them now. "Who were you, Arthur? How did you end up with a bullet in the back of the head, and such a rude burial? Were you a good guy or a bad guy?"

"Who are you talking to?" said Patty Perkins, coming into the lab. The two old friends embraced, and Bernice held up the photo she'd been peering at. "I'm talking to Arthur, our skeleton."

"Ah, I see. He didn't happen to mention how he died or who shot him, did he?"

"Nope. He's the strong, silent type. We're going to need some help from the lab. Curt should be almost to Corvallis by now—that's assuming the road is passable. I don't have any way to contact him. We just have to wait."

"And we're both so good at that, aren't we?" Patty rolled her eyes. "What's your gut telling you on this one? Did you and Matt see anything that Ed and I missed?"

"No, you covered it. Matt poked around the circumference of the lighthouse footprint, but he didn't find anything. But finding the bullet still intact and Arthur's bones gives us more to go on than you might think. If Matt is right about the body being placed there before the lighthouse's foundation was laid, and if the radiocarbon test on the bone fragment backs that up, you'll at least know where to begin."

"And the isotope test can tell us if Arthur lived around here or someplace else, right?"

"Within a range, depending on how old the skeleton is. Why are you here, by the way? Not that I'm not delighted to see you."

"I've been here all day, and thought I'd see if I could catch you before I left for home. Our favorite district attorney asked me to come over here and check on the Anselmo girls, make sure they all survived the earthquake."

"That was unusually thoughtful of him," Bernice said.

"Not really. He was worried about bad PR if anything happened to those girls while Chinook County is still involved with them."

"That sounds more like Mr. Dalrymple. And are they all right? Everyone accounted for?"

"Thankfully, yes," answered Patty, nodding. "With the help of the county's Human Services staff, we placed about three dozen of them with families in the valley and in Portland, and I don't know how they are faring, but all the girls in our county are fine. Shaken up obviously, but safe and sound. You wonder what other misfortune could possibly befall these young women this year, and it's a relief to know they're OK. Dalrymple also wanted me to make sure the road repairs between Twisty River and Buck Bay got done by the county guys. They did a good job filling cracks and holes, removing trees, and even starting some blacktopping in crumbled places. You still need to watch where you're going, but the road is safe now for everyone."

"Why wouldn't the D.A. ask his own employees if the job was done?" Bernice asked, raising an eyebrow.

"Yeah. I asked him, and he hemmed and hawed and said he didn't trust them to get it done. Probably doesn't trust his own mother."

Bernice laughed. "That. And the county maintenance guys probably don't talk to him."

"He's lucky I talk to him. Hundreds of our people dead and missing, and he's worried about PR," Patty said, shaking her head.

"How is Ted feeling?"

"He's much, much better. I told him he has a hard head, and in this case it served him well."

"He's home now, right?"

"Yep, I brought him home yesterday afternoon with strict orders to stay put while I'm working. He can't drive yet because of the concussion. He's dying to see his cottage on Ocean Bend Road, but he really must rest for a few days before that excitement."

"It survived the quake?" Bernice said incredulously.

"Go figure, huh? Ed and I went by the day after, and I couldn't believe it when we came around the corner and it was still standing. The motel next door was a pancake, and part of the bluff across the road is gone. Vicky's restaurant looked seriously damaged. The road is cracked all along the ocean side, including in front of Ted's place, but it's passable if you have the right vehicle, like Ed's truck. We didn't go in, but it looked like only a part of his chimney was damaged, and maybe one or two of the front windows. It's solidly built of stone, but I was still surprised. It's probably the best surviving structure in the whole town."

"I'll bet Ted was thrilled. I know he loves that cottage."

"We both love it. It's where we met, after all," Patty smiled. "And now,

I need to take off and hit for home. I'll fill in Matt tomorrow morning about Arthur."

"Thanks, hon. Tell him it will be a day or two most likely before we know anything. And, he needs to get some rest. He's not fully himself yet."

"Meaning?"

"He had a bad woozy spell yesterday. Says he's OK now, but he won't be if he doesn't take care. I didn't tell you this."

"Right. I'll keep my eye on him."

"Once I've got some test results," Bernice said, "we should get the gang together, don't you think? Is city hall habitable yet?"

"Yes," Patty answered, "the National Guard shored up the foundation and built a new partial wall where it got washed away. It's not perfect by any means, but the PD and the city employees have moved back in. Roughing it, for sure, but better than that damn tent on the highway! Sheriff Earl wants to meet, too. He's intrigued by Arthur, and has been poring over old records of missing persons. He said to tell you to 'get a move on'."

"You can tell him I said 'fuck off, Earl'", Bernice replied sweetly. "And, tell him to work on getting the dang electricity back on so I can see what I'm doing."

Patty gave her friend a little salute on her way out the door. "Will do, Dr. Ryder."

• • •

Curt showed up back in Buck Bay at noon the next day, and handed the report to Bernice, who eagerly took it from him and retreated to her office. She donned her white lab coat from the coat rack in the corner; she wanted Arthur to know she cared. She pulled up the blind, and brilliant sunshine poured into the good-sized office. Bernice had a view of the hospital parking lot, but today she was grateful her window faced south and there was plenty of natural light to read by. This no electricity thing was starting to wear on her, like it was for the thousands of Oregonians still without power.

According to the test results, Arthur was an adult male, approximately forty at the time of his death, maybe a little older. He died roughly 125 years ago. There was no hint or suggestion of disease, and he appeared to be in good health.

The oxygen isotope tests indicated that Arthur began his life and lived most, if not all, of it in the Pacific Northwest, and the results were consistent with the local area. He definitely spent his last years in this area. His ethnicity was Native American.

"Whoa!" Bernice said out loud. "Looks like we'll have to find a new name for you, Arthur."

. . .

"Did she say 'we *are* married', or 'we *were* married'?" Walt asked Fern the minute Susie Longworth was out of earshot.

"*Were* married," Fern replied. "As in ex-wife."

"Man, if I were married to her, I wouldn't let her get away," Walt sighed and then hurriedly added, "Don't tell Sophie I said that. Or Matt either, for that matter. Forget I said it, OK?"

Fern laughed and punched Walt in the arm. "She is a beautiful woman, no question."

"Did you know about her? Does Matt ever talk about her?"

"I knew he had a former wife, but he doesn't mention her often. I got the feeling that they weren't married very long."

"Looks like maybe she hasn't forgotten him as much as he has forgotten her," Walt speculated.

"It's nice of her to come here and volunteer her services, for sure. I knew she was a nurse, and I think that's how she and Matt met. He got injured playing football, and she helped him with physical therapy."

"Do you think he'll be happy to see her?"

"No idea," Fern said, playing with the beads on her necklace. "We should try to find him to let him know, don't you think?"

"He and Ed took Jay, Rudy, and a couple of the guys out to map the downed power poles for the county. The utilities are organizing county maintenance employees and some of the National Guard to help them restore service. Sylvia said they'd be back here by 3:00 p.m. or so."

"Well, then I guess we'll have to wait to tell him about Susie."

. . .

Bernice called Matt on the satellite phone.

"Did you get results on the bone?" Matt asked.

"Yes, I just finished reading the lab report. Dead about 125 years, give or take a few years in either direction, approximately 40 years old at the time of his death—adult male, as I suspected—lived around here, otherwise healthy, and he was Native American."

"That's intriguing," Matt said.

"I thought so too, and that never occurred to me, although now that we know, it's not altogether surprising. There are several tribes in this region. Two or three have thrived in recent years after former Senator Mark Hatfield got them recognized and restored reservation lands that the federal government had seized. I don't remember all the details, but it was an important thing for the tribes, and some of them are economically stronger now than ever."

"Wonder what it was like 125 years ago? Let's talk to the historical society lady. Also, Sheriff Earl is chomping at the bit to look at old records once you give him an approximate dating."

"Yeah, Patty mentioned that. I've got more news, too, on the bullet. Shall we meet later this afternoon? I can get there, and so can Patty. Where are you guys?"

"Yeah, that's a good idea, now that we have some info on our victim. I'm north of Port Stirling with Ed and Jay—helping the county guys work on the power poles. I told my department we'd be back at city hall mid-afternoon. We can meet there. The building is not ideal yet, but it's coming together. Can you call Earl? Let's say four. Wear your boots."

Bernice laughed. "Haven't had mine off for four days now," she told Matt.

"At least they're your boots. Mine belong to some guy I'd never met until four days ago."

"Costco up on the hill in Buck Bay is open as of this morning, I heard. Their warehouse survived. You have to bring your own flashlight and pay with cash or check because their credit card system isn't working, but I thought I might swing by at lunch time and pick up some things for me and hubby. Do you want me to buy you some clothes, shoes, or whatever?"

"That would be great. Although I really appreciate the loaned clothes, I'm getting tired of the same stuff. And I'm going to have to go to Fern's parents' house and do laundry soon—they have a generator—and I'm not looking forward to that. I do have cash to repay you. My grandfather always told me to carry cash because you never knew. I can hear him saying that now."

"Ha," said Bernice. "May turn out to be the best thing he ever taught you if the ATMs and banks don't work for another week or two. We have our checkbooks but I don't suppose you do."

"Nope. I did have the presence of mind to grab my wallet, and somehow it stayed put in my jeans pocket during everything. And Bill Abbott is working on all our paychecks in cash this month, so I'll be fine. Here's what I need and my sizes. And thank you, big-time!"

• • •

After a week of eighteen-hour workdays, and with immediate crises somewhat under control, Matt allowed himself to ponder his own post-disaster situation.

He was so grateful for the community help, and particularly for Fern's love and hospitality, but he did need to start thinking ahead.

For starters, where would he live? Other people in Port Stirling had the same problem, of course, but Matt felt that the sooner he could get settled somewhere, the more help he would be to everyone else. The only thing he knew for sure is that Port Stirling was his home now.

When he first took the job earlier this year, Matt believed it was a short-term, interim solution to revitalize his career before he would move back to Texas and resume his former life. But Port Stirling had gotten under his skin. He wasn't sure if it was because of Emily's murder and how the town had come to rely on him so soon after his arrival here, but he felt welcome from his first day in town. Sure, there were people who didn't like Matt, but the past few days had shown him friends he could lean on in a disaster.

Matt had good friends in Texas, of course, but the kind of friendship that comes with surviving a harrowing ordeal—and there had been two since his arrival—had made Jay Finley and Ed Sonders his friends for life. When he wasn't hanging out with Fern, Jay or Ed had taken him fishing, or hiking in the woods, or, more often, beer tasting at the local hotspots.

Add to that, he had realized during the Anselmo case how attached he'd become to Fern. It had snuck up on him slowly, but when she was at risk, he knew he wanted her and couldn't imagine a life without her in it. When he thought she might be dead, it was like a sucker punch to his gut. He tried to hold it together and be professional until the case was resolved, but he had been devastated and at times felt like he could barely breathe.

He supposed they could live in Texas together, but it wasn't only Fern, the job, and his friends that made Matt want to stay—he loved the ocean completely after only a few months.

The locals all told him that the Pacific would grow on him after living at its shore, and, boy, were they right. Looking out his big windows was the first thing he did every morning, and the last thing every night. He was now into his fourth season in Port Stirling—beautiful fall—and Matt was recognizing the ebb and flow of the sea and its rhythmical patterns. He understood the tides, and how they varied and left the beach changed nearly every day. He was beginning to see how the atmosphere and the weather changed the color of the water from sparkling cerulean blue to cold steel gray to angry brown foam.

The weather. Good God, the first month he spent in Port Stirling— January—he remembered thinking that he would never get used to the weather. Pounding sideways rain that went directly down the back of your neck and soaked your pants legs, relentless wind that made keeping a cap on while jogging virtually impossible, swirling, deep fog that made it seem as if the world ended five feet in front of your eyes.

The weather was overwhelming to Matt at first, but he quickly realized it was simply a case of having the right apparel, and learning when to stay inside and when to go out. There was a reason why outdoor sports-wear companies were born and thrived in Oregon, and that reason was the Oregon coast and the rest of the wild, rough state with its mountains, deserts, and water features of every imaginable kind.

Matt had come to appreciate a rainy, cold night inside his cozy cottage with a fire burning hot in the massive stone fireplace—the only thing in his former home still standing. And he had become even more apprecia-tive of the warm, windless days—and there were more of those than out-siders realized—when he could go for a run down his beach at low tide. In the lengthy summer daylight, his after-work routine had been to go for a long run that helped release job stress. He'd finish off with a stretch out on his bluff, followed by a favorite Oregon craft beer in his Adiron-dack chair perched on the edge, while he watched the ships far out to sea on the horizon.

He even had a pet in the Pacific Ocean, Roger, the seal who showed up most days, bobbing in the shallow waters directly in front of Matt's house. What Roger must have been thinking when the tsunami came! Had he survived?

Matt hadn't had time yet to survey the scene below his house. He knew that a big chunk of his bluff was gone, and tomorrow morning at low tide, he and Fern had planned to go there and see if by some miracle he could recover any of his things. He had low expectations, but Fern thought it might be good for his mental outlook if they at least inspected the area. He had put off thinking about his future, and she was probably right; if he saw with his own eyes that his former life was gone, he might be able to start planning a new one.

• • •

Matt, Ed, and Jay arrived back at city hall at 3:15 p.m. and had just enough time to clean up before the Chinook County crime team met to discuss their skeleton. Sheriff Earl, Patty Perkins, and Dr. Bernice Ryder were on their way to join them, and new permanent member of the crime team, Detective Fern Byrne was already in the building. Matt had asked

Bernice to not invite the other local chiefs of police yet until the core team could see what they were dealing with. Besides, travel throughout the county was still not a piece of cake, and limited to essential.

Matt checked in with Sylvia, the department's admin assistant. "Anything exciting happen while we were gone?" he asked the 70-something woman dressed entirely in red today. Everyone in the department was wearing jeans and boots, with the exception of Sylvia, who had, if anything, exceeded her usual pulled-together fashion status. Matt had told her it was OK to dress more casually until their building was completely cleaned up, but she had declined, saying, "And let that damn tsunami win? Not a chance."

"Not unless you consider a visit from your ex-wife exciting," Sylvia replied now, and smiled up at him.

"What are you talking about, Sylvia?"

"Do you know a woman named Susie Longworth? From Texas?" She waited.

"Yes. I was married to her once upon a time."

"Well, she apparently remembers you, too, and has come to Port Stirling with four of her nursing mates to help us out. Darn nice of her if you ask me. She was here looking for you earlier today."

"Are you making this up?" he grinned at her.

"No, Chief, I am not. Fern and Walt talked to her. Walt appears to be in love with her. Fern probably not so much."

CHAPTER 15

The Chinook County crime team hunkered down together in their usual meeting room, which did not look at all usual. The boring, utilitarian gray carpet had been ripped up because of the water damage it sustained when a portion of city hall's north wall had collapsed during the earthquake. The massive conference table had survived, but the chairs were ruined, and Bill Abbott had rounded up a bunch of folding chairs to use in the interim. The National Guard had repaired the foundation and wall, but the cosmetic stuff would have to wait in line behind higher priorities.

"I want to take a minute," Matt started, looking around the room at his six colleagues, "and tell you how happy I am that you all made it through the events of this week. Perhaps because of my near miss, I have a stronger sense of what's really important in life, and a lot of it for me is you guys. Working with people you like and that you know you can count on doesn't happen every day, and I feel fortunate."

"Cut the mush, Chief," growled Sheriff Earl, "we're glad you made it too. You should probably have washed up in Japan by now, but it wasn't your time."

"Nope," Matt agreed, smiling at the curmudgeonly sheriff. "I'm supposed to be here, probably to solve a murder that no one in this county has solved for over one hundred years. Bernice, tell these nice folks what we've got."

135

Dr. Ryder handed around copies of her report, including a description of the crime scene, and the forensic tests results. Once everyone had a copy, she said, "Adult male, Native American ethnicity, about forty years old at the time of his death, which was approximately 125 years ago."

"What's the range of years since his death?" asked Jay.

"It's not an exact science," answered Bernice. "But it's accurate within a decade or two. He's been laying there for no longer than 125 years; it could be less, as much as twenty years less, but likely not much more. So, I'll put it at between 1896 and 1916. Plus, everything is consistent with him having lived all of his life around these parts."

"The four of us who have been to the site," Matt said, "have a hard time imagining how the body would have been placed there after the building of the lighthouse. Not impossible, but difficult. And the lighthouse was built in 1901."

"Do we know if there are any Native American burial grounds in the area?" Jay continued.

"I was about to ask you the same question," Matt said, stirring in his chair. "I'm ashamed to admit that I didn't realize there was history in this regard here. Anyone have any clues?"

"I know a little about this subject," Ed Sonders said. "I know there's a famous historical burial grounds near the mouth of the Umpqua River, but I've never heard of anything around Port Stirling."

"Mae Walters at the historical society could help us," Patty said. "She was with Ed and me when we found the skeleton. I thought I would stop by there after our meeting once I know what we have on our plate."

"After we see if we can identify the victim," Matt said, "is there a local tribal group or groups we could reach out to?"

"Yeah, the tribe that owns the casino in Buck Bay is a big organization, and the Twisty River tribe is the largest in the area," Fern added. "Their HR Director is a friend of mine, and she would be interested in this case, for sure."

"What's her name, Fern?" Matt asked with his pen poised over his notebook.

"Susan Mulcahy. She's a descendant of the tribe on her mother's side, and her family has lived in Chinook County for at least five generations. I'll be happy to contact her when you think we're ready, Chief."

"Yeah, about that," Bernice interjected. "We're not ready to take this outside this room yet. If you'll keep reading my report you'll see that our victim was shot in the back of the head, probably at close range. The bullet was still lodged in his skull, and we recovered it."

"Good Lord," said Patty. "After all this time? Metal and bones—amazing to me."

"Arthur had a nice roof over him," mused Bernice. "And, yes, I realize I need a new name for our skeleton. Not sure Arthur suits him, and he likely wouldn't appreciate such a British name. I considered the burial grounds theory too, Jay, but I don't think it washes in this case."

"Agree with you, Bernice," Matt said. "First off, he was definitely a homicide victim. It would be very difficult for a person to shoot himself in the exact center of the back of the head, and that's what happened here. Plus, wasn't the jetty where the lighthouse sits built specifically for it? I got the feeling that it hasn't been there for centuries. He could have been murdered somewhere else and deposited here when the killer knew the lighthouse was about to be built, and would hide the corpse potentially forever. In fact, that's my theory. And, it would have worked if not for one of the biggest earthquakes and tsunami in recorded history."

"Pretty good plan," agreed Ed. "Earl, how many open unsolved homicide cases or missing persons do you have at the county? I'll check our state police records as soon as I leave here."

"I've been scoping out the county records since I heard the news, and I've found thirteen so far. But I didn't go back far enough based on Bernice's test results. Plus, narrowing it down to a Native American male helps a lot. If Arthur was murdered, surely it would have been reported at the time he went missing."

"Maybe it's like Jimmy Hoffa," said Jay. "Reported missing, but no body."

"Perhaps I should take another look around the site," Bernice grinned at her young pal Jay, "and see if Jimmy's there, too."

"It never ceases to amaze me how you two can always find something amusing in murder," said Patty, shaking her head.

"Aw, c'mon, Patty, you were smiling, too," Jay said.

"I was laughing at you, not with you," Patty said in a fake pretentious voice.

"Bernice is right about keeping this quiet for now until we identify Arthur," Matt said. "But here's where it gets really tricky for me. Bernice, tell them your thoughts on the bullet."

"So, I've been to the site with Matt, and I agree with him that killing Arthur there AFTER the lighthouse was built doesn't seem possible. But we have this nice bullet as a souvenir," Bernice said, holding up a plastic bag with the bullet.

"Bullets like this one," she continued, "were consistent with use in a bolt-action rifle like the kind used in the first half of the twentieth century."

"Like a Springfield rifle?" asked Sheriff Earl.

"Could be," said Bernice nodding vigorously. "But I already thought of the Springfield rifle, and therein lies one problem Matt and I have. That particular rifle wasn't really in use until 1903, two years after the lighthouse was built. We know about it because it's one of the more famous of the old rifles."

"I have one," Earl said. "My grandfather used it in World War 1, and it came to me after my dad died. It's a beauty."

Matt and Bernice looked at each other, and then Matt spoke.

"I'll need to see that rifle, Earl. Maybe you've got our murder weapon." Matt smiled to show the sheriff he was kidding.

Some of the color went out of Earl's usually ruddy face, and he said, "OK".

"Now let's go find out who this gentleman was," said Matt, dismissing the team.

• • •

Fern placed her hand on Matt's arm after the others filed out, and said, "Can I talk to you for a minute?"

"Sure. What's up?"

"You had a visitor today, and I wanted to tell you about it."

"Ahh, you're too late—Sylvia already spilled the beans," he smiled. "My former wife is in town, apparently."

Fern stared at him, trying to decide how he was taking this news. "Will you meet with her?"

"Sure. She came to help, so, yeah, I'll see her and thank her for her service."

"Not sure that's a good idea right now," Fern said haltingly.

"Why not?"

"You're a little vulnerable," she fidgeted.

"I'm not vulnerable."

"You almost died. It doesn't get any more vulnerable."

"You think I'm too wimpy to deal with my ex-wife?"

"That's not what I said, Matt."

"What, exactly, did you say then?"

"You went through a violent, frightening, traumatic episode. In case you don't know, almost dying, the death of a loved one, and divorce are three of the most upsetting things that can happen to a human. I'm just saying that revisiting your divorce in the same week you almost lost your life is not the healthiest coping mechanism. That's all."

"I don't intend to revisit my divorce. But it would be extremely rude to not acknowledge her presence and her help to our community."

"Who wanted the divorce?" Fern asked. "We've not really talked that much about your marriage." She looked a little pale.

"Susie requested a divorce, and I didn't fight it," Matt said calmly. "We had grown apart, mostly because of my new profession, law enforcement. When I played for the Cowboys, it was all fun and games, and we were a great couple. But that all changed when I became a cop on the beat. Odd hours, stress of the job—you know. Take what we deal with here in Port Stirling and multiply it 1,000 times, and you've got the Plano PD. It wasn't what she bought into."

"Would you say you're still friends, or was the split bitter?"

"I never hated her, if that's what you mean. I understood her point of view. I was just disappointed that she didn't love me enough to adapt."

"Do you still love her?"

Matt hesitated, and looked at a spot on the wall behind Fern. "No, I don't love Susie. I'm fond of our time together, but that's all, and it's a distant memory." He reached out, took Fern's hands in his, and locked eyes with her. "I love you. And what I feel for you is deeper than what I ever felt for her."

Fern started to weep softly.

"Sure, it took me a while to recover from the divorce," Matt continued. "But I can honestly say that since I moved to Oregon, I've hardly thought of her. Once, when I put on my 'good' jacket to tell the Bushnells their daughter was dead, I thought of Susie because she'd bought that jacket. That could be the only time she's entered my mind since I've met you."

"You don't have to say that," she said, gaining her composure, and giving his hands a squeeze. "I'm not jealous of your relationship with her. I'm just concerned about the timing on your psyche. And I'm uneasy because I love you, too." She tried a smile, and it kinda worked.

He squeezed back. "OK then, we love each other, we're confident about us, and a visit from Susie is not going to change that."

Fern hoped he was right.

CHAPTER 16

B ingo!" exclaimed Sheriff Earl Johnson, pulling the file from the cabinet. "I think we have a winner."

He held in his stubby-fingered hands a police report, hand-written and dated July 28, 1904. The top page had a tan stain on the upper right-hand corner. An adult male had been reported missing without a trace two days previously by his wife, Rochana Kouse. The missing man was Tyee Kouse, and he was forty-one years old. The Native American husband and wife had four children at the time of Tyee's disappearance: three sons, Elan, Jobe, and Dyami, and one daughter, Enola.

The family lived east of Port Stirling in the Twisty River valley on property that abutted the river. Earl thought it ironic that the earthquake and tsunami wave that uncovered Tyee's remains had likely covered his family's homestead with mud and debris.

According to the report, Tyee had left the family farm in the early afternoon of Tuesday, July 26, to take his homegrown fruits and vegetables to markets he regularly supplied in Twisty River and Port Stirling. Tyee usually took his children with him on his deliveries because they loved to ride on the steamer upriver to Twisty River, and then back down to Port Stirling. But, it had been a beautiful summer day and they had been happily playing in the river, so he went alone.

Tyee never returned, and his family never saw or heard from him again.

His horse, Harvey, had returned alone to the family farm at some point that night, with its wagon still filled with the week's goods.

Rochana knew in her heart that Tyee would never leave his beloved family voluntarily, but she had trouble convincing the local law enforcement authorities of that fact. The two-page report, which, to Sheriff Earl showed an alarming lack of any real investigation into Tyee's disappearance, concluded with a verdict of 'voluntary disappearance'. There was only the one report in the file—no follow-up, nothing else.

"You were right, Rochana," Sheriff Earl murmured to himself, "your husband did not leave you voluntarily. Someone put a bullet in the back of his head, and hid his body in a damn good hiding spot. And I'm going to find out who."

* * *

"Hi, Earl," said Matt into the satellite phone. "What do you have?"

"I think I know who Arthur really is," Earl said excitedly, at least as excited as the sixty-three-year-old, jaded sheriff ever got. "When I looked through our archived files before yesterday's meeting, I only went back as far as the 1940s. But this morning I started looking back into the late nineteenth century, and I found our guy in 1904. July 28, 1904 to be exact."

Earl filled him in, and Matt suggested a strategy for how to proceed. "Let's start with finding out who owns the Kouse property now. That should be in your county records, right?"

"Yeah, I can figure that out."

"You should also look up death records for Rochana, and for the four children. Plus, any marriage or birth certificates for the kids. I'd like to know if there are any living descendants. The fact that they had four kids means our chances of finding one or more are pretty good, don't you think?"

"If they stayed in the area," Earl agreed. "But kids started leaving Chinook County in the 1940s, 50s, and 60s to go to colleges in the valley. The populations of Buck Bay, Port Stirling, and Twisty River were all larger in the 1930s than they are now. And the Native American populations have declined around here, too. But maybe we'll get lucky."

"I'm generally a lucky man," Matt said, "and I'm overdue for a break."

"Yep, I would say that you are due after this week. I'll do some research here and let you know soon."

"And, don't forget, Bernice wants to look at your old rifle."

"I haven't forgotten. I got it out of the case last night and put it in a sleeve for travel. I'll pop it over to Buck Bay this afternoon. But first, I want to find Tyee Kouse's descendants. We owe him. Our predecessors on the job didn't properly investigate his disappearance. It's a crying shame."

"Why do you suppose that was?"

"Obvious. He was a Native American. Probably not much more important than a cow in those days."

"But the man had a family and a thriving farm. How could that not warrant some attention?"

"Oh, they probably made the right noises, but in those days, one less Indian was nobody's problem."

"That's disgraceful," Matt said. "How do you call yourself a cop if you don't value human life? But Teddy Roosevelt was president then, right?"

"You mean old 'The only good Indian is a dead Indian' Roosevelt?"

"I remember my history, and he really did say that, didn't he?" Matt said. "And he presided over removing tribes from their land and ruining their cultures."

"Exactly. And Oregon didn't do right by the Natives either. Not a historical record to be proud of. Which is why the law didn't bend over backwards to find out why Tyee disappeared."

"Can you imagine how frustrating that must have been for his wife and kids?"

"Which is why you and I are going to find out what happened to him and who did this," Earl said. "Especially if any of his grandkids or more likely, great-grandchildren are still around here. I hope that bullet didn't come from my grandfather's rifle."

"It didn't, Earl. It's just a formality," Matt assured him.

"Hope so. What are you working on the rest of today?"

"Still helping the National Guard and our volunteer crew put up power poles. People are getting antsy about restoring electricity. Oh, and I have to go find my ex-wife."

"Huh? Didn't know you had one."

"Yeah. In Texas when I was younger. Apparently, she's come to Port Stirling to help the effort. She's a nurse."

"Well, that's certainly a story for another day," Earl chuckled. "But right now, I owe Tyee Kouse's family some answers."

. . .

Matt left city hall and drove up the hill to the makeshift hospital. He had cleaned up as best he could in the bathroom, which had running water as of two days ago. Somewhat uneasy after hearing the news about Susie being in town, he felt more comfortable after talking it through with Fern.

No matter how much Fern protested, he could tell she was jealous of Susie, and nervous about him seeing her. And why wouldn't she be? Susie's looks caused both men and women to go a little cuckoo. He was used to it. But it no longer had a hold on him, and he meant what he told Fern.

And, it wasn't as if Fern was chopped liver, as his father said when he and Beverly, his mom, had come out during the summer to visit. It had been their second trip to Oregon since January to visit him. Matt cooked dinner for them and Fern in his cottage one night because he wanted them to meet her in a comfortable, casual setting. As he knew they would, both of his parents had loved Fern. She was easy-going around them from the minute they met.

Fern had offered to take them both for a walk on the beach after dinner in the long summer twilight, and she and Beverly had taken off; his dad had stayed with Matt to help him clean up the dishes.

"Well, Fern is a winner, son," his father had declared.

Matt laughed. "If I recall, you said the same thing about Susie."

"Yes, I liked Susie—what a beautiful woman. But Fern isn't exactly chopped liver either," he grinned. "And she's nice. A warm, caring woman.

Good sense of humor. Your mother took to her immediately, I can tell. How long are her legs anyway?" he asked, giving Matt a playful elbow in the ribs.

"Long," Matt returned his dad's grin. "I always liked blondes, but this redhead stole my heart." Turning serious, he said, "When she was in trouble during the Anselmo case, I almost lost it. I honestly think I fell for Fern the first time I laid eyes on her back in January, but it took her being at risk for me to really understand how deeply I felt."

"Thank the good Lord that turned out all right. It must have been awful for you."

"About as bad as it gets in this business," Matt agreed. "And we still haven't wrapped it up fully, although the feds are in charge now."

"Have you met Fern's parents? They live here, too, right? What are they like?"

"Yeah, they're great. Irish heritage, and all four of Fern's grandparents emigrated from Dublin. Her mother and father grew up together in the same neighborhood in Boston, married, and moved out here to start a new life away from their families. They're smart, fun people."

"I figured they must have a good sense of humor—'Fern Byrne' was my tipoff." Dad smiled.

Matt laughed. "Yeah, can you imagine growing up with that name, and constantly having to explain it? Bottom line is that I could do much worse for in-laws."

"Are you that far down the road, son?"

"No, not quite yet. We're both aware that what we have now might be a reaction to all the shit that went down during the Anselmo case. We don't want to move too fast." Matt smiled. "Fern keeps psychoanalyzing us as a couple to explain where she thinks we are on the 'survivor' charts."

"She's an intelligent young woman, and gorgeous—don't blow it," he said, giving his son a quick hug.

That had been in early August. Was that only last month, Matt thought? It seemed forever ago. Matt had managed a quick call to let his parents know he was alive once he borrowed one of the county's satellite phones, and as soon as his brain fog cleared.

He would ask Susie to give them further information on Port Stirling and their situation once she returned to Dallas. Beverly had cooled on Susie after the divorce, but his dad was still friendly to her, and Matt knew they all saw each other at their country club.

Pulling into the temporary hospital parking lot, his Texas country club seemed like a million miles away. But still, he spotted Susie from a distance.

She saw him, too, the minute he got out of his vehicle, waved, and came running toward him, her blond ponytail swinging wildly.

Aware that there were people he knew milling around, Matt attempted to sidestep the embrace he knew was coming from his former wife. To no avail.

Susie threw her arms around Matt's neck, and pulled him tightly to her. "I am so relieved to see you!" she exclaimed. "Sweet Jesus, I'm so happy!"

Despite the comforting familiarity of her hug, Matt broke out of the clutch, stuck his hands in his jeans pockets, and smiled. "It's nice to see you, too, Susie. Thanks for coming to help us—we need all the help we can get right now."

"I figured y'all could use more hands on deck. I talked a few of my fellow nurses into coming along for the ride, and Dallas Memorial was real sweet about giving us time off. Aside from this flippin disaster, how are you?" It sounded like 'yew'. "You look good, Matt."

"I looked better before the earthquake sent my home down a 300-foot cliff, and that damn wave tossed me around."

She grabbed his arm, her face etched in pain. "Stop. Please don't talk about it. I can't bear to think of you being in that danger. It's over now, and you're safe. That's all that matters."

"Well, my safety is not the only thing that matters; we still have people at risk. People inside here", he nodded toward the stopgap hospital, "and families with no home to return to."

Susie closed her eyes and shook her head, as if to make those people go away. "Are you happy here, darlin? Do you like Oregon?" She pronounced it 'Oregone'.

"No, I don't like it here. I *love* it here," he smiled. "My job is the best, and I couldn't ask for nicer co-workers. I've got talented people in the jobs I need them to be in, and we've had some good early success. The town has welcomed me."

"They certainly should have," Susie said. "You saved them from some real nasty people."

"Oh? You've heard about our latest case?"

"I know you've solved two murders. I keep up with you. We have this thing now called the internet, you know?" she teased.

"Yeah, I know, and I'd kill for it about now. Once we take care of our people, getting the utilities up and running is job one."

"Your last little problem made the front page of the Dallas papers. They pointed out that you were a hometown boy. You're a rock star in Texas now. Again, I should say."

"Ha. I was never a rock star in Texas," he laughed.

"Why, of course you were, darlin'. When you played for the 'Boys you were. And even when that messy thing happened in Plano, people still looked up to you. I looked up to you."

Matt stared at her. "No you didn't."

She pulled her ponytail over one shoulder and twisted the end of it around a finger. "I may not have always shown that to you, but I did respect you and your work. Always."

"You divorced me, Susie. How's your new husband, by the way? I forget his name."

"Benjamin. I divorced him, too."

"Already?"

"Turns out he liked to watch porn online." She looked down at her shoes. "That didn't set well with me."

"No, I don't imagine that would set well with many women. I'm sorry, Susie. You deserve better."

"Maybe I *had* better and foolishly let it slip away."

"Is that why you're here?"

"Not entirely. We really are on a humanitarian mission. But I did have a hankering to see with my own eyes that you're OK."

Matt spread out his arms wide and said, "I'm OK!" like in an old Hollywood movie.

She laughed. "Yes, I can see that you are fine. So this godforsaken place suits you?"

"It's not godforsaken, it's the Promised Land," he said seriously. "Honestly, I don't miss Texas much. Except for my family. And maybe a little sunshine in January. The ocean has gotten in my blood, and I love it."

"Even after what it did to you?"

"Yes, even after the horror. I still want to be here. You're seeing it at its worst. It's such a beautiful place normally. I've taken up fishing again, and you wouldn't believe the bounty from the sea and the local rivers."

"Don't you miss a good ol' Texas beef brisket?" she teased.

"I can cook, you know. I have a grill." He paused. "Make that 'had a grill'. I'll be starting over, but I'm staying."

"Where will you live, Matt? And are your parents going to help you out financially until you get back on your feet?"

Again, he stared her down. "I don't need their help, Susie. I have plenty of money of my own. You know that."

"Well, I don't know that. You gave me a lot of your money."

"It was the right thing to do when we split up. It wasn't your fault that I wanted to change my life. It was important to me that you continue to live the way I'd promised you."

"Still, it was a lot, and now I worry about your future."

"Don't. I have lots of problems right now, but finances aren't one of them. I'm not sure yet what I'll do for housing, but I'm good for now, and will make a plan for myself once things calm down for everyone."

"Where are you staying?"

"I'd rather not say."

Out of the corner of his eye, Matt saw Patty Perkins approaching them.

"Patty, hi! How are things going?" he said.

She looked first at Susie and then at Matt, taking off her red-rimmed sunglasses. "I'm sorry for interrupting, but there's someone I want you to talk to in the building. Are you coming in soon?"

Patty turned her shoulder to Susie. Matt could see the twinkle in her eyes, and he knew what she was doing.

"Yes, I'm headed inside now. Patty, I want you to meet an old friend of mine who's come from Texas to help us. Susie Longworth, this is Patty Perkins, and next to me, she's the best detective in Oregon."

The two women shook hands politely.

"A woman detective," Susie smiled. "Good for you."

"I believe you have female detectives in Texas," Patty smiled back.

"Not very darn many," Susie said. "We could use more. Things would get done faster."

Patty laughed. "Gotta agree with you there."

"Very funny, ladies," Matt said. "I'll follow you in." He turned to face Susie. "I can't thank you enough for coming. Do you have a good place to stay, and are you set up?"

"Yes, we're staying in that motel that's open up on the hill. They're letting us use their kitchen and they have a generator. Some of the National Guard guys are staying there too. I suspect it will be one big party."

The circumstances hardly warranted a party, and Susie's face didn't look like one either. She looked sad as Matt gave her a quick hug, and said, "I'm sure we'll see each other around town," and walked away.

CHAPTER 17

Sheriff Earl Johnson decided he finally needed to tell the district attorney about Tyee Kouse. Earl, like the majority of county employees, didn't much care for D.A. David Dalrymple. The down-to-earth, crusty sheriff thought Dalrymple was a pompous jerk. More often than not, all he did was get in Earl's way and make his job more difficult. Worse than that, in Earl's book, was that the D.A. was always overdressed. *Who wore a suit and tie to work every day in Chinook County?* Nobody, that's who. And oily…Dalrymple definitely had an oiliness about him.

The sheriff didn't give a rat's ass about public relations when it came to doing his job. As long as the crooks got what was coming to them, and the victims got justice, Earl was happy. Dalrymple only cared about himself, Earl thought, and mainly about how the voters saw him. The sheriff's position was an elected one, too, but Earl believed that politicking was bullshit, and he either deserved to be re-elected or not based on his job performance. That approach had served him well for twenty-two years.

But now, he approached the D.A's assistant's desk, nodded at her and said "Is he in?"

"Why, Sheriff Johnson, we don't see you much around here," she smiled at the gruff man standing in front of her with his hands on his hips, feet apart.

"I'm busy, Carla," he replied, but did offer up a slight smile.

"I'll tell him you're here. Be right back."

Dalrymple was seated at his enormous walnut desk, and didn't bother to rise when Sheriff Earl came in. His scalp was just visible through his thinning blond hair.

"Sheriff, what can I do for you?"

"I'm fine and my family all survived the earthquake," Earl said. "You and yours?"

Dalrymple blanched. "I was going to ask," he said. "We're all good at my house, and I'm happy you're OK. My garage got knocked off its foundation, and I've got a couple of trees down, but otherwise no damage." He motioned to the chair in front of his desk, and Earl took a seat.

"Yeah, we had some tree damage, too. Sure glad I don't live down by the river. Patty and Ted have quite a mess to clean up, I understand. Same with Ed Sonders, who lives up the road."

"It will take months for us to complete the clean-up around here," the D.A. agreed. "But first we've got to get the utilities going. My constituents are starting to complain about our pace."

"Count me in that group," Earl said. "My beer's starting to get warm."

Dalrymple actually laughed. "If that's the worst thing that happens to you, I think you'll survive."

"Unfortunately, there's something worse. That's why I came to talk to you."

Dalrymple, immensely relieved that they were off personal matters and on to business, said, "What's happened, Earl?"

"Patty and Ed found a skeleton in the ruins of the Twisty River lighthouse. Bernice has run tests, and tells us it belongs to a Native American adult male, and he's been there for over 100 years. Got a bullet in the back of his skull."

"What the hell?"

"Yeah. It gets worse. I found a missing person's report from 1904, and it matches up with Bernice's results. What really stinks is that the law enforcement in charge back then didn't properly investigate the case. They told the wife and family that he took off voluntarily, and dismissed the case. They never saw him again, and he was obviously murdered and buried where Patty found him."

"Oh, for God's sake. So now we have no choice but to investigate, and it's going to make our county look bad. Right?"

"'Fraid so, David."

Dalrymple slapped his open palm on his desk. "We do not need this right now. We have people hurt in the earthquake, we have newly homeless and displaced families that we have to help, our food supply is not back to 100 percent yet, and we don't have electricity for crying out loud! You've got to take care of our folks first."

Earl cleared his throat. "I understand all that, and my department has been working around the clock to help people get back to some sense of normalcy. But I also have an obligation to Tyee Kouse's family if he has any descendants still in Chinook County. They have a right to know that he didn't abandon his family, even if it does go back several generations."

"Yes, I agree, it's the right thing to do. It's just that we have to prioritize."

"What do you mean?" asked the sheriff, in spite of the fact that he understood precisely what the D.A. meant.

"The investigation of your skeleton can wait until life is back to normal."

"Matt Horning and I have prioritized Kouse's murder," Earl said firmly. "We are both committed to helping Port Stirling and the county function, but we have to try to find Kouse's descendants. It shouldn't take us too long—we have resources to call on."

Dalrymple frowned at the sheriff's obstinacy. "What kind of resources?"

"Patty tells us that the Port Stirling Historical Society has some good info on the earlier Native American tribes in the area. The director, Mae Walters, was with Patty and Ed when they found the skeleton, and she's very interested in the outcome."

"OK, that sounds good. What else are you doing?"

"The county clerks are looking at all the birth, marriage, and death certificates starting with Tyee and his wife, Rochana, and their four kids. The names of the children were in Tyee's missing person's report, so we at least have that to start with. I'm also talking to Hugh over at the newspaper. He's got a generator, and is hoping to get out a one-sheet bulletin tomorrow with earthquake info from us and each of the towns around here. Kind of an update on where we are, and how to get help."

"Yes," interrupted Dalrymple. "I talked to Hugh yesterday, and he said he was close to getting something out. Said he and his staff will distribute it at the food markets, and go door-to-door as much as they can. Why were you talking to him?"

"I asked him to put a notice in it about Tyee Kouse—asking if anyone has any knowledge of him or his family to contact me. That's why I'm telling you now."

"Dammit, Earl, you should have talked to me first," shouted the D.A. "Do you really want to add to the chaos with the news of a Native American skeleton? You should quietly investigate first and see what you turn up."

"Disagree. It's our best chance of finding out if any of his descendants are still in the local area. It's up to Chief Horning and me to investigate, David, and we're planning to do our jobs." He stood to leave.

"You never give a shit about the optics, Earl," Dalrymple said, shaking his head.

"No, sir, I don't. I'll make sure you get a copy of Bernice's forensics report."

The D.A. pointed his index finger at Earl's face. "And I want to know the minute—the minute!—you get any intel on possible local descendants. Is that clear?"

"Of course, David." Sheriff Earl left the room.

. . .

Fern and Jay were working on finding housing for six families who formerly lived in the vicinity of Ocean Bend Road. Almost every house on that bluff collapsed during the earthquake. Their height above the sea saved them from the tsunami, but most of the houses were either flattened or uninhabitable.

Fern had touched base with several families who survived and most were temporarily living with relatives or friends in other area towns. But there were still six families, twenty-two people in all counting the children, who had no place to go, at least in the short term. For now, FEMA had set up an emergency shelter at the fairgrounds north of town for them, but in Fern's view, it wasn't very comfortable. She and Jay had spent the day knocking on doors of some of the village's larger homes, and inquiring about their ability to take in a family.

Fern and Jay were well-known because they had both grown up in the area, and they were able to cash in some of their goodwill on behalf of the displaced families. By the end of the day, with Fern's Fitbit registering 19,000 steps, all six families were moved into real houses with real roofs over their heads.

Insurance company reps were in town, and were sorting out the details. For residents who had lost everything, but who had no earthquake insurance, several Go Fund Me accounts had been opened, and donations were pouring in from around the world. Habitat for Humanity had arrived, and were meeting with officials to determine need and develop a plan.

The nurses from Dallas were not the only volunteers; smart, caring people were coming in from neighboring states and further flung locales to contribute their skills and labor. Fern and Jay would have preferred their town not suffer this unimaginable disaster, but it warmed their hearts to see this kind of response. It was like a fresh wind blowing in from the sea to discover that people would still look out for each other in times of tragedy.

"Matt's ex-wife is real nice, don't you think?" Jay asked Fern with the start of a little smirk on his needing-a-shave face. They were walking along a street between the bluff and the highway that had survived the quake intact. There were several nice homes in this section, and the two detectives knew several of the homeowners.

"She seems nice."

"And killer pretty," Jay persisted.

"She's very attractive."

"You're not going to bite, are you Red?"

"Whatever do you mean, Detective Finley?" Fern said softly with a Texas twang, looking up at the gangly young cop with a coy demeanor, and batting her eyelashes.

"C'mon, she doesn't act like that," Jay said.

"I'm kidding you."

"Why do you suppose she's here?"

"I'm taking her at her word—she wanted to help. She did go to all the trouble to organize her colleagues, and make the arrangements to get them here. It has the feel of a humanitarian cause about it."

"And?"

"And, I think she probably felt a need to see her ex-husband with her own eyes to know he was safe. I know that if I were in her shoes, I would probably do the same thing. I think it's admirable, and she doesn't deserve my scorn or yours."

"Matt seemed surprised."

"I'm sure he is. I'm equally sure that he will handle the situation well."

"Is there a chance they could get back together?" Jay knew this was an awkward question, but he honestly wanted Fern's opinion. He'd grown used to them as a couple after the Anselmo case, and their relationship was important to him. He counted the two co-workers among his best friends, and he didn't want either one of them to get hurt.

"No," she answered firmly. "There is no chance. Matt never mentions her at all, and I think he's almost forgotten they were ever married. And besides, between us, he and I are solid. We've been through a lot together in a short period of time, and that might have colored things in the beginning. But now we know where we stand, and it's good."

"But they *were* married," Jay said.

CHAPTER 18

This is great!" Matt said, holding the *Twisty River Bulletin* in his hand, and skimming it. Cup of coffee in one hand, and the abbreviated newspaper in the other, he read aloud to Fern, who was still in her robe.

"The Chinook County Sheriff's Office and the Port Stirling Police Department request your assistance in locating any descendants of former Port Stirling resident Tyee Kouse. Mr. Kouse disappeared in 1904, and the local police have new information about the case. If you know anyone who might be a descendant or have knowledge about his family, please contact Sheriff Earl Johnson in Twisty River, or Chief of Police Matt Horning in Port Stirling."

"That should help," Fern nodded. "Even though it was decades ago, someone around here will know something."

"That's what Earl and I are counting on." He put the *Bulletin* on the kitchen table, and reached over to take her hand in his. "How are you this morning? Everything OK? You seemed a little restless during the night."

"I'm good," she smiled. "Jay and I did some wonderful work yesterday, and I was a little over-tired last night. Sometimes I have trouble sleeping when that happens. I know, you'd think I would go out like a light when I'm really tired."

"Well, it's an unsettling time, for sure. I've stopped having nightmares about that damn wave, but my sleep is still not quite back to normal either."

"I think we're putting too much pressure on ourselves. We've been through hell and back, and it's typical that we don't feel normal yet."

"I'm sure you're right, but I'm usually tougher than this," he smiled.

"When's the last time you lived through a 9.1 earthquake and a killer tsunami?" she teased.

"Point taken. Now that we've identified all the dead and missing, I want you and Jay to continue with the displaced families."

"Is FEMA tracking down the missing's families?"

"Yeah. They've made good progress. Unless any bodies wash up in the weeks ahead, they're presumed drowned. Every collapsed building has been checked, and we don't believe there are any further earthquake victims."

"How many locals are missing?"

"Forty-four, and they all lived on the ocean-front side of Ocean Bend Road."

They sat there holding hands for a minute until Fern whispered, "We were so lucky."

"Yeah," he wiped a stray tear off his chin, and reached for his coffee. "Take Walt and Rudy with you today, too—they aren't needed on the utilities work anymore…they got more help yesterday from utilities in California and Colorado. Experienced crews."

"Does that mean we'll have power soon?"

"I think we're getting close. Olive Joiner told me that she talked to her sister a couple of days ago, and stressed that getting the power back on was crucial down here. The governor has asked other states for utilities help, and that's what did the trick apparently."

"Thank you, Olive!"

"Amen to that."

"What are you going to do today? And what day is it?" she grinned.

He scratched his head. "Saturday, I think," he smiled, and held up the county's satellite phone. "First, I'm going to stay close to this, and to my office in case there are any leads on Tyee Kouse. I found *The Bulletin* on your front porch this morning, which means they're doing a great job distributing the news. If nothing shakes loose by this afternoon, Earl and I are going to the Kouse homestead and look around. Earl delivered his old family rifle to Bernice for testing yesterday, and he's a wreck. I can tell he's worried that his grandfather or great-grandfather might have had something to do with Kouse. I thought it might help him if I spent some time with him today."

"That sounds like a plan. There must be other old rifles like that still around, don't you think?"

"I'm sure there are. But it is interesting that Earl has one."

"I hope for his sake, Bernice is able to rule it out as the murder weapon," Fern said running her hand through her chin-length auburn hair, mussed from sleeping. "I need to get moving, and I'm getting tired of taking showers in cold water."

"It could be worse—you could have no water like the first couple of days."

"I know, I know. But next to a big bowl of oyster stew from the Crab Shack Café, a long, steaming-hot shower is the thing I want most in the world."

"Why don't you go to your parents' house tonight and borrow their shower? I'm sure they wouldn't mind."

"I might. I'm going to really miss that café. Do you suppose they'll rebuild?"

"I actually talked to Gina yesterday—ran into her down on the harbor front. She said her dad owns the land, and that they would likely rebuild the café if they get what they need from the insurance company. But there is nothing left, and they'll have a real clean-up job first to even get ready to build. Not to mention getting all new equipment and furnishings here somehow." He shook his head at the task ahead.

"We've got real work to do, but I know these people, and this town will bounce back. We have to."

"*We* don't have to. *We* could move."

"Leave Port Stirling?" Her eyebrows shot up.

"It's one option."

"But it's our home. At least, it's my home." She frowned.

"It's my home, too. I love this place. But there are other nice places in the world. You and I have skills that travel, and we could go almost anywhere we want."

"I'm not leaving. Especially now. This town has been here for both of us when we needed it, and now it needs our help. I'm surprised you would even consider leaving. You're the most popular person in town!"

"No, you are," Matt said.

"No, you are."

He smiled. "OK, people like us, I get it. What are we going to do when Abbott finds out we're shacking up together? It's against city policy, you know."

"We are not *shacking up*. I am sheltering a displaced resident," she said, straight-faced. "Although, I do rather like having you here." She pinched his cheek.

"I'm serious. The shit's going to hit the fan when I tell Bill we're together. He warned me back in April, and I'm shocked he hasn't heard about us, since everybody else seems to know."

"Who knows? We've been so careful."

"Patty and Bernice know. Bernice's husband saw us one night in Buck Bay when we went to dinner over there. Jay knows…just because he does. Ed and Sylvia knew before we did, I think," he smiled. "My point is that it's going to get sticky. One of us may even have to leave the department."

Her face turned pink. "Our friends would never let that happen! Not after the Anselmo case. We're a team. Maybe I could report to Walt instead of to you," she suggested.

"No good. I thought of that, too, but Walt reports to me, so it doesn't change anything. In fact, it would be worse because it would put Walt in an uncomfortable position."

"I suppose." She turned quiet.

"I think the best thing for us to do is to approach Bill together. Tell him straight up before he hears it, and let him know that it won't get in the way of our work. Sort of throw ourselves on his mercy, and see what he comes up with. What do you think?"

"Does this mean you're not going back to Texas with Susie?" Fern was serious.

Matt's heart skipped a beat, and he looked at her for a moment. "I'm not going anywhere unless it's with you," he told her, trying to keep his exasperation out of his voice. "This is not about me leaving you or Port Stirling. I just know what's coming when Abbott hears that we are, in everyone's lingo, a 'hot item'. And I'd like to head it off at the pass."

Fern smiled broadly. "We *are* a hot item. All right then, I like your method. Honesty is always the best choice, and I'm with you. What did he say in April? We weren't together then."

"It was a misunderstanding. Someone told David Dalrymple they saw your car parked in front of my cottage on a Saturday night and assumed. Dalrymple, of course, ran to Abbott to complain. I explained to Bill that you and Jay and I had been meeting to discuss the Anselmo case in private. Bill was relieved, and told me he didn't want to have this conversation again."

"A lot has changed since then. And we have a right to be happy. We're both darn good at our jobs. A stupid policy from last century can't get in our way, it wouldn't be fair, and I won't let it."

"One of the things I love most about you, Fern Byrne, is your sense of justice. You and I both know we can handle our relationship and our jobs. We just need to convince Bill."

• • •

A youngish man, about 30, walked into the first open door he found inside Port Stirling city hall and asked the two people meeting there where he could find Police Chief Matt Horning. They asked his name, and he replied "Del Kouse." He was casually, but nicely, dressed in jeans, with a heather blue wool sweater over an open-neck blue and grey plaid shirt. His hair was black, as were his wide-set eyes, and his complexion was bronzed and glowing. The overall effect was dramatic. He had a confident air about him, and smiled easily.

One of the city employees walked Del Kouse down the hallway to Matt's office, where he was seated at his desk which formerly looked out two large picture windows at the glorious Twisty River, the jetty, the lighthouse, and the Pacific Ocean beyond. Even if Matt wanted to see the devastation of his former view, he couldn't because the windows had blown out during the earthquake and were now boarded up, awaiting repair. He had two lanterns on his desk because his usually brightly-lit office was dark.

"This is Mr. Del Kouse," said the employee. "He's here to see you, sir." She gestured at Matt, and said, "This is Police Chief Matt Horning."

Matt jumped out of his chair and sprang to greet the young man. "Thanks, Marcia," he said. "I'll take it from here. Please come in, Mr. Kouse. I think I know why you're here, but do tell me. Have a seat," he gestured to the chairs in front of his desk.

"Tyee Kouse was my great-great-grandfather," he started slowly. "I never met him, but one of his sons, Dyami Kouse, was my great-grandfather, and I did know him when I was a little boy. Dyami's oldest son is my grandfather, Hakan Kouse. I saw that you might have some information on Tyee's disappearance. Is that correct?"

Matt reached across the desk to shake his hand. "I'm happy to meet you, Del. I do have some news for you, and you should brace yourself. I'm not sure if it's good or bad news." He paused to let the young man digest what he'd said.

"Tell me the truth, and give it to me straight. Any news on my great-great-grandfather will be welcomed by my family."

"OK. Chinook County Sheriff Earl Johnson and I believe that we have found your great-great-grandfather's remains. A skeleton was found in the ruins of the lighthouse after it was destroyed by the tsunami. We have run forensic tests on the bones, and have pinpointed an approximate timeframe of the death. That timeframe is within the window of 1904, the year Tyee Kouse disappeared." Matt paused. "Can I get you a bottle of water?"

"I'm fine," Del said firmly. "Please continue, Chief."

"Additional forensic tests confirm that it's an adult male of Native American ancestry, and that the victim lived in the Pacific Northwest his entire life."

"Victim?" The young man swallowed hard.

"Yes. The skull had a bullet lodged in it—in the back—and it is our contention that your great-great-grandfather was murdered and buried under the lighthouse with the hope that his remains would go undetected."

Del Kouse took a deep breath, and let it out slowly.

"My great-grandfather Dyami loved his father very much. His mother, too. He had a happy childhood, and was beloved by both parents. He went on to live a full, productive life, but my grandfather told us he was never the same after his father left them."

"Tyee didn't leave his family," Matt said, and looked directly at Del. "What happened to him is still a mystery, but the one thing we know at this point in our investigation is that he didn't leave willingly. He was killed by a person or persons unknown."

"Will you investigate further?"

"You bet your darn right we will," Matt said. "The manner of his death and subsequent burial have not set well with the sheriff and me. Our earthquake and tsunami were violent and tragic for our village, but I promise you that one good thing will come out of it. We will investigate Tyee's death, and we won't stop until we have some answers for you and your family."

"I hear you're good at this," Del smiled.

"I am," Matt smiled, "and so is my team. Sheriff Earl, in particular, does not appreciate how his predecessor handled Tyee's disappearance. And, take it from me, you do not want to piss off Earl Johnson."

Del chuckled. "According to family legend, my predecessors didn't appreciate the so-called investigation at the time either. My great-granddad's mother was said to have remarked that nobody cared about a missing Indian. Do you think that's true?"

"Our sheriff said almost exactly the same thing, and said Tyee's file indicated that no one spent any time trying to understand what happened to him. So, yes," Matt said, nodding, "I do believe that no one in power at the time did care, and they took the easy way out, saying he left of his own free will. However, I do have more evidence than my predecessors had—human remains, a bullet, and much more science and technology at my fingertips than they had in 1904. We also know something about the weapon. We believe it to be an old rifle, and there may be some still around."

Matt didn't tell him about Earl's rifle. No point in muddying the waters yet.

"Can we…" Del started and cleared his throat, "are we able to retrieve his remains? Is it just a pile of bones, or something more recognizable? My family will all want to know."

"We found a mostly intact skeleton and skull. One of the larger bones and the skull are currently in Buck Bay with the county medical examiner. She is taking good care of them while the tests are underway. As soon as Dr. Ryder is finished with her work, she will return them to me. I made the decision to leave the rest of his remains in place for now, in the hopes that what has happened today would occur, that someone from your family would appear. If you and anyone else you designate would like to view the site, it would be my honor to escort you there."

"Many of my relatives are still in the area, Chief. My grandfather, who is spunky and healthy at eighty-eight, and his younger sister are the two surviving members of their generation—Tyee's grand-children—but my father and his two siblings, also direct descendants of Tyee, all live in the county. I have cousins and two sisters, some of whom still reside here. I think it would be best if I collect my grandfather and my great aunt, Meda, and the four of us go to view the land where he died. And my father, too."

"Whatever you want, Del. Your family is owed a great debt which local law enforcement can never fully repay, but the sheriff and I will try our hardest to make it as right for you as we can. Come here tomorrow morning and we'll go out together. Does 9:00 a.m. work for you? How are you holding up from the earthquake, by the way?"

"Yes, tomorrow morning will work. I will collect the elders and bring them here. As for me, I'm pretty much screwed, if you'll pardon my language. I work remotely for a Silicon Valley tech company, and without power I can't do my job. And my sister is hurting, too. She works for the casino in Buck Bay, and it was destroyed by the quake and mostly by the tsunami—it's just gone. But no one in my family was badly hurt, and we all have homes, so it could have been worse."

"Several people died in the casino I understand, but your sister made it out OK?"

"Yes, she works days in the fancy restaurant, so she was safely home when it hit."

"Does anyone live on or near the old family homestead out on the river?"

"You know about that?" Del looked surprised.

"Yes, the sheriff found Tyee and Rochana's address in the police report of his disappearance. Earl knows the place, and we were going to go out there this afternoon if no one turned up from *The Bulletin's* mention."

"That's where my grandfather lives. He never left. My father was raised there, too, and now owns the adjoining property. My sister and I each have an outbuilding on dad's property. We've lived there for about two years. You know, to keep an eye on our parents and granddad. I'm the best cook of the lot of them, and now they won't let me leave," he smiled.

"That sounds similar to my situation before I came to Port Stirling last January. My folks own a ranch outside of Dallas, and I lived on the property, too. My siblings still do. Not very many people do that anymore, but it worked great for us."

"It's more common in my culture," Del said. "We take care of our elders, and they like to make sure that we are living proper lives. Spying on us, really. Keeping us in check."

"My mom says 'keeping us responsible citizens'," smiled Matt.

"You're the police chief, so it must have worked."

"And talking to you, I can tell it worked on you as well."

Del stood and Matt walked around his desk to give the young man a hug. "And tomorrow, I'll take you to meet your great-great-grandfather."

CHAPTER 19

Rochana Kouse spread out the family blanket on their favorite spot down by the Twisty River near the bottom of their property. It was a warm July evening by coastal standards, with no wind or fog, and she had decided to take advantage of it by serving the evening meal next to their beautiful river.

As she prepared the space, she could see her husband Tyee and the two oldest boys, Dyami and Elan, working in the big field just above the river. *I swear my husband is the hardest working man I know*, she thought, and smiled. Tyee and the boys had been working amongst their crops for most of the day, and she had only seen them briefly at lunchtime in the house.

As she limped back up to the house to retrieve the food—she had slipped on a rock yesterday while washing some sheets in the river, and twisted her right knee—she called to her husband. She paused, food basket in hand, smiled broadly and waved to him as he looked up at the sound of her voice. She pointed with her free hand down toward the river, and he nodded in understanding.

Later, Rochana settled her two youngest children, Jobe and Enola, on the blanket, and gave them each a piece of dried salmon to chew on until Tyee and the boys arrived. She was careful to situate the blanket so that Tyee would be able to watch the sunset in the west toward the Pacific Ocean. Near the end of the sun's journey over the ocean, the day's last rays would reflect off the Twisty River surface, and the whole family would delight in watching the fish and frogs jump in the abundant river.

Rochana cooked a chicken earlier in the day, and it would be the star of tonight's meal. As the keeper in charge of the chickens, she spent several months fattening up a few of the hens for slaughter. The one she'd chosen for tonight had been on the low end of egg production, so too bad for her. Accompanying the poultry was Tyee's favorite squash dish, potatoes from her storage bin, and a roasted camas root. She had cooked extra potatoes because not all of the children liked squash. Tyee would insist they eat some squash, but she knew the extra potatoes would be far more popular. The first of the season's huckleberries, to be eaten out of a large bowl by the handfuls, would be a delicious dessert for her family.

Tyee and the two boys trudged across the field to join the others. Rochana could tell that the boys wanted their father to race them to the blanket, but she could also see the exhaustion on his face. The boys took off running, leaving Tyee behind. Dyami, older and bigger than Elan by two years, and with a longer, more powerful stride, won easily.

Tyee patted Rochana on the head, and stroked her long, dark, glossy hair. He sat in his appointed seat facing west, his shoulders sagging a bit as he finally gave in to the tiredness of his workday. The early evening's sweet, soft air washed over him, and Rochana could see him relax into it, the sun on his sharp-boned, handsome face. He removed the dirt-streaked bandana holding back his black hair, and brushed the hair behind his ears.

"Run to the river and wash your hands, boys," Rochana said.

"I am clean, mother," Dyami protested.

She reached over and grabbed his arm, where there was visible dirt. "You most certainly are dirty. You will do as I say." Her tone was like thunder, but there were creases of humor around her eyes, and Dyami knew his mother loved him well. Still, he didn't move, nor did Elan, following his older brother's lead.

"If you think Dyami should wash before we can all eat, raise your hand," she said, letting her eyes rest on each of her other three children. Five of the six raised their hands.

Knowing he was defeated, and listening to his stomach's rumbling, he ran to the river, dragging Elan with him. They sloshed water onto their hands, rubbed them briskly, and sprinted back for the towel their smart mother held out for them.

The other children got quickly in line behind him. Tyee winked at Rochana, and she began to serve the chicken.

"How does your knee feel today?" Tyee asked his wife, softly rubbing her shoulder.

"It's swollen, and it slowed me today," she answered, pulling up her skirt so he could see it. "But it will heal in a day or so, do you think?"

Tyee looked at the puffy knee, and gently touched it. She winced.

"Perhaps we should ask my sister to look at it," Tyee said. His sister was the tribe's medicine woman. "She might recommend an herbal treatment with meditation to begin the healing. Shall I fetch her for you tomorrow?"

Rochana hesitated. "Let's see what tomorrow brings," she finally said. "I am in harmony with my world, and will do what sister has taught me. But if I am still unwell by the next day, we will ask her for help."

Tyee nodded in agreement with Rochana. He valued his wife's intellect, and her strength. Not to mention her expert touch with the family's food.

"This chicken is very good," he smiled at her. "It must have died a happy hen."

"She died, that's all I can say," Rochana smiled at him.

"Children, eat some squash," Tyee said.

Rochana and the children laughed at Tyee because he said that almost nightly. It had been an excellent season for squash so far, and it would be on the menu frequently. Tyee loved all squash, but the summer ones were his favorite. He didn't understand why his children didn't love it as he did.

All four children knew it was pointless to resist, and quickly ate some before both parents would start telling them how important squash was for their bodies and overall well-being.

A bee landed on Enola, and Tyee reached over and swatted it away from his daughter's head.

"Thank you, papa," the four-year-old said sweetly, as her face turned stern. "I don't like those bees. They make a noise, and they like to land right here." She pointed to her bare arm.

"I agree with you daughter," Tyee smiled at her. "Bees have a necessary role to play on our earth, but it would be nice if they would leave us alone. They won't hurt you, but if you get too bothered, come and tell papa. OK?"

"OK."

Tyee ruffled his charming daughter's hair and said to Rochana, "We have a bountiful harvest coming this week. The weather gods have been good to us this season, and we will have much to sell to our customers."

"That's good news," Rochana replied. "Are the lettuces holding up during the past two warm days?" She knew that a streak of hot weather could cause the lettuces to bolt skyward.

"They are holding well, and are bigger than usual. The colors are deep, and the leaves are firm. They will fetch top market dollar. So far this year, we have no failures in any of the crops. Only the spinach is growing weary. Whatever is left over from my trip to market this week you should plan on using for us."

"I will look forward to a large spinach salad first, and then will cook the rest with some of our storage garlic." She paused, and looked up to the dimming sky. "I think we will get some rain soon," Rochana said, and Tyee perked up. He trusted his wife's weather instincts. "See the difference in the light off to the southwest?" she asked. "And those thin lines?"

"I do."

"Those trails often are followed by clouds. And, the air smells heavier to me tonight than it has for the past few days."

"I hope you are right, mama," said Dyami. "Tomorrow is our watering day."

"And you would love for rain to come tonight, so you get out of some work tomorrow," smiled Tyee at his oldest son.

Dyami, sitting next to his mother, took her hands in his, and said, "Please, please, be right, mama!"

They all laughed.

After that, the family sat quietly in the early evening twilight and waited for the frogs to begin their chorus. Rochana counted her blessings while listening to the frogs' entertainment. She loved her husband above all others. Her children were healthy, strong, and happy. Their business was flourishing. Her home, while basic, was a palace to her. And, most important, their family was held in high regard, and she and Tyee were widely respected.

A passing cloud created a sudden shadow overhead, and Rochana shivered involuntarily. Everything in their lives was so perfect now, but that shadow gave her a sense of dread.

CHAPTER 20

Sunday morning, two weeks and two days after the earthquake, the blazing blue sky and dry conditions that had aided the cleanup skedaddled. The day dawned with stormy, dark clouds out to the southwest, and a brisk wind that presaged a distinct change in Port Stirling's weather.

By the time Matt and Fern enjoyed a lively cold shower together, the rain lashed against the windows. He braved the patio to make coffee and start breakfast on the propane gas grill while he waited for her to finish dressing. Back inside, he set the kitchen table with her white modern china and some yellow linen napkins that he found in a drawer next to the currently useless oven. The napkins picked up one of the muted colors in the area rug that warmed up the wide-plank floors. Fern's kitchen had quickly become a place of companionship for the two of them, a place to plan their days together, and to come back together at the end of the day to relax.

Matt loved waking up with Fern, and they were both grateful for her patio grill that had helped keep them eating and alive, but he really missed mornings in his cottage. He found himself thinking more and more about Roger, his 'pet' seal, and wondered about his fate during the tsunami. He'd been down to the beach below his former home twice since the night he left running from it, mainly to look for any remnants of his life that may have been brought back in by the tides. Nothing so far, and no sign of Roger.

But it was always early morning when he used to see him bobbing in the water from his window, and he thought he might go by there this early morning on his way to meet Del Kouse.

"Good morning, handsome," Fern said, coming into the kitchen.

"Good morning, gorgeous," Matt replied, their standard greeting. "I'm cooking bacon on your patio. Sick of cold cereal."

"That sounds so good. Is there coffee?"

"On the grill."

She grabbed her favorite mug from the cupboard, the one that read 'All you need is love and, of course, coffee', and went to the patio. "I'll make some eggs, too," she said.

Over breakfast, their talk was mostly about the day's logistics. "I need to get rolling," Matt said, smearing one last bite of butter on a baguette he'd found thawed in her freezer. "I want to stop by my old place before I meet Del."

"You miss your cottage, don't you?" she said, and there was heartache in her eyes.

"Yes," he answered truthfully. "I loved waking up and looking at the ocean." He placed his hand over hers. "But I also love waking up and looking at you," he smiled. "Doing both would be my perfect world."

"Well, maybe someday we can make that happen," she said, trying to not sound too serious. "But not today. You need to get your fine ass in gear if you don't want to be late."

"Yes, ma'am," he said, rising from the chair.

"Good luck this morning with Del and his family," Fern told him as she walked him to her front door. "I hope it's not too painful for them. Or for you."

"There's no telling how Tyee's grandson and granddaughter will react, of course, but Del is a pretty amazing guy, and he will steer them through this."

"You really like him, don't you?"

"I do like him. This town has its share of rednecks…"

"Hey! You can't say that about my town," she groaned, "even if it is true."

"Not everyone, but you know we have some, and Del Kouse stands out from that crowd. He's highly intelligent, even-keel, and with an optimistic, upbeat personality. I like him a lot, and I'm eager to meet his relatives.

My gut is telling me that the Kouses are an interesting family, and I can't wait to hear their stories."

"Wish I could go with you."

"You'll meet them all soon. It's important you help Patty and Ed today. Get this big 'lost and found' tent set up, so people will have a central place to dump any found items and look for their missing stuff. And, if you happen to spot a pair of size eleven black and green running shoes, they might be mine, and I'd be thrilled to have them."

She laughed. "Do you want me to go over to Buck Bay and see if I can find some shoes for you? I know you're getting tired of wearing Mitch's boots. It was nice of Bernice to pick up some clothes for you, but I could go at noon tomorrow and spend my lunch hour shopping for you."

"You're sweet to offer, but I can go a few more days. Too busy to go for a run right now anyway. And mine might turn up. Folks are saying that stuff is coming in with the tides. That's why this lost and found is important. People are missing way more important things than my running shoes."

"Can you imagine how long it's going to take us to make everyone whole again?" she said. "Sometimes it gets me down and feels overwhelming."

"Don't let it. We have to stay positive. And the help is pouring in every day; we don't have to do this alone. Besides," Matt said, taking her in his arms, "I know you, and you have enough energy for half the town."

Squeezing him hard, she said, "And you have the other half covered, handsome. Every day, I think how flat-out lucky we were that you came to us when you did. Think about this year! What would we have done without you, my darling Matt?"

"You might not have had your run-in with Octavio," he said seriously.

"That's my point. We got through that, the worst possible thing that could happen. We can handle this."

"I keep getting all the credit for that, but it was really your smarts and actions that made the difference in that case."

"Which is why we're such a great team, and why Bill wouldn't dare come between us!"

"I hope you're right, sweetie. But now, I've got to introduce some people to a relative. I'll see you tonight, and good luck with the lost and found center. Make it happen."

. . .

Matt pulled over to the edge of Ocean Bend Road and parked at the start of his former driveway, shutting off his engine. The wind buffeted his car, and the rain was so heavy that his windshield, without the wipers moving, was immediately blurred. His borrowed jacket had a hood, and he was happy about that today, as he stepped out of the vehicle and into the first nasty fall squall.

The rain pelted him, and blew sideways into his face, drenching him. The wind was evil, and flung more rain at him as he hurried to fully zip up his rain jacket and secure the tie under his chin.

The upper part of his driveway was unscathed. It wasn't until he'd walked about twenty yards that he could see that more of the bluff had crumbled away since he'd first visited his former house the day after the earthquake. There was a new chunk missing on the southwest corner of the property.

About nine days after the big quake, they'd had the third aftershock that Matt later learned had clocked in at 6.0—again, substantial. He and Fern had still been in bed that Sunday morning, awake but chatting, and it had given them a fright. The bedroom windows had rattled and her chandelier swung ferociously, but it only lasted a minute or so.

Fern was the first on her feet, running to the window and pulling back the draperies to see what was happening outside. "Stop it!" she'd yelled at the universe, standing there in her naked glory. "Stop it right now! We'll never surrender to you, you fucking earthquake."

In spite of his fear, Matt had to laugh. "Your neighbors might be getting an eyeful." He rarely heard Fern swear, and it was obvious that she'd reached her breaking point with nature.

"That is so the least of my problems," she said, turning to face him. "What if this keeps happening? What if everything still standing falls down now?"

"Your house didn't fall down," he observed, looking around the room, "and I suspect we're finished with the worst of the ground shaking.

Aftershocks after a big one are common, but they usually peter out in a matter of days."

"I know that, smarty pants, I'm just ticked off."

He got up and stretched. "I'd like to say 'come back to bed' but I suspect we had better get a move on and see what's happening out there."

Now, in the fierce rain and blustery wind one week later, Matt could see that the last aftershock had taken more of Port Stirling's ocean-front real estate. But as he squinted from his driveway south down the coastline, he realized that the view was even more spectacular than it had been. He had notified the owner of his rental house, and she told him she would decide what to do after talking to her insurance company.

As he stood looking out to the horizon, in spite of today's brooding weather, or maybe because of the power of it, Matt knew this was where he wanted to be. The ocean was throwing up brutish grey waves, and they were crashing ashore one after the other, so quickly that several were breaking onto the beach simultaneously. From his view, he could see to the stormy north, too, where Emily's tunnel was mostly underwater in this morning's high, frothing tide. This land, this sea, had become important to him, and he decided then and there he would talk again to the owner and see if she might want to sell him her property instead of rebuilding.

But for now, Matt picked his way down the steep pathway further south of his house. The beach had been rearranged since his last visit, and was compressed now because of the tide. His focus was on the wrack line of marine debris deposited near the bank. In and among the usual kelp, crustacean shells, and small logs, Matt spotted several household items, battered by the surf.

He fit some of the items in the large trash bags he'd brought with him—a small end table, an antique hairbrush, a silver teapot among them—selecting things that looked to be repairable, and leaving the rest for now. The cleanup crews Bill had assigned continued to patrol the beach after every high tide, and Matt left the obvious junk for them.

He secured the two trash bags, and placed them near the grassy path that led to the bluff, and then walked north on the beach, paralleling the water until he reached the spot directly below his house. As he walked, the robust wind at his back occasionally lifted him slightly and actually pushed him forward. *Going back into the wind is going to be a bitch.*

He heard a sound. Turning toward the ocean, Matt spotted three Pacific harbor seals playing in the surf just offshore. One of them was calling out, presumably to him. Matt locked eyes with the noisy seal.

"Roger!" he yelled, and was thankful there were no people around.

The big seal bobbed up and down, as if to acknowledge his buddy, Matt. Matt noted his gleaming silver coat and friendly, ebony eyes, and hadn't a doubt that it was Roger, one of his first 'friends' in Port Stirling.

"I'm happy to see you, Roger," he said, not at all embarrassed to be talking to a seal. "I bet you had quite a ride last week, huh?"

Roger ducked under water and came up a little closer in to the beach. Matt had never seen him this close up, it was usually from his cottage window, and he was interested to see how big he was. Matt knew that the harbor seals often lounged on the beaches and rocky headlands around here, but he'd only seen Roger in the surf.

"Did you duck under the tsunami and swim back out, or did it carry you ashore with it? It almost got me, you know."

Roger crinkled his nose engagingly, almost like a dog.

"Looks like we're both tough SOBs. Shall we grow old together here in this spot?" The seal bobbed up and down again, and Matt was convinced they were communicating on some level.

Yes, he would definitely speak to his landlord about the property.

· · ·

Matt drove onto the road leading to the lighthouse. It was a much more foreboding place on this howling, menacing morning than when he and Bernice had been there. Grim and unwelcoming. Perhaps because he now knew there was death out here.

Del Kouse, his father, his grandfather, and his great aunt were in the SUV behind him.

Del strode up to Matt and extended his hand. "Thanks for bringing us here, Chief Horning. It means a lot."

"Please call me Matt. Have you told your family what to expect?"

"Yes, and they are prepared. You told me that you didn't know if this was good or bad news, but I assure you that it is very good news for my family." Del turned to the three people behind him.

"This is Chief of Police Matt Horning," he said to the oldest of the three. "Chief Horning, this is my grandfather, Hakan Kouse, and his sister, Meda. And this is my father, Robert."

The old man came forward and shook Matt's hand. "My grandfather was a tribal chief when he disappeared, and we've had to live for generations with the disgrace that he left us. If you prove that to be untrue, you will be a true hero to my tribe." A broad smile lit up the old man's still-handsome, chiseled face, and Matt could see where Del got his good looks.

Meda, using a cane, came forward next, somewhat wobbly on the rocky terrain. Matt reached out to take her arm and steadied her. "My grandfather used to take me fishing close to here," she smiled. "I was only three, but I remember it like it was yesterday." She had thinning grey hair pulled back in a bun, but very few wrinkles, brilliant turquoise earrings, and a smile that was perfect on this stormy, gloomy day.

"Do you still fish?" Matt asked.

All four Kouses laughed.

"Have I said something funny?" Matt asked.

"Aunt Meda is the fisherman of the family," Del explained. "She has her own fishing hole on the Twisty River, and the rest of us are not allowed near it. We eat her catch once or twice a week. She's the bomb," he said, giving her an affectionate fist bump.

Matt turned to Robert. "It was good to meet your son yesterday. He's been the only bright spot in this wretched week."

Robert smiled at Del. "He's OK, I guess. We give him grief about reading all the newspapers every day, but today we're happy he's so diligent about it. With no TV, I'm not sure the rest of us would have seen your announcement about my great-grandfather. Obviously, it's important to us, and we are so grateful you've reached out. My wife, Linda, and my mother, Fala, want to meet you too, but my mom fell during the earthquake and is mending at home. Linda is staying with her while we're here."

"If you're all ready, let's go to the site," Matt said. "Please watch your step, it's uneven walking. The tsunami really did a number on the lighthouse and the jetty as you can imagine..."

"The tsunami knew what it was doing," said Hakan, with a wise air about him. "Sometimes we must tear down to rebuild."

Silence followed them as they approached the lighthouse ruins. Matt held up the yellow crime scene tape so the Kouse family could walk under it. Bernice and Matt had left Tyee Kouse in the position they found him. Matt hung back, giving the four family members the space to process what they were seeing and feeling as they circled the remains.

Meda spoke first. "It is my grandfather, Tyee," she whispered, looking upward to the sky and letting the persistent rain fall on her face.

"Yes," agreed her brother. "It is he."

"How can you be sure?" Del asked.

"We just know," Hakan and Meda said simultaneously.

Matt stepped forward. "Sheriff Johnson and I are fairly certain, too. The forensic tests and the police report on Tyee's disappearance match up. "We believe these bones belong to Tyee Kouse."

"What happens next, Chief?" asked Robert.

"Once the county's medical examiner is finished with her tests, which will be soon, we'll hand the skeleton over to you, Hakan, as Tyee's oldest living relative, if that's what you want."

"Yes, that is our pleasure," said Hakan. "Our customs would have us wrap grandfather in cedar bark and place him in a cedar box. We will then have a proper burial on our family property. Tyee's head will be pointed to the west. That will allow for an easier departure for his soul." He pointed down at the bones. "This is an insult to a great man—face down and pointed east. We will remedy it." His voice shook with anger.

"Is there anything in your family's history that could provide us with any clues about who could have done this?" Matt asked. "Stories from the tribe about the past?"

"My father, Dyami, used to tell me that this site," Meda said, waving her arm around the lighthouse ruins, "was important tribal fishing grounds in his father's time. They were opposed to building the jetty and the lighthouse, preferring to let the waters do as nature intended."

"I remember that, too," said Hakan. "It seems ominous that Tyee would be buried on this very site."

"As if it was a warning to others who were hostile to the construction?" inquired Matt.

"Perhaps," allowed Meda. "But why would the killer place his body under the lighthouse, where he would likely never be found if his death was to be a warning?"

"Yeah, that doesn't make any sense," Matt agreed.

CHAPTER 21

Dr. Bernice Ryder returned Earl's Springfield rifle to him. The sheriff greeted Bernice's news that his family rifle was not a match with the bullet found in Tyee's skull with a wall-to-wall grin and a "Hot dog!" In fact, Bernice had never seen Earl quite so happy.

"Thank the good Lord!" said Earl, wrapping Bernice in a big hug. "I don't know what I would have done if my family had a hand in the death of Tyee Kouse. Crummy enough what the sheriff at the time did."

"It's clear-cut, Earl. Your rifle is not the murder weapon. I'm keeping the bullet, but we'd need to get really lucky to find the weapon."

After making Earl's day, Bernice drove to Port Stirling and presented Tyee's bone fragment and skull to Matt. The two of them went to the lighthouse, and retrieved all of Tyee's bones, meticulously cataloguing each piece and its proper order. Then they reassembled the skeleton at police headquarters, carefully wrapped it in a blanket that Sylvia brought from her home for the occasion, and placed it in their conference room, where it would await repossession by his family.

"This feels very sad to me," said Matt, locking the conference room door behind him.

"We've seen death before, Matt," said Bernice. "More than I want. But I have to agree with you, this does seem particularly sorrowful. I wonder if it's because I know nothing about my great-great-grandfather, but the Kouse family knows everything about theirs, and is taking this so personally."

"Yeah, it's like Tyee was murdered yesterday instead of 117 years ago. We've got to make some progress on who killed him and why. When you meet the family, you'll understand."

"Where will you start?"

"Tyee's granddaughter mentioned that when the lighthouse and jetty were constructed, their tribe was opposed to it. Something about keeping the waters natural. Fishing rights, and so forth, I believe. Jay and I are going to interview the director of the historical society. Patty's coming, too, because she knows her. I suspect that the building of the lighthouse was a big deal in 1901, and there's likely a store of information on the process. So, we'll start there."

"My firearms examiner is also available to you to analyze any rifles, if you do get lucky on the weapons front. He showed me how he came to reject Earl's rifle, and it's good stuff. Both the bullet and Earl's rifle are mostly intact, and the ridges didn't match up. My guy says that even if the murder rifle shows up, it will have to have been well-cared for, cleaned regularly like Earl's, and so forth for any forensic tests to be successful."

"But it's possible, is what I'm hearing."

"Possible, but there are some big 'ifs'. You will have to get lucky."

"Well I am lucky," he smiled, "but I think this case will resolve more on motive and opportunity than means. But you never know," Matt said, shaking his head. "Maybe I should ask everyone in town to bring in their old rifles and see if we can get a match. It's not like we're suspecting them of any crime. We might catch a break."

"Personally, I'm too cynical to ever believe the cops are on the up-and-up," she grinned. "I'm not bringing my rifle in to you."

"Yeah," he said, "you're probably not alone in that sentiment."

· · ·

Unfortunately, the Port Stirling Historical Society was among the older structures that collapsed during the shaking. Mae Walters, the director, explained to the cops that about 750 items locked in a safe survived, but nothing related to the Native American tribes was in it.

"So, there are no documents from approximately one hundred years ago that might help us?" Matt asked her.

"Nothing specifically about the local Natives," Mae answered. "We have papers and historical items from the early tribes, but it will be hit or miss to find anything in the rubble of our building. It's a devastating loss."

"What about the construction of the lighthouse?" Patty asked.

"Fortunately, documents and photos from that period are primarily what's in the safe. It was such an important event for the area at the time."

"Why was that?" asked Jay.

"The construction of the jetty and the building of the lighthouse meant that boats could navigate the mouth of the Twisty River for the first time. The jetty created a deep channel that meant larger boats could make it over the bar. It allowed goods to be moved inland faster. It also led to an expansion of the harbor at Port Stirling, which meant more traffic for the local area. It was a big deal that helped the entire region," Mae said.

"But the tribes opposed it," said Matt. "Why do you think that was?"

"Yes, it's well-documented that the local tribal leaders were hostile to the plan from the very beginning. The south bank of the river close to where the lighthouse is—was," she sighed, "were important fishing grounds for at least one of the coastal tribes. There is a lot of information written about the importance of fish in tribal culture; you can read up on that easily. There was also chatter about not messing with nature. That the meeting of the river and the ocean was somehow sacred and shouldn't be interfered with. And my own personal feeling after meeting some of the local descendants is that they simply didn't want the additional boat and people traffic going up the river. Many of them lived along the river further inland…"

"Some still do today," Matt interrupted.

"Yes, so it was sort of a NIMBY thing," Mae said. "Can't blame them on any count, really."

"Do you recall if the historical society housed any papers or photos that named any tribal leaders?" asked Matt. "It would have been prior to 1901."

"So, in the buildup to construction, you mean?"

"Yeah. We're looking for any names that could give us a lead or some kind of starting point."

"We had an old newspaper article that I recall had one or more photos of tribal leaders meeting with the U.S. Army. We might find it when we are finished cleaning up here, but I wouldn't hold my breath if I were you. Sorry."

"No, it's us who are sorry for the loss, Mae," said Matt gently. "This must be so tragic for you."

"I've given most of my adult life to restoring and preserving our town's heritage," she said, and her face reddened. "We've recovered some things as we continue to sift through the debris, but many, many things are lost forever. It is heartbreaking."

Standing next to Mae, Jay reached out and put his arm around her, giving her a squeeze. She looked up at the tall detective and smiled. "So," she said with new energy in her voice, "we'll have to start over, won't we? It's not like we don't have a new defining event in our town's history, huh?"

"Right," said Patty. "One hundred years from now, people will probably refer to Port Stirling as 'pre-and-post earthquake'. I'm sure as we speak, residents are out there documenting it. Will you have help with that?"

"I've already spoken to Bill Abbott about it," Mae said. "He's assigning another city staffer to help us…first, with cleanup, and then with research. Our organization will be fine."

"I would really, really like to find any print articles or photos around the time of the lighthouse construction," Matt persisted. "Do you have any ideas where we could start looking in this mess?"

"I will personally go through every item in the safe," she promised. "Tell me exactly what you're looking for."

"Our victim was a Native American adult male," Matt told her. "We think the forensic testing on his bones matches up timewise with a forty-one-year-old man who disappeared from Port Stirling in 1904."

"Are you talking about Tyee Kouse of the Twisty River tribe, by any chance?" she said, her eyebrows raising.

The cops exchanged glances. "You know his case?" Matt asked incredulously.

Mae nodded in the affirmative. "Tyee Kouse was a tribal chief, and a very important man. His family was among the early settlers in Chinook County. His disappearance was a source of great speculation for many years, and not just within the tribe. He was highly thought of as one of the founders of modern-day Port Stirling. His family and the tribe were prominent farmers and fishermen, who supplied a very large percentage of the food for the communities throughout the county."

"I'll be damned," said Matt.

"Yes. Residents who have lived around here for generations will know Tyee's story, and most, including me, don't believe he just took off. There would have been no reason, no reason at all, for him to do that."

"That's what his family says, too," Matt said.

"It was probably glossed over at the time," Mae said. "The early white settlers didn't pay much attention to the Native Americans, only when they needed their help."

"Sheriff Johnson found a one-page missing persons report in the county archives. Law enforcement at the time marked his case 'voluntary disappearance'."

"Doesn't surprise me," said Mae. "Well, now I guess the mystery of Tyee's disappearance has been solved. Someone put a bullet in the back of his head. Have you told his family? There are still lots of Kouses around."

"Yes, his great-great grandson responded to *The Bulletin's* announcement, and I've met him, a good guy. And this morning, I met Tyee's grandson and granddaughter, and his great-grandson, too. They are thrilled at the discovery. We'll be turning over the skeleton to them for burial."

"Wonderful," Mae enthused.

"So now you can see why I'm so determined to understand what was going on prior to 1904," said Matt. "What could have led to Tyee's murder? His death was not accidental, so who could have wanted him dead so much to shoot him in this manner, and then hide the body?"

"Who stood to gain the most from the jetty and lighthouse construction?" asked Patty.

"Well," said Mae, pausing to think, "I suppose it would have been the white traders in the region. Once the channel in the river was created, and their boats could safely navigate with the help of the lighthouse, their markets would have expanded. And many of them did get rich quickly thereafter. It also opened the gateway to the lush timber stands upriver that had been mostly inaccessible before they could get bigger boats up there. Some of your early timber barons got their start after the jetty was built."

"It's almost always money," said Patty. "Money or love."

"Or revenge," chimed in Jay.

"So, maybe Tyee, as a tribal leader, had a lot of influence over the tribes, and they were fighting against the plan to build it," mused Matt. "The white guys didn't like it, and figured if they got rid of Tyee, their problem would go away."

"That sounds entirely logical to me," Mae said. "He was a thorn in the side of some wealthy white people."

"It's certainly a theory," Patty agreed. "Now, how can we prove it?"

CHAPTER 22

Susie Longworth knew there was still a spark between her and Matt, and she didn't appreciate him avoiding her. *What was I thinking divorcing that man?* She had truly loved him when they married. He had changed some after his football injury, but they were still good together.

It was only after he became a cop that their trouble started. The long hours, the danger—she wasn't proud to admit it, but it had gotten to her. In retrospect, she really hadn't been fair to Matt. She should have been tougher and ridden it out. Her whole life, Susie had been a woman who cared about others, and took care of them. And then, when it came to her own marriage, she had been unusually selfish, putting her needs above her husband who'd tried so hard to save them as a couple. She'd been foolish, thinking she could change him, when it was she who needed changing, not Matt. Was there such a thing as a second chance?

Look at him now! Look how fabulous he is! Susie thought it absolutely amazing that he was still single. *What was wrong with the women around here?* He would have been eaten alive in Dallas within weeks of their divorce.

Oh, dear, it dawned on her. *Of course, he must have a girlfriend, and that's who he's staying with now that he's homeless.* Well, she would have to find out who she was, and nip that little romance in the bud.

• • •

After hours of sifting through debris and historical treasures, as usual it was eagle eye Jay who spotted the torn page under some broken glass. He'd developed his reputation for finding important evidence during the Emily Bushnell case, and it had continued during the Anselmo action.

This time, Jay spotted the front page of an old newspaper. The masthead read *Port Stirling Recorder*, and had an illustration between the words 'Stirling' and 'Recorder'—a one-story building with water in front of it. It was mostly text on the page, but there was one photo in the middle of the second column, and one advertisement for a furniture store on the far right of the page. Under the masthead was the date: December 3, 1899.

"Hey, guys, look at this," Jay said, carefully moving the broken glass off the newspaper page.

Matt's eyes went immediately to the photo, which featured three males, two white middle-aged men in suits and top hats, and one younger Native American man who was wearing a fringed buckskin jacket. They were posed, staring at the camera, hands at their sides, with serious expressions.

The caption below read *Lyndon Carmichael, Ronald Percy, Chief Tyee Kouse Discuss Building Plan for Jetty*.

"Oh, my," said Mae, coming up beside Jay and Matt. "I remember this newspaper. We have several editions from around the early twentieth century, about eight of them if I recall. They were all placed behind glass and kept in a window-less interior room of the museum for preservation."

"Let's search this immediate area," Matt said to Patty and Jay. "And be careful—we might be able to save some documents."

"There might be copies at the University of Oregon Library in Eugene," Mae said. "They have brilliant archives from most of the state's newspapers going well back into the 1800's. But, yes, let's be careful!"

In all, the cops and Mae, working deliberately, unearthed fewer than ten pages of the *Port Stirling Recorder* that were readable. Many more pages were found, but they had too much water damage to save.

When they decided they'd done as much in that area as they could, Patty took a hard look at the first page that Jay had found, and said, "I know a bunch of local Carmichaels. Wonder if they're related to good ol' Lyndon?"

"And I know some Percys, plus a local Carmichael family, too," added Mae. "Chances are they descended from these two gents. Unless the grandchildren and greatgrandchildren went off to the valley to college and never returned, many of the old-time families still have a presence in the county."

"Patty, can you go home early and stop at the courthouse? See what records you can find on Carmichael and Percy?" Matt asked.

"Sure."

"Are we crazy looking for a killer from over one hundred years ago?" said Jay. "It's not like we'll catch the murderer, after all. I have to ask." He sounded uncomfortable, as if he wasn't sure it was a good idea to challenge Matt.

"It's a valid question. And some in our community will see this as a big waste of time."

"I'm not saying it's a waste of time."

"It's OK. I asked myself the same question last night. But then I met some of Tyee's family, and, for me, there was no longer a choice in whether or not to pursue this case. It's true that we won't catch a murderer, but it's really about justice for the family. They were treated badly by local law enforcement in 1904. We can't make up for how Tyee's disappearance was dismissed then, but we can show them Port Stirling has a heart now, and that their family matters."

"It's important that the county respond, too," added Patty. "I understand why Earl is taking it personally, he should. I read the so-called report his predecessor wrote, and even considering the times, it was a disgrace. I'm all in, and if people think we're wasting our time, tough titties. Ask them how they'd feel if it was their family history."

"History is important," said Mae. "Of course, I would think that," she smiled. "I'll do my part on research. I have a good contact at the U of O Library, and she'll help me."

"That sounds good—thank you both," said Matt. "Jay?"

"I just wanted to hear your rationale." He grinned. "And, you *are* the boss. Do I look stupid?"

They all laughed, and Matt punched him in the arm.

• • •

"How nice to see you again, Miss Longworth," said Sylvia to the beautiful woman standing in front of her desk. How on earth anyone could look this gorgeous in the earthquake aftermath was beyond her.

Although, Sylvia had tried her best, and put together a nice outfit this morning. She had given up her trademark flowing skirts and long sweaters in the short term because of practicality in the face of the ongoing mess in their office, and today wore charcoal grey trousers tucked into her oh-so-glamorous khaki wellies. A pale yellow sweater set, topped off with a yellow and grey art deco print scarf finished her look.

"You'll have to remind me of your name," Susie said. "I'm terrible with names."

"It's Sylvia. Just remember it starts with the same first letter of your name, dear." She smiled.

"That's a good tip, Sylvia. I'm looking for Matt today—is he here, by any chance?"

"I'm afraid not. He's out working on a case."

"Is he somewhere that I could pop in and talk to him for a minute? I have a car."

"The Chief doesn't like to be disturbed while he's on a case."

"Oh, that. Well, he wouldn't mind me," she smiled.

"I believe that he might," Sylvia smiled back. "In any event, I'm not sure precisely where he is right now. He had a couple of stops to make, and his agenda may have even changed since we spoke earlier. I'm sorry, but it's not a good day for him."

"In that case," Susie said, changing tactics, "might you know where he's staying at night? Perhaps I could catch up with him later."

Sylvia looked over Susie's shoulder and her eyes widened.

"The chief is private about his comings and goings," Fern said coming up alongside Susie. "It's a security thing with him. None of us know where he is since his cottage was destroyed."

Bald-faced lie, thought Sylvia, but it tickled her heart.

"I see," said Susie, facing Fern. "That makes sense—don't want the bad guys to know where he is, I suppose."

"Yes," replied Fern. "Can I help you with anything? I'm Detective Byrne, and we met last Wednesday when you arrived in town."

"I remember you and the sergeant," Susie said. "Just between us girls," and she looked over at Sylvia, too, "do you know if Matt is involved with anyone? Is he dating?"

"Why?" asked Sylvia. "Are you hoping to give it another go with him?" She smiled.

Susie pushed a strand of her shiny blonde hair over her shoulder, and laughed.

"Maybe," she admitted. "We were very happily married."

"Right up until your divorce?" asked Fern. She was not smiling.

"Well, that was all my fault. I was stupid. Matt didn't want our divorce, and we'd still be married if I hadn't been so dumb."

"It usually takes two to tango," Fern said calmly. "I'm sure he had a hand in things going wrong between you, too."

Susie took a hard look at Fern, and glanced quickly at her left hand. No ring. *Of course, she's the only attractive single woman in town.*

"Whatever our reasons were, it doesn't matter now," Susie said. "In the face of disaster, our real feelings come out. This is probably too much information for his employees," she smiled sweetly, "but we've never really stopped caring for each other."

"Don't you dare try to take him back to Texas," Sylvia laughed, somewhat nervously, "we need him here. He's been a godsend to our town."

Susie laughed, too. "I wouldn't do that to you, Sylvia. At least, not now. He's a very competent man, and I can see how much the town needs him to get through this disaster."

Sylvia, not to mention Fern, didn't care much for that reply. "Maybe you're not his type anymore," she suggested.

Susie looked directly at Fern and said, "Oh, I'm every man's type."

• • •

Working together at the Chinook County Courthouse in Twisty River, Patty and Sheriff Earl scoured the old files, searching for any reference to

Carmichael and Percy. There was a lot of information about both, as Lyndon Carmichael and Ronald Percy had been important timber barons in the late 1890s and throughout the early 1900s.

Both families were well-established in the county, and it looked as if they lived near each other on the eastern side of Port Stirling. The two patriarchs both had large families, and Patty and Earl figured it might be relatively easy to trace their descendants in the area.

"Let's start with Carmichael," Sheriff Earl said. "He was a little younger than Percy and more prominent, it appears. Let's see if we can track his brood through to today."

"Works for me," said Patty.

Lyndon and Winnie Carmichael had five children, four girls and one boy, the youngest. "They obviously kept trying until they got their son," Patty chuckled. "Men. You're so obvious."

"What?" asked Earl. "Someone to carry on the family name? What the hell is wrong with that?"

"If you didn't insist on women changing their names to yours when they marry, it wouldn't be a problem. In fact, it would be far more efficient to have men change their names to their wife's since she's the one having the children to carry on."

Earl stared at Patty. "You're nuts, Patricia. You know I love you, but you have some of the goofiest ideas on the planet. Can we please just agree to disagree on this one?"

"You old fart."

"You nutter."

"What are the names of Lyndon and Winnie's offspring?" Patty asked. Earl was going through the birth records from the 1880s forward. "Here it is," he said. "Louise, Blanche, Norma, Anna, and Elroy." Patty jotted down the names, and their dates of birth as Earl recited them.

Next they looked for marriage certificates for all five children, starting fifteen years out from each birth. Four of the five children were married, starting with Louise in 1905, and ending with Elroy in 1916. Only Blanche had not married, and they found a death certificate for her in 1906 at the age of eighteen.

They continued to follow marriage, birth, and death certificates through 1956, when Earl said, "We're losing light. Shall we continue tomorrow morning?"

Patty looked up from the file she'd been reading. The soft afternoon light from the single window was fading. She had a small flashlight with her, but Earl was right, better to start fresh tomorrow morning.

"This no-power routine is starting to be a real drag," she said. "Any progress from the utility guys?"

"They're getting close," Earl answered. "At least, that's what they tell me. I've heard there are a couple of big sub-stations out of Bonneville that need a fix, and then we should be in business pretty much everywhere statewide."

"Thank God. Ted and I are out of candles, and I'm getting sick of cooking on our gas grill."

"Not to mention, no football on TV."

She laughed. "Yes, even my intellectual husband is bemoaning that fact. He was inconsolable on Sunday. I'll see you tomorrow. Does 8:00 a.m. sound about right?"

"Yeah. I think we're close to something, Patty. I can feel it."

CHAPTER 23

The next morning dawned with fog laying low over the valley. It swirled around the Twisty River, hovering over the water's surface. It was a light and airy fog, however, and Patty, looking out her bedroom window to the river, knew it would burn off soon, leaving a bright, sunny day.

Ted, who was feeling better every day now, had made coffee, and was retrieving milk from their cooler for their breakfast cereal.

"You know what I want?" Ted asked Patty as she came into the kitchen, dressed for work.

"Let me guess. You want country sausage, eggs, and those crispy, perfect hash browns that The Grill makes for breakfast," she said, pecking her husband on his cheek. "And you miss your morning coffee klatch."

"That's it! That's exactly what I want," he exclaimed. "I'm sick of cereal. They feed it to cows to fatten them, you know. And, yes, I miss seeing my friends."

She ran her hand over her slightly protruding belly. "Thanks for that bovine reminder."

He handed her a cup of black coffee, strong and steaming. "I wasn't referring to you, my pretty."

"You could have been. Do you feel up to some fishing today? We've been eating too much junk since the earthquake. I'm going to track down some fresh vegetables this afternoon, even if I have to go over to Buck Bay. If you could land us a nice trout or two, I'll fix us a healthier dinner tonight."

"You're on, lady. Buy some more candles, too, if you can. Sorry you're still our shopper."

"You'll be able to drive next week, and it's OK. Do we have vodka left? I'd like to do it up right tonight with a cocktail, and we'll pretend we're at The Grill."

"Not only do we have vodka, I believe we have a jar of Costco garlic and jalapeno olives in our pantry."

"Party time! I'll be home early. And you be careful to not fall in the river, OK?"

"Yes, mother," he said.

. . .

Patty's satellite phone rang as she was backing out of her driveway. "Are you at work yet?" asked Matt.

"On my way in now. I'm meeting Earl at the courthouse. What's up?"

"After sleeping on it, I think Lyndon Carmichael and or Ronald Percy must have had something to do with Tyee's murder, or at the very least that they knew something about it. The only other thing that makes sense is that there was some kind of feud in the tribe. But based on what Mae and Tyee's family told us about the historical perspective, it sounds like Tyee was a hero within the tribe, and pretty much beloved by much of the Port Stirling community."

"So it narrows down to someone who had a reason for wanting him dead."

"Right. And it appears to me that two of Oregon's biggest timber barons back then had the best reasons for wanting to create a larger shipping channel at the mouth of Twisty River."

"And if Tyee was a vocal community leader opposed to the construction of the jetty, he was in their way."

"Don't you think that makes sense?" asked Matt.

"I do. It kept me up last night, too," Patty agreed. "This morning, I watched a tugboat towing a barge loaded with logs going down the river. In 1899 when that photo was taken, I think only a sternwheeler boat could have navigated this river. That jetty, followed by the lighthouse, would have opened the river to all kinds of commerce."

"Carmichael and Percy could see it. The whole world needed Oregon lumber, and they would log it, mill it, and ship it. They would be rich men."

"But there was one Indian in their way."

"That's what I'm thinking. OK if I come over this morning and help you and Earl track them until we find a local descendant?"

"Sure. The more the merrier. Everything all right with you?" Her antennae were up.

"Let's just say that it would be a good day for me to be out of Port Stirling for a few hours."

"Okayyy."

• • •

Earl and Patty were knee-deep in the Carmichael family tree when Matt arrived, noting everyone still in Chinook County in the mid-1970s. He brought sandwiches and chocolate cake from the Safeway deli.

"I figured if I was going to crash your party, I should at least bring goodies," Matt said. "Word is Safeway's the only place around with a generator that's got their bakery going."

"You are a prince among mere men," the rotund sheriff said, slapping him on the back, and taking his sack of food. "I was wondering what I was going to do for lunch today. The wife says we're getting low on supplies, and I need to make a run before I go home tonight."

"Same here," chipped in Patty. "Ted and I have decided that we need to up our post-earthquake eating habits. He's fishing today for the first time, and we're doing trout and veggies tonight. Thanks, Matt, that was thoughtful of you."

"Hey, we're all in this together," Matt said. Pointing at the files in front of them, he asked, "Where are we?"

"Mason Carmichael, 1983," Patty said. "Lyndon's great-grandson. Married Marilyn Johnson in 1981, and had two children, Dianne and Nick. I think Dianne Carmichael might be Dianne Dobbins now, a manager at First River Bank. I'm looking for a marriage certificate with her name on it now. This would be a hell of a lot easier if our computers were working!"

"Tell me about it," Matt said. "I've heard the utilities are getting close."

"Yadda yadda yadda…we've been hearing that for two days now. Show me the money!" Patty said.

"Here you go," Earl said, pointing at the file in front of him. "Dianne Carmichael married Duane Dobbins April 3, 2006. Certificate of Marriage granted in Twisty River, Chinook County. You think you know her?"

"Yes, Dianne started as a teller in my bank, and worked her way up quickly. She's now the branch manager. Nice woman, always friendly and helpful."

"Is your bank open yet?" asked Matt. "Do you know?"

"They weren't as of Friday," Patty said. "I wanted some cash, but there was a sign on the front door saying they hoped to reopen yesterday. There were some guys working around the back of the building, doing repairs. I asked them how it was going, and they said 'almost done'. They're probably open today."

"Yeah," said Matt. "People need cash, and with the ATMs not working, the banks need to get their act together fast."

"Do you want to go over there now?" asked Earl. "See if we get lucky and catch her?"

"Patty and I will go," said Matt. "You keep looking and see if you can find any Percys still in the area, OK?"

"I'm going to eat this nice lunch you brought first," grinned Earl, pulling out a sandwich.

. . .

First River Bank, located on the busy intersection with the one stop light in town, was open. It was an attractive, cedar-clad low-slung building with a green and blue sign featuring, naturally, an illustration of the town's river.

Dianne Carmichael Dobbins was one of three employees helping customers. Patty walked across the watery blue carpet and approached the counter, flashed her badge, and asked if Dianne could take a few minutes to talk with them. She introduced Matt.

"I know you, Chief Horning," Dianne said, smiling at Matt. "Nice work on that drug cartel." She shook his hand. "I've heard that you had a role in it, too, Patty. Thanks to both of you. We don't need that going on in my hometown!"

"You live in Port Stirling?" asked Matt.

"My husband and I just moved there last year from Buck Bay, but my family has long-called Port Stirling home. My brother lives outside the town in my parents' old home on the river. Duane and I wanted to get back to Port Stirling since we both grew up there. We'd been looking for the right property and Nick, my brother, told us about a house with a view of the Pacific. It was perfect. We bought it about fourteen months ago." Her lower lip trembled and her eyes got wet. "Our house was destroyed by the earthquake."

Matt reached out to her. "I'm so sorry. I lost my house, too, although it was a rental. I'm sure you are devastated."

Dianne wiped her eyes with a well-used tissue she retrieved from her pocket. "It's the worst thing that's ever happened to us," she squeaked. "Mom and dad's place took a hit, too, mostly from the tsunami, but Nick says it only needs mud and gunk cleanup, and a few repairs. He and I loved that house as kids, and he'll do what it takes to fix it. But the ocean just took my house."

"Mine too," said Matt. "Ocean Bend Road. All gobbled up."

"That's where we lived! What was your address?"

Matt told her, and Dianne said, "Oh my gosh. Duane and I owned the sprawling white one with the big lawn in front on the bluff. I know your little yellow cabin. It was about seven or eight houses south of ours. Can you believe what happened?"

"I was lucky to get out alive; sound asleep when the quake first hit."

"Us too." She shuddered.

"Well, we're all right now," Matt said. "We can replace houses and our stuff, and we're determined to rebuild Port Stirling even better than before." He looked over at Patty and gave her a slight nod.

"Dianne, we want to ask you a few questions about your family. Are you up for that now?" Patty asked.

"No problem. Let's go in my office," she gestured to an open door about ten feet away. "Peggy, I'll be a few minutes," Dianne said to one of the tellers. "Call if you need me."

They took seats around a small round table in the office. Patty spoke first. "We want to confirm a few details about your family, Dianne. Are you the daughter of Marilyn Johnson and Mason Carmichael?"

"Yes," said Dianne, adjusting one cuff of her navy blouse. "Why? What's this about?"

"Is Mason, your father, the great-grandson of Lyndon Carmichael? Have you heard his name previously?" Matt asked, ignoring her question.

"Yes, Marilyn and Mason are my parents. Mom and dad live in Palm Desert now. Why are you asking about my parents?" she asked again, a little more aggressively this time.

"We're looking for descendants of Lyndon Carmichael, and our research led us to you," Patty explained. "Do you know that name?"

"Of course I know that name. Lyndon Carmichael was my great-great-grandfather, and he is a legend in Port Stirling. Surely you've heard of him, Patty, you've been here forever."

Matt could have sworn that Dianne's nose tilted ever so slightly upwards as she addressed Patty.

"I've never heard of him until yesterday," Patty said. "Why don't you tell us why he is a legend. Fill us in." She leaned back in her chair with her hands clasped together over her stomach, prepared to listen.

"Lyndon Carmichael built the jetty and the lighthouse in Port Stirling. He was the first man to have the vision of what this area could become."

"In what terms?" asked Matt.

"Logging, commercial fishing, agriculture, tourism—my great-great-grandfather made it all happen, almost single-handedly."

"The Native Americans didn't help him? Weren't they already doing that when the white settlers came to Port Stirling?" Matt asked.

Dianne snorted. "If you call growing a little corn, and sticking a fishing net into the river, then, yes, I suppose they started it. But I'm talking about business. Lyndon recognized that the Twisty River bar had to be tamed in order for boats to make it upriver. Getting the jetty constructed and the channel deepened made all the difference in the world. My great-great-grandfather pretty much invented the timber industry in Oregon because he developed a national and, later on, international market for our lumber. The same with agriculture. You think those Indians knew what to do with their crops? They did not. It was all Lyndon's expertise. By all accounts, he was an amazing man for his time."

"Did your father or your grandfather—was his name Raymond Carmichael?—ever meet Lyndon?" asked Patty.

Dianne bristled, and it was clear that she was tiring of being questioned. "Yes, Grandpa Raymond knew Lyndon, but Lyndon died before my father was born. Most of what I know about him I heard from Raymond. He spent lots of time with his grandfather when he was a kid."

"Have you heard of Ronald Percy?" asked Matt.

"Yes, the Percy and Carmichael families have always been friends. Lyndon and Ronald were friends, and later business partners, and their children all grew up together. Nick is still friends with one of Ronald's great-great grandsons—they went to school together from the first grade through high school. Why are you interested in them? I think it's time you told me why you're here."

"We have an old photo of Lyndon and Ronald together with Tyee Kouse, a local Native American tribal chief from that time period," said Matt.

"Oh, I know who Tyee Kouse was," she said, sticking out her chin. "And we didn't call them Native Americans then; he was an Indian."

"Who was he?" asked Matt. "What do you know about him? And, now we recognize Native Americans by calling them by the proper name."

Dianne shrugged as if it didn't matter to her what Matt said. "He was a troublemaker, that's who he was. Grandpa told me that the Indians did everything they could to stop the construction of the jetty. They set white people's barns on fire, and they used dynamite on the construction site. Tyee was one of their leaders, and he hated my great-great-grandfather."

"Was it mutual?" Patty asked.

Dianne hesitated. "Yes. Yes, it was."

CHAPTER 24

Matt and Patty glanced at each other, and then Matt leaned forward onto the small table, his face closer to Dianne's, and his muscular arms and shoulders taking up space.

"Do you know if there are any old rifles in your family that may have survived for several generations?" he asked her.

She stared at him, and cleared her throat. "This is beginning to feel a little threatening to me." She turned to Patty. "Do I need to call my lawyer? Where is this going?"

"You are not at any risk, Dianne," Patty soothed. "We're just trying to learn about the past and put a puzzle together."

"Why are you interested in Tyee Kouse?"

Matt looked at Patty and almost imperceptibly shook his head 'no'. Then he said, "We're intrigued by the historical relationships between the Native Americans and the early white settlers. We would also like to know what happened to Tyee Kouse. It's our understanding that he just disappeared."

"Up and left his family, you mean," Dianne said. "Everybody knows he took off and was never seen again."

"Well, see, as cops that bothers us. Why would he have done that?" Matt asked her. "A family man, a well-respected tribal leader? It doesn't make sense to us."

"You asked me if there was a mutual dislike between Lyndon and Tyee, and my answer was 'yes'. Based on my family stories, I would even call it a feud. The two battled for years, over the Indians' so-called fishing rights, and then over the construction of the jetty. But my great-great-grandfather wasn't the only one who didn't get along with Tyee. Nobody liked him."

"Why do you say that?" asked Matt.

"He was a thorn in everyone's side," said Dianne.

"And by that you mean every white person's side?" asked Patty, but it came out sounding more like a statement of fact than a question.

"I suppose, yes, mainly that's what I mean. The Indians loved him because he was aggressive on their behalf. He even tried to claim the forests upriver as Indian territory. That was when Lyndon and Ronald Percy joined forces, because they had both staked forest property that Tyee was claiming belonged to the tribe."

"Did it belong to the tribe?" asked Matt.

"No. And the Indians had no proof it did."

"They were here first," noted Matt.

"Ownership depended on more than that," Dianne said in a huff. "You had to have money and resources. Lyndon and Ronald had that; Tyee did not. End of story."

"So Lyndon and Ronald wanted to get rich, and Tyee Kouse was in their way," said Matt. "Is that a fair statement?"

Dianne glared at him. "Lyndon and Ronald wanted this region to thrive. They were entrepreneurs with the skills and resources to develop Port Stirling and Chinook County. They deserved their wealth. It was hard-earned."

"And if the Indians lost everything along the way, it didn't really matter, right?" Matt was beginning to get pissed off and it showed.

"It's a dog-eat-dog world, Mr. Horning," she said formally, "probably even more so back then than now. But if you're smart and work hard, you will succeed—that's what my family taught me."

Spoken like someone born on third base who went through life thinking she had hit a triple, thought Matt. "I'm going to ask you this again, and I'd like an answer this time, please: Are you or anyone in your family in possession of one or more older rifles that might go back generations?"

Dianne tapped her index finger on the table while she thought. "There is a cabinet in Nick's house that has several old guns in it," she finally answered. "I can't tell you specifically whether they are rifles or what—I'm not a gun person."

"Thank you," Matt said, and made a note in his police notebook. "What is the address of Nick's home, and is his full name Nick Carmichael?"

The address of Dianne's family home rolled off her tongue without a thought, and she confirmed her brother's name.

"Where are you and your husband staying now?" Matt asked. "Do you need any help with housing in the short-term?"

"Thank you, but we're fine. We're staying in a suite at a Buck Bay hotel for now, just until Nick gets the repairs done to his house, and then we'll move in with him while we rebuild. The house is quite large, and it will work well for all of us."

"Why did Nick get the family home instead of you?" Matt asked.

Her face flushed, and it was clearly an uncomfortable topic.

"I'm not sure that's any of your business, but there were several reasons. Nick is more the farmer type than I am, and the property is really a ranch. Dad thought Nick would do a better job managing it. As you can see, I have my own career. And, my husband wanted us to start fresh, not beholden to our families when we married. My parents still own it, and Nick and I will get equal shares when they're gone."

"It sounds like a great place," Patty said to lower the tone.

"It is!" Dianne said. "I will miss my ocean-front home, but I'm looking forward to moving back home for a while."

"Do you know any good contractors or builders?" Matt asked. "I might need one, too."

"Of course. We have the best builder. Ray Thompson—he's amazing. We're first in line, and he's going to be very busy, so you should make your plans as soon as you can. Here's his number," Dianne said, jotting it down on a Post-it note.

"Will you build back on Ocean Bend Road?" Patty asked Matt.

"Not sure yet. I don't actually own the land where my cottage stood. I've been renting it since January. But I already miss my ocean view, so I'll figure out something. Been too busy. I saw that Ted's house survived. He's on the other side of the road," he said for Dianne's benefit.

"Ted is my husband and he's thrilled his small house withstood the earthquake. He was so upset until we knew it was safe. I can't even imagine what the two of you are going through."

"It's awful, Patty," said Dianne. "We lost almost everything. Our brand new beautiful home and everything in it."

"Think of the fun you'll have rebuilding and buying all new things," Patty said cheerfully. "I wish I could throw a couple of Ted's old chairs into the ocean."

They all laughed, and it seemed a good time to end the meeting.

• • •

The sun was setting as Matt drove back to Port Stirling, and the bright glow was in his eyes most of the way as he headed west into it. He took his time and enjoyed the pastoral scenes along the way. Yes, there was clear damage from the tsunami and the raging river, but there were a few cows back in the fields, and signs of life rising through the watery remains. Being alone in the car was about the only time he had to think these days, and he enjoyed the solitude. He lowered his window and breathed in the soft air.

His thoughts turned to Susie, even though he really didn't want to think about her. Fern had been upset last night, and when he'd pressed her, had confided her unsettling run-in with his ex. According to Fern—who could not tell a lie if her life depended on it—Susie came to town with the intention of reuniting with her former husband. Matt found this surprising, and he didn't want any part of it.

Susie had let him down when he needed her most. His NFL career had ended abruptly, and it had been a tough realization to Matt that he would never play football—a game he truly loved—again. Susie sympathized with him, and stood by him as he recovered from his injury, and took the time to decide what his next career would be.

When he first became a cop, things were good. He quickly advanced through the ranks, had regular hours, and developed a good reputation.

Susie was part of a thriving physical therapy practice, and the two were happy.

The trouble started for two reasons. Matt wanted children, and Susie wanted to wait a while longer, claiming she wanted to get more seniority at work. In truth, she had no maternal feelings, and Matt was beginning to suspect that she didn't really want kids at all.

And then Matt got promoted to Homicide Chief Detective, and everything changed. Overnight, they couldn't plan a social life; his schedule was very erratic, and they fell behind with all their friends and travel. Matt loved the work, however, and he didn't mind the sacrifice for now.

Susie reacted differently. The country club, their exotic trips, and the Dallas social life with their friends turned out to be the glue that held their marriage together. When those things were no longer the constant in their lives, the union crumbled. Susie became pouty and resentful, and downright angry at him.

Matt didn't blame her. She had grown up expecting a certain lifestyle, and when he snatched it out from under her, the outcome was probably predictable. He tried to convince her that his work hours were temporary, and that it wouldn't always be this way. But she grew impatient. And, late one Sunday night, when a planned BBQ with friends had to be postponed because of a gangland shooting in Plano, Susie told Matt she wanted a divorce.

He didn't fight it. No point. He chose his profession, and he would make that choice again. Which was why he was surprised at Fern's take on their encounter yesterday. His current job might be more low-key than in Texas, but his role was important in the community, and he was essentially on the job 24/7. Did Susie think that would ever change? Or did she believe she was better equipped to deal with his career now? It didn't matter—it was too late for them. He loved Fern, for all the reasons he didn't love Susie anymore.

As the setting sun dropped into the sea, creating a series of pink and orange clouds overhead, Matt let out a whoop. There were lights on in town! The power was back!! He drove down Deception Hill into the village, and couldn't stop yelling. There were lights on in most of the buildings still standing!

As he made his way to Fern's house, he rolled his window down and laughed and waved at all the people outside banging on pots and pans and shouting for joy. Several people were dancing in their front yards, even amidst remaining muck and mud, and all the kids were running around shrieking and jumping up and down.

Tragically, they'd lost friends and neighbors, and it would be months before they would realize 'normal', but they were going to be all right. They would rebuild. Port Stirling would be better and stronger than ever, and Matt was home.

Fern was standing in her front yard, one hand shading her eyes while she watched the sunset when Matt pulled into the driveway. The last of the sun's rays caught her red hair and turned it golden. She waved at him.

Matt was happy.

• • •

Dianne Carmichael Dobbins entered her brother's home without knocking and yelled, "Nick, it's me. You home?"

There were lights glowing in the huge, sprawling house, and Nick came out of a swinging door to the far left of where Dianne stood in the grand central foyer. It was a log home, built by Marilyn and Mason Carmichael in 1963 on the site of Mason's parents' home which had burned to the ground during the big fire in the 1950s. But it wasn't just any log home; it was the size of a resort lodge. Two stories, high ceilings, several fabulous river rock fireplaces, and a wall of windows that looked out to the river.

Marilyn and Mason, tired of Oregon winters, had decamped to Palm Desert when Mason retired from his family's various businesses. His focus was primarily on the company's timber stands, the fourteen sawmills around the state, and the manufacturing, sales, and exporting of lumber. Mason's sister ran the agricultural side of the family's holdings, which encompassed everything from cranberry bogs to blueberries to hazelnut orchards. The family's reach was deep into Oregon, and their cumulative wealth was second only to a well-known shoe salesman. Lyndon Carmichael had given his family a nice head start.

"The electricity is back on!" Nick grinned at his sister.

"Hallelujah," she replied, giving him a quick hug. "I turned the bank's ATM on, and it was working beautifully when I left. I was getting really tired of dealing with the hoi polloi asking when the ATM would work again."

The siblings looked a lot alike. Both had thick, glossy brown hair, and dark brown eyes. They also had matching clefts in their respective chins, and both had apple-shaped bodies on the somewhat pudgy side.

"To what do I owe the honor of your visit?" Nick asked. "And where's Duane?"

"I want to tell you about a meeting I had this afternoon with our local police, and Duane doesn't need to know about this." Nick thought Dianne looked a little nervous, unusual for his older sister.

"What's up?"

"You know Patty Perkins, right? The detective for the Twisty River police?" Nick nodded, and dried his hands on the dishtowel he'd been holding. "Well, she and the chief of police for the Port Stirling PD came to the bank to talk to me."

"What for?"

"They were interested in Lyndon Carmichael, and his relationship with Tyee Kouse. Said they were intrigued by Tyee's disappearance all those decades ago, and they'd found a photo during the tsunami cleanup of Lyndon, Ronald Percy, and Tyee posed together."

"OK, but what does that have to do with you?"

"They asked me a bunch of questions about the Carmichaels and the Percys, and their association with Tyee. Whether they got along, things like that."

"What did you tell them?"

"The truth. That we hated the Indians and they hated us."

"No use trying to put lipstick on a pig, I guess," said Nick. "What do you think they're up to? In my experience, cops don't do anything without a reason."

"That's why I'm here. The Port Stirling cop asked me if we had any old family rifles that had survived. I got the feeling that he and Patty weren't telling me everything, and that question rattled me. Do we?"

"Do we what?" Nick could be a little thick sometimes, which drove his sister nuts.

"Do we have any old rifles around?" She crossed her arms over her chest and waited.

"Hell if I know," Nick said, not a gun person either. He started walking to the huge great room behind Dianne. "Let's go see what's in that cabinet in dad's den." Dianne followed, her heels clacking on the highly-polished wood floors.

Mason's den was designed after one he'd admired in a Scottish castle. He and Marilyn had been the guests of the fourteenth Lord MacCleave ("please call me Hugo") at his ancient home in the Scottish Highlands. Mason Carmichael and Baron Hugo MacCleave were business partners; Mason imported MacCleave Highland Whisky, and Hugo imported Oregon lumber.

The room, smelling of wood smoke and old books, was Dianne's favorite. It was large but cozy, and featured carved wood walls and a handmade barrel ceiling. A large library table was placed in the middle of the room with a substantial ornate chandelier hanging over it. A massive walk-in fireplace stood at the far end of the room with four well-used mahogany leather chairs grouped around it. Built-in bookshelves lining one wall held hundreds of leather-bound editions. Mason's desk came from an estate sale in Dublin, and was stationed to the right of the door. Leather ottomans were placed around the room, and Dianne remembered plopping on them to read when she was a child, a fire roaring in the room.

Nick tried the door on the antique gun cabinet, but it was locked. "Wait a sec," he said, and migrated to Mason's big desk. "I think the key is in dad's top drawer."

It was.

He fit the old-fashioned key into the lock, and unlocked decades of legacies and secret histories. Opening the cabinet door, Nick reached for one of the older rifles. "Wait!" yelled Dianne. "Here, use this," she said, pulling out a tissue from her handbag. "We don't want your fingerprints on any guns...just in case."

"Good thinking," her brother said. "What about this one?" he said holding out one age-old, worn rifle for her to inspect.

"It looks ancient. So does that one next to it, for that matter."

"The others look more recent, don't you think?"

"Yes. If the police are looking for a gun that might have belonged to Lyndon, it has to be one of those first two. How do you feel about stashing those two guns somewhere?" She turned to face him.

"Why would we do that? These guns have nothing to do with us," he said logically.

"Nick, honey, you and I have a lot to lose if things go south with the Carmichael name. What if one of these guns was used for a bad purpose, and the police can link it to our family?"

Nick's face clouded over for a moment while he processed Dianne's question. "I suppose you're right, sis. But it would have been decades ago. We surely can't be blamed for anything like that."

"But imagine that this gun was used to kill Tyee Kouse," Dianne said. "What if Lyndon killed him? You need to think further ahead, and what that could do to our brand. The Carmichael name is our gateway to everything, Nick. If it's sullied in any way, it could hurt our businesses. People are real sensitive these days to the rights of people who aren't like us. We could have problems overnight if Lyndon killed Tyee and the media made a big deal about it."

"Lyndon Carmichael did *not* kill Tyee," Nick said, his color rising. "You're worried about nothing."

"What if he did? What if he did, Nick?"

CHAPTER 25

Port Stirling city hall was back in business, and Matt couldn't be happier. The utilities had been restored, his broken picture windows replaced, and everyone in the building was in a sunnier mood. Most knew that normal was still months away, but there was a sense that the worst was behind them.

Commissioner Olive Joiner had worked nothing short of miracles for Port Stirling with her sister, the governor. They had procured badly-needed supplies from all over the country, everything from food to furniture, distributing equitably to the hardest hit areas. The southern coastal region of Chinook County-the most westerly part of the state-had been the worst hit, with Seaside/Astoria in the north taking the second worst blow, and they had been the governor's top priorities. The cities in the Willamette Valley were also hurting, but the coast issues were life-threatening, whereas the valley and eastern Oregon were mostly infrastructure problems.

The delayed school year would resume next week, almost six weeks after the September 23 disaster. Cleanup and necessary repairs had been finalized at nearly all of the state's schools. Many towns had one or more teachers killed during the quake, and it would take more time to hire replacements, but the survivors vowed to take on their kids.

Matt turned on his computer, and was surprised at how the simple act was so satisfying. He busied himself with reading the recently uploaded reports from his staff on minor criminal acts since the earthquake, housing reports on where the displaced families had gone, and new policies from the Oregon State Police and other police departments around the state. Matt made sure he knew about all the available resources to help their destroyed businesses and schools, and passed along the pertinent ones to Bill Abbott and his staff.

Once he'd taken care of the living in his town, he turned his attention to the dead, specifically Tyee Kouse and his mysterious case.

* * *

Susie Longworth had taken great care with her appearance this morning. She dressed in a powder blue silk blouse with a ruffle around its low-cut, V-neckline, and tucked it into a straight, close-fitting black skirt. Black, pointy-toed pumps rounded out her look. She wore her long blonde hair in loose waves today, which beautifully framed her fresh face. A soft peach lip gloss was her final touch.

She checked herself out in the mirror. *Lookin' good, Susie-Q.* If she lost out to a tall, skinny, freckled redhead, she wasn't worth the earrings she just put on.

* * *

Fern had looked like hell every day since the earthquake. She couldn't seem to get past grabbing her favorite jeans, or make an effort of any kind. Part of it was due to the trauma of what her town was going through, and how exhausted she was trying to hold everything together. It also felt shallow to Fern to worry about her appearance right now when others all around her were re-learning how to live.

But something this morning was telling her it was time to up her game. Or at least get back in the game. Yes, it was likely driven by her encounter yesterday with Matt's ex-wife. She knew that Susie Longworth meant business, and her being in Port Stirling to 'nurse' was just an excuse to wiggle her way back in with Matt. He might believe their marriage is over, but clearly she doesn't. And Fern wasn't going down without a fight.

She pulled out an old forest green dress that she knew Matt liked on her, and traded in her mud-caked boots for real shoes. Best she could do.

• • •

"Earl, it's Matt. How are you?"

"I'm good. Isn't it nice to have electricity again? Everyone is walking around here grinning ear to ear."

Matt laughed. "Same here. I guess it's a case of you don't know what you've got until it's gone. I've got some news for you on the Tyee Kouse case."

"Yeah?"

"Patty and I had a chat with the great-great-granddaughter of Lyndon Carmichael, and it was informative. But first, I want you to get a search warrant for this address." He gave the sheriff Nick Carmichael's home address.

"The Carmichael place?"

"You know it?"

"Everyone knows it. It's the nicest house in Chinook County, maybe in the state."

"Well, then we'll get to see inside it. There's a chance they may have an old rifle or two that belonged to Lyndon, and I want to go in and get it before his descendants do something with it. I don't know Nick Carmichael yet, but my gut feeling is his sister might not be cooperative. I'll explain when I see you. Can you talk to the judge and get the warrant right away?"

"On my way now," Earl said. "Is this just a weapons search?"

"For now, yes."

• • •

Matt and Earl met in the long driveway that curved in off the Port Stirling/Twisty River road, and ended in a large tiled forecourt that could park about twenty vehicles. The driveway, unusual for this rural area, was beautiful, and meandered through a stand of old oak trees that formed an arch over the narrow drive. The trees were under-planted with hundreds of ferns and hostas, to lush effect.

I could live here, Matt thought, even before he reached the house with its stunning view of the river and meadows beyond.

There were no cars visible, and if anyone was at home, they had parked in the six-car attached garage at the far end of the entry. Matt could see leftovers from the tsunami between the house and the river, but the immediate vicinity of the house was spotless. He got out of his car and waited for Earl who had pulled in behind him.

The sheriff waved the search warrant as he approached Matt. "All set. The judge said "weapons only", but if we get suspicious, she's willing to go further."

"I don't think we'll need anything else—we'll either find an old rifle or we won't. It's not like we're going to catch a killer today."

"It's odd, huh?" said Earl. "Don't think I've ever worked on anything like this."

"Me neither. But think how great it would be to tell Del Kouse and his family that we found the gun that killed Tyee," Matt said. "It could be the first step in helping piece together what really happened to him."

"A house like this might even have a gun room," speculated the sheriff, looking over Matt's shoulder at the impressive home. "It was kind of a thing with the lumber guys when Mason Carmichael built this place."

"That would certainly make our job easier. Ready?"

"Following you, Chief."

Matt rang the doorbell to the right of the large door, under a bronze plaque that read 'Carmichael House-Established 1956' in an elaborate font, and waited. The control freak part of him always hated this moment because he never knew for sure what was going to happen next. But the cop-on-a-mission part of him liked it because, either way, it was progress on a case.

Nick Carmichael opened the door and said, "Yes?" He wore an apron over jeans and a grey crewneck sweater. Matt was briefly taken aback at how much he resembled his sister.

"Hi," Matt said. "I'm Matt Horning, the police chief in Port Stirling, and this is Chinook County Sheriff Earl Johnson. We have an odd reason for being here today. May we come in?"

Nick said, "My sister told me you might come by. Please come in."

The two old-hand cops exchanged a quick glance. *A warning from the sister. Interesting.*

Matt was used to luxury. He'd grown up with it in Texas, but he hadn't seen much overt luxury since he'd moved to Oregon. He was seeing it now, and he felt a tiny pang missing it in his own life. Instinctively he'd realized that a show of wealth from the new chief of police might not endear him to the people he needed to win over. But perhaps now that he had some street cred in town, he could live a little better than he had been.

"Did Dianne tell you what we're looking for?" Matt said pleasantly.

"An old gun? That might have belonged to my great-great-grandfather?"

"That's right. The sheriff has a search warrant issued by Judge Cynthia Hedges that gives us permission to search the premises for an old rifle." To lighten that intimidating statement, Matt added, "Your home is beautiful, Mr. Carmichael."

"Thanks. It belongs to my parents, but I live here now. Kind of a glorified caretaker," he grinned. Happy guy. And why not?

"We won't mess up anything, and we won't be long," Matt promised. "Is there a gun room anywhere in the house or on the property?"

Nick looked puzzled for a minute. "No, not that I know of. We do have a barn out beyond the garage complex that has a couple of finished rooms in it, but I don't remember seeing any guns there. Mom used one of them as her potting shed, and the other one is used to store things like outdoor furniture in the winter, that sort of thing."

"Any ideas where any guns might be kept?" the sheriff asked. Earl, remembering how much money Nick's parents had given to his reelection campaign tried to not sound like his usual gruff self. It was becoming increasingly difficult for the curmudgeon to be pleasant.

"Yes, dad has a cabinet in his study where he kept guns. It's locked, but I think I know where the key is. Follow me."

Nick went into his father's den for the second time that day. "You'll have to excuse my apron," he said while walking down the hallway. "I'm making an apple pie for tonight's dessert. Our orchards are bursting with apples."

"Like I said, we won't take up much of your time," Matt reiterated.

"I can't imagine that we would still have one of my grandfather's old guns, but I guess you never know unless you look."

Mason's den was the stuff of Matt's dreams. His former cottage—rest in peace—would have mostly fit into this room. "What an amazing room," was all he said now.

"Yeah," agreed Nick. "Little over the top for me, but dad wanted to replicate a den he'd seen in a Scottish castle while on a business trip back in the sixties. I guess this room turned out just like its Scotland counterpart."

Matt and Earl spotted the gun cabinet when they entered the room. Nick hustled to the big desk and fished out the key. "Ah, here it is. Right where I remembered dad keeping it."

The first thing Matt noticed in the good-sized cabinet was the two empty slots on the far left. Earl, too. Both cops pulled on latex gloves, and pulled out two of the rifles to inspect, ignoring Nick who stood watching them with a certain fascination.

After a minute had passed, the sheriff said, "Mine's too new."

"Mine too."

They reinserted the two, and pulled out the next two.

"Same with this one," Matt said.

"Yep," agreed Earl.

Matt looked a bit longer at the next rifle he removed from the cabinet. "This one is older," he told Earl, "but probably from the 1920s or so."

Earl had yanked out the rifle next to the one Matt was holding, and nodded. "This one is older, too, but nowhere near old enough."

Working their way to the left, they decided that none of the guns in this cabinet could have belonged to Lyndon Carmichael, although there were some fine earlier rifles in the collection.

Matt turned to Nick and said, "So, I see that there are two empty slots on the left here. Any ideas if there used to be guns in them?"

Nick hesitated. "Don't think so. I remember being a kid playing in here, and the cabinet was never completely full up." He stared at Matt, and then looked over to Earl. The sheriff thought he was daring them to challenge what he just said.

"Your father seemed to be a rather precise man," Matt said slowly. "I'm surprised that he would custom-build a gun cabinet that had two extra spaces."

Nick shifted his weight from one foot to the other and scratched his head. "Well, I see what you're saying, Chief, but I think he was planning to buy two more guns."

"Really? For this cabinet? When he now lives in Palm Desert?" Matt said as lightly as he could manage.

"You know how it goes with some projects. You never quite finish them," Nick laughed. It sounded hollow to Matt.

"Guess we're on a wild-goose chase, sheriff," Matt said jovially. "Thanks so much for your time." He reached to shake his hand, which had flour remnants on it. "We'll get out of your hair now."

"No problem," said Nick. The relief on his face was unmistakable.

"Someday soon, though, I'd like to come back and have a real tour of your home. It's amazing," Matt said.

"I'd love to show you around," Nick said. "Any time, just let me know."

"Oh, I will."

. . .

CHAPTER 26

"Guess we have to do it the hard way," Matt said to Earl as they walked to the vehicles.

"Figures. Why can't things ever be easy?"

"Aw, c'mon, Earl, you know better than that," Matt snickered.

"It's so obvious," Earl said. "Nick or his sister took the two oldest rifles and hid them somewhere."

"Yeah. That's exactly what they did. The question is why? Did I spook Dianne into action, or do they know something? A family secret passed down through the generations?"

"I'll go back to the judge for a broader warrant," the sheriff said. "But I don't like this. The Carmichaels are a very prominent family, and this is going to rock a lot of boats."

"Do I look like I care about rocking boats?"

"S'pose not," Earl conceded. "But I'll have to tell the D.A. that we're going to search the Carmichael property, and he will be apoplectic."

"We're just doing our job. The district attorney should try it sometime. Would it go easier on you if I ask for the warrant?"

Earl stared at him. "I am the sheriff of Chinook County. As you rightly pointed out, easy is not part of my job description. I'll get the warrant, and I'll meet you back here tomorrow at 8:00 a.m. with some of my deputies." He turned and strode to his car without another word.

• • •

Back in his office as the sun dipped lower in the western sky, Matt took a quiet moment to sit and look out his new windows. The view, although altered by the tsunami devastation, was still breathtaking.

The Chinook County Board of Commissioners, working with the Port Stirling City Council, had unanimously voted to rebuild the Twisty River jetty. They would start work as soon as the area's business and housing infrastructure was repaired, and construction crews became available.

A decision on whether to replace the iconic lighthouse was tabled for now. With modern navigational tools, the lighthouse had been decommissioned years ago. But it was a symbol of the region, and there was some sentiment that it should be rebuilt as a show of resiliency when priorities and budgetary requirements allowed. Matt had mixed emotions about the lighthouse now, and wondered if those in favor of rebuilding it would change their minds when the facts of Tyee's murder became known.

But that was for another day. Today's cloudy, rainy morning had blown over, and the sky had cleared. Matt's view was to the north and west. The river's mouth was wider now without the jetty forcing it into a narrow channel. It had spilled over into the marshy areas where Clay Sherwin's body had been found last April. Matt, his mind wandering back to his second homicide in Port Stirling, wondered if the egrets would return in time for their annual spring counting.

In the intervening months since the Anselmo case had wrapped, Matt had become friendly with the marine biologist who had the misfortune of discovering Sherwin's body. Once the case was resolved, Matt had taken the poor man and his wife out to dinner to tell them the entire story in the hopes that it would make his grisly discovery recede over time. He had since been invited to their home, and the three had struck up a nice friendship. They were an intelligent, interesting couple, and Matt had enjoyed their company.

He'd run into the biologist downtown yesterday, and was happy to learn that the couple had survived the earthquake and were fine. Matt ran his hand through his curly black hair, and turned back to his desk and the city's list of the residents who had been displaced when their homes were destroyed. Fern and Jay, working with FEMA, had done an excellent job finding new housing for the worst off in Port Stirling. Checking off the updated list now, he knew that everyone who wanted or needed a roof over their head had one. It would take time for construction crews—even with all the out-of-state help—to catch up to the demand, but they would eventually get there. In the meantime, all the survivors were safe for now.

He reached for the buzzing intercom on his desk at the same moment his office door opened and Susie Longworth entered. Sylvia's voice said, "Your ex is here." He replied, "Yeah, I see that. It's OK, Sylvia."

"I'm sorry to interrupt you, darlin', but I wanted to see you before I leave for home tomorrow morning," Susie said, coming up and perching on the edge of his desk. "Your clinic is fully operational again, and our work here is finished. We're going home."

"Thank you for coming to help. It was a nice thing to do, and my town appreciates it."

"I don't care about your town, I care about you. That's why I came here."

Matt coolly appraised her. *Be careful what you say next.* "Whatever your motives were, it was still commendable of you."

"Commendable?!?" she laughed. "Are you going to give me a key to the city?" she teased, crossing her legs.

"The only key to the city I've given out is to the dog who discovered a child's murdered body. He deserved it."

She shuddered. "Your job is mind-boggling to me."

"It always has been," Matt said. "That's why we're divorced." He leaned back in his chair.

"About that," she said. "I was thinking that maybe you should take a vacation and come home for a couple of weeks. We could spend a little time together and see if there's anything there. What do you think, hon?"

There it was, finally on the table. "There's nothing there, Susie," he said calmly. "I'm sorry. And I couldn't leave here now even if I wanted to. Which I don't."

"How can you be sure? We fell madly in love once. There could still be a spark if we tried to see if we could find it. I won't beg you, Matt, but I want you to know that I still feel it. I was stupid, and I deeply regret how I let you down."

"We let each other down. But what's done is done."

"I'm asking for a second chance. A second chance at happiness for both of us."

She shifted off his desk and onto his lap, clasping her hands around his neck. "Are you going to sit there and tell me you don't feel a thing for me?" she smiled. "Nothing? Are you sure?"

Forcefully, he put his arms around her, kissed her hard, and then broke away. "Good-bye, Susie."

"That's a start," she smiled, inches from his face. Then she moved in, and kissed him back even harder, drawing it out.

"Hey, Jay and I are going out for a beer, do you want…"

He heard Fern's voice behind Susie, and knew she'd entered his office. He pushed Susie off him, and faced Fern, his heart beating fast and nearing explosion in his chest.

Fern's face turned redder than a fully-ripe tomato, and she blinked. Then she stammered, "Excuse me. I didn't mean to interrupt you." She turned and hurried from the room, a streak of green wearing Matt's favorite dress.

• • •

"Oops," laughed Susie. "You probably don't like your staff seeing you making out."

He glared at her. "You need to leave. Now." His voice was cold, he had noticeably paled, and she knew he meant it.

She straightened her skirt, and picked up her handbag from his desk. "I'll go, but you need to acknowledge what happened here. That was not a make-believe, good-bye kiss you gave me," she said evenly. "I know the difference, and that was a hungry kiss. You need to think hard about that, Matt. Good-bye for now."

Susie walked down the hallway into the squad room, and glanced over at Fern, who had returned, shaken, to her desk. Susie gave a smile and a little wave, and left the building.

Fern wanted to run away, but her pride wouldn't let her. She was a detective in the Port Stirling police department, and she would act like one.

At Matt's request, she had been researching old newspaper articles featuring Lyndon Carmichael before she and Jay had decided to call it a day and go out for a beer. She returned to that work on her computer, and tried to quiet her racing heart and erupting skin.

Jay, back from the men's room and putting on his jacket walked over to Fern's desk. "Are we going now?" And then, looking at her distraught face, said, "What's wrong? Are you OK?"

Fern looked up at him, and Jay thought he had never seen a more heartbroken face in his lifetime. Her eyes welled up, and she was unable to speak. Jay had been through hell and back with Matt and Fern, and he intuitively knew that only one thing could upset her this much. He reached down, took her by the arm and said, "Let's go. Get your coat."

Jay and Fern left the squad room just as Matt came out of his office. Jay looked back over his shoulder and his look said 'what the hell have you done?'

Matt gave Jay an agonized look, but it was too late, as the squad room door slammed shut.

Sylvia and the other officers all looked down at their desks and shuffled papers. It was their way of saying 'whatever this is, it is none of our business.'

• • •

Fern and Jay tucked into a back booth in the lounge at the newly reopened Inn at Whale Rock restaurant just as the sun sank into the Pacific. Vicky had come into the room, distributing small candles on each table as she did every day at sunset. She set one down between Jay and Fern, and said, "Your usual? Pelican beer for you, Jay, and our best chardonnay for you, Miss Fern?"

"No," whispered Fern. "I'll have a double Beefeater martini, please, Vicky."

Vicky did a double-take at Fern, nodded, and scooted quickly toward the bar.

"Are you able to talk yet?" Jay asked gently. Fern had not said one word in the car.

She looked up at him. "That fucking snake," was all she said.

"Who? Susie, Matt's ex?" Jay had seen Susie leaving as he came out of the men's room.

"Matt. I expected it of her. Matt's the real snake." She clammed up as Vicky returned with their drinks. The waitress placed napkins in front of the two cops, set a drink on each one, patted Fern on the shoulder, and said, "It will be OK. You'll see."

"It will *not* be OK," said Fern icily, staring at her drink. "It will *never* be OK."

Vicky looked at Jay, shrugged, and mouthed 'I'll be back'.

"It's obvious that Matt has done something to upset you," Jay said. "You have to tell me what happened before I can help you."

Fern took a big swallow of her drink, gulping it greedily. "Why do I always go for men with wives? What is that about?" she cried.

"Matt doesn't have a wife. He has an ex-wife. There's a big difference," said Jay.

"Oh really?" she snarled. "And ex-wives sit on your lap with their skirts hiked up and their tongues in your mouth? Is that what it means to be an ex-wife?"

Jay sat in stunned silence. "Matt would never do that," he said finally.

"I saw him." Tears streamed down her ashen face.

"He loves you, and he would never do anything like that to hurt you."

"I saw him, Jay!"

"In his office?"

"Yes. In his chair. I barged in to invite him to come with us. Serves me right, I guess."

"There has to be an explanation. Something."

"There is," Fern said. "And it's simple. He still loves her." She was openly sobbing now.

Jay reached across the table and took her hand. "I don't know what the hell this is about, but I know he doesn't feel *anything* for Susie. If you could have been with him the night you went missing, you would know what I know. He loves you so much. I have no idea what this is all about, but you'll talk to him and straighten it out."

Fern wiped her cheeks with both hands, and locked eyes with Jay. "I know what I saw. I not only will not be talking to him to 'straighten it out', I won't be talking to him ever again."

CHAPTER 27

Matt stumbled to his car in the city hall parking lot, got in, locked the doors, and sat there quietly in the growing darkness. *What the heck just happened?* How could he have ruined his life in thirty seconds?

He had to talk to Fern and try to explain. It didn't look good, he admitted, but he'd been trying to get rid of Susie once and for all. He thought a good-bye kiss-off would put an end to her nonsense about giving their marriage another go. To him, it was the final dismissal.

Once he told Fern that, everything would be all right.

. . .

At Fern's insistence, Jay took her to her parents' home, where she planned to spend the night. She refused to go to her own house in case Matt was there.

"I can't drive," she told Jay as they left the bar. "Too much to drink." She'd had two healthy martinis before Vicky switched her to a small glass of white wine. *At least she's still with it enough to know she's messed up,* Jay thought.

"That's OK," Jay told her. "I'll drop you at your parents tonight, and we can get your car in the morning. You're sure you don't want to go home and talk it out with Matt?"

"Not gonna happen. I'm done. I don't need a snake in my life. I've already experienced that, and I don't need it again."

"Well, there is the slightly inconvenient factoid that he's also your boss."

"I realize that," she said. "And I love my job. I'll figure out something… just need some time to think it through."

"Right now, you just need some sleep. I'll cover for you tomorrow. I'll say you're sick, taking a PTO day."

"Could you do that for me? I've welcomed the long shifts and the sacrifices since the disaster, but I can't handle this. Too raw. I'd really appreciate it while I figure this all out. Guess Abbott was right all along."

• • •

Matt let himself into Fern's house with his key. She wasn't home, and all was dark. He turned on the lights, made some coffee, and sat on the living room sofa to wait for her.

It was about 2:00 a.m. when he realized she wasn't coming home. *OK, this is bad. What should I do?*

He was certain he could straighten out everything with her, but it was too late to go looking for her tonight. He pulled off his shoes, walked into their bedroom, and stretched out on top of the bed. He'd just close his eyes for a few minutes.

The next thing Matt knew, a shaft of sunlight was coming in through a slat in the bedroom blind that covered the east-facing window, directly into his eye. He reached his arm out to Fern's side of the bed. Empty and cold.

He got up, showered and dressed quickly, and headed to the office. Fern's car sat alone in the middle of the parking lot. The sight of the baby blue VW hit him hard. He knew her well enough to know she wouldn't have done anything stupid last night…but where was she? In the light of day, Matt could puke. He'd really screwed up.

He locked his car, and headed for the building, when another cop car turned into the parking lot. Jay.

He watched Jay pull up beside Fern's VW, and waited for him.

Jay spied him, got out of his car, and walked briskly to where Matt stood waiting for him.

"What the hell were you thinking?!?" Jay exploded, inches from Matt's face. The tall, gangly detective had a good three inches on his boss, and used it.

"Calm down. It's not that bad. I can explain." Matt tried to sound low-key, but he was churning inside.

"It's bad." Jay stared at him.

"Where's Fern now? She didn't come home last night. As soon as I can talk to her, I can clear this up."

"You need to get a fucking clue, man! She doesn't want to see you or talk to you."

"Where is she?"

"I can't tell you. She said, and I quote, 'I'm done. I don't need another snake in my life', and I'm pretty sure she meant it."

"Where is she, Jay?"

"Are you ordering me to tell you, sir?"

"Of course not. I'm asking as your friend."

"My friends don't have sex with their ex-wife in their office." Jay glared at him.

"For Chrissakes, I wasn't having sex with Susie," Matt said. "I was trying to get rid of her."

"That's not the way Fern saw it."

"Well, that's the way it was. The truth. I'll explain it all when she gets here. You'll see."

"She's not coming to work today. Taking a PTO day. You love her, Matt. How could you do this to her?"

"Yes, I do love Fern, and I've done nothing to hurt her."

"She's devastated," Jay said softly. "I thought you two were perfect. And now it's all fucked up. I'm going to work," and he headed to the building's side door.

Matt stood there, thinking, in the now brilliant sunshine. *I need to fix this before it gets completely out of control. Where could she be? She couldn't have stayed at Jay's, his place is too small. Maybe her parents? It would hurt her pride, but maybe she was so upset she didn't care.*

It was worth a try. He got back in his car, and tried to remember the street the Byrnes lived on. He'd been there a couple of times, and although Fern had been driving, he could find it again. He ran into one roadblock where the pavement had cratered during the quake, but found the house on his second try.

Her dad answered the doorbell. He had red hair, too, which had recently started to grey a bit at the temples.

"Hello, Matt." He neither smiled nor frowned, and his tone was neutral.

"Hi. Is she here?"

"She is."

"May I come in? I'd like to talk to her."

"She says she doesn't care to speak with you."

"She doesn't mean it, Mr. Byrne. I can fix this," he pleaded.

To Matt's surprise, the older man laughed. "If you think she doesn't mean it, you don't know my daughter as well as you think you do. Wait here. I'll go tell her you're here."

Fern's dad liked Matt. He didn't know—and didn't want to know—why his daughter was so angry with him, but the chief deserved a chance to explain.

He closed the door, and Matt paced the porch, zipping up his jacket against the breeze that had started blowing from the southwest. He'd been here long enough now to know that a southwest wind meant some weather was blowing in. He looked in that direction and, sure enough, dark clouds were forming out to sea and bullying their way toward the coastline.

The door opened and Mr. Byrne came out shaking his head. "Nope," he told Matt. "No go. Sorry."

"She refuses to talk to me?"

"I'm afraid so, son."

"What should I do?" He was honestly bereft.

Fern's dad looked at him for a moment and then said, "You might try writing her a note. I got into hot water with Fern's mother once when we first became engaged, and she called off our wedding. Refused to speak to me 'ever again!' Truth was, I deserved it, probably more than you deserve whatever's going on now. Anyhoo, I wrote my wife a letter explaining myself and begging for forgiveness."

"Did it work?"

"Ten months later Fern was born. So, yes, it worked."

"Wait here. I've got my notebook in the car. It won't take long." Matt sprinted down the sidewalk to his car.

He wrote:

Dear Fern,

I was only trying to get rid of Susie once and for all. What you witnessed was a good-bye kiss-off, which is a Texas thing. I knew what Susie was up to, and I needed to stop it. I have no feelings for her. I love you without reservation, and can't imagine my life without you. Please meet with me when you're able to, and let me convince you of my feelings. I'm telling you the truth.

Love, Matt

He folded the note in half, and went back to Mr. Byrne on the porch.

"Thank you for suggesting this," Matt said, handing it to Fern's father. "I hope it works for me, too!"

"I'll make sure she gets it." And he quietly went back inside the house, and closed the door.

Matt drove back to city hall. He didn't blame Fern for being upset at him. He hadn't handled Susie gracefully, and he knew he was partly to blame for what Fern witnessed. There was a part of him—buried somewhere deep inside—that wondered if he truly had zero feelings for his former wife. *Why, after all, did I let her go as far as she did?*

CHAPTER 28

Matt took his sergeant, Walt, with him to meet Sheriff Earl and his deputies to conduct the further search of the Carmichael house and property. He normally would have taken Jay with him, but thought it best to let him cool off a bit.

Plus, Jay was doing a great job on helping to repair Port Stirling, both people and infrastructure. He really was an asset to Matt's department—smart, productive, and people responded well to Jay, everyone liked him. It was obviously important for Matt to keep the trust of all of his staff, but he particularly needed Jay's good will. Had he tarnished it?

The sheriff and his crew had just arrived at the Carmichael home when Matt and Walt pulled up.

"How do you want to handle this, Earl?" Matt asked.

The sheriff patted his inside pocket. "First, we'll show Nick the warrant, so there's no misunderstanding about what we're allowed to do this morning. The judge has given us more leeway, and we're pretty much free to go anywhere on the property."

"Good. Personally, I like the barn as a hiding place for the two rifles," Matt said. "If I were a Carmichael, I'd want them out of the house in case they became relevant."

"Agreed. Let's start there."

The two cops approached the front door, but Dianne opened it before they could ring the doorbell.

"This seems like an official operation," she said, waving her hand at the cars and deputies in their parking apron. "What could possibly justify this kind of attention from you boys?"

Boys? thought Matt. *That seems a bit insulting.* "We're still looking for older rifles, Dianne. We think there are two missing from your father's gun cabinet, and we want to have a further look around, if you don't mind."

"Or even if you do mind," the sheriff added. He was not amused.

She looked at Earl quizzically. "I assume you have a search warrant, or something that gives you permission to invade our privacy?" She was dressed for work in a black suit with an ivory blouse, and large gold earrings. Her dark hair was pulled back in a severe bun, and her face and mood were as dark as her suit. Dianne's husband and brother were nowhere to be seen.

The sheriff produced the warrant from his pocket, and she took it from him, reading it carefully. Thrusting it back at Earl, she said, "We have nothing to hide, Sheriff Johnson, so please feel welcome to do your job. We'll be interested to see if you find any old family heirlooms, too. Nick and I are now responsible for the Carmichael brand, and our family history is very important to us."

"Is your brother here this morning?" Matt asked. "Anyone else on the property we should be aware of?" *And how fucking weird to refer to your family as a 'brand'.*

"Nick is around somewhere. He's planning to start harvesting the potatoes today, and he'll have a crew here at some point. My husband has already left for work, and I'm on my way now. You have my number if you need anything, correct?" she addressed Matt.

"Yes, I know how to reach you. We'll get started now, and thank you for your cooperation."

The sheriff waved at his guys, and all the cops headed out beyond the garage complex to the barn.

Matt had seen a lot of barns, but he'd never seen one quite like this one. It was huge, at least the length of one football field. The entire inside was finished with oak wood paneling and dozens of cabinets along the length of two walls. There were skylights placed periodically in the roof, so the inside was light and bright.

The room Nick had referred to as his mother's 'potting shed' was spotless. Divided glass shelving held compartments for seed packets, which were organized alphabetically, arugula to watermelon, and asters to zinnias. Tools were cleaned and hung from wall hooks. On one countertop was a master plan drawing of the property.

Matt ran his finger over the segment of the map that had the words 'Vegetable Garden' superimposed over a large square area that was segmented into four plots. *These people have too much time on their hands*, he thought, while at the same time acknowledging to himself that this garden was also his dream. He missed digging in the Texas soil. *I need to get my stuff together and figure out what the rest of my life looks like.*

The cops conducted a thorough search of the barn, including one hidden trap door, but found no guns.

"Time to think like Dianne," Sheriff Earl said. "Nick would have hidden the rifles out here somewhere. Where would she have put them? I still like your thought about getting them out of the house. Garage, maybe?" He scratched his ear.

"Maybe," said Matt. "Let's have a look."

One of the five vehicles in the six-car garage was a vintage Bentley, pale yellow with tan interior. Walt had spotted it first, and peeled off the protective tarp, laying it aside. He said, "Whoa, check this out, Matt. Isn't she a beauty?"

Walking up, Matt let out a low whistle. "Wow. My first thought is thank God the river and the tsunami didn't come up this far."

Walt chuckled. "You know it."

"Did you check the trunk and under the car?" Matt asked his sergeant.

"No," Walt admitted. "I'm afraid to touch it."

Matt walked around behind it and opened the trunk. Inside was a bulky package wrapped in sheets. Two antique rifles. "Guess the Carmichaels thought we would be afraid to touch this car," he said with a smile.

"How predictable am I?" Walt moaned. "What a dope."

"If it's any consolation, I was afraid to touch it, too," laughed Matt.

"I knew it!" said Earl, coming up to Matt. "Wonder how long these two rifles have been in that gun cabinet?"

Matt, wearing gloves, unwrapped the sheets and placed them on the garage floor, and then laid the rifles down on top. "Probably since Mason Carmichael built the house," he said. "Who knows where they were before that. They look pretty old, don't they?" he asked Earl.

"This one here," he pointed, "looks even older than mine, and mine goes back to the turn of the twentieth century."

Matt examined both rifles, and then photographed them. "Walt, try to find Nick Carmichael. Look in the area of the vegetable garden first. Tell him to come here if he wants to see his family's rifles before we take them to Dr. Ryder."

Earl snorted. "He saw them last night before he hid them here."

"I'm being polite, sheriff," Matt smirked. "I'm thinking of your re-election campaign coffers."

Nick huffed and puffed and sputtered about 'never seen those guns before'…blah, blah, blah. Not one cop present believed a word of it.

"I'm going to take these over to Buck Bay, to the county's medical examiner for testing. Dr. Ryder is very careful with historic artifacts, and she'll make sure your property is cared for."

"What kind of tests?" asked Nick.

"Ballistics and dating of the guns." Nick didn't need to know anything more at this point.

"I'll have to tell my father," Nick said. He stood with his legs apart, hands on hips, and frowned. "They're his."

"Please share with your father that both rifles will be returned here in a couple of days," said Matt. "Unless, of course, we believe they were used in the commission of a crime."

"What does that mean?" Nick said, waving his arms in the air. "What am I supposed to tell dad?"

"I'm sorry, but I can't say anything further until our investigation is completed," Matt said.

The cops left the building.

• • •

"Knock knock. Can I come in, sweetie?"

"I'm awake, mom," Fern said. "Come in."

At the age of sixty-six, Fern's mother was still a stunning woman. She wore her silvery grey hair cropped in the 'Judi Dench' style. Her eyebrows, always perfectly groomed, framed dark blue eyes, and she had the same soft 'English Rose' complexion as her daughter. She was rarely without a smile, as now.

"I'm not judging you, mind, but it is after 10:00 a.m. I thought a mug of dark roast might help you kick start your day," mom said, handing her daughter a steaming cup.

Fern had to laugh in spite of how she felt, which was beyond awful. "Since when do you say kick start?"

"I'm a hip woman for my age," she smiled at Fern. She placed her hand on Fern's shoulder. "How are you feeling, honey?"

"Do you mean because my guts have been ripped out by the man I love, or because I drank too much last night?"

"Both, I suppose."

"I'm heartbroken, my stomach is upset, and my head hurts."

"You look pretty good for all of that."

"I do? Maybe I just needed some sleep. Some real sleep." She took a sip of the hot coffee. "Thanks, it's delicious. And thank you for the bed. Honestly, it's the first great night's sleep I've had in weeks, since before the quake, I think."

"Sometimes coming home—and I know this isn't your home anymore—but sometimes it can take all the weight off your shoulders. You've had so much responsibility lately, all while conducting a red-hot love affair. It's a lot. Maybe you let it all go last night. What are your plans for today?"

"Obviously, I'm not going to work. Jay is covering for me, and letting the department know that I'm taking a PTO day. I've got three weeks I need to use up by the end of the year—haven't taken a day off yet."

"You haven't taken one day off since January? Goodness gracious," she wagged her finger.

"Maybe that explains a lot, huh?" smiled Fern. "Can I stay here for a couple of nights? Catch up on my sleep?"

"You don't have to ask. Stay as long as you want. What are you going to do about Matt? By the way, your father just told me that our cell phones are working!"

"That's awesome. Trying to do our jobs with no cell service has been a real bitch."

"Did you read the note he left for you?"

"I read it."

"And?"

"And, I believe his explanation for what I saw."

"I hear a but coming."

"*However*, believing him isn't enough. I don't trust him now."

Her mother frowned. "Matt Horning is one of the most trustworthy men I've ever had the pleasure of knowing. He saved your life, Fern."

"I'm well aware of that. But I'm talking about a different kind of trust. I don't trust that he truly understands his own feelings about Susie and maybe about me. He once chose her over all others. And, she left him—he was happy in their marriage. It's entirely possible that he still has feelings for her."

"What are you going to do?" Her mother looked worried.

"Well, what I'm *not* going to do is pretend I didn't see them together, resume our relationship, and wait around for him to someday possibly understand his real feelings. Maybe that's not fair to Matt, but if it all goes south, it's most definitely not fair to me. And, right now, I can only worry about myself."

"You're just going to walk away from him?"

"For now, yes. I don't ever want to feel again what I felt yesterday when I saw him kissing her. Can you understand that?"

"Yes, I hear you. But I think you're assuming a lot about him without giving him a chance. What would it take for you to give him an opportunity to mend things?"

Fern leaned back against the headboard and sighed. "I can't answer that yet. Maybe if he gets a restraining order against his ex-wife," she said with a wan smile.

Her mother laughed. "Is she that bad?"

"Worse," answered Fern. "Thanks for the chat. It helped. And, now, I need to get dressed, get some food in me, and think about how I will approach my job. He's not going to take that away from me, too."

"I'll make you some breakfast while you get cleaned up. And, Fern, you're going to be fine. Because you're my daughter, which makes you as tough as they come."

Fern blew her a kiss, and headed for the shower.

CHAPTER 29

Matt called Bernice, and told her he was bringing two old rifles for her to test.

"Your name came up on the satellite phone screen," was the first thing she said. "Are you calling me on your cell phone?"

"Yes! They're working! County-wide, I've been told," he said. "Have you tried yours?"

"It hasn't been out of my handbag for weeks. Guess I'd better charge it up. How exciting. Tell me about the rifles."

"They belong to Lyndon Carmichael's family, and we found them during a search of the garage of the family home. They're old, could have been around in 1904, and put the bullet in Tyee's head."

"You're not talking about Mason and Marilyn Carmichael's home, are you?" asked Bernice.

"Yep. Their son, Nick, lives there now. His parents moved to Palm Desert several years ago. Nick's sister, Dianne, and her husband are staying there now, too, because they lost their home during the earthquake. Turns out they were sorta neighbors of mine, further north on Ocean Bend Road."

"Oh, boy," said Bernice. "Pretty prominent family."

"I know, I know," whined Matt. "I've been told. They can't hurt me...I don't think so, anyway. But Sheriff Johnson is my partner on Tyee's investigation, and I'd sure hate to see this mess up his reelection bid."

"Earl is bullet-proof," she laughed. "He'll die wearing the Chinook County Sheriff's badge."

"Hope so. But my story gets worse."

"Oh?"

"So, yeah, Mason Carmichael's den has a gun cabinet, which the son took us to when we went in with the warrant. Except that there were two empty slots, and we could tell that the guns got older as you worked your way from right to left. The two empties were the far left, so someone hid the two oldest rifles."

"But you found them?"

"Hidden in the trunk of a $300,000 vintage Bentley."

"Oh, my."

"Good hiding place, no?"

"Do you have proof who hid them there?"

"Nope. Other than my gut instinct. Dianne was agitated when we asked her about old family guns the previous day. And when Patty and I interviewed her, it was obvious that she and her family didn't care much for the early Indians in Port Stirling. I think she was worried that great-great-grandpa Lyndon may have dealt with Tyee and we might figure it out."

"Bring them to me and let's get this show on the road," Bernice said. "I'm dying of curiosity."

"That's what makes you such a good ME. I'll be there soon."

• • •

Fern, dressed and breakfasted, went outside to her parents' covered patio and sat in one of the chairs around their teak dining table. She jotted some notes on her mom's kitchen note pad, and then sat quietly for a few minutes thinking about the task ahead of her.

She picked up her cell phone and dialed.

• • •

Matt always enjoyed the scenic drive north from Port Stirling to Buck

Bay. What little traffic there was today consisted of a few pickups and trucks, as the repair and rebuild action took over in Chinook County.

What the heck was he going to do about Fern? He hadn't heard from her since he gave his note to her father this morning. Surely she had read it by now. He was convinced they could work this out.

While he waited for her to come around, he'd rented a suite with its own kitchen at the Port Stirling Links resort. The two golf courses at the resort were unplayable and under repair, so they weren't accepting guests from outside the local area, except for the FEMA employees. Bill Abbott had worked out a deal with the owner, who lived in Philadelphia, for the city's rainy day fund to rent some of their accommodations for housing for displaced residents. In addition, the resort owners' LLC had also made a generous cash donation to the city's emergency relief fund. Abbott and his wife, Ruth, were staying there while they figured out what was the next move for them. The Abbotts and Matt paid for their own accommodations so as to not create an image of impropriety.

Matt had been comfortable there last night, even with his brain in turmoil, but he hoped he wouldn't be staying there for long. Sylvia, understanding without him saying a word, had asked him yesterday morning where he was staying. When he told her, she had offered to drop off some groceries for him on her way home this afternoon—she lived further north of the resort east of the highway.

"That's hardly in your job description," he told her. But God bless her for making the offer.

"Of course not, but it is in my 'friend' description. And from the looks of you, you could use a friend about now."

"What do you mean? I'm smiling." He attempted one, but it flopped compared to his usual megawatt smile.

"You can fool some of the people some of the time, but you can never fool me," Sylvia said.

The two had become close during the intense work on the two murder cases since Matt had arrived in Port Stirling. Matt respected her work, both from a skill set perspective, as well as her doggedness and creativity in getting the job done. Sylvia, for her part, had worked with many incompetent people during her seventy-something years, and she recognized competency and professionalism when she found it in her new boss. Outsiders saw their relationship as a substitute mother/son-type rapport, but it wasn't like that at all. It was grounded in mutual business respect.

Sylvia wanted the police department to run smoothly, and helping her boss in his hour of need was second nature to her. "Leave it to me, Chief," she said now. "You keep doing your thing, and let me do this one thing to help."

Knowing further protest would do absolutely no good whatsoever, he'd said "OK, thanks", and left to meet Sheriff Johnson at the Carmichael home. He had to admit it had been nice to arrive 'home' last night, and find his fridge full, and a bowl of fruit on the counter.

Matt pulled into the parking lot at Buck Bay Hospital, and carefully transported the two rifles to Bernice's lab in the basement. Saying "let's have a look at your goodies," she laid the package on a slab counter, and unwrapped the guns.

"I'm not a gun aficionado," said Bernice, "but these are real beauties, aren't they? Antiques."

"Yes. Earl thinks they're both easily more than one hundred years old. Nick, Mason Carmichael's son, said he'd never seen them—which we don't believe—but all the other guns in the cabinet had been handed down from generation to generation."

"They've obviously been well-cared for. That will make our testing easier."

"When will you have something for me? I'm not in a big hurry."

"I believe that's the first time you've ever said that to me," she said.

"Well, I don't have a scary killer on the loose this time, do I? You should take advantage of my laid-back approach because it's probably the only time it will ever happen."

"As it turns out, it's looking like a slow week for me here," she said. "We're finally caught up from the earthquake and tsunami paperwork, and there's no one in intensive care upstairs currently. If you don't turn up any more dead bodies, I might have some actual quiet time for this."

"I'll do my best."

• • •

Matt had forgotten, and left his cell phone in the glove compartment of his car when he went in to see Dr. Ryder. He always placed it there while driving so he wouldn't be tempted to look at texts or email. He pulled it out now and saw that he'd had a call and a voicemail while he'd been in the lab.

Fern!

He quickly hit 'play' on the voicemail and put the phone to his ear.

"Hi, Matt. It's Fern. Thank you for the lovely note you wrote. I do appreciate it. But it doesn't change my mind about not wanting to talk to you further about our relationship. I was already wondering about your feelings for Susie even before I saw the two of you together. I just can't take the chance that you still love her, so...I'm done here. I've been down this road before, and it's too painful for me. I'd like you to use your key and go into my house to get your things, and then leave the key under the doormat. I will stay at mom and dad's until you text me that you've done so. I also ask that you remain professional at work, and not try to corner me when I come in tomorrow. My job is important to me, and I need you to respect that while we regain our friendship footing. Thanks. Bye."

He sat still for a minute, and then replayed the voicemail. Maybe he didn't hear her correctly the first time.

But he had heard correctly.

CHAPTER 30

Matt returned to the office in a daze. He had been taught by his parents that when he was hurting for any reason, the best medicine was to do something nice for someone other than himself. Sort of the opposite of today's 'self-care' mantra.

He called Del Kouse to give him a brief update. Matt wished he had more to tell him, but he knew Del would be happy to hear that they were working on Tyee's case. He was.

"I'm so relieved to hear that you and Sheriff Johnson are serious about helping my family learn what really happened to Tyee," Del told Matt.

"Don't get your hopes up sky-high," warned Matt, "but we're currently testing two old rifles we've found locally. If the guns are in good condition, and we believe they are, and the bullet is as well-preserved as it appears to be, we have a good chance of making a match to the murder weapon."

"That's incredible," said Del. He'd been pacing around the front porch of his home, but now sat down on the floral-cushioned bench swing originally purchased by his grandmother. A large oak tree at the corner of the porch shaded it from the late afternoon sun. "Where did you find the guns?"

"I can't say at this point. It wouldn't be fair to the owner if they turn out to not be a match."

"How long will it take you to know anything?"

"Only a couple of days, I think. They're at the lab now."

"What are your instincts telling you?" Del asked.

Matt hesitated. This could be a crazy wild-goose chase, and he didn't want Del to think it was a done deal. On the other hand, he wanted to be truthful and let him know what he was really thinking.

Truth won out. "This could be a wild-goose chase," he told him, "but my gut is telling me that one of these rifles might be the one we're looking for. The guns' location lines up with some of the historical evidence and stories we've learned about Tyee and the early white settlers. I could be dead wrong, but I'll be surprised if one of these two guns doesn't turn out to be what we're looking for."

"I think you understand how much this would mean for my family."

"What happened to your family was flat-out wrong. The sheriff and I are determined to pursue any leads we develop. Seeing as your case is 117 years old, we'll probably run into a brick wall at some point. But I'm going to stick my neck out now, and tell you that I believe we can get you some answers. Maybe not the final answer, but we're gonna come close."

"Thanks, Chief. I want you to know that we're going to proceed with a proper funeral for Tyee's bones. I've checked state law and local zoning laws and there's nothing to prevent us burying him on our land. So, my father has chosen a spot near the river, and the funeral will be there on Saturday. I'd like you and Sheriff Johnson to come."

"I will let the sheriff know, and we'll be there," Matt promised. He hated funerals, but this one would be special.

• • •

At 6:00 p.m. Matt told Sylvia, who was the only person in the squad room, "Let's go home…such as it is."

"Just leaving," she said, reaching for her tote bag.

"I'm going to get in a run before the sun sets," he told her.

"What kind of shape is the golf course in?" The resort was a major driver of tourism in Port Stirling, and most of the town knew it was important to get it up and running as soon as possible. Port Stirling Links had its detractors, but they were mostly the left-over hippies who didn't want anyone coming to town.

"The ocean-side course got chewed up bad by the tsunami," Matt answered. "It's going to take a while to rebuild the fairways and greens. I've heard the inland course isn't quite as bad, although they've got some fissures from the earthquake in the wrong places. Word is they're going to redesign around the damage on both courses and incorporate it rather than try to return the two courses to their exact original designs."

"They got the cabins and the lodge repaired quickly, I thought, considering the destruction."

"Yeah, Bill Abbott told me the owner brought in additional construction crews from Pennsylvania. He's losing money every day, so I understand the urgency."

"Let's go," Sylvia said, flipping off the lights. "I'll walk you to your car."

He smiled.

• • •

Matt hadn't told Sylvia the full truth. He wanted to swing by Fern's house first and pick up his stuff. On the drive back from Buck Bay after listening to her voicemail one more time, he'd decided that his only course of action was to honor her requests. He had to trust that time would heal these wounds, but, for now, there was no point in his pressing the matter.

He unlocked the front door and walked into the stillness of the empty house. It was Fern who brought the warmth and energy to this place, and without her it was just a bunch of walls.

He packed his things as quickly as he could, and stopped only long enough to place a note on her bed pillow. It read simply 'I love you'.

• • •

Back at his new lodgings, he changed into his running gear. It was a mild, early evening with no wind, so he opted for shorts and a long-sleeved tee. He laced up his sneakers, and then paused to send a brief text to Fern:

"Chief Horning has left the building. The coast is clear."

Maybe he could win her back with charm and humor.

While he would much rather be staying at Fern's house, it was handy having the golf course to run on outside his front door. He needed to avoid mud and debris still left from the tsunami, but it was a joy that he was the only one out here. And the view! No wonder golfers came from all over the world to play here. It was impossible to imagine that you could pay for a better view anywhere.

For the first time since the tsunami had deposited him on the forest floor, Matt considered his future. Running in the balmy coastal air, a treat in late October, the cobwebs seemed to clear from his brain. Maybe because of the Susie/Fern fiasco, or maybe because of the intensity of bringing his town back to normal, or the tragedy of the Tyee Kouse case, Matt realized he'd been in a fog the past couple of weeks, drained and outta gas. Now, for the first time in weeks, he had a glimmer that life would go on. He needed to think about his own situation.

Where would he live, for starters? *Let's recap. Port Stirling is my home now. That's the one thing I know for sure.* Alone or coupled, he loved it here, and his job was important to him. He loved the lifestyle, outdoor-oriented, laid back, friendly. He'd even learned to if not love, at least adapt to the weather. What was that Norwegian saying: 'There is no bad weather, only bad clothing'?

OK, so I'm staying. Now what? He had truly loved living on the ocean. In some ways, it had changed his perspective on the world. The vast expanse and the drama of it all appealed to him. But now he wondered if he would feel safe living that close to the killer Pacific again? Would he go to bed every night wondering if another huge wave would rise up and eat him alive?

As he ran, he weighed the pros and cons, and, essentially, it came down to the odds. Matt knew that the last 'Big One' in Oregon had been 300 years ago. *The odds are in my favor.*

Maybe it was seeing the Carmichael family home that triggered a desire in Matt for something grander than his little cottage of the past nine months. It had suited his purpose, especially considering the circumstances of his job since the day he set foot in Oregon, but Matt had always lived in a larger, more luxurious space since he left the University of Texas and began his adult life. He didn't need a six-car garage, but he wanted a real house on a decent-sized piece of property.

And he wanted his view back. While it was possible he might have occasional tsunami flashbacks, the everyday beauty and tranquility would be a balm to him, and the risk was worth it. *OK, calling my landlord first thing tomorrow and talk about the property.* He didn't know how big the lot had been, or even how much of it was left, but he did know he didn't have close neighbors before. And, if that didn't work out, there were miles of coastline surrounding Port Stirling. He would buy ocean-front property somewhere and hire a builder.

. . .

The balmy, no wind October weather had disappeared during the night. Matt awoke to a banging sound. One of the shutters on his room's big window had blown loose and was thumping against the wall. They were mostly there for looks, but he staggered to the window and could see that they could close, and he did so now, pulling them firmly together.

Back to bed, and the next thing he knew, his alarm was going off.

While it felt beyond trivial to him to even think it based on the circumstances, he really needed to go shopping. He had virtually nothing of his own to get through the days. Bernice had bought him some basics that first morning after the earthquake had deposited all of his worldly goods in the Pacific, and he and Fern had found a few of his things on the beach—his sneakers!—several days later, but he didn't really have any bad weather apparel. Maybe he should take a few days off after Tyee's funeral, and get his life in order. Maybe he should consider going home to Texas for a quick break.

He'd think about that later, but now he was due in the office, and he wanted to get there early in case Fern did come to work. He was determined to show her that he would respect their new boundaries. Plus, no matter what happened between them, Fern was one of the best assets not only in his police department, but in all of city hall.

Seated at his desk, Matt was the first to arrive, and all was quiet in the squad room. He organized his day around further Tyee Kouse research, and some upcoming personnel reviews. He had just begun the paperwork for his first annual reviews of his officers as their chief when the earthquake hit, and now that things were settling down in town, he would get back to that task.

Most of his staff had acted with courage and dedication during the disaster, but one of his officers had been a disappointment. He'd been with the department two years before Matt arrived, and had a couple of black marks in his file, including a traffic stop that he'd handled badly a few weeks before the earthquake. He didn't seem to like the 'community' part of his job, and it had showed when the village needed him most. Matt would have to have a serious discussion on that issue, and he wanted to spend some time thinking about how to handle it. It was tricky with personnel he'd inherited from the old chief, especially this guy who Matt knew didn't much like him. *Tough, I'm not wild about you either.*

Bill Abbott wanted all budget requests for the next year on his desk by December 1, and the personnel reviews were tied into that process. Matt wanted to get his request in early because he had a couple of bigger ticket items in mind, and he wanted to ensure that they got serious, early consideration. He and Jay had fallen in love with drone technology during the Anselmo case, and they really wanted one for the department. And now, there could be no denying how much they needed at least one satellite phone.

His cell phone rang now, and he saw that it was Dr. Ryder. "Bernice, good morning," he said.

"Howdy."

"How come you didn't buy me a rain jacket?" he teased.

"Because when I shopped on your behalf it was seventy-five degrees and beautifully sunny, not fifty degrees and raining like a banshee," she laughed. "Oops."

"Well, I'm a grown man and it's time I did my own shopping."

"Does that mean you're wrapping up taking care of your town?"

"Almost. We've had so much outside help that it made everything go faster. We're not totally out of the woods yet, but the worst is over. Everyone has a roof, and we're starting on planning for the future. Me included. But first I need some boots and a jacket. I kept one chief's uniform here in city hall, and it's the only warm thing I have. Enough about my clothing woes, what do you have for me?"

"A perfect match."

"What?"

"One of the rifles you brought to me yesterday shot the bullet we found in Tyee's skull. It's a perfect match."

"You sure?"

"Positively, one hundred percent sure," Bernice said. "It can't be this easy, can it? Solving a 117-year-old murder case?"

"Wow." Matt thought for a minute about the ramifications of this discovery. "Well, we don't know who actually pulled the trigger, but we can sure narrow it down now."

CHAPTER 31

MONDAY, JULY 25, 1904

Rochana placed the towel around Tyee's neck and securely tied it. He sat in a straight-backed chair on his front porch, and watched his wife take out her sewing scissors from their cloth wrap. He was shirtless on this warm summer day, and his torso was bronzed and strapping.

"You look good, husband," she'd told him at breakfast. "But your hair is too long and unruly. I will cut it today."

Tyee laughed. "I have no choice in the matter?"

"Not if you don't want to scare your customers tomorrow."

"Well, we can't have that, I suppose."

Now, using her comb and scissors, she worked efficiently, the glossy black hair falling to the porch floor.

"There," she said. "You are tidy and respectable once more."

He rose and embraced his wife. "I'm going to jump in the river to clear off the hairs. Come with me," he smiled.

"You tempt me," she returned his smile, "but the children…"

"The children will be fine. Dyami is in charge today. Come with me."

They left their clothes on the river bank, and waded into the cool, refreshing water. Tyee ducked under, shaking his head as he surfaced. Rochana laughed at him, and he took her in his arms.

CHAPTER 32

When Matt got off the phone with Bernice, he could tell there was action next door in the squad room. Lights on, people talking. Fern. He felt the tightening in his stomach. *No point in stalling the inevitable.*

"Good morning, all," Chief Horning said, strolling into the squad room. "Welcome back, Fern. Are you feeling better?"

"Yes, thank you," she replied. "Much better this morning." She looked down at her desk and shifted a file from one side to the other.

"I want to give everyone an update on the Tyee Kouse case," Matt continued in his normal chief voice. "Dr. Ryder just called me, and one of the rifles we found during the Carmichael home search is an exact match with the bullet we found in Tyee's skull."

Fern looked up with wide eyes.

"Is there any room for error?" asked Jay.

"Not according to Bernice. She said that the rifle is in pristine condition, having been well-cared for. Plus, the bullet was perfectly preserved. It's the gun. Sheriff Johnson and I believe the rifle has been in a sealed gun cabinet in Mason Carmichael's possession for decades."

"Tell 'em where we actually found it, Chief," grinned Walt.

"You mean, where *I* actually found it, don't you?" Matt smiled back at his sergeant.

"Might as well get this humiliation over with," Walt said, shaking his head.

"Your sergeant," Matt said, addressing the rest of the room, "pulled a tarp off a vintage Bentley in the Carmichael's garage, and was so taken with the stunning car that he neglected to search it. I suggested we might want to do that."

"And, of course, we found the rifles wrapped up in the Bentley's trunk," Walt said to much laughter. "Which is why Matt is the chief and I'm not."

"We think that the current residents of the house tried to hide their two oldest rifles because they knew we were looking for something," Matt continued, patting Walt on the back.

"Do they know anything about Tyee?" Jay asked.

"They know that their great-great-grandfather Lyndon Carmichael and his buddy Ronald Percy—remember that photo you found?—were foes of Tyee and the other Natives in the region in 1904. Needless to say, they take Lyndon's side."

"So what happens next?" asked Walt. "It's not like we have a killer to arrest, right?"

"We poke around some more, and see if there is any local, and especially family, lore about the relationship between Lyndon and Tyee," Matt told them.

"Don't we already know they didn't like each other?" Jay probed.

"Anecdotally that's true," Matt agreed. "But we can't just assume that Lyndon killed him. I want us to talk more to the Kouse elders, and we'll need to go back a generation or two in the Carmichael family as well. Family stories, history passed down, that kind of thing."

"Mae Walters at the historical society is working with the newspaper archives folks at the University of Oregon," Jay added.

"Yes," said Matt, "and I'd like you to talk to her today and see if they've found anything new. Patty is my next call, and I want her to go back to Dianne Carmichael at the bank and dig deeper on the family lore angle. Walt, you and Rudy are in charge of researching more about the gun. Go over to Buck Bay and bring back both rifles, and then see what you can learn about our murder weapon online. When was it made, how many, that sort of thing."

"What can I do?" Fern spoke for the first time, looking directly at Matt.

"If you're up to it, I'd like you to talk with Mason and Marilyn Carmichael. Mason is Lyndon's great-grandson. He and Marilyn live in California now. Sylvia's got their phone number and email." He looked at Sylvia to confirm that. She nodded.

"Of course I'm up to it," Fern snapped.

Matt visibly paled, and Jay broke the uncomfortable moment. "What are you going to do, Chief?"

"Earl and I will talk again with the Kouse family and see if they know more about the two men's connections. Del Kouse told me a lot, but I want to delve deeper into the family histories. I'll tell the Kouse family that we've identified the murder weapon, and who it belongs to, but the rest of you please hold back that info until I've had a chance to tell them and a few other key people. Any questions anyone?"

"When are we getting our annual reviews?" asked Rudy, sweeping the room like a stand-up comedian. "I wouldn't mind if all of my file was lost in the earthquake."

Everyone laughed.

Matt said, "Glad you brought that up. When I'm not lost in 1904, I'm working on reviews and budget now. I'll be in touch soon." He looked over at Jay. "And, yes, Jay, I'm requesting a drone in our 2022 budget, so you can quit bugging me about it."

Jay punched the air with his fist.

• • •

With a quick glance in Fern's direction—she was staring at her computer screen—Matt headed back to his office. She looked so beautiful, it grabbed his heart. She clearly aimed for professional today with her sharply-cut navy pantsuit and crisp white blouse, but she couldn't harden her soft complexion, bright eyes, and shiny auburn hair. He even loved how her long, slender fingers tapped on her keyboard.

Just give it time. But, what if... He wouldn't let himself finish that thought.

He made quick calls to Sheriff Earl and to Patty to update them on

Bernice's findings. When he and Patty hung up, he could almost visualize her grabbing her badge and bag, and racing out the door. Dianne Carmichael would not know what hit her.

Earl was hugely relieved. "I've had this squeezing feeling inside since we discovered Tyee," he said to Matt. "Being a man of the law, I almost couldn't stand how officers treated the Natives and let down Tyee's family. But if Lyndon Carmichael shot him, I could almost understand the climate in 1904 that would allow a powerful man like him get away with it."

"I doubt if anyone ever knew what really happened. Remember, they had no body. All they knew was that Carmichael and Percy hated Tyee and he hated them. No body, no witnesses coming forward, no one saw anything, according to the report. They probably interviewed Carmichael and Percy, they said they knew nothing, and that, unfortunately, was the end of it."

"I'm glad to at least know who the murder weapon belonged to, and really glad to know my ancestors didn't use my old Betsy on him!"

Matt smiled into the phone. "Your elders are in the clear, Earl. Your rifle was government issued in 1914—too late to have killed Tyee. Wanna go with me to meet some Native American elders? See if they can tell us any stories?"

"I'm all yours. Tell me where and when. It'd be real nice if we could give the Kouse family a little something more in terms of closure."

• • •

Walt and Rudy picked up the rifles from Bernice, and carefully transported them back to Port Stirling city hall, where Matt locked them in the evidence room. The three cops spent some time inspecting the murder weapon, which Rudy had dubbed "Old Clarence".

"The barrel is so clean," Matt noted.

"Old Clarence has been oiled and properly maintained throughout his life," said Walt. "It would work as well today as it did in 1904."

"Old Clarence will not be used again, at least, not in my lifetime," Matt promised. "I think when we wrap this up, this rifle and the bullet in Tyee's skull need to go to the historical society. Both men were important to the times in their own way."

"The Carmichaels aren't going to like that idea," said Walt. "But I like it. I like it a lot."

"Does everyone in town know this family?"

"Most people in Oregon, probably. If I were you, I'd share the info about Old Clarence with your boss as soon as you can. He will have people he needs to tell, too."

"You're not telling me that Bill Abbott will want us to keep this quiet, are you?" asked Matt.

"No, he won't. Too strong on ethics, that guy. But there are people in this town who won't like this news."

Matt stared at Walt. *Great. First Fern leaves me, and now I've got a popular murderer to expose.*

. . .

Fern sent an email to the California Carmichaels that read, "This is Detective Fern Byrne with the Port Stirling Police Department, and I would like to speak with Mr. and Mrs. Mason Carmichael as soon as possible. Please reach me at this number at your earliest convenience."

Her phone rang about twenty minutes later. Mason Carmichael.

After the introductions, Fern asked, "Is Marilyn Carmichael available to talk?"

"She's on the golf course. Where she is most days," her husband answered. "What's this about? Your note sounded serious. Are my kids OK?" He sounded worried.

"They're fine, as far as I know," Fern said. "I'm sorry, I should have mentioned this call wasn't about them. But it is about your family." She paused for effect.

"How so?"

"We're interested in one of the rifles that we believe was taken from the gun cabinet in your den recently and hidden in the trunk of a car in your garage. Do you know anything about that?"

"Nick—my son—told me that the police had found two rifles in the Bentley, but neither one of us knows how they got there," he said, his voice casual. "Why are you interested in them?"

"I'm not at liberty to disclose that information. Just so I'm clear, you know nothing about how two antique rifles ended up in the trunk of that car?"

"That's correct. I don't know, and neither do Nick or Dianne, my daughter. So there's no point in talking to them any further on this matter. Am I clear?" Not so casual now.

"This is a police investigation, Mr. Carmichael. We don't usually let people dictate to whom we can talk. Am I clear?" Not a good day to annoy Fern. Moving on, she said, "It's my understanding that your gun cabinet has two empty slots, on the far left. Is that correct?"

"Yes."

"Was your cabinet custom designed when you built your house?"

"Yes."

"What were or are your plans, then, for the two empty slots?"

"I thought I would add to my collection someday."

"But you haven't, and now you no longer live in the house," Fern noted, and let that hang there for a moment. "How is the display of your guns organized?" Fern asked.

"I'm not sure I remember," he said.

"Let me see if I can refresh your memory. Are they ordered chronologically by age, with the newest on the right, the oldest guns on the far left?"

"That sounds right, but I really can't remember."

"We believe that the two rifles found in the car trunk have been lodged in the empty slots in your cabinet for quite some time, Mr. Carmichael, and someone tried to hide them from us when they knew we had an interest in them."

"Why are you interested in two old rifles?" he asked, sounding agitated. "Neither of those guns has been fired for years. Decades!"

"We know that," Fern said, her voice even. "Who did you inherit them from?"

"My father, Raymond Carmichael."

"And who did he inherit them from?"

"His father, Elroy Carmichael. And he inherited them from Lyndon Carmichael, the founder of our family in Oregon."

"Was there ever a time when these rifles were out of your family's custody? Can you prove their provenance?"

"Yes, I most certainly can prove their origin," he said haughtily. "I have the original bill of sale on Lyndon's account at the mercantile. Historical items are honored in my family, and we treat them with respect."

Fern made a note. "OK, has your family passed down stories about the early days of Lyndon's time in Port Stirling?"

"Naturally. My family considers him one of Oregon's founding fathers. He was an amazing man. What specifically are you referring to?"

"Well, as an Oregonian, I'm interested in his commercial ventures, and particularly his role in building the jetty and the lighthouse."

Fern settled back in her chair while Mason began to talk about his favorite subject, Lyndon Carmichael. He did have interesting, fun stories to tell, and Fern enjoyed hearing about the early days of the white settlers. At one point, he mentioned Lyndon's good friend, Ronald Percy, but there was no acknowledgement of Lyndon's dealings with the Native Americans.

"I remember seeing a photo of Lyndon, Percy, and a Native chief, Tyee Kouse," she lied. "How did they get on with the Natives in those days?"

"Not well, as you can imagine," Mason said. "The Indians resented the changes that Lyndon and his friends were making. They stood in the way of progress as much as they could until it became inevitable."

"Did you ever hear any stories of violence between the whites and the Native Americans?" Fern asked.

Carmichael paused. "Not directly, no. But the early days of Oregon were a rough time, and I'm sure there were incidents along the path to development. But nothing involving my family that I know of."

"Teddy Roosevelt didn't help smooth relations, did he? At least, not if I remember my history correctly."

He laughed. "No, he had about as much use for the Indians as Lyndon did."

"Doesn't that seem a bit harsh to you now?"

"I don't like to think of people being hurt certainly, but Port Stirling and the state would not have moved forward if the settlers had let the Indians push them around."

"Did Lyndon Carmichael murder Tyee Kouse, Mr. Carmichael? Was he in the way, and needed to be disposed of?"

Dead silence. "Is that what you think?" he said finally, his voice cold as ice. "That's the most ridiculous thing I've ever heard. Lyndon Carmichael was the epitome of an upstanding citizen. He was a man of strong values, family values, and a devout Christian. How dare you even suggest such a thing! You'd better watch yourself, Miss Byrne."

"That's Detective Byrne."

CHAPTER 33

Matt and Sheriff Earl spent an interesting afternoon with Del Kouse, Robert and Linda, his father and mother, Hakan and Fala, Robert's parents, and Meda, Hakan's sister. They met at Hakan's home because Fala was still recovering from her nasty fall during the earthquake.

Hakan and Fala's home was situated on raised ground about 200 yards from the river, not far from the Carmichael's house. But the comparison ended there. It was more of a family compound, with three additional simple structures dotting the property among several tall fir trees. It was pleasant and comfortable, but not palatial like their neighbor.

"It's nice to meet you two ladies," Matt said to Linda and Fala, who had not made the trip to the lighthouse to view Tyee's remains. "I hope you're feeling stronger now, Fala." A piano behind Fala was covered in family photos, all in plain silver frames, and one wall displayed a large artistic quilt.

"I am," she replied with a broad smile. "I hated to miss the trip to the lighthouse, but this old body was talking to me the day you all went to visit Tyee. It was more important for Hakan and Meda to view their grandfather."

"We have news," Matt started, looking at Earl, who nodded. "We've found the rifle that fired the bullet into Tyee, and we know who it belonged to."

There was a collective gasp in the room from every Kouse.

"Where was it found, Chief Horning?" asked Meda. "Tell us," she instructed, pointing her cane at him.

"In the trunk of a car in a garage on Mason and Marilyn Carmichael's property, not far from here, actually. It had been hidden there when we started asking questions about old rifles."

"Mason Carmichael is Lyndon's great-grandson," said Hakan slowly. "I knew his father, Raymond."

"Yes, he is," Matt confirmed. "One of my staff is talking to Mason now. We want to find out how the rifle got in the trunk, and where it's been since 1904. We hope to have more information for you soon."

"The Carmichael home is on the next property down river from us," Meda said, frowning. "When Mason and Marilyn Carmichael built that monstrosity of a house, they said it was on land originally owned by Lyndon. It was land he took from Tyee's widow, my grandmother, Rochana."

"Did Lyndon live on the property when Tyee lived here?" Earl asked.

"We think so," Hakan answered. "I first met Raymond fishing on the river when we were kids. He told me that his grandfather used to have a house around here that burned down. But Raymond still came to this fishing hole that he remembered as a kid."

"Is Raymond still alive?" asked Matt.

"No," said Hakan. "He died about four years ago. He lived up in Buck Bay, I think. Very wealthy man. I last saw him about five years ago at a meeting at the casino. He told me he had lung cancer, and I felt bad for him. He was a nice man, unlike his idiot son."

"Mason?" asked Matt.

"Yes. No use for that man," Hakan said, shaking his head. "He's a shadow of his ancestors. Accomplished nothing of importance in his lifetime."

"Did you and Raymond ever discuss your grandfathers?"

"Yes, a few times. We knew they didn't like each other much. We used to laugh about it."

Added Meda, "Raymond once told me that his father and grandfather told him that the world would be a better place with no Indians. But Raymond was not like them, and we were all friendly. Mason seems to take after his grandfather and great-grandfather more. Always looks down his nose at us. We tried to be friendly when he was building next door, but he wanted nothing to do with us," she said, glowering.

"Aunt Meda's right," spoke Robert for the first time. "I tried real hard to be friendly with Mason—we were in school together—but he didn't have the time of day for me. Our family has steered clear of him and his two kids. No point."

"Same with me and Dianne and Nick," added Del. "Our generations don't mix either. Nick still hangs out with Ronald Percy's great-great-grandson—the Percy's lived around here, too—and it's like they think they're Lyndon and Ronald. Weird, if you ask me."

"Bad blood all the way around, then," said Earl. "Hakan, do you remember if there was ever any talk about Lyndon being responsible for your grandfather's disappearance? Any gossip?"

"My father was convinced that the white settlers made Tyee 'disappear'. He didn't know what happened, but he was sure they were to blame somehow," Hakan said.

"Father was always ranting about Lyndon," Meda added. "We all thought he was a little crazy and we didn't pay that much attention to him, but he was convinced they, in his words, 'disappeared' Tyee. I can remember it plain as day."

Hakan laughed. "Our father Dyami was a little crazy, but maybe now not so crazy, huh?"

"Maybe now not so crazy," Earl agreed, and, unusual for the grumpy sheriff, reached out and hugged both Hakan and Meda.

* * *

"Dianne Carmichael is on the warpath," Patty told Matt, "and that pun is on purpose."

"Great," said Matt, "just what I need, another woman mad at me. Forget I said that," he added hurriedly.

"Woman problems, uh-oh," Patty hoped that Matt would somehow feel her warmth and sympathy for him through the phone lines. "She said to tell you and Earl that you'd better back off, and that if her family name gets dragged through the mud, she's holding you personally responsible."

"Ooh, threats," Matt said. "Did she admit to removing the rifles from her daddy's gun cabinet and hiding them in the car trunk?"

"No, 'fraid not, and I pushed her on this point more than once. I even asked her why she would do such a dumb thing as trying to hide the rifles. She just sat there and stared at me. She's not going to fess up. She did mention that they were her father's most treasured possessions, and she and Nick were worried you'd take them away and they would never get them back."

"Any admission that her family might have been responsible for Tyee's murder?"

"Nope. Just that the rifles are family heirlooms, and they didn't want you and Earl to have them. Do you want me to arrest her for obstruction of justice?"

"Good God, no…at least, not yet," Matt said. "Let's see how this plays out over the next day or so. Earl and I got some info from the Kouse family, and I wanted to hear from you, Fern, and Walt first. Earl and I will put it all together tonight, and decide on a course of action. Sound good to you?"

"No," Patty whined. "I want to go back and arrest her. She's a very unpleasant woman."

"Last time I checked we can't arrest people for being unpleasant," Matt laughed.

"If I were queen, we would. Should be a law. Be pleasant or go to jail."

"I doubt Dianne will become any more pleasant, especially when she probably has to tell her dad what's happened. Likely not looking forward to making that call."

• • •

This time, Fern knocked before entering Matt's office. Of course, she tensed up first, recalling what she'd seen the last time she was here. Her throat felt tight, and she knew her face was turning pink. But that was then and this is now, so she squared her shoulders, and went in.

During the uncomfortable, terse meeting, she reported in a few succinct sentences her phone call with Mason Carmichael.

"He was very defensive," she told Matt. "Swatted away any suggestion of violence on the part of Lyndon toward Tyee, and insisted that Lyndon was the finest human being who ever walked the planet."

"Yeah, the family seems determined to maintain their brand's image— Dianne and Nick were the same. Did he fess up to hiding the guns?"

"No, but he's smart enough to know you have him cold turkey on that front. Did Nick or Dianne admit they hid them?"

"Nope," answered Matt. "Deny, deny, deny seems to be the family's strategy."

"Figures. Mason did establish that the rifle in question belonged to Lyndon and has been passed down from father to son ever since." Fern consulted her notes. "Says he has the original bill of sale under lock and key."

"Did you ask him if the gun had ever been out of the family's possession?"

"Do you think I'm stupid?" she said sharply and glared at him. "Certainly I asked him. The answer is no."

"Just confirming," Matt said quietly.

"He wants his rifle back."

"Tough cookies."

Fern almost smiled, but caught herself. "I told him you would say that, not in those exact words."

"I told Earl that I believe that rifle and the bullet from Tyee's skull should go to the historical society."

"Whether we can prove Lyndon shot him or not?"

"Yes. We know that gun fired the bullet that killed Tyee, and we now know that gun belonged to Lyndon Carmichael. And we know that Lyndon considered Tyee a troublemaker who was in his way on the road to riches. If nothing else, it's an interesting bit of Oregon's history, don't you think?"

"I do," Fern agreed. "I wish there was some way to prove Lyndon shot him, and to know why and, especially, how Tyee ended up buried under the lighthouse. But I've racked my brain, and I don't see a way forward to solving this mystery."

"I'm with you, and it's probably going to drive us both crazy the rest of our lives." He paused. "Speaking of..."

Fern held up her hand, palm facing him. "Don't. Please. Don't."

He looked forlorn, but said in a strong voice, "I'm sorry. I'll respect your wishes."

"Anything I left out?" she said briskly, rising from her chair.

"No. Very thorough briefing. I'm just waiting on Walt and Rudy to report on what they've learned about the rifle. Thank you."

"You're welcome," she said, and left his office.

. . .

In the end, it was Sergeant Walt's report on the rifle that gave Matt pause. He and Rudy, after researching online, had identified the gun. It turned out to be a Springfield rifle, similar to Earl's. But therein was the problem.

"It's the M1903 Springfield," Walt told Matt. "Caliber .30-06. It was the standard U.S. service rifle between 1903 and 1936. After that, the Army used it as a sniper rifle."

Rudy added, "The Coast Guard has used it, too."

"Right," said Walt. "It was officially approved by the U.S. military in June, 1903, and was used in World War 1. They made the model between 1903 and 1949, and it's still popular with gun collectors."

"So Lyndon Carmichael was an early-adopter," said Matt.

"Maybe Roosevelt gave it to him to shoot Injuns," remarked Walt. Rudy laughed. But Matt said, "That's enough, Walt," although he smiled when he said it.

"Do you see our problem, gentlemen?" asked Matt.

"Plain as the nose on your face, Chief," said Walt. "Lyndon shot Tyee in 1904 with this rifle, but how in the hell did his body end up under the foundation of the lighthouse that was built in 1901?"

"Nail on the head, Walt."

. . .

Fern purposely left out one thing from her report to Matt about her telephone call with Mason Carmichael: that he'd threatened her. 'Watch yourself' could mean a lot of things, but after what happened to her during the Anselmo case, Fern would never take a threat lightly again. She didn't tell Matt, however, because she knew how he'd react, and this case didn't need any more drama. But she would keep a close eye on the Carmichael family from here on out.

. . .

Matt's phone rang. Earl.

"Howdy, Sheriff. What's up?"

"I've found something fairly interesting. Do you have a minute?"

"Yeah. I have a couple of updates for you, too. Go ahead."

"I went back through the county's criminal files between 1900 and 1910 to see if anything jumped out at me."

"And did it?"

"Yes. It may be nothing, but after sleeping on it last night, it's still niggling at me. Like you, I like to listen to my gut—which, in my case, is prodigious—and it's screaming at me today. In 1901, they had a big community ceremony to mark the grand opening of the lighthouse on the new jetty. French champagne, cake, the whole nine yards. Apparently, Ronald Percy drank a bit too much and got belligerent. Thought Lyndon Carmichael was taking all the credit, when, in fact, it was mostly Percy's company that did the construction work."

"On the lighthouse or the jetty?" interrupted Matt.

"Both, actually. Percy owned all the rock quarries around here, for starters, and he employed over one hundred men. The old newspaper articles that Mae Walters found at the U of O indicated that it was Carmichael's planning and Percy's construction working together that got it done in the end."

"So what happened at the grand opening?"

"Lyndon and Percy had words and it got out of hand, and Percy took a swing at him. It connected, and broke Carmichael's nose and one cheekbone. Classic sucker punch, sounds like. Percy was arrested on the spot, and spent the night in the county jail."

"Guess Tyee wasn't the only thorn in Lyndon's side," said Matt.

"Yeah, Carmichael filed a charge of assault and battery against Percy and it went to court. Because there were about seventy witnesses, Percy was convicted. There was no weapon involved, and the witnesses all said Percy was drunk, so he was convicted of a misdemeanor, not a felony. He was fined $200 and spent an additional five days in jail. Plus, he had to apologize to Carmichael in a public setting."

"Ha! I thought they were always great buddies?"

"Apparently, not always," Earl said. "Like I said, I don't know exactly why this is bothering me. I guess it's the lighthouse connection. It just seems that Tyee's case revolves around that darn lighthouse, and I'll be damned if I can figure out why."

"Nick Carmichael and Ronald Percy's great-great-grandson—I can't remember his name—are good friends and have been since childhood. You could follow up with them and ask if they knew about this episode. And maybe if they've heard any other stories. You didn't find any other criminal records?"

"Only Percy's arrest. I will talk to these kids," Sheriff Earl said. "All we've got now is the descendants' memories and family lore."

"My news is about the rifle. Walt and Rudy researched Lyndon's gun, and it was manufactured sometime in 1903 at the feds' Springfield Armory. Tyee was killed with it in 1904, so how did his body get buried under the lighthouse in 1901?"

"Clearly, it didn't."

"Right," said Matt. "I'm baffled."

"Well, let's see what the families say. I'll let you know. Where will you be tomorrow morning?"

"Depends. I'm meeting with an architect at 10:00 a.m. I've bought the land that the bungalow I rented sat on, and I'm going to build me a house."

"That's good news. About time you put down roots here. How much of the bluff is left to build on?"

"My former landlady owned about three acres on that spot, mostly running north to south, all ocean-view, and the quake took out about 40 feet of the bluff. There's still about 300 feet between Ocean Bend Road and the new bluff. Plenty of room for me to build my dream house. She took

my offer last night. I'll have to wait until the Building Code Division cer-
tifies that the new bluff is stable, and then get in line with all the other
construction projects, but that's OK."

"Happy for you, Chief. Talk soon."

CHAPTER 34

att called Ed Sonders and Jay, and asked them to meet him at the site of his former home at 6:00 p.m.

"Why?" asked Ed.

"We're going to drink a beer and watch the sunset."

"I'm in," said Ed.

"Will there be food?" asked Jay.

• • •

Fern was about to leave the squad room and head for home. Her parents provided what she needed after the shock of Matt's behavior, but she was anxious to be back in her real home by herself to process some things.

Her phone rang, and it was an unknown number with an out-of-area code. She was tired and it was late, but she couldn't not pick up.

"Detective Byrne," she answered.

"Hello, detective, this is Marilyn Carmichael. You talked with my husband earlier today, is that correct?"

"Yes, hello, and thanks for getting back to me," said Fern, surprised.

"I would like to clear up something that I understand he told you in error. Is this a good time for you to talk?"

"Yes. Please go ahead."

"Mason filled me in on your conversation. He said that you asked about any stories that may have been passed down about violence between the settlers and the Native Americans."

"Yes. He said 'nothing specific' if I recall without checking my notes."

"He lied to you, detective."

"Excuse me, but does Mason know you're calling me?"

"I'm a grown woman, and I don't share everything with my husband anymore."

"I didn't mean to imply that you needed his permission," Fern said hastily. "Of course you don't. It's only that my experience so far has been that the Carmichaels stick together."

"I don't have Lyndon's blood in me," she retorted. "I'm an outsider."

"OK." *Where are you going with this, Marilyn?*

"The truth is that there were several instances of violence in Lyndon's generation against the Natives, and Mason is well aware of that fact, and specific incidents. I'd hate to see him get in a position where he's lied to the police."

"Well, yes, I'd say that is a problem," Fern told her. "I'm more interested in any stories you could tell us, specifically any involving Lyndon and Tyee Kouse, a Native American Chief, who also lived in Port Stirling. We know he had a difficult relationship with Lyndon."

Marilyn Carmichael laughed. It was a guttural laugh that sounded like a woman who spent days on the golf course, and evenings in old, mid-century Palm Springs restaurants and bars, smoking and drinking martinis.

"Difficult is not the word I would use to describe those two," Marilyn said. "They despised each other, and were constantly at war over something. Sometimes trivial and sometimes major. Sometimes Tyee won the battle, but more often than not, it was usually Lyndon who had the new laws on his side."

"But a war of words and out-and-out violence are two different things," Fern offered.

"Mason likes to tell the story about Lyndon and Tyee fighting over upriver timber rights. They got into a knock-down drag-out fight over it, and it ended with no winner and two losers. Both men were pummeled within an inch of their lives, before they were pulled apart. A bloody mess."

"Good grief."

"Yes. The government eventually stepped in and decided it was actually Ronald Percy, Lyndon's close friend, who owned that property. Wouldn't you say that nearly beating a man to death is an act of violence?"

"I would say that, yes."

"It was the Wild West, however, and I suspect events like this weren't totally unique to Lyndon and Tyee. Why, if I may ask, are you interested in this old history?"

"I appreciate your call and your honesty more than you can know, but I'm not at liberty to discuss our case yet," Fern said.

"I understand. Case, huh? That sounds serious. Should my family be worried?"

"No, none of you is at risk, I can tell you that. We're interested in some things that happened many decades ago," Fern said. "But you might tell your husband and kids that hiding guns and lying to us will not help."

"Gotcha. Thank you for your time, Detective Byrne. I hope we can meet some day."

"I'd like that, too, Mrs. Carmichael. Thank you so much for your call. I will pass this along to our chief of police."

. . .

Finally, a little after 8:00 p.m. Fern drove into her garage, and sat in the dark for a few minutes. She'd made it through a day without Matt… but it had been excruciating. Her stomach hurt, her eyes burned, and the loss felt like a body part missing.

They had such a good thing going. *How could he do this to me?*

He says he didn't. It was her.

He could have pushed her aside. He let it happen.

She was on top. Very aggressive woman. Maybe he was trying to get rid of her once and for all.

Ha. He's a man who shot a cold-blooded killer in the middle of the forehead. And he can't handle a blonde from Texas?

It's a totally different situation, and you know it.

All I know is how I feel, and I feel like hell. I love him, I hate him, I miss him, I hate him.

You need a drink.

First smart thing you've said.

• • •

The men sat in folding chairs in the dirt where Matt's living room had been. The stone fireplace, looking smaller and lonely, still stood in its place, now dangerously close to the edge of the cliff.

"I'm as sentimental as the next guy," Ed said, "but why are we here when there's a perfectly good bar open down the road?" He looked down at his usually spit-and-polish shoes which were now covered in dust. "We shouldn't even be here."

"Good question," said Jay.

"What a couple of wimps," said Matt. "I thought you were both tough cops, and you're whining about a little dirt on your shoes? Can you see this from your precious bar?" he waved his arm out to sea.

It was a glorious sight, the sun just beginning its descent into the Pacific. A few linear white clouds on the horizon started to turn pink and orange. The sea was calm, single waves lapping quietly at the shore 300 feet below them.

"S'pose not," admitted Ed, who both men knew loved what was Matt's former cottage and yard perched above the ocean. "I am going to miss this place," he said seriously now.

"You won't have to," Matt said, beaming.

"What's up?" said Jay, suspicious as always.

"I bought the land last night and I'm going to build my house here," he burst out with it, spreading his arms out wide.

"No shit?" said Ed.

"No shit. My landlady has in her words 'had it with Oregon', and was delighted to sell me this parcel. We'll probably see a lot of people fleeing in the months ahead."

"That's terrific," said Ed. "Congrats! How much land are we talking?"

Matt stood and pointed north up the coastline. "See that stunted tree that's blown backwards? That's the north end of my property, and it runs from there out to Ocean Bend Road. And south, it ends where the bluff takes that little jog outward, past that about twenty feet."

"Wow, that's a big lot," said Jay. "This is cool."

"It's just over three acres total," Matt said, still beaming.

"That's plenty of room for a house, even a big one," Ed said.

"And a garden," Matt added. "I miss my Texas one."

"Does Fern know about this plan?" Jay had to ask. "Have you told her?"

"Nope. She isn't much interested in talking to me right now." He looked down and rubbed his hands on this thighs, pushing hard.

"She'll get over it," Jay said. "Just needs some time."

"She either will or she won't," Matt said. "I thought it might help if I made a big statement about staying in Port Stirling. I think she thinks I might go back to Texas."

"What in the hell are we talking about?" Ed asked.

"Fern saw Matt and Susie making out in his office, and she broke up with him," Jay told Ed, sounding like he was in the seventh grade.

Big Ed stared hard at Matt, took a sip of his beer, and said slowly, "Please tell me that isn't true."

"Part of it is true," Matt said. "But I wasn't making out with Susie," he glared at Jay. "Fern saw something unfortunate, and took it the wrong way. She doesn't want anything to do with me outside of the office."

"Jesus Christ! What were you doing? How could you let this happen?" Ed yelled. "Fern is worth all three of us put together."

"I know that. Jeez, please don't yell. I was trying to get Susie to leave and to realize that we weren't ever getting back together, and it kinda backfired."

"Can you fix it?"

"Not based on today, I'd say. Fern has asked me to not corner her in the office. To let her do her job, and not try to talk about us. I have to respect that."

"Yes, you do," said Ed. "Fern is a serious woman, and she doesn't act frivolously. Sounds like you're just going to have to wait it out."

"Well, I'm not doing that," Matt said raising his chin. "I have a life to live, in case y'all hadn't noticed. I'm going to build a house and do my job and see my friends. Fern will do what Fern will do."

"Have you heard from Susie?" asked Jay.

"Repeatedly," Matt muttered. "She wants me to come home for a vacation, and see if we still have a spark."

"Oh, for Chrissakes," Ed said disgustedly. "Maybe you should slap a restraining order on her."

"I can't do that. I was married to the woman."

"Or," said Jay, grinning ear to ear, "you could not do it, but I could tell Fern you did."

The three cops laughed. "What are we, fifteen years old?" Matt said through his laughter. "Does this male female stuff ever get any easier?"

"No," said Ed. "Most definitely not."

CHAPTER 35

M att had called together a meeting of the Chinook County major crime team, and they all sat around the table in city hall on beautiful new chairs that Olive Joiner had donated to the city.

"It's the simple things in life that are important," Matt started. "Like having a decent chair to sit in during a meeting instead of a folding chair with your butt falling through."

Laughter and head nods around the table. "Let's not take our calm, peaceful existence for granted ever again," offered Patty, seated to Matt's right. "I noticed driving into town today that things are looking much better in Port Stirling. Cleaner and new. I know it's probably bittersweet, but you guys have done a nice job bouncing back."

"We're not there yet," Jay said, "but thanks, Patty. It's been a slog."

"We've had a lot of outside-the-area help, too," Matt said. "Especially cleanup and construction teams—that's what you're seeing evidence of. But I agree with you, never taking our small-town vibe for granted again. How are things going in your towns?"

"Twisty River is almost there, too," said Sheriff Earl. "There's just a couple of businesses and the mill down by the river that still need repairs. The tsunami pretty much leveled them, but they're all rebuilding."

"What's needed most right now," added Patty, "is landscaping help, including at my house! The big wave left a mess for miles anywhere close to the river. Ted and I did a little work last weekend, but we need professional help."

"I heard there's a garden center in Eugene that's volunteering their employees to help in Buck Bay," said Fern. "Maybe you could tap into that."

"Good tip," said Patty. "I'll follow up. If we don't hurry up and replant somewhat along the river, it's going to be a real mess once the fall rains start."

"We have updates for you on the Tyee Kouse murder case," Matt changed the subject. "I'll tell you about the firearm first, and then Earl, Fern, and Patty can report on their conversations with some of the principals in our investigation."

He brought the team up to date on the latest information on the gun, and then turned the floor over to Fern to talk about her calls with both Mason and Marilyn Carmichael.

Fern was wearing a royal blue sweater, slim black pants, and black booties. Her hair needed a cut, but her salon had permanently closed and her hairdresser had fled Port Stirling, so she pulled it back in a ponytail today, set off with small gold hoop earrings. She was twitchy as she described her conversations with the Carmichaels, but calmed down as she got into it.

"There goes my campaign contribution from Mason," said Earl with a straight face when Fern finished her update. The sheriff was the only one in the room who didn't know about the tension between Matt and Fern, and so didn't recognize the uneasy atmosphere.

"We'll let you return the one vintage rifle we aren't keeping to him," said Matt. "Maybe that will get you back in his good graces. If not, we'll all have to pony up before the election, I guess."

"He's running unopposed," Bernice said. "Like always."

"Because no one wants this job," Earl said. "Some days I don't want it either. But yesterday was not one of those days. Matt and I spent the better part of the afternoon with Tyee Kouse's family, listening to old stories about the white settlers and the interactions with the Natives. Good stuff for a history buff like me."

"I didn't enjoy my job yesterday," Patty jumped in. "Dianne Carmichael is not a bowl of cherries."

"Did she admit to hiding the rifles?" Earl asked.

"Nope, and she's not going to, even though we've got her red-handed on that front. It sounds like Mason, her father, came close to admitting his kids had done it. Was that your take, Fern?"

"Close, but no actual cigar," Fern replied. "He hinted that Nick and Dianne were worried we would take the guns and he wouldn't get them back, but I couldn't get him to say that the two of them hid them in the car trunk."

"But we know they did," Patty said. "Dianne was quite hostile toward me, and wouldn't give an inch. It's clear the Carmichaels are worried about their family name and Lyndon's sainthood. It remains to be seen how far they'll go to protect it."

"I've got one extra nugget of info," Jay said. "I talked to Pete Percy, Ronald Percy's great-great-grandson yesterday. He and Nick Carmichael are pals. I asked him about the fight between Lyndon and Ronald at the lighthouse grand opening. He confirmed that it was a well-known event in his family's history. He also told me that while Lyndon and Ronald did work together on many early projects around the county, and were neighbors and knew each well throughout their lives, they weren't always the best of friends."

"Mae Walters at the historical society confirms that," Patty said. "She says that Lyndon and Ronald were very competitive, and they both wanted to be 'King of Chinook County'. They each had their own slice of commerce, but they fought over most everything that came their way."

"But the families socialized together, according to the old newspaper clippings," said Matt. "So they must not have been true enemies."

"Maybe," said Patty. "But society was important then, and they would've put up a good front no matter what was going on behind the scenes."

"Remember," Jay continued, "that Pete doesn't miss a chance to jab at Lyndon, and Nick does the same about Ronald. It's like they're still competing through their family history."

"I'm at a loss as to where to go next," Sheriff Earl admitted, running his hand over his crewcut. "We certainly don't have any eyewitnesses."

"And all we do have is circumstantial evidence," Matt joined in. "We know the rifle that killed Tyee belonged to Lyndon Carmichael. We know the two men were bitter enemies trying to share the same land. But we can't prove that Lyndon actually pulled the trigger. Tyee's grandson, Hakan, and his granddaughter, Meda, both believe it was Lyndon who 'disappeared' their grandfather, but they have no proof either, other than their father's lifelong conviction it was Lyndon's doing. And, of course, Dyami, Tyee's son, is dead now."

"To me, it doesn't seem fair to even 'out' that the rifle that killed Tyee belonged to the Carmichaels," said Fern. "What if it had been stolen, and then Lyndon got it back somehow? I know Mason said it had been in his family's possession the entire time, but he doesn't really know where it was prior to his father giving it to him."

Matt looked at her. "That's a strong point. Since before Raymond Carmichael gave it to Mason, no one on this earth today knows where that rifle might have been."

Fern looked pensive for a moment. "Unless Mason or Marilyn tell us that Raymond confessed that Lyndon killed Tyee, and he heard it directly from his grandfather, we'll never know. And Mason is not going to tell us even if he knows. I asked him point-blank if Lyndon murdered Tyee, and he got all huffy, and said it was the most ridiculous question he'd ever heard. So, if Mason knows what really happened, it's going to his grave with him."

"Is it enough for Tyee's descendants to know that he didn't abandon them but was murdered? And who owned the rifle that killed him?" asked Bernice.

"They are thrilled with the news," Matt answered. "Knowing that he didn't leave of his own free will has fixed decades of anguish for the family. I'd love to present them with a foolproof case of what happened that day to Tyee, but it's just not possible. They always believed that Lyndon was responsible, and finding the rifle in his descendant's home sealed it for the family. I think they're good, Bernice."

"Man, this is hard, though," said Jay, shaking his head. "They deserve to know what happened. So unfair."

"We all feel that way," said Matt. "But sometime in a cop's life he has to accept that he's come to a dead end. As much as I hate this—and I do—I believe we're at that stop sign on Tyee's murder."

"Then the next question is what do we do with the facts?" Fern said to the group. "At the very least, I think we need to publicly announce that the 1904 disappearance of Tyee Kouse has been solved, and that he was murdered."

"Strongly agree," said Earl. "It's the least we can do officially for the Kouse family. We'll also have to explain how and where we found his body. It's important historically, in my view."

"Yes, we'll tell the tale, for sure," Matt said. "I think it should come from your org, Ed. It's really a state-wide story of interest, and you were there when the skeleton was discovered. And bring in Mae Walters from the historical society, too, and include some early photos of Tyee. I'll ask Del Kouse if he wants to comment on the finding."

"I'm happy to have this come from the Oregon State Police, my boss will love it, but there's an elephant in the room," Ed said. "What do we say about the rifle and the bullet in Tyee's skull?"

"What do you think we should say?" asked Matt.

"I get your point totally, Fern, but I think we have to show the police work you all did to test the bullet, track the rifle, match the gun to the bullet. And not just because doing our job makes us look good—although it does. It's highly relevant to the story."

"Let's consider this," said Patty, "what if, say, two years from now, someone comes forward and says 'my great-grandpa told me he stole Lyndon Carmichael's gun and killed Tyee Kouse with it, and then gave the gun back to him'?"

"I'm inclined to go with the odds," said Ed, "and the strong odds are that Lyndon Carmichael shot Tyee in the back of the head."

"But it's going to hurt the Carmichael's reputation," argued Fern. "There's no denying that."

"We'll make it perfectly clear that this is a history lesson, and it has nothing to do with the descendants of the family," said Ed. "Beyond that, I don't really care if the Carmichaels have their little feelings hurt. From all we've learned about that family, they've run roughshod over everything and everyone who's ever gotten in their way of getting richer and richer."

"I'm with Ed," said the sheriff. "Maybe it's time the Carmichaels know what it feels like to be on the other end of the stick."

"Revenge?" said Fern, raising her eyebrows, her eyes widening. "That's not like the two of you gentlemen I know."

"It's hardly revenge," said Earl. "It's telling the story as we know it. Ed's right, the odds are that Lyndon did it. I've thought about nothing else since we learned about the rifle, and I'm having trouble coming up with any other plausible scenario. Lyndon shot Tyee, and I agree with Jay, Tyee's family deserves to know what really happened. It's the best we can do," he said gently.

She sat looking across the table at Earl. The two of them had been good friends going back to Fern's days at the county. "I trust you, Earl, and you too, Ed, and we're all in this together. Who will tell the Carmichaels what's coming? They should have advance notice."

Matt noticed that Fern did not say she trusted him, and it felt like a knife in his belly. He looked over at Bernice, and she was already looking in his direction. *Does that woman know everything I'm thinking the minute I think it?*

Matt spoke. "Let's roll this out this way. Bernice, Patty, and Jay, are you guys comfortable with going public?"

The three nodded affirmatively.

"OK, then it's unanimous. Earl, you and I will take the second rifle back to the Carmichaels. You'll be the good cop and I'll be the bad. Fern's right, we don't need them to be blind-sided. You give them back the gun, and I'll explain to them that we're keeping the other because it was used in the commission of a crime. I will also tell them that the Oregon State Police will be releasing details of Tyee's death with some historical perspective. I'll go as easy as possible, and make sure they understand we won't drag Lyndon's name through the mud."

"Patty, Ed, and Bernice will go—if you want to—with Earl and me to tell the Kouse family what we're doing. Ed and Patty found the body, and Bernice did…well, what Bernice does. They may have questions for one or more of the three of you, and with your involvement, it feels like the right way to handle it. Or is it overkill? What do you say?"

"I'd really enjoy meeting them," said Patty. "And since I had to deal with Dianne Carmichael, I think I'm owed part of the good times," she grinned.

"Me too," said Ed. "I want to make sure that I get their story straight for the public."

"Yeah, me too," said Bernice. "My job will probably scare the daylights out of them, but they may have some forensic questions."

"The proper burial of Tyee's bones is happening tomorrow morning on their ancestral land," said Matt. "Earl and I have been invited to the family ceremony, and we're going. Let's get through that first and give the family some peace. I'll call them the following day and arrange a visit with all of us."

"It feels incomplete," Earl mused.

"It is," said Matt.

CHAPTER 36

Y ou really need to quit calling me, Susie," Matt said into the phone. "I'm busy, and I don't like the interruptions at work."

"You can make me stop bugging you," she said.

"Oh, yeah? How?"

"Come to Texas for a visit. You need a vacation after everything you've been through. It would do you so much good to see your family and unwind from the horror of the earthquake."

"Not to mention spend some time with you, right?" he said.

"Maybe once or twice, so we can make sure we don't want to revisit our marriage. I know you believe it's over, but I'm not so sure. I'd like us both to be sure we're completely done. I'd like to move on, too, you know."

He snorted. "You've already moved on, Susie—you married again, remember?"

"That was obviously a rebound thing. Which I now deeply regret. He's such an ass."

"I'm sorry you picked the wrong guy," Matt said. He did feel badly that her second marriage was a disaster. She deserved to find the right man. But he knew it was no longer him.

"If I come and we work through this, will you promise to leave me alone?"

"Yes, I will. I just want us to be sure, Matt." She sounded sincere. "We had a sweet love going once, didn't we?"

"Once upon a time, as it turned out. OK, you win, I'll wrap up some things here and I'll come visit. I'll let my parents know—they'll be thrilled."

"Hooray! If you'd rather not stay at the ranch, you can stay with me. I ramble around in this big ol' house."

"No, I will stay at the ranch, that's non-negotiable. And it will be a quick visit, I have lots going on here. Do you understand?"

"Whatever you say, darlin'."

. . .

After the men left the crime team meeting, Patty and Bernice appeared in no hurry to leave, so Fern stayed for a while and talked to them.

"Did you get your garage door fixed?" Patty asked her.

"Yes, a contractor who's been working on the high school swung by my house last week on his way home and fixed it for me. He lives down the street from me, knew about my issue. It's good as new. How are things at your place? I heard you and Ted were surrounded by a sea of mud."

"You heard right. What a friggin mess," Patty said. "I'm going to talk to that Eugene nursery you mentioned and see if we can get some help this weekend."

"Doesn't Twisty River have a nice little garden center?" Bernice asked. "I seem to remember going there as a kid with my mom."

"*Had* a nice little garden center," Patty said. "It was down by the river and they got completely wiped out by the tsunami. They're an older couple and have decided to call it quits. He told me they'd been thinking about retiring anyway, and the quake made the call for them."

"Ted should open a new one!" Bernice exclaimed. "He'd be so great at that, and it would give him something to do until you retire."

"That's a good idea," agreed Fern. "Did you ever see his back yard on Ocean Bend Road?" she asked Bernice. "It's the most amazing place. Totally unexpected when you look at the house from the front."

"You mean because it looks like a dump from the front?" smiled Patty. She knew what everyone in Port Stirling thought of Ted's old place.

"Nooo," said Fern, stretching out the word. "That's not what I meant at all. His back yard is like this tropical oasis almost. Matt took me there a while back, and I couldn't believe what I saw. Palms, roses, hibiscus, vegetables—it was all so beautiful."

"Do you want to talk about it, hon?" asked Bernice quietly, reaching across the table and placing her hand on Fern's outstretched arm. Fern could see the sympathy in her eyes.

She put her face in her hands and burst into tears. "There's…nothing to talk…about," she said between sobs.

"We know you well, and we know you're not yourself," said Patty, choosing her words carefully. "Bernice and I have good shoulders to cry on."

"Don't be nice!" Fern said with tears streaming down her red face. "It makes me feel worse."

Bernice reached behind her and grabbed a box of tissues off the small table against the wall, and pushed it to Fern. "You'll feel better if you get it—him—out of your system," said Bernice. "Although, if it's any consolation, Matt feels like you feel."

Fern looked up in desperation. "How do you know that?" she said, with a lump in her throat.

"He has a sadness in his eyes, and for a strong man, he's moping around too much. Not everyone knows about you two lovebirds, but Patty and I could see it early on. You and Matt have a real connection, and us old hags knew it was just a matter of time before the two of you realized it."

"You're hardly old hags," Fern said to the two attractive women sitting across from her. She dabbed at her eyes with a tissue, and tried a wimpy smile.

"Bernice may be, but I'm not," cracked Patty, and that got a real smile from Fern. Then serious, "We hate to see you suffer, and want to know if we can do anything to help you navigate whatever is going on." She exchanged a glance with Bernice. "We don't want to interfere. But we hate seeing you both moping around."

"It's her," Fern said. "Susie, his ex-wife. She's after him, and I witnessed them together before she went back to Texas. He tried to explain it away, but I know what I saw, and it makes it impossible for me to continue our relationship. You won't say anything, will you? I haven't shared this with anyone except my parents. But you both always seem to know what's going on," she added.

"It's my job to read people," Patty said. "That's all. Our lips are sealed. This is about you and Matt, nobody else."

"And it's my job to read between the lines," Bernice said. "We want to help you because who hasn't had a broken heart?"

"Have you?" Fern asked.

"How much time do you have?" Bernice laughed. "I've been married three times, and please don't spread that around. It makes me look flaky. But there were good reasons why the first two didn't take. Until I met number three, I thought I wasn't cut out for romance. Maybe like you're feeling right now, huh?"

"We've all been there, Fern," Patty said. "Before I married Pat Perkins, I was engaged to a local mill foreman. I was young, he had a good job, and was well-respected in town. Two weeks before our wedding, he beat the crap out of me one night. I can't even remember why. Sent me to the hospital, though."

Fern's eyes widened. "A man beat you up? *You?*"

"I know. Hard to believe a tough old broad like me could be beaten by a mere man, isn't it? Needless to say, it was the one and only time. Wedding cancelled, gifts returned. I'm not saying that my fiancé beating me up is any worse than whatever you perceive Matt has done. I'm only saying that Matt is one of the good guys, and I have built-in radar on this issue. Perhaps he deserves the benefit of the doubt."

"He was kissing Susie," Fern said glumly, "while he was living with me. I can't get that picture out of my head." She twisted a ring on her pinkie finger. "And I'm afraid of getting hurt even worse."

"You should always protect yourself against getting hurt," Bernice said. "But sometimes, like Ed said in the meeting, you have to go with the odds. I'm betting that Matt's explanation for what you saw is closer to the truth than what you're imagining. Isn't he worth a second chance?"

Fern's tears came again and her lower lip quivered, as she shook her head. "I am physically and mentally unable to risk it," she whispered. "I'd rather be alone."

Bernice and Patty exchanged startled glances.

"Then you will be," Patty said.

• • •

"Hi, mom. It's Matt. And Happy Halloween."

"The same to you, son. Everything all right with you?"

"Yes. We're recovering out here on the left coast. Slow but sure. I've even heard that some parents are organizing a big trick-or-treat tonight. They want the kids to feel normal again."

"That's a terrific idea. Poor kids, having to go through this awful ordeal."

"Yeah, lots of nightmares and residual effects."

"Are you sleeping through the night yet?" she asked.

"Yes, I'm fine. Busy, but manageable now. The big deal was getting the utilities back up and running. You don't realize how dependent on them you are until you can't communicate with the outside world. How are you and dad doing?"

"We're good. Healthy, happy, and no major disasters here to report."

Matt laughed. "That's a good thing. I'm thinking, now that things are slowing down here, that I might come for a visit. A short one, to check in with you."

"This doesn't have anything to do with Susie Longworth does it?" his mother asked him in THAT tone.

He blanched at the question. "Why do you ask that?"

"Because Alice told me that Susie has been talking about you at the club. Like you're back together, or some other such nonsense."

Matt swore under his breath. Alice was one of his mother's best friends. "It is about her, but it's not what you think." *I've been saying that a lot lately.* "Susie and some of her nurse friends came out to Oregon to help with our injured after the quake. And she made a nuisance of herself where I'm concerned."

"Oh, for cryin' out loud! She's the one who divorced you. That damnable woman."

"I pointed that out, mom. Seems she now regrets our divorce."

"How do you feel?"

"I'm solidly in love with Fern, but that took a wrong turn when Susie was here. I need to do something to prove to Fern that Susie and I are the past. That's one reason I'm coming home."

"Port Stirling is your home now, Matt, not Texas. But you're certainly welcome to come here for a visit. When will you be here? I'll make sure your wing is ready for you."

"I'm aiming for early next week. I have a couple of things here in the department I need to finalize first, and I will let you know as soon as I have a flight confirmed. Transportation is still a little tricky, but I can get there. I've got something else I want to talk to you and dad about, too… I'm building a house here and I need some design help."

"Well, that's wonderful news. It's time you had your own home. I can't wait to hear all about it! And, I shouldn't say this but I'm going to anyway: I am very fond of Fern Byrne. So's your dad. I don't expect that to factor into your decisions at all, and it shouldn't. I just needed to say it."

"I'm very fond of her, too, mom. But you need to know this could go either way. She's really pissed off at me. And I probably deserve it."

CHAPTER 37

The wind rattled the shutters on Matt's window early Saturday morning and woke him from a dead sleep. It was still dark. He tried to snuggle down into the resort's luxurious bedding and go back to dreamland, but it was no use.

Tyee's funeral was today. He was looking forward to it, but had conflicting emotions; equal parts joy and dread. Joy that they were bringing Tyee's bones back where they belonged, but dread that he didn't have all the answers.

He stayed in bed until he could see a crack of light through his curtains. Looking out, the clouds were slate and sinister looking. *Please don't let it pour down rain today...today, of all days.*

Matt wasn't sure when he would be able to eat again today since he and Earl had a full schedule, so he sliced up a leftover baked potato, fried it with some butter, and added three eggs. A banana for dessert. Some days his coffee tasted better than usual, and this morning was one of those days. He drank two cups of the strong roast brew, and took part of a third into the shower with him.

It was a good thing his police dress uniform had ridden out the earthquake safe in his city hall office closet, because all of his other 'nice' clothes had perished in his bungalow. He thought he would allow some time in Dallas to do a big shop for himself; he was getting tired of the same few clothes he owned.

But now he put on the crisp white shirt, suit, tie, and hat, and looked at himself in the mirror. The hat was a snug fit over his curly black hair—he needed a haircut, but his barber shop wasn't open yet. And the only shoes he had were his sneakers he and Fern had found on the beach, and the boots he borrowed from her friend. He chose the running shoes. *I look like a serious cop as long as no one looks at my feet.*

· · ·

By the time he and Earl met at the Kouse home, the foreboding sky had broken up and the sun was peeking through the clouds. And something smelled wonderful…smoked fish?

"We didn't deserve to have a rainy day today," Earl said.

Matt laughed. "I thought the exact same thing this morning when I first looked out my window. Wouldn't be fair."

"Where are you staying these days?"

"I have a suite at Port Stirling Links. One of their cabanas. It's nice."

Earl's disdain for the ritzy resort was well-known throughout the county. "Humph. Can't stay there forever, can you?"

"I'm going to build a house. Just bought the property from my former landlord on the bluff in Port Stirling."

"I hope you got a deal."

Again Matt laughed. "Yeah, she couldn't unload it fast enough once she knew her house was in the Pacific. I've had the land inspected, and all of Ocean Bend Road is stable now. I'll build to earthquake standards in case our little event wasn't a 300-year quake like the experts say it was."

Earl gave him a brisk little salute. "Smart man. Glad to hear you're putting down roots. I'm not real good at saying it, but I like working with you. And I don't like working with many people."

"I've heard that," Matt grinned at the crusty sheriff, whose eyes were crinkling at the corners.

Meda Kouse came out to greet them. She was wearing a ceremonial Indian dress that looked old, but had been taken care of. Matt thought it was buckskin, a tan color. He admired the pattern of brown, blue, and white beading on it, and the fringe on the sleeves. A beautiful beaded belt made of suede encircled her ample waist.

"Welcome sheriff. Welcome chief. Please wait here. We'll be going down by the river in a moment. And we hope you'll stay after the ceremony for some refreshments." Her smile was as big as the sky. "We're all so happy you came."

Both cops took off their hats and gave Meda a nod. "Thank you for inviting us, Meda," said Matt. "It means the world to Earl and me. And the weather is cooperating!" he waved up at the sun.

"It wouldn't dare not," she said, "not after making us wait all these years. Grandfather Tyee will be smiling on us soon."

Four men—Hakan, his son Robert, and his son, Del, along with a man Matt didn't know—came around the corner of the house carrying a cedar box. It was similar to a casket, but not as formal and a bit smaller in size. They, too, were dressed in buckskin, and all four wore some sort of headdress.

Hakan's was the most elaborate. It covered his head, and was conical in shape, with eagle feathers pointing straight up. The base was a decorated headband, trimmed in fur, beads and shells. It was adorned with a band of flaming-red feathers from the crest of the pileated woodpecker. Matt wondered if it had belonged to his grandfather.

The men carrying Tyee's remains headed across the wide lawn toward the river. The other forty or so guests, including Matt and Earl, walked behind them, and the procession proceeded to the riverbank. A grave had been dug, and they carefully placed the cedar box in the hole. Several of the women stepped forward and placed colorful flowers on top of the box. Meda placed a necklace of some sort at the end of the box pointing west.

The ceremony was moving, with a quiet drum beat and melodic chant-ing. The third, fourth, and fifth generations of Kouse men eventually tossed dirt on top of Tyee's box, and then the procession shifted back up the lawn. During the ceremony, tables had been set up and decorated around two large oak trees alongside the house.

Refreshments consisted of the best salmon Matt had ever tasted, and heaping bowls of corn with melted butter. A variety of salads with fresh cabbage and dill, kale and garlic, and assorted greens and tomatoes were placed on each of the long tables. Baskets of bread, small plates of pickled cucumbers, and pitchers of sweet lemonade also graced each table. After Matt and Earl had feasted until Matt thought he'd never eat again, and Earl worried the buttons on his shirt would pop, blackberry pies were brought out.

As they walked to their cars at the end of the perfect afternoon, Matt was grabbed from behind in a bear hug. Del Kouse.

"Thank you feels insignificant," he said, "but thank you Chief Horning and Sheriff Johnson. My family is indebted for what the two of you have done for us. If there is ever anything you need, please call on us."

Matt smiled at Del, and shook his hand. "The only things I need right now are a builder and a good rain jacket, but thank you, and we will remember this day forever."

"What are you building, if I may ask?"

"My house went down the cliff in Port Stirling during the quake, and I've decided to build a new one. But all the contractors are busy with more important projects, like the schools and repairing the businesses we lost that night. I have to wait my turn."

Del was quiet for a moment. "No. No, you won't have to wait," he said breaking into a smile. "Our family's mantra is 'community before self', and it was important to Tyee, just as you have shown that you live by it, too." He turned and pointed, "See that man over there? That's my uncle Ned. He's married to dad's sister, Sarah, who led the chant. He builds custom homes and developments in Buck Bay. He will help you."

"I can't ask you to do that," Matt protested. "I'm sure he's really busy." But he snuck a hard look at Ned and thought the man looked competent.

"You have money?" Del asked with a grin.

"Lots," laughed Matt. "Does that make a difference?"

"Ned commands a high price, but he builds the most beautiful homes in the area. I'll arrange a meeting between you two…does tomorrow work?"

"I can't ask him to meet me on a Sunday."

"No days off now, everyone needs help," Del told him. "Besides, Sundays don't matter to Ned and Sarah—all they do is watch football. They don't go to church. Ned says football is his religion."

Earl laughed. "Well, then he'll love this guy," he said, slapping Matt on the back. "He played in the NFL until he wimped out with a bum knee."

"This sounds like the perfect partnership," Del said. "Wait right here."

And so, with full bellies around, a partnership was indeed made. Matt had a builder.

• • •

Matt and Earl turned right out of the Kouse property instead of left toward the Twisty River road. The road went straight for about one-half mile, and then took a sharp left when they reached the river. Another three-quarters mile paralleling the river brought them to the Carmichael's house.

All of these decades, and only a little over a mile separated these two families. *It could mean a lot or nothing*, thought Matt.

Earl unpacked the antique rifle from the back of Matt's squad car, and they approached the front door. A man Matt didn't know opened the door.

"I'm Chief of Police Matt Horning and this is Chinook County Sheriff Earl Johnson," Matt said.

The man smiled. "I know Earl," he said pumping Earl's outstretched hand. "I don't believe I've had the pleasure of meeting you yet, Chief, but welcome to Port Stirling. Come in, please."

He ushered the cops into the giant foyer and introduced himself to Matt. "I'm Dianne's husband, Duane Dobbins. I understand we used to be almost neighbors until that damn quake destroyed our homes. I've heard about you, of course, the Anselmo—what a deal that was!"

Matt didn't quite know what to think of the friendly welcome. Duane was a handsome guy, open-necked golf shirt with a nice tan underneath, jeans, and Converse Chuck Taylors. Too-perfect blond hair, and fit.

"What can we do for you gentlemen today? Nick and Dianne have filled me in on the guns—is that the reason you're here?"

"We're returning one of the two old rifles we removed during our search," Earl said, and held up the gun wrapped carefully in a blanket. "We took good care of it, and I'd be happy to place it back in Mason's gun cabinet where we think it's supposed to be. If that's OK with you, that is." The sheriff much preferred dealing with Duane Dobbins rather than Dianne, whom he'd never much cared for, even before this case.

"Let me get Nick," Duane said hurriedly. "Dianne went to Buck Bay this afternoon to do some shopping, but Nick is here." He reached into his jeans back pocket, pulled out a phone and dialed. "Hey, Sheriff Earl is here and he's returning some of your property. Could you come down?"

Moments later, Nick came bounding down the imposing central staircase. It was six feet wide, and curved beautifully to the landing. "Ahh, the guns," he said approaching the cops.

Earl cleared his throat. "Well, actually, it's just the one rifle. Do you want me to put it back in Mason's cabinet?"

"Where's the other one?" Nick asked, his voice chilly.

Matt's turn. "We're keeping it, I'm sorry to inform you. The Springfield rifle was seized as evidence in a criminal case, and we have determined that it was used in the commission of a deadly crime. Even though no one in this house was involved or will be charged with the crime, we deem the gun to be a nuisance and it will not be returned."

"But that gun is worth a lot!" Nick exclaimed. His face turned crimson and he blinked furiously. "You can't do this!"

"I believe the rifle has historical value, and I intend to release it to the Port Stirling Historical Society. You, Dianne, or your parents are entitled to request a court order to release the seized firearm which you lawfully possessed and did not criminally misuse. But I think a better solution is that the historical society and the City of Port Stirling reimburse you the gun's economic value, and you let it go quietly. I will fight you in court, and the story will get a lot of play."

"Dad won't let you do this." Nick glowered, and beside him, Duane Dobbins shook his head in disbelief.

"That gun killed Tyee Kouse…beyond a shadow of a doubt," Matt said. "Do you and your family really want it back in your home?"

CHAPTER 38

Travelling between the coast of Oregon and Texas was never easy under the best circumstances. On the Tuesday that Matt left, it was almost impossible. The Buck Bay airport was still under about two feet of mud from the tsunami, and the Eugene airport was not operational yet either—their control tower had collapsed during the earthquake. So, he had to drive to Portland, which normally takes four to five hours, but today took eight hours, and he missed the flight to Dallas.

He overnighted at an airport hotel, and caught a flight at noon on Wednesday. His sister, Miranda, picked him up at DFW, and drove him to the family ranch. The flat, no-trees terrain looked foreign to Matt. Even though it was early November, it was a pleasant seventy-three degrees, almost twenty degrees warmer than when he'd left Oregon.

"Mom's got a brisket on the BBQ," she told him. "Your favorite, right?"

"You know it is," he smiled. "It's good to see you. It feels like I've been gone for years instead of just ten months."

"Not to me," said his sister. "It feels like yesterday we were celebrating your forty-third birthday at the ranch. November 1? I swear that was last week!" she laughed. "But you've certainly crammed a lot into the nine months you've been gone."

"You look good, Miranda," he said. People called her 'Randi' these days, but his sister would always be Miranda to him. She had the same curly

305

black hair as her brother, but today it was blown-out straight and to her shoulders in a more sophisticated style. Big designer sunglasses covered much of her face, and she wore dangling silver earrings with her black and white outfit.

"So do you, Mr. Wild West. Clearly, almost being killed in an earthquake and tsunami agrees with you," she joked and then turned serious. "We were scared out of our minds, Matt. I'm still dreaming about that huge wave drowning you."

He patted her on the arm. "I'm fine. And my town is going to be better than ever. Tough people out there. Resourceful and relentless."

"You love it, don't you?"

"I do. And I'm planning to stay as long as they'll have me."

"Understand you're having female troubles. Anything I can do?"

His big sis had been his 'go to' for problems with girls growing up. "You could find a new man for Susie Longworth...that would help a lot."

She threw back her head, let out a whoop, and laughed hard. "I knew that woman would regret dumping your ass someday. I tried to warn her about hubby number two, but she wouldn't listen to me. She was 'madly in love'."

The former sisters-in-law had stayed friends, even though, in Matt's mind, they were nothing alike. Miranda was a hard-driving corporate attorney, and didn't put up with the old Texas ways. She and her husband, Larry, also a successful attorney, were active in Democratic politics, and determined to move Texas forward.

"She's messed it up big-time with Fern and me. I think it's the real thing between us, and now she doesn't want anything to do with me. I'm devastated."

Now it was her turn to pat her brother on his arm. "She'll come around."

"Why do people keep saying that?!? You don't know how pissed she is, and she's got all this anger in her directed squarely at me."

"Because you're a hunk, and she loves you, according to mom and dad. Not the hunk part...I threw that in," she smiled. "Seriously, bro, you're a catch. Great looking, nice guy, fun personality—the total package. There's only one other guy like you I know and I'm married to him. Pickings are

slim out there these days, and I'm going out on a limb and say they're probably *really* slim in Port Stirling, Oregon."

"Fern has a lot of character, and a strong sense of right and wrong. Part of
why I'm so crazy about her. I screwed up, and I don't see her backing down."

"Winter's coming. There's going to be some long, cold, rainy nights.
You'll start looking better and better to her. I practically guarantee it."

"I hope to hell you're right. In the meantime, I've got to get rid of Susie
once and for all, and I want you to back me up."

"Right behind you."

. . .

Drifts of Big Bluestem grasses surrounded the low-slung Horning ranch.
Its blue-green color was beginning the change to winter russet. Fragrant
asters, Texas gayfeathers, black-eyed susans, and white and purple alliums
dotted the landscape around the large patio. Dinner there on this silky
Texas evening was so good.

Matt had taken a swim in the long Olympic-sized pool first, and changed
into clean clothes, tan slacks and a white golf shirt. The two days of travel
had left him wilted.

Dad always kept a full keg of beer out by the pool, and Matt and his
younger brother, Sam, tapped into it now. Miranda and his mother drank
Chardonnay that mom was now ordering from an Oregon winery she and
dad had visited last summer.

The family was relaxed and the conversation was happy and cheerful.
Soft white lights around the patio's perimeter came on as the sun set.

"First, please join me in a toast," said Ross, hoisting his pint glass high
in the air. "It takes more than a big, bad earthquake to get my son. Here's
to you, Matt."

"Cheers! Hip hip hooray! Take that, 9.1 shake!" The family joined in,
drinking and laughing.

"Matt's going to build a house in Port Stirling," Ross told those gathered.

"Does that mean you're not coming home?" Sam asked. He was fairer
than Matt and Miranda, as if the black hair wore out by the time it got

to him. Sam was also softer around the edges, and looked like he'd had an easier life than his siblings. He wore a turquoise Hawaiian shirt, white shorts, and was barefoot.

"It does," Matt answered. "Never say never, I guess, but I really love it out there."

"What's wrong with Dallas?" Sam persisted.

"Well, it doesn't have an ocean, for starters," he laughed. "That sea air gets in your blood. I bought the three acres my former rental house stood on." Out of the corner of his eye, Matt saw his mother flinch. "Don't worry, mom, most of the land sits well back from the new bluff, and the county inspectors have taken a look at the whole region. After a couple of healthy aftershocks in the immediate aftermath, we're stable now, and I'm good to go."

"Is there anything left of the bungalow?" his mom asked. "I treasured that little house."

"One thing," Matt answered. "Can you guess what it is?"

"The stone fireplace," his parents said in unison.

"Yep. But it's perched on the very edge of the new cliff now. I'm having it moved stone-by-stone, and it will be featured in my new house. Speaking of, I'm going to take some money out of my trust, dad. I had enough on hand to buy the property, but I figure if I'm going to build my house, I should do it the right way."

"It's about time you spent some of your dough," dad said. "Do you even look at your reports?"

Guilty, Matt said, "Not often. Am I broke?"

Miranda and Sam laughed. "Not unless you call $18 million plus change broke," Miranda said.

Matt's eyebrows raised above wide eyes. "How can there be that much? Last time I checked we each had about $11 million."

"While you were busy out west catching crooks, we hit another oil well on the southern edge," Ross reported. "I transferred about $7 million more to each of you kids' accounts last spring. Only Sam has spent anything; you and Miranda need to start living your lives before you get too old like your mother and me."

Sam lifted his glass toward Matt. "Here's to the good life," he smiled somewhat sheepishly.

"You may be too old but I'm certainly not," his mother huffed.

"I don't know what to say," Matt started. "Thanks, mom and dad." To Miranda and Sam he said, "We did a good job picking our parents, didn't we?"

"Let's eat," said mom.

As Matt dug into his brisket, he thought, *maybe I'll buy a Scottish study for my new house, too.*

• • •

Matt's next evening wasn't nearly so pleasant. He agreed to meet Susie for dinner at a restaurant near her Greenway Parks home. She wanted to meet him at the country club they all belonged to, but Matt nixed that idea. He didn't need all their friends speculating about their relationship.

She insisted he pick her up instead of meeting her at the restaurant, but he said 'no' to that, too. He knew that trick, and he wasn't about to end up at her house after dinner. It was difficult to be so mean to her, but he couldn't let down his guard, or the purpose of the entire trip would be wasted.

During the drive to the restaurant, he thought of Fern, which made tonight's resolve much easier. His heart ached to repair things with her, and he was frustrated that she wouldn't talk. It was so unlike her to not talk things through—it was one of the things he most loved about her. She was a calm, rational woman (in spite of her red hair, that was their joke), and they had successfully navigated any little bumps in first their friendship, and later, their relationship.

So the fact that Fern had now clammed up meant that Matt had really hurt her. He knew she'd had an unpleasant affair with a married man in San Francisco before she'd come back home to Port Stirling. On the board of directors of the museum Fern worked for at the time, she had no idea he was married, a fact which he'd successfully hidden from all of his previous mistresses, too. His wife had caused a stink when she discovered her husband's infidelity, and took it out on Fern, causing her to get fired from her museum job.

Matt understood that Fern had been reluctant to get involved with him once she became part of the department, but the bond between them had been too strong to deny after the Anselmo case ended. They needed to be together then, and Matt felt strongly that they *still* needed to be together.

But if he forced it, he knew enough about Fern's character makeup that she would resist him even more. That's where the frustration came in—he just had to wait. Going about his life, especially with a new project like building his house, was the best way for him to proceed. Be professional and cordial at work, and leave her alone to work through her feelings. *Easier said than done.*

Now, seated in one of the restaurant's dark red leather semi-circle banquettes, Matt fervently wished he was in Fern's kitchen cooking dinner for the two of them instead of in this white-tablecloth, high-ceilinged restaurant. The walls were paneled in a rich mahogany wood, the gold patterned carpet was deep and cushy, and potted palms dotted the room. Depending on where you were in the room, it either smelled of expensive perfume or roasted prime rib. The chandeliers operated at low light, and tiny lamps on each table added to that ambience.

Susie stopped just long enough at the maître d's stand for everyone in the room to get a look at her before making her way to Matt's table. Dressed to kill, she looked gorgeous in a sleeveless black lace dress, with a low scooped neck, and straight skirt falling gracefully to the floor. Matt could see her diamond pendant necklace from across the room. Guess that was the point of it.

He stood to greet her and helped her onto the padded seat next to him. "You look beautiful," he greeted her. "Like always."

"Well, I don't wear this little number like always," she smiled at him. "Special occasion. You look nice, too. New suit?"

"As a matter of fact, yes. I went shopping today."

"I've often wondered if you still have that yummy Brooks Brothers navy suit I bought you when we were first married. Do you?"

"I did, until September 23," he smiled, "when the Pacific Ocean decided it needed that suit more than I did. I lost everything that night. I can smile about it now, but it's a horrible feeling that I wouldn't wish on anybody. I last wore that suit at a funeral back in January, soon after I arrived in Oregon, so it did its job."

"Did you get some nice things today?" she asked.

"Yeah, I cleaned out a couple of stores at Galleria, and am having everything shipped to Port Stirling. I was getting tired of living out of a suitcase and with a few borrowed items, but I don't have much free time when I'm on the job to shop. As you know."

"Yes, I remember that life. But I've grown up, and it wouldn't bother me now."

"So you say. Let's order," he said more brusquely than he intended.

Susie seemed to know everyone in the restaurant, and several people stopped by their table to say hello. It was uncomfortable for Matt to be seen as a couple, but he kept his cool demeanor.

They both ordered rib eye steaks, his with mashed potatoes and collard greens, hers with a Caesar salad. There was no point in thinking he would eat anything other than beef while visiting home, and he just rolled with it. They both ordered lemon cheesecake for dessert.

Matt had kept their conversation on a friendly note. A time or two, after she'd drunk a vodka tonic and a big glass of red wine, Susie had nuzzled closer and tried to hold his hand, but he rebuffed it as gracefully as possible. *Not going there.*

As they waited for their dessert to arrive, she asked him where he was going to live going forward.

"Port Stirling," he answered. "I thought I'd told you that."

"You did. Sorry, that's not what I meant," she smiled. "I assume that your employee, Fern, kicked you out after she saw us together. I meant where in Port Stirling are you living now, and is it temporary?" She leaned toward him, exposing even more of her cleavage.

"How did you know where I was living?"

She laughed. "I guessed. Good guess, huh?"

Matt scowled, but turned to greet the waiter with a smile as he brought their cheesecake.

"I'm living at the golf resort currently, but I've decided to build a house close to the ocean. I miss it."

"Do you own property?"

"As of four days ago, yes. I bought the property where my rental house was. About three acres of ocean-front on the new bluff."

"Well, that's big news. What kind of house will you build? Will there be room for me?" She lowered her chin, but looked up at him through dark lashes.

Matt ignored her attempt at seduction. *Sooo not interested.* "I'm going to do it right and build the house of my dreams. I'm going to design it myself and put everything I want in it." He took a bite of his cheesecake.

"Guess you can afford it now. I heard your ranch hit another oil well a few months ago. Suspect the money is rolling in for all the Horning clan." She looked at him expectantly.

He stopped eating the cheesecake, his fork suspended in midair, his dark eyes blazing. "Is that what this is about? What it's been about for weeks? The money?" He glared at her so hard she shrank into the banquette.

"No. No," she stammered. "Of course not. I love you, Matt. I loved you when we were married and before I knew about your money. You know that."

"That's not actually true, Susie," he said calmly but with pure steel in his voice. "I had a juicy NFL contract when we married, and you knew my family had money. You don't love me, maybe you never did."

"I do love you!"

"Don't think so, darlin'. What a fool I've been. We've always been about the money, you and me, but I was too blinded by you to see it. I thought we were partners in life, but you were just running your business."

"That's not true, Matt. Please give me another chance and you'll see how much I love you. Let's start tonight," she said, placing her hand on his thigh. She could feel it slipping away. Out of her grasp.

He grabbed her arm under the table, and shifted closer to her face. His face was pinched with his mouth set in a tight line. "You—we—are out of chances, and there will be no tonight or any night for the rest of my life. I don't love you, Susie. I love Fern, and even though you tried your darnedest to destroy her, she's so much stronger than you, and she will prevail."

"Don't say that," she whimpered. "I'm better than she is."

He squeezed her arm firmly until she said, "Ow!" He hadn't meant to hurt her; just get her attention.

"I'm sorry, I didn't mean to hurt you," he apologized, "but here's what's going to happen, Susie." In a low voice he said, "I'm going to walk out of this place, and fly home tomorrow. I expect to never hear from you again. You will not bother me in Port Stirling. You will not bother my family here. You will not talk about me ever again. If, after six months, you accomplish your end of this bargain, I will deposit $1 million into your bank account. If you break one of my new rules, you will never see that million. I will not give you another cent. I'm feeling less generous in my old age. Do you understand the deal?"

Unable to speak, and with tears running down her face, Susie nodded.

Matt paid the bill and left the restaurant, the ranch, and Texas.

Susie cheered up immensely when, six months later to the day, her bank account swelled handsomely.

CHAPTER 39

In the weeks and months following the earthquake, things slowly and wonderfully began to return to normal in Port Stirling and throughout Oregon. Insurance companies, aware that the world was watching, had for the most part come through for the Oregonians who had lost everything. Where they didn't, the government stepped in to help make people whole again.

The response had surprised Fern somewhat. There was a new sense of creativity around Chinook County. It was like the natural disaster had forced them to take a hard look at their surroundings, and many of them decided that they could do better. There was some actual architecture springing up in select projects around town. People, while still very casual, were dressing a little better when out in public. Wearing pajama bottoms to the grocery store no longer seemed to be a thing. The restaurants and hotels, competing against each other to win the rebounding tourist trade had committed to not only repairs of their buildings, but some long-over-due and tasteful remodels. The entire town was starting to sparkle a bit, and Fern had never been prouder of her hometown.

And the harbor! The fishermen who had lost all during the tsunami took the opportunity—and the insurance money—and upped their boat game. Every watercraft in the harbor, including the spanking new Coast Guard cutter, six months after the quake, was new. The gleaming boats sat amid the newly-built port, and to Fern's eyes, the scene was postcard material.

The police department was almost bored, and Fern was glad it was Friday night. She was looking forward to her first normal weekend in months. There had been virtually no crime in town, and barely any in the county since the disaster. She was grateful for that fact because it gave her town the focus they needed to rebuild their lives without distraction. Matt had asked her to conduct a review of their policies and procedures this week, and make any recommendations, and she finished that project this morning, placing it on his desk.

She was just reaching for her coat when Sylvia came over to her desk. "Chief Horning would like the two of us to talk about how we can keep this community policing and goodwill we've got going on now. Shall we set a time to discuss on Monday? I've got some thoughts."

"I've got a better idea," said Fern. "Why don't we go have a drink now? End the week on a high note. Are you available?"

Sylvia smiled. "Can't think of a better way to kick off a weekend. Let's go, Red."

They settled into a corner table by a window in the bar at the Port Stirling Links resort. Fern knew that Sylvia lived nearby on this side of town, and she wanted the older woman to have a short drive home after their drink.

Once the waiter had brought them each a glass of wine, accompanied by some warm cashews, Sylvia said, "What do you think about holding a monthly town hall-type meeting, staff taking turns to run it? If we would all commit to it, I believe we could keep on everyone's good side."

"I like it," said Fern. "We could launch it as part of disaster follow-up. Some folks are still struggling, and this could be a good forum for people to come up with solutions to help those still in need."

"It never would have worked before," Sylvia added. "We didn't have the right people in the department to pull it off. But now we do, starting at the top. Chief is really good at public engagement, and we should take advantage of that, don't you think?"

Fern was so relieved that she and Matt had somehow managed to regain their friendship. She still loved him, and had caught him looking longingly

at her a time or two, but this was really for the best. They were an excellent team at work, there was no trouble from Bill Abbott, and everyone
seemed to accept that their romance was over, and she was just another
officer in the PD.

Everyone except Sylvia, that is. "Speaking of, are you almost done
being mad at Matt?"

"I'm not mad at him. I just don't want to get involved again."

"You can't still be afraid of his ex-wife."

"I'm not afraid of her," Fern said. "But I think they're not done, and I
don't want to be entangled."

"He went to Texas to make sure she understood she's out of his life forever. You do know that, right?"

"Yes, I know he went, and I also know that we were all relieved when he
came back without her. But we don't really know what happened between
them, do we? At least, I don't know. Maybe I don't ever want to know."

Sylvia stared at Fern, and then opened her arms wide to encompass
the room. "Do you see any blondes from Texas here? No, you do not. She
gave him the full-court press when she was here in October, and you sure
as hell know she gave it to him again when he went to visit. To visit his
family, I might add. We have no actual proof that he even saw her while
he was there, and he only stayed a couple of days."

Fern played with the stem of her wineglass. "Is she still calling him all
the time?" she asked, and hated that she did.

"Not a peep. And he hasn't mentioned her once. Not that he tells me
much. Nor do you, for that matter."

Fern laughed. "It's not in your job description to listen to our lonely
hearts club whining."

"Jesus! You sound just like Matt! Not in my job description; can we
all move past that please? We're a small department. We care about each
other, we depend on each other. We're friends. Matt helped my grandson get squared away, and it meant a lot to my family. Why on earth can't
I help him? Huh?"

"We're not going to solve this tonight," Fern said.

"It hurts me to see you both miserable and lonely. That's all."

"I'm actually not lonely," Fern whispered. "I'm dating a new teacher in Buck Bay. Nice guy and I like him."

Sylvia leaned forward, her elbows on the table and said, "What?"

"I have a boyfriend."

"Why didn't you tell me?"

"Because I don't want to combine my personal and my professional lives ever again. The woman always suffers, Sylvia. You know that better than anyone. But I'm telling you now."

"How did you meet him? And what do you know about him?"

"Bernice Ryder introduced us. She's on the Buck Bay school board, and interviewed him before he was hired. He's a little older than me, about mid-forties, and a recent widow. His wife died of breast cancer two years ago, and he wanted a change of scenery…he's from Colorado. He teaches science and is the new high school football coach. He's cute."

Sylvia gawked at Fern. "I had no idea. I'm sorry I interfered, and good for you! I'm going to tell you the truth. I love both you and Matt, and I was thrilled to learn you were a couple. But it's none of my business, and if you don't make each other happy, then it's time to move on. You're doing the right thing."

"Thank you. Can we drink our wine now?"

* * *

Monday morning it was back to reality. Matt and Sheriff Earl were due in court at 10:00 a.m. Mason Carmichael had sued them to get his rifle back, and because the parties couldn't come to an amicable settlement, it would be decided in front of a judge at the Chinook County courthouse in Twisty River.

Judge Cynthia Hedges was all business in her long black robes. Lawyers and defendants alike feared her courtroom, even though she was soft-spoken and very pretty. All present were quiet as she settled into her chair, and then motioned to both parties to take their seats, and the hearing began.

The Carmichael's case was solid. Mason owned the gun, and while he didn't dispute that it had been used in the commission of a crime, he proved he wasn't involved in the crime. Their side also made a strong argument for how the Port Stirling police department could not establish that the rifle had been fired by a member of the owning family. Plus, the gun's value had been confirmed at between $1500-2000, and Mason wanted to understand why he should forfeit that value.

The answer, according to Judge Hedges, seemed to be that, in her view, because of the last-century murder of a prominent tribal chief, the rifle did have historical value to Chinook County, especially when it could be matched up with the bullet found in Tyee's skull.

Therefore, it was ruled that the rifle would be surrendered by the Carmichael family and given to the Port Stirling Historical Society for their museum. The city would reimburse Mason Carmichael $1750 for his loss of value, unless he wanted to donate it to the museum. He did not.

Mae Walters, also present in the courtroom, went out to lunch with Earl and Matt following the trial, where they cheered, laughed, and ate heartily.

Two days later, the Oregon State Police sent the story of Tyee Kouse out over the wires. Virtually every media outlet in the U.S. picked it up. Although it was mentioned that the murder weapon had belonged to Lyndon Carmichael who was a contemporary of Kouse, that fact was mostly buried under two more interesting facts. The public was more fascinated by the tsunami destroying the lighthouse, and the discovery of a 117-year-old skeleton than they were by the actual murder. And the question that really captured their imagination turned out to be how Tyee's body was placed underneath the stone lighthouse nearly three years after it was built.

Case closed.

CHAPTER 40

Patty Perkins and hubby Ted Frolick put the finishing touches on his sturdy bungalow that had survived the earthquake on Ocean Bend Road. They had been working all weekend to clean it up after the displaced family they'd rented it to back in September had returned to their permanent home. The Gillis family's home, just down the road from Ted's place, had been knocked off its foundation, and they were happy when Ted had offered his bungalow to them while their home was repaired.

Now, six months later, Ted was eager to make the little cottage and garden his again. Patty had convinced him that it was a good time to buy some new furniture, draperies, and bedding, and he had to admit that, along with a fresh coat of paint in the kitchen, his beloved bungalow had never looked fresher and better.

And, it was time to plant his peas! He'd already planted some at their Twisty River house, but peas seemed to love the sea air, and he wanted two crops this season to compare. Still newlyweds in spirit, Patty and Ted decided to "honeymoon" for a week at the bungalow while Ted did his thing in the garden, and reconnected to his little house.

It made Patty happy to see Ted happy. Plus, she loved the new bed she'd bought to replace Ted's old lumpy one. Life was good again.

• • •

Matt, his architect, and his builder, Ned Childs, met on Ocean Bend Road to walk Matt's property. There was a light drizzle and overcast skies on this Tuesday afternoon in mid-March, but the view from almost every inch of the property was still dazzling.

"I really appreciate you making time for me, Ned," Matt said. "I know how in demand you are right now." Matt had researched Ned Childs' work around the county, going to see some of his latest projects in person. He had also been surprised to learn that Ned had a reputation and clients in other parts of the U.S, too, and a couple of breathtaking projects recently completed in Mexico.

"My contribution here is nothing compared to what you have done for Sarah's family," Ned said seriously. "Repairing Tyee's reputation, and therefore, the entire Kouse family is priceless. Nothing we could do would properly repay you for that gift. Besides, I've always wanted to build on this bluff, but never had the right opportunity."

"He means he never found a client with the right budget," the architect grinned.

"Until now," Matt said, beaming, and clapping Ned on the back. "Let's walk and I'll share my vision with you guys."

"You're from Texas originally, is that correct?" asked Ned.

"Yes, lived there all my life until last year when I moved here. Most of my life in the same house—my parents' ranch outside of Dallas."

"So, are we building a Texas ranch house here?" smiled the architect.

"We are not," said Matt. "I want this house to be Pacific Northwest, contemporary, but not starkly modern. Local materials whenever possible, although I realize with the earthquake that sourcing might be tough on some things." He turned to face the road and said, "I want my house to, in essence, turn its back on the road. It needs to look attractive to the road for sure, but I want the focus all out this way." He turned to face the ocean and held out his arms to it. "I want almost every room to have a view. Is that possible?"

The architect and the builder exchanged glances.

The architect spoke first. "Yes, it's possible. But it will require a larger footprint than most houses today because we have height limits on new ocean-front homes."

"You mean I can't build a four-story house?" Matt questioned.

"Not even a three-story," said Ned. "City won't allow it in this location, even for their favorite police chief."

"So what are my options?"

"Well, you've got a lot of width to work with," said the architect, "because your property is mostly north to south rather than east to west. I would suggest a long, low structure that parallels the bluff, and depending on how much square footage you want, perhaps a second story on one end. We could get away with that as long as the second story is not too obtrusive."

"What kind of square footage could you fit on the ground floor if we used up a lot of the land from north to south, leaving a nice set-back from the road and from the bluff?" Matt asked. His architect took off walking in yard-long strides, first south and then north.

After a few minutes, he returned to Matt and Ned. "Without seriously crunching numbers, I would say that you could easily do a one-level, 8,000 square foot house, up to 10,000 if you didn't care much about a privacy land buffer on both ends. That's probably more house than you would need."

"It's not about need," grinned Matt. "It's about want. And this house is going to be fully loaded. If we do 8,000 on the ground floor, could I do a 1,000-1,500 square feet second story master bedroom and bath on one end? Would it look funny, or is it realistic?"

"I like it," smirked Ned. He looked positively delighted.

"I like it, too," said the architect. "That way, you'd still have plenty of room on either end for landscaping to give you all the privacy you'd want. Plus, you'd have the most beautiful master bedroom suite in the world with a million-dollar view."

Matt laughed. "Let's do it!"

CHAPTER 41

TUESDAY, JULY 26, 1904

Lyndon Carmichael drove his fancy new Studebaker Model C with its white chassis, tufted red leather interior, matching red wheel spokes, and a gold-flecked steering wheel from his house situated on a beautiful curve of the Twisty River. Because the automobile had no roof, Lyndon only drove it on sunny, dry, tender days like today.

He was headed for the harbor at Port Stirling with his wife, Winnie, and three of their five children, Norma, Anna, and Elroy. The oldest two daughters, Louise and Blanche, had stayed home to attend to the house. The far rear of the vehicle was piled with two large trunks. The five Carmichaels would leave their automobile at the harbor, where their servant would hike into town later, pick it up and drive it back home. They had booked the steam schooner to ferry them up the coast to Astoria, where Lyndon would meet with U.S. Senator Charles W. Fulton to discuss fish processing, timber stands, and the lumber industry. The family would take a one-week vacation in the bustling seaport with its population of about 8,500.

Once they had the children settled with snacks and puzzles in their cabin below decks on the schooner, Lyndon and Winnie made their way forward to the captain's small lounge. They were welcomed aboard, served a glass of sherry and a small plate of cheeses and apples before the captain left them to perform his duties.

The couple, excited to be going on a trip, talked animatedly about their plans for the week ahead.

"It's good to get away," said Lyndon. "Don't you feel as if we've been surrounded by chaos of late?" he asked his wife.

"I do," she replied, taking a sip of her sherry. "Everyone seems to want something of us these days." She tugged at the band collar of her black-and-white pinstriped blouse. "I swear, Lyndon, our housekeeper is stealing from us. Every time I look in the pantry for something I know is there, it's not there. Should I confront her?"

"Oh, I wouldn't," said Lyndon. "It can't be Annie, she's as honest as the day is long. Maybe cook is pilfering a little here and there, but don't we expect that?"

"Suppose so." She smoothed her long black skirt.

"It's the same in business these days, Winnie. Men are greedy, and no one is satisfied with their piece of the pie. I don't know what our world is coming to anymore. We must teach the children to be strong so they will fight for what is rightfully theirs after you and I are gone."

She smiled and reached forward to take his hand. "We're not going, dearest."

He leaned back in his chair and laughed. "I already feel more relaxed being on the water with you and away from cooks and servants and friends. We'll have a wonderful holiday."

"Speaking of friends, what in heaven's name was wrong with Ronnie Percy last night?" She rolled her eyes.

"I know," he said serious now. "Ronald had his knickers in a twist over a stand of timber upriver from our place—just before you get to Twisty River. He says he claimed it and it belongs to him."

"Does it?" Winnie tried to stay out of Lyndon's business dealings, but sometimes he wanted her opinion.

"Do you know the stand I'm talking about? It's north of that big turn in the river about one mile before the steamer landing. Very old growth, beautiful forest."

"Yes, I know of where you speak."

"Ronald says it's his, but I claimed it over five years ago," Lyndon clenched his fist.

"Well, that's that then, isn't it?"

"It's even more complicated. According to Ronald, he says Tyee Kouse has a deed that says the Indians own it. Says he's seen it. Tyee showed it to him, but then snatched it back and put it in his pocket."

Winnie sniffed. "I think those Indians are getting above themselves. I saw Rochana walking on our road like she belonged there. I told her it was private property and she said, 'we share this road, Winnie'. Called me by my first name! Have you ever?!?"

"That is troublesome, my darling. It's best to avoid the Kouse clan in total. Take no measure."

"Why was Ronnie so angry?" she asked her husband. "I don't believe I've ever seen him act quite like that."

"He was unusually distraught. I worry that his business dealings are not as strong as they appear to be on the surface. But it would be insulting for me to inquire."

"What will you do about the disputed land?"

"I will discuss it with Senator Fulton when we arrive in Astoria. He will understand my position in the matter. I believe that Ronald understood that was one of the purposes of our trip today, and that was part and parcel of why he was upset."

She smiled. "How much did you donate to the senator's campaign?"

"Enough," he returned his wife's smile.

• • •

Ronald Percy woke in a foul mood. *Damn it to hell and back. I need that timber.* He laid in his soft bed, looking out through his cotton curtains. Percy could tell that the morning had dawned bright and cheery, but his disposition did not match it.

Percy was tired, bone-deep tired, of Lyndon Carmichael always winning. Every battle. Every war. It all seemed to go Carmichael's way. *Half the money Carmichael made in the past year should have been mine. It was me who found the deals, me who greased the skids, me who could have done a better job running it.*

But Lyndon Carmichael would always swoop in at the last minute, and use his connections to steal Percy's deals. And now he was about to do it again. Oh yes, Ronald Percy knew why the Carmichaels were going to Astoria. It was to convince that senator that they had the rights to that timber stand. And it would probably work—birds of a feather flock together.

And that damnable Injun. If it wasn't Lyndon Carmichael in his way, it was Tyee Kouse. This time they were both in his way. Lyndon with his political clout, and Tyee with a piece of paper. But maybe there was a way to kill two birds with one stone. *This time, I won't stand for it. By God, I won't! It's my turn to win.*

Percy dressed hurriedly, and grabbed some breakfast from the food on the dining room credenza that his wife Hazel had left for him. She had already retreated to her sewing area in the corner room on the top floor. Hazel was in the final stages of a new quilt, and she was determined to finish it this week. She was a good woman and didn't deserve to always play second fiddle to that mean, pompous Winnie Carmichael.

Ronald Percy headed across the fields separating his property from Lyndon's. The grasses were high and waving in the soft wind, and he could tell it would be a warm day. Filled with rage, he'd still had the presence of mind to grab a fishing pole to disguise his intentions. He wore a hat to hide his distinctive ginger hair that immediately identified him.

He knew the Carmichael house would be unlocked; no one ever locked their doors, no reason to. He also knew where Lyndon kept his favorite rifle. All he had to do was avoid the household staff. The Percy and Carmichael houses had been built around the same time, and were similar in size, design, and layout. Carmichael had added more refined touches, but the Percy home had larger rooms.

Percy went around to the back of the house, and slipped quietly through the kitchen door, his heart hammering in his chest. No one in the kitchen! It was a large room with two work stations, and on this sunny early morning was well lit with four gas lights and a big window facing east. An eat-in trestle table with benches for the staff had been cleared of breakfast dishes. The wood floors were highly polished, and every surface sparkled.

From the kitchen, he had only to navigate a short hallway to his right, and slip into Lyndon's office. He poked his head into the hallway. No one in sight there either, but Percy held his breath for a moment, and listened to the stillness. *Where was everyone?* He knew there were four household staff employed by Lyndon, but he couldn't see or hear anyone. The only sound was his own scared breathing.

Ten tiptoe steps and he was alone in Lyndon's office. The rifle lifted easily off the wall-mounted shelf. Percy checked that it had ammunition—it did—but he looked frantically around the small room for a box of bullets, in case he needed more. *Quick! Where could they be?* He opened every drawer, making more noise than he wanted, and paused his actions when one squeaked loudly. He stood stock still, listening. When Percy could hear nothing, he resumed his hunt, and found the box in the back of a drawer in the table behind Lyndon's desk. He stuffed them in his pocket, picked up the rifle, and scrambled silently back through the kitchen.

He was in and out of the Carmichael house in under five minutes. No one saw him enter or leave.

• • •

Tyee Kouse asked his children if they wanted to accompany him on his deliveries this week. They were torn, since they loved riding the steamer with their father upriver to Twisty River. They loved waving to people on the riverbanks as the steamer passed them. They loved the wind in their hair, and the nature smells along the way.

But today, on this warm July day, they were having so much fun playing and fishing in the river they didn't want to stop. Tyee smiled at them, and said, "Next week, children."

He loaded up his buggy with this week's produce—a bumper crop. The mild coastal valley climate coupled with Tyee's magnificent loamy soil, tended lovingly over the years, made his farm one of the best in southwestern Oregon. Today he filled his bins with luscious lettuce, the last of this season's spinach, huckleberries, camas root, onions, squash, potatoes, and corn. He also had some beautiful herbs: fennel, dill, oregano, and rosemary. Last but not least, Tyee threw in some summer flowers to give as a bonus to his lady customers.

He hooked up his old horse—he called him Harvey—to the buggy and set off for the port.

He never made it.

Ronald Percy knew that Tyee Kouse took his goods to market every Tuesday. He also knew that he traveled the dirt path behind the Percy property that led to the coastal road and then to the village and the port. He didn't know for sure, but he suspected that Tyee, like most of the Indians, carried important papers on their person when they traveled around the county.

Holding Lyndon's rifle, Percy settled in comfortably behind some bushes next to the pathway to wait. He could see down the road and would be able to spot Tyee's horse well in advance. There was no one else around, and a hush fell on Percy as he waited, his insides a turbulent mess.

He shot Tyee in the back of his head as he passed by with Lyndon Carmichael's rifle.

• • •

Percy calmed Tyee's horse, and tied him to a nearby tree. Hurriedly, he rifled through Tyee's pockets, pulling out several papers, one the deed to the timber stand. He placed the documents in his own pockets, and pulled the body into the underbrush to hide it until darkness. Then he calmly walked back to the Carmichael's, cutting through the forest that separated their properties.

When he came to the clearing on the west side of the house, he crouched behind a tree for ten minutes or so to see if there was any activity in and around the house. All was still. Percy slipped back in through the same kitchen door and repeated his earlier movements, only in reverse this time. He wiped down Lyndon's rifle with his shirt tails, and coolly placed it back on its rack. And then he left quickly, traveling through the forest to his own home where he would wait for night to come.

Percy's eighteen-year-old son was working in their barn when Ronald arrived back home. Closing the barn door behind him, he said, "Son, I need to talk with you."

• • •

Late that night, under cover of darkness, but with a half-moon in a cloudless sky to light their way, Ronald Percy and his son quietly loaded Tyee's body, wrapped in an old tarp, into the back of their Auburn Runabout, and headed to the port. Percy kept a nice boat in the harbor, and he and his son frequently went deep-sea fishing.

At the hour of 2:00 a.m., when all good folks were sound asleep in their beds, they did not encounter another person about. The two men transferred the body from their automobile to Percy's boat, and silently eased into the Twisty River. They headed down the newly-created channel toward the open sea.

But just before they reached the jetty, Ronald steered his boat through the mist toward the lighthouse. They pulled even with the shore, and the boy jumped out, pulling the boat in between two large rocks. He was shaking fiercely with fear, but did what his father instructed him to do.

Once the boat was secured, the two carried Tyee's body up a short path, no more than fifteen feet from the water. He motioned to his son that they should lay the body on the ground. Then, Percy shined his lantern along the lighthouse's foundation, searching for the small door he knew was there. There it was! He sprung open the hatch and motioned to his son.

The portal led to a trap door under the floor of the lighthouse. *You fought this lighthouse tooth and nail, Tyee, and now you can stay here for eternity,* thought Ronald.

"How did you know this was here?" his son whispered, although there was no one around to hear them. The fog horn, with its occasional bursts, was the only sign of life. "I built it, didn't I?" he replied to his son.

CHAPTER 42

SUNDAY, JULY 24, 2022

At the building site on a balmy July morning, Matt was dressed in khaki shorts and a short-sleeved black polo, his favorite sneakers on his feet. He carried the architect's drawings as he walked through the ground floor of his taking-shape new house.

After a busy week at work, this Sunday morning was Matt's first opportunity to check the week's construction progress on his house. He inspected the walls and window openings to make sure they were where they were supposed to be. About the third time he found himself stopped at a window opening, mesmerized by the endless view out to sea, he knew his architect and builder had gotten it right. More than right, it was perfect.

He walked through each room and examined the dimensions, now that walls were beginning to appear. Every room felt good; spacious, open, and airy.

He drifted to the southwest end of the structure to see if work had begun on the large deck designed for this end of the house. Not yet, but he could see stakes in the ground representing the boundaries. He planned to be one of the few people in Port Stirling to have an outdoor swimming pool—even most of the resorts didn't have them. The idea of swimming laps in the rain and wind in the narrow lane pool he'd

designed appealed to him. It would be heated year-round, of course—
he wasn't a masochist.

Matt paused at the triple-wide glass doors opening that would lead
to the deck, stared at the shimmering blue ocean and gentle white waves,
and thought about Tyee. Two days from now, on the 118th anniversary
of Tyee's death, the village of Port Stirling would dedicate the new lighthouse. The U.S. Army Corps of Engineers, Portland District, working in
concert with the Governor's Office, and Chinook County Board of Commissioners, had rebuilt the jetty and its iconic lighthouse in record time
following the devastating earthquake and tsunami.

Once the governor had learned of Tyee's skeleton and its placement,
and the story of the rifle, she drove the effort to rebuild the lighthouse.
Matt had suggested that they rename it, and Mae Walters at the historical
society agreed. They took their suggestion to the county board, where it
passed unanimously. Instead of the Twisty River Lighthouse, after Tuesday it would forever be known as the Tyee Kouse Lighthouse.

Matt was looking forward to Tuesday's ceremony to be led by Del
Kouse, with all sorts of VIPs in attendance. Word had it that the Carmichaels would not attend. *Good, no fistfights at this lighthouse dedication.*

"Knock, knock," Matt heard behind him in the vicinity of what would
be the front door of his new home. He turned abruptly, thinking he was
all alone on the site.

"Can I come in?" Fern asked. Her face blushed a soft rose, her chin
tilted downward, and she looked up at him expectantly.

"Yes, ma'am, you certainly may," Matt beamed at her. His stomach
flipped, and he was unable to blink in case the beautiful scene in front of
him disappeared.

Things had begun to thaw somewhat between them, but Fern still took
pains to not be alone with Matt. He had given up completely when Bernice let slip that she'd introduced Fern to a new teacher in Buck Bay, and
it seems they'd hit it off.

Now, they stood briefly paralyzed looking at each other, and began
to laugh. Fern was also wearing khaki shorts and a black polo shirt. The

only difference in their attire was that she wore leather huaraches instead of running shoes.

"Everyone in town is talking about your new house, so I thought I'd better come take a look," she smiled.

He looked into her familiar, kind eyes. She looked terrific, and it bruised his heart.

But Matt wasn't the sappy sort.

"Do you want to see the master bedroom?" he grinned.

"Maybe."

Authors thrive on reviews. If you enjoyed *Code: Tsunami*, please take a minute and write a review wherever you bought it. I will be deeply grateful.

The fourth book in the Port Stirling mystery
series will be published in early 2022.

So you don't miss out on the latest news and updates, please go to

WWW.KAYJENNINGSAUTHOR.COM

and sign up for my occasional newsletter.

ACKNOWLEDGEMENTS

When—not if—the Big One hits the west coast, there is likely to be even greater devastation than I have depicted in this story. If you, dear reader, live in this region, particularly in the coastal areas, please stop reading now, and assemble an earthquake preparedness kit. Make sure you know about your region's warning system. The 1964 Alaska earthquake generated a tsunami wave runup of 220 feet in the Valdez Inlet. If you want to understand what's truly possible, read about Lituya Bay, Alaska, in 1958.

I relied on several studies that have been published on the Cascadia fault zone that give more detailed projections of the aftermath of a potential 9.0-range quake. Many are readily available to read online. I also highly recommend Bonnie Henderson's excellent non-fiction book, *The Next Tsunami—Living on a Restless Coast*.

I want to thank the Bandon Historical Society, and especially Executive Director Gayle Propeck Nix and historian Jim Proehl. Their assistance in helping me understand life in 1904 was invaluable. If there are any historical oddities, they are mine in service of the story, and not errors on their part. I also want to thank my Native American consultant, who wants to remain anonymous, for their help on early Native dress, food, and names.

I want to give a special thanks to cover and illustration designer Claire Brown. As she did with *Midnight Beach*, Claire designed the perfect cover for *Code: Tsunami*. She somehow knows what I'm thinking before I think it. How does she do that?!?

Jessica Morrell is a tough, but fair, editor. Thanks to her for her meaningful, thorough, and thoughtful edit.

Special shout-out to my four beta readers who have helped me on all three of my books—they know who they are. Each bring something different to the cause, and I highly value each of them.

I have lots of Texas girlfriends, and except for being gorgeous, they are nothing at all like Susie in this work of fiction.

Other authors often talk about the lack of emotional support they receive from their families regarding their writing careers. I am not in that group. My husband continues to cheer me on daily, helps me make marketing decisions, orders take-out on the days when I'm on a roll and don't want to stop writing, and is convinced I can write novels until my one hundredth birthday. We'll see.

Printed in the USA
CPSIA information can be obtained
at www.ICGtesting.com
LVHW091453101123
763181LV00110B/221/J

9 781733 962667